UNDER THE A

Also by Anna Belfrage

Praise for In the Shadow of the Storm (first book in The King's Greatest Enemy)

"Overall, this is a story will suck you in from the very first page and refuse to let go. I can't even think of one bad thing to say about it!" *So many books, so little time*

"The character cast is plentiful and rich, the historical details – fascinating and illuminating, the tension is ever-present and the fast-paced plot line is sure to leave you breathless. I really loved everything about this book." *Bookish Lifestyle*

"A twisted affair of mistaken identities, power struggles, and political strife, In the Shadow of the Storm gives readers a gripping novel that continuously pushes the boundaries of what they think they know and what's really coming." *A Bibliotaph's Reviews*

"Belfrage's writing is wonderful, her ability to transport the reader to the setting along with her fully developed and motley characters create an enthralling reading journey." *Unshelfish*

Praise for Days of Sun and Glory

Praise for The Graham Saga

"A brilliantly enjoyable read" *HNS Reviews*

"This is a series that will take both your heart
and your head to places both light and dark, disheartening
and uplifting, fantastic and frightening,
but all utterly unforgettable" *WTF are you reading*

"Anna writes deep, emotional historical novels, adding the
fantastical element of the time slip and a "what if?" scenario,
and creates for us a world in which to be lost in on rainy days
and weekend reading fests."
Oh for the Hook of a Book

"It seems Belfrage cannot put a foot wrong.
Long may she continue to give us installments
in this truly wonderful series." *Kincavel's Korner*

"An admirably ambitious series" *The Bookseller*

Further to excellent reviews, The Graham Saga has been
awarded multiple B.R.A.G. Medallions, five HNS Editor's
Choice, has been shortlisted for the HNS Indie Book of the
Year in 2014, and the sixth book in the series won the HNS
Indie Book of the Year in 2015.

ANNA BELFRAGE

UNDER the APPROACHING DARK

Matador
9 Priory Business Park,
Wistow Road, Kibworth Beauchamp,
Leicestershire. LE8 0RX
Tel: 0116 279 2299
Email: books@troubador.co.uk
Web: www.troubador.co.uk/matador
Twitter: @matadorbooks

ISBN 978 1788035 095

British Library Cataloguing in Publication Data.
A catalogue record for this book is available from the British Library.

Typeset in 11pt Bembo by Troubador Publishing Ltd, Leicester, UK

Matador is an imprint of Troubador Publishing Ltd

This book is dedicated to Kathryn Warner, a lady who generously shares her impressive knowledge of everything related to Edward II, thereby inspiring people like me to write.

England in the early fourteenth century was a complicated place…

A king should not be ruled by favourites, but Edward II was prone to indulging the men whose company he enjoyed. By 1321, the barons of England had had enough of the king's grasping favourite, Hugh Despenser, and rose in rebellion. For a short while, it seemed the barons would prevail, but for once in his life, Edward II acted with speed and determination. The uprising was crushed, Despenser became the most powerful man in England bar the king, and the rebellious barons were executed, one by one.

Except one. Edward II committed the mistake of his life when he chose not to execute Roger Mortimer. Instead, he allowed Mortimer to languish in captivity, but in August of 1323, Mortimer escaped the Tower and fled to France.

Edward II further compounded his mistake by alienating his wife, Queen Isabella. After stripping her of her dower lands and exiling her French household, Edward and Despenser thought they'd tamed the young queen — so much so that Edward sent her to negotiate on his behalf in France.

Queen Isabella successfully brokered a peace treaty with the French king. Edward was requested to come to Paris and do homage for his French lands. Instead, he sent his son, and just like that, the English King had handed his affronted wife the weapon with which to destroy him.

In 1326, Isabella returned to England, accompanied by her son — and by Roger Mortimer, by now the queen's lover and trusted advisor. Isabella promised to rid the realm of the tyranny imposed by the Despensers, and instead of resistance she encountered support wherever she went. The king and Despenser fled west, but in November of 1326 they were captured.

And now, in early 1327, Despenser is dead, while Edward II is held in captivity. A new day dawns for England, a new king will soon sit on the throne. A young king—too young to rule—and instead of Hugh Despenser, it is Queen Isabella and Roger Mortimer who control the kingdom. Not, necessarily, a good thing.

Chapter 1

Adam de Guirande was in the bailey when his brother, William, was sighted at the top of the lane. It was three days before Twelfth Night in the year of our Lord 1327, and Adam should have already been on his way to Westminster, but he had delayed on purpose, not wanting to leave until his priest brother returned from his recent excursion to Tewkesbury Abbey.

It was wet rather than cold, and dark clouds to the east promised more rain. Adam sighed: it would be a long ride to Westminster, but he was not in a position to refuse. He had been summoned back to court, by both Prince Edward, his present young master, and Lord Roger Mortimer, his former master. From the terse wordings in the two separate messages, delivered by two different and exhausted messengers, Adam gathered his two lords were not seeing eye to eye on things. They rarely did lately. Ever since Mortimer—or rather Queen Isabella—had led the invasion that had deprived King Edward of his throne, the prince's relationship with his lady mother's champion and lover had cooled. Now King Edward was held prisoner at Kenilworth—an honourable and comfortable captivity, to be sure—and this had further distanced the prince from his mother.

Adam strode over to the gate to welcome William, stopping for a moment to take in his manor with proprietary pride. Tresaints was not a large place: it consisted of the manor house, several buildings that housed barn and stables, kitchens and storage sheds, and, to the left of the house, a chapel, built some centuries earlier by a returning crusader ancestor of Kit's. The thought of his wife made him smile, and he glanced at the solar window, the opaque horn panes lit from within by candles and fire. His Kit, surely sitting up in bed with their newborn son at her breast. A son, a little bundle he had already taken to his heart, holding him for hours as he slept.

William held in his horse and gave Adam a weary nod. He was covered in mud and drenched to the skin, shivering violently as he dismounted. Gavin, Adam's squire, was there to take the reins and lead the tired horse off towards the stables.

"Accursed wind," William said. "It drives the rain like nails through your skin."

"We'll have you in a bath soon enough." Adam studied the donkey that William had been leading. "Is that…" His mouth dried up.

"It is." William scrubbed at his face, the normally well-shaved cheeks bristling with fair stubble. "I would not recommend that you look inside."

Adam walked over to the donkey. A newborn son indoors, and here, in the darkening dusk, stood a donkey loaded with a wooden box that contained the remains of his eldest son.

"No coffin?"

"He was buried in haste. There were too many to bury to coffin them all, and what with the pestilence…" William left the rest unsaid, but Adam nodded. An unknown illness claiming several lives—the monks would be in a hurry to inter them.

"How do we know it is him?" he asked instead, caressing the rough grain of the wood.

"He was buried under his own name." William closed his eyes. "And I looked."

"You looked?" Adam studied the box. What was there left of a four-year-old lad after more than six months in the ground?

"The hair," William said curtly, and Adam didn't want to hear more. He lifted the box off the donkey, and something rattled inside. It made his stomach heave. So light, nowhere close to the solid little body that had been Thomas de Guirande, all blue eyes and fair hair and a disarming smile.

He had not wanted to do this, but Kit had begged and pleaded, saying it was only right that their son be brought back to rest at Tresaints. Adam cradled the little box. He'd had no desire to exhume his son's body, disrupt his peace, but when William had sided with Kit, he had given in with ill grace, fearing that this would only open wounds that were half-healed. And he'd been right. To stand in his bailey clutching the nondescript box that contained his son's—he swallowed—bones, it was near on unbearable.

"I'll take it." William held out his hands. Adam shook his head. No, this he would do himself.

"I'll put him in the chapel."

William frowned. "By the door, Brother. There's enough left to smell." Adam threw him an angry look. His brother just looked back, his face grey with exhaustion and grief.

Once Adam had deposited his burden in the chapel, they made for the hall, entering together. Adam sent one of the maids off to arrange for a bath. William made straight for the large fire in the central hearth, pulled up a stool, and sat down, extending his sodden boots towards the heat.

"Were they helpful, the monks?" Adam asked, serving his brother wine.

"Not particularly." William's mouth twisted into a little smile. "The monks of Tewkesbury owe a lot to the late Despenser and his lady wife."

Adam flexed the toes of his damaged right foot, a constant reminder of Despenser, now safely dead—if unburied still, various rotting parts of the man decorating different locations. Even now, close to five years since Despenser had his men drive a red-hot stake through Adam's foot, he could recall the pain, and even more, the stench. He cleared his throat.

"A child is not to blame for Despenser's fate."

"No, but you are—or so they see it. They'd all heard that Adam de Guirande was one of the men who captured Despenser and led him off to meet his unsavoury death."

"I did as I was told to do." Adam drank deeply. The execution of Hugh Despenser still caused him nightmares, in particular the disturbing image of Mortimer and the queen dining as they watched the man die, piece by piece.

"It doesn't matter anymore." William held out his goblet for a refill. "England is now ruled by the victorious queen."

"Aye." And the equally victorious Mortimer, but Adam chose not to say that.

3

"So," William said, smiling at him. "Has the babe arrived?"

"He has—four days hence." Adam smiled back. "A healthy lad, with hair as red as his mother's."

"Ah." William chuckled softly. "A temperamental son, then."

"For now, all he does is eat, shit, and sleep, so I can't tell."

"And Kit?" William asked.

"Recovering, but still abed."

"No, I'm not." Kit's voice startled Adam, who rose to his feet, as did William. She was not dressed for visitors, her dark red hair hanging in a thick braid down her back. Her kirtle was loosely laced, and she grimaced as she sat down, brushing at her swollen breasts. A right picture, his wife, her milky skin tingeing with pink under his appreciative eyes.

"A son, I hear." William smiled fondly at Kit. At times, it irked Adam that his wife and brother had such a close relationship, and he didn't like that there were things she'd talk to William about but not to him. "I can't very well talk to you about you, can I?" she'd said when he aired this with her, and that comment had not made things any better, rather the reverse.

"A son? More like a starving wolf," Kit said. "He eats all the time."

They said nothing for a while. Finally, Kit turned to William. "Did you find him?"

"I did."

Kit closed her eyes, but not before Adam saw the spark of hope extinguished. He sat down beside her and took her hands.

"He's home, sweeting. As soon as we can fashion him a coffin, we will bury him here, where he belongs." More or less the same words she'd said some weeks ago, but from under her eyelashes a tear or two seeped. He disengaged one hand and captured one of them with his thumb. "You knew he was dead."

She opened her eyes, brilliant pools of blue that glittered with unshed tears. "But I hoped." Kit leaned her head against his chest. "I hoped, Adam." He stroked her head, fingering her heavy braid.

4

"So did I." He drew her even closer. "God help me, so did I."

Kit insisted they go to the chapel, overriding Adams protests that it was too cold, too dark, and that there was nothing to see—not really.

"I can't leave him alone in the dark," she replied, so, with a sigh, Adam got to his feet, found a cloak for his wife, and led her over the muddy yard with William trailing them.

As always, entering the little chapel imbued him with a sensation of peace. Kit greeted each of the three saints that guarded the entrance and then they were standing on the tiled floor, facing the altar. One single candle illuminated the entire room, casting most of it in shadow. In the gathering dusk, the stained-glass window on the eastern wall was mostly a collection of dark blues and black, and the flickering flame of the candle reflected on the polished floor.

Kit crossed herself and lit four more candles—one for every year of their son's life. Hesitantly, she approached the little box.

"I want to…"

"No." Adam was not about to open this makeshift coffin.

"But…" She stooped, placing a hand on the lid.

"No."

Kit rocked back on her heels, a crease between her brows as she studied him.

"No, sweeting," he said, hearing how his voice shook. He sank down to his knees. "Leave him be. You—we—should remember him as he was."

Very slowly, Kit sank down to her knees. "He really is dead, isn't he? And I'll never see him again."

"Sweeting, hush." He cleared his throat. "Our son is safe now, free of the pains and rigours of this world." A scant comfort: his son should have been learning to ride, collecting bruises and scrapes as he played. By now, he'd have had his first wooden sword, and Adam would have taught him how to use it. Not to be.

"Sometimes, God is very unfair," Kit whispered to Adam. "Why did he have to take our son? Why not one of Despenser's children?"

"God's ways are unfathomable," William put in, sounding more like the priest than the brother. He knelt down beside them, shivering in his damp clothes.

Kit didn't reply. Tears streamed down her face as she commended her son's soul to God.

Once indoors, Kit gestured them up the stairs to the solar. A tub had been placed before the fire, the steaming water sprinkled with rosemary and lavender. Kit dismissed the maid, gently disengaged little Ned from Meg's arms, and handed their son to Adam.

"Time for bed, child," she said to Meg, brushing a wisp of dark hair off their daughter's forehead. Not quite two, Meg was as temperamental as Adam's trusted old stallion, Goliath. At her mother's words, Meg's lower lip jutted out, her finely shaped brows—so like her mother's—pulled down in a frown. She opened her mouth to protest.

"No." Kit sounded firm. "You heard me. Now go with Mabel, and if you're biddable, I am sure she'll tell you a bedtime story." She ushered the child towards the door and the waiting Mabel.

Adam nodded approvingly. For the first few weeks after being reunited with their daughter, Kit had hovered round the child as an apologetic shadow, but a recent confrontation involving Meg, Kit's favourite veil and some shears had re-established the natural orders of things, Kit a firm and loving mother, Meg a wilful handful of a child.

Kit turned to William. "Why aren't you in the water yet?" she scolded, helping William with his thick robe before turning her attention to his boots and hose. "And the shirt."

William shook his head. "I'll keep it on."

Adam raised a brow. "Why?" He'd seen his brother naked often enough, as had Kit.

"Because I want to," William snapped before getting into the tub. He hissed at the heat, sitting down very carefully while his shirt billowed like a sail around him.

"I can't wash you with that on," Kit said.

"I'll wash myself." William snatched the soap pot out of her hand, grunting as he did so.

"William?" Adam placed Ned on the bed. "What ails you?"

"Nothing!" But the way he washed himself, hands skating carefully over his arms and shoulders, told another story.

"Your shirt, Brother." Adam crossed his arms and stared down at William. With a muttered expletive, William drew the shirt over his head, displaying a series of welts and bruises, the skin broken in several places.

"What happened to you?" Kit's hands hovered over him without touching.

"As I said; not everyone welcomes a de Guirande with open arms." William gave Adam a mulish look. "I gave as good as I got."

"I'm sure you did," Adam said. "But I'm assuming this wasn't the monks."

"No." William looked away. "This was a band of ruffians." He grimaced when Kit washed a long, seeping gash. "Despenser men. Peace is as yet a fragile thing, and I heard much muttering along the way. As long as the king remains at Kenilworth, he remains a rallying point for the discontent."

"So what would you propose be done with the king?" Adam sat down on a stool, rested his shoulders against the wall, and extended his long legs before him, crossed at the ankles.

"I don't know." William gave him a tired look. "But while he remains alive—"

"Shh!" Kit scowled. "What are you saying? That the king be killed?"

Adam shared a look with his brother. Much better for the realm at large if King Edward were to die—but impossible to contemplate. The prince may have acquiesced to being his mother's puppet—for now—but he would never countenance killing his father.

"Lord Roger will restore the peace." Adam smiled crookedly at the irritated expression on his wife's face.

"May God help him," William said.

Some while later, the manor was sunk in sleep. William had been given a bed in the hall, and in their solar Kit was lying in Adam's arms, her head on his chest. The babe snuffled in the cradle, one of Adam's hounds sighed as it stretched out by the hearth, the glowing embers the single source of light in the shadowy room.

Adam toyed with her braid, wrapping and unwrapping it around his hand. She yawned and moved closer, her heavy, warm breasts pressing into his side. Tomorrow, he would be gone from her, and God alone knew when next he'd share a bed with her. He smiled ruefully; he had never expected to develop such a dependency on his lady wife, and he had no intention of ever admitting to it, but this was how he slept the best, with her at his side. He tightened his hold on her hair.

"Once Ned is old enough to travel, I can come and join you." She raised her head to look at him. "Do you think that would be all right?" And he could hear it in her voice that she detested being separated from him.

"I don't see why not." He brushed a finger down her nose. "Our prince has already decided he expects you to be on hand to welcome his bride." He chuckled. "Little Philippa is inordinately fond of you, isn't she?" Their future queen was all of twelve, and at present remained with her parents in Valenciennes, waiting for the papal dispensation required for the marriage to happen.

"She's a sweet child. She will make him a good wife—a gentle and sweet wife, very different from his lady mother."

"Mmm." Adam smiled at the ludicrous thought of Queen Isabella as a demure wife.

"Will the queen be at court when you return?"

Adam laughed out loud. "Queen Isabella *is* the court." He tugged at her braid. "For now. Her son will not always allow her to eclipse him."

"And rightly so."

"You don't like her much, do you?" Adam lowered his voice despite knowing they were alone.

Kit shrugged. "She is like a flame, and those who fly too close may end up singed and burned." She frowned. "And I like Lord Mortimer much more than I like her."

"So do I." Adam sighed. Truth be told, he loved Lord Roger.

The next morning, Adam set off for Westminster. He didn't want to leave, all of him screeched in protest at riding away from his wife and their home. And as to Kit, she clung to him, and he kissed her repeatedly, promising he would be back as soon as he could.

When he swung astride Raven, his coal-black stallion, she stood beside him, gripping his stirrup.

"Ride safely," she said. "And beware of the wolves."

"The wolves are all dead, sweeting," he said with a smile.

"The wolves never die, Adam. When one is killed, a new one takes its place." She patted his leg. "God's speed—and hurry home to me."

"I will return as soon as I can." Which, he admitted ruefully, was utterly imprecise.

Chapter 2

Prince Edward had grown—or so it seemed to Adam, who was taken aback at the sight of his young lord. It was not much more than six weeks since he'd seen him last, but in the intervening time Edward had filled out, and in a dark blue tunic of finest wool that hung to well below his knees, in boots of red leather and a heavy golden necklace set with gems that sparkled in the candlelight, he looked more royal than ever before.

But the smile that lit up his face at the sight of Adam was still that of a young lad, as was his hasty, undignified approach.

"You're back! At last," the prince said, enfolding Adam in an embrace.

"My lord, this is not seemly." Over Prince Edward's head, Adam caught more than one displeased look: the future king embracing a minor knight!

"I don't care."

"But I do, my lord. I don't want to wake up with a dagger at my throat."

"They wouldn't dare. And Lady Kit? Is she well?"

"She is." Adam grinned. "And very proud of herself, on account of presenting me with a son. As you suggested, we've called him Edward."

"My first godson." The prince clapped his hands. "My congratulations, Adam. And maybe this little one will make the grief over Tom more bearable."

"I hope so."

"It was God's will," Prince Edward said.

"Aye." Adam studied his feet. "But that doesn't help much, my lord."

"No, I suppose it doesn't." With this statement, the prince clearly thought the matter closed and went on to discuss other matters as they walked towards the dais, on which sat the queen, deep in conversation with Lord Roger.

"They mean to make me king," the prince said in a hushed voice. Of course they did. Thereby they eliminated any risk posed by the captive king, and as the prince was only fourteen, the reins of government would remain in his mother's capable hands. Adam bowed from some distance away; the queen inclined her head, eyes as green as emeralds studying him. "But I won't let them," the prince added. "How can I, when my father still lives?"

"My lord, your lord father will never rule again," Adam said, as gently as he could. Keeping the king alive was a risk, but to have two crowned kings in England was the equivalent of opening a Pandora's box of strife and bloodshed. So if they planned to crown the lad, what would happen to the king?

"I know." Prince Edward's shoulders slumped. "I want to see him, but Maman says he doesn't want to see me." Thick eyelashes shielded his eyes. "Do you think that's true?"

"I don't know, my lord." Adam cursed the queen to hell and back for her insensitive comment, true or not. "Could you not write him and ask?"

Prince Edward gave him a bleak look. "Do you truly think he'd be allowed to read it?"

It was a lively court Adam returned to. Over the coming days, he met most of the prince's new companions, a colourful collection of lads and young men who were all somehow related to the important families of the realm. Some were of an age with Edward; quite a few were closer to Adam in years, as was the case with Roger Mortimer's eldest son, Edmund. Not that Edmund aspired to a place among the prince's companions—rather, he maintained a careful distance. But upon seeing Adam, he shone up.

"A son, I hear."

"Aye, a healthy, squalling lad." Adam scanned the room. "Your lord father?" He had not seen much of Mortimer these last few days.

"Not here. He and the who…— the queen—are busy elsewhere." It came out very bitter.

11

"Beware, Edmund," Adam said in a low voice. "The queen—or her son—will not have her spoken of like that."

"But that's what she is," Edmund hissed, his fine features contorting. Adam sighed. Edmund and his mother were close, and Lord Roger's open love affair with the queen was tearing Lady Joan asunder. Edmund leaned closer. "Four years locked away from the sun and the wind, all because of him and his ambitions. Or should I say his and her ambitions?" He broke off, cursing softly. "And after all those years, he returns—to England, to his lands, but not to his wife. How can he? It was us, not him, who paid the price. It was us—me, my mother, my brothers and sisters—who were locked away. But now he no longer cares for us, not now that he has that Babylon whore in his arms."

"Shush! Besides, that's not true." Adam placed a hand on Edmund's arm, causing him to flinch. "Your father loves his children—and Lady Joan. But this thing with the queen…" Adam cast about for words. "It's like a poison, a fire burning through his veins. I don't think he can help himself—and God have mercy on him for it."

Edmund didn't reply. His fingers picked at the embroidered edges of his sleeves, dark eyes flitting constantly around the room. The fine velvet tunic hung off his frame, and Adam could only imagine what several years as the king's prisoner had done to him.

"Will you be staying at court?"

Edmund shook his head. "Thank the Lord, no. I am off to Wigmore within the week." His face shone up. "Spring at home, eh? And even more importantly, spring as a free man." He studied his hands. "It is difficult getting used to."

After some further conversation, Edmund excused himself and left the hall, trailed by a young man Adam belatedly recognised as yet another Mortimer son, this one being John, at most sixteen or so.

"Consorting with erstwhile traitors?" someone said from behind him.

Adam turned, scowling. "Traitors? Edmund—"

"It was a jest," the man standing in front of him said.

"In bad taste," Adam snapped. "Especially to a man who has paid the price of so-called treachery."

"Ah yes. But it was treachery at the time, was it not?"

"The king broke his vows," Adam replied curtly. "What can men do but rebel against such a king?"

"So a king must live up to a higher ideal than the rest of us?"

"Yes." Adam looked him up and down, trying to place the dark hair, the long face and dark eyes. "Don't you agree?"

The man pursed his lips. "I do. A king is set to rule and must do so by example." He laughed. "That would, however, disqualify many a king from being king, don't you think?"

"Probably. Montagu, is it not?" Adam asked. The man bowed.

"William Montagu, at your service."

"And I at yours, my lord," Adam replied, bowing somewhat lower.

Not all of the prince's friends were as polite as Montagu. Many of them made it clear they considered Adam nothing more than an upstart man-at-arms, and more than once he was aware of eyes digging into his back, now and then accompanied by a whispered comment about him being Mortimer's spy. Adam chose to ignore it all, focussing instead on his young lord, who was more than delighted to have Adam back.

"Look," Prince Edward said, holding up a squirming pup. "A gift from Lord Mortimer. Its dam is half wolf." He stroked the pup over its brindled back. "I aim to call him Lancelot."

"Lancelot?" Sir Henry Beaumont, the prince's tutor and guardian, rolled his eyes and muttered that he doubted such a renowned knight would be pleased at having a dog as his namesake.

"He's dead. If he existed at all, that is." Edward gave his tutor a challenging look.

Sir Henry stroked his beard. "Well, let us explore other heroes today." He gestured towards the solar. "Virgil awaits you."

Edward groaned but followed obediently, the pup cradled in his arms.

"And what will it help him to read Virgil?" Montagu slid down to sit beside Adam in the window seat. "How will the story of Aeneas make him a better king?" He produced a couple of figs and offered one to Adam who shook his head.

Adam lifted his shoulders. He had little Latin and had never heard of Aeneas, but he had no intention of sharing this with Montagu.

"He loves you," Montagu said.

"My lord?"

"The prince. In his eyes, you stand first among men."

"And does that trouble you?"

Montagu bit into the fig and chewed. "Not as such. I find it surprising, no more."

"It will pass. He will grow out of his former protectors."

"Of course he will." Montagu gave Adam a cool look. "At some point, he will rid himself of all reminders of Mortimer."

Adam's gut clenched. What exactly did that mean? "Like his mother?" he enquired mildly and was quite pleased by how stricken Montagu looked.

"The prince should be accompanied by his peers," Montagu muttered.

"Men like you." Adam nodded. "Like Ralph Stafford and the de Bohun brothers. But not men like me, a mere knight, no more."

William Montagu flushed. "I don't mean to disparage you."

"But you did." Adam rose. "I shall ask the prince's guidance on this matter."

"What?" Montagu leapt to his feet. "No, no, I didn't mean to imply—"

"Of course you did," Adam cut him off. "I am the prince's man. Until he releases me or casts me out, I stay." To his surprise, Montagu threw back his head and laughed.

"I stand chastened, de Guirande." He extended his hand. "Start again?"

Reluctantly, Adam took his hand. He needed a friend—or at least a neutral acquaintance—among the men closest to his lord.

14

One such ally he already had, Adam reflected some hours later, bowing in greeting as Thomas, Earl of Norfolk and uncle to the prince, came towards him. Adam owed the earl his life, and for all that Thomas of Brotherton had problems keeping his eyes to himself whenever Kit was close, Adam liked the man—a lot. In difference to his incarcerated royal brother, Earl Thomas was level-headed and an intelligent man who thought before he acted. He was also a skilled fighter and a good drinking companion, more than capable of holding his wine.

"You're back!" Thomas slapped Adam on the back—hard. He always did. As always, Adam pretended not to have felt anything, and the earl's mouth twitched into a little smile. "One day, I'll clout you so hard you fall on your face."

"You can try, my lord," Adam replied.

"A challenge, de Guirande?" Thomas chuckled. "You know me, I can't resist a challenge." He sobered. "How are things with your fair wife?"

"Kit is doing well, as is our son."

"Ah." Thomas bowed slightly. "A son; I am glad for you." He guided Adam to the side, keeping a cautious eye on the various groups of courtiers. "I hear you're to accompany Mortimer tomorrow."

"I am?" Adam studied Lord Roger, at present standing beside the seated queen. The fairest amongst women, Adam thought, watching Queen Isabella tilt her head back to look at Lord Roger. A long, beautiful neck, visible through the folds of her sheer veil, an elegant figure highlighted by the tight fit of her newfangled cotehardie, for the day in deep red; her face, her mouth—her catlike eyes, gleaming green in the light of the candles—no wonder she held a man like Lord Roger enthralled.

"You ride for Kenilworth." Thomas sounded curt. "You and half the parliament, to hear it." He tossed Adam a walnut. "Ned insisted you accompany the party."

"What for?" Adam asked.

"To inform the king that the barons have renounced their loyalty to him and force him to abdicate in favour of his son."

"And then what?"

15

Thomas grimaced. "I don't know, but God help and sustain my brother in these, his darkest days." He nodded in the direction of the queen. "She will not allow any harm to come to her husband."

"No, she wreaks her vengeance on the Despensers instead." Adam was sickened by the story Sir Henry had told him earlier, describing in hissed detail how three of the Despenser daughters had been forcibly dragged from their mother not yet a fortnight since.

"Children!" Henry Beaumont had exclaimed. "The eldest no more than ten, the youngest four, and now they've been veiled, locked away to live out their lives as nuns."

"Together?" Adam had asked, hoping that the three girls had at least been afforded that source of comfort. Henry had merely looked at him, slowly shaking his head.

"What about Lady Eleanor?" Adam asked Thomas.

"What about her? My dearest niece remains in the Tower, at the queen's pleasure. I dare say they won't let her out until they've found her a suitable husband. Eleanor de Clare is much too precious a marital price to be allowed any say in her future."

Adam shrugged. That was the way things were ordained. Wealthy women were wed as it suited their family best, and a woman as comely as Lady Eleanor would attract a number of suitors. Politically, the queen would be foolish to allow Lady Eleanor to choose for herself.

On the dais, the queen laughed. She lifted her goblet to her mouth, drinking deeply.

"More spoils of war," Thomas murmured. "Our fair queen has appropriated dear, dead Hugh's collection of golden goblets. I think she finds it most satisfying to drink from them."

Adam studied the tableau on the dais. To one side, the queen and Mortimer, Lord Roger smiling down at his lady love as if oblivious of their audience. He wasn't, of course. Lord Roger rarely did anything in public without a purpose. On the other side of the dais, the prince was lounging in his chair, listening intently to whatever the tallest of his companions was saying. But now and then he glanced at his mother and Lord

Roger, and Adam felt an icy finger travel up his spine at the look in the prince's narrowed eyes.

"Dearest God, it isn't over," he muttered.

"Over?" Thomas lowered his voice. "Of course it isn't over. The play for power has just begun." He nodded at his nephew. "He hasn't found his claws yet. God help them when he does."

"She's his mother!"

"Aye. And the man you're riding to strip of his crown is his father."

Chapter 3

"He won't accept it, he says." Mortimer spat to the side and handed the pitcher of wine to Adam. "Silly brat! Parliament offers him the crown, and he says he will not touch it unless his father abdicates." He shook his head. "He has balls, our young king." His face clouded. "Too big, perhaps."

"It is difficult for him, my lord." Adam glanced at his young master, at present laughing with his friends and his younger brother. It was getting late, the fire in the large hearth had dwindled to glowing embers, no more, and other than Edward and his companions, the large chamber was empty, wise men seeking their beds rather than more wine. Adam would have preferred his bed, but Lord Roger had asked him to stay, and so here he was, sitting on the shadowy dais with his former lord while his present lord made sport with the jester and his dog.

"Does him credit," Mortimer muttered. "Had the whelp leapt at the crown, I'd have been in two minds about him." He emptied his goblet. "And so I am yet again burdened with the task of being the bad wolf. Me, not Isabella, not young Edward. Oh no, it is me that must ride to confront our former liege, put the fear of God in him should he choose not to cooperate." He scowled. "Knowing him, he'll not make it easy. He may have made an utter mess of things, but he has quite the stubborn streak in him—and is foolish enough to hope that he will be granted an opportunity to yet again turn the tables on me. Us," he corrected himself, smiling down at the ring the queen had recently given him, thick gold adorned with a red jewel.

"It could still happen." Adam crossed himself. Dear Lord, not that: not a kingdom torn asunder between father and son.

"No." Lord Roger's voice was flat. "Edward, second of that name, will never rule again. Never."

Adam's brows rose. "My lord?" No man knew what the future might hold.

"You heard. Never—not as long as I live and breathe." Lord Roger grinned. "Besides, parliament has already decided to depose him. Edward may still make things difficult, but he can't stop them—not now."

"And the Despensers?" The daughters had been cloistered, but there were sons as well. Sons who would have every reason to avenge their father. The Despenser lands had been divided up, and it stuck in Adam's craw to admit Mortimer had proved as rapacious as Despenser when it came to land, demanding the lion's share of Despenser's Marcher lands.

"Finished," Lord Roger said. "You were there, remember?" As always, when he recalled Hugh Despenser's death, something thick and furry clogged Adam's throat.

"What will you do about his sons?"

"Despenser died attainted, and the sons are imprisoned," Lord Roger replied. "Well, bar the fool still holding out at Caerphilly, but it is but a matter of time before he submits. And that's what they'll all do—submit or remain behind walls for the rest of their lives. And even if they don't, what threat can they pose to me?" His eyes crinkled into a smile. "I have the lady of the realm by my side."

The ride to Kenilworth was cold. Too cold, January winds laced with icy rain penetrating cloaks and woollen tunics. By the time the distinctive red keep rose before them, several days after setting out, Adam's hands had frozen in place round the reins, and Raven's thick black mane was dotted with ice crystals, glittering under a pale winter sun. Even his legs felt sheathed in ice despite both hose and leather breeches.

Once through the main gatehouse, they walked their horses over the causeway, ice making the ground treacherous. To their left, the great mere was silent and frozen, tufts of reeds rattling their frost-encrusted heads in the relentless wind. They slowed at the inner gatehouse, were inspected one by one by men in Lancaster tabards, and were then allowed to enter the lower bailey. They dismounted. The bailey rang with noise; shod hooves clattered over cobbles, men laughed and talked, and here and there a dog barked, a sword clattered. Mortimer led the way towards the inner bailey, guarded by yet another gatehouse. Henry Lancaster came out to meet them, standing at the top of the stairs that led to the massive keep.

By the time Adam made it up the outer stairs, Mortimer was already deep in conversation with Lancaster, throwing but a cursory glance at Adam before continuing with what he was saying.

"I'll see him first," Lord Roger said. "See if I can knock some sense into him."

Adam raised a brow but said nothing, noting several displeased looks. Lord Roger best beware—in the eyes of the men assembled, Mortimer was an unknown and dangerous quantity, and comments such as this would not endear him to those who feared the power of Queen Isabella's lover.

"I'll go with you, my lord." Adam was here not only for Lord Roger, but first and foremost for his lord and master, Prince Edward. The prince would not like it if Mortimer entered his father's rooms unaccompanied.

"As you will." Lord Roger sounded amused. He leaned closer. "And no, I wasn't planning on murdering him," he added in an undertone.

"I know." Adam gestured discreetly at their travelling companions. "They don't." Mortimer's expression hardened.

King Edward was standing by the window when Mortimer and Adam entered the room. It was freezing, the fire in the hearth a pitiful source of heat in a room where the shutters stood wide open, the northerly wind gusting snowflakes onto the floor near the window.

Henry of Lancaster had provided a sizeable chamber for his royal captive, but had not gone out of his way to furnish it beyond necessities. A large bed, covered by an assortment of blankets and pelts, one armchair facing the hearth, a table, a stool—on the table a goblet, a pitcher, a plate with a half-eaten roll of bread. The room reeked of loneliness, of hours spent in solitude.

"Mortimer." King Edward did not turn fully to face them.

"My lord." Mortimer bowed, and Adam followed suit before hastening over to fasten the shutters.

"What do you want?" The king sounded tired. "Come to complain about the she-wolf?"

Mortimer bristled, dark eyes narrowing. "Your son refuses to accept the crown unless you willingly abdicate."

"Good lad." Edward ambled over to the hearth, found a poker, and dug into the embers. "So now what? Aim you to put a leash on me?"

"No." Lord Roger kept a cautious look on the poker, as did Adam. "You abdicate, of course."

"I do?" The king brought the poker down, hard. It made Adam jump, but Lord Roger didn't so much as flinch. "Why should I?"

"Why?" In a swift move, Lord Roger grabbed the poker and threw it into the corner. "Because otherwise I will set myself up as king."

"You wouldn't dare! No one would accept it." Edward of Caernarvon drew himself up to his considerable height—he overtopped all but Adam—and glared.

"No? Do you wish to put it to the test? Of course, first I must rid myself of the other contestants, so both your sons must die, and your daughters I will force to take the veil." Mortimer grinned, and in the flickering light he looked akin to the devil. Adam wiped his hand on his tunic: Was Lord Roger serious?

"You wouldn't!" Their former liege shook his head, fingers fussing at the fine fabric of his robe. For all his bare surroundings, Lancaster was ensuring his prisoner was adequately dressed, his surcoat trimmed with fur, the robe beneath in velvet. Somewhat sombre, the black material caused the king to look wan and ailing.

"You think me less ambitious than your precious Despenser?" Lord Roger advanced on the king, who shuffled backwards. "What would he have done, do you think?"

"He would never have threatened my children! Never!"

"No, he threatened other men's children instead," Lord Roger replied, and the king deflated, sitting down on the chest at the foot of the bed.

"I loved him. Loved him so much, and now he is dead, and I will never…" He bit off the rest of the sentence, raising a shaking hand to his hair—far more grey now than fair, but vigorous and curly.

"You loved him too much—more than you loved your children or your kingdom, and much more than you loved your honour. A king cannot allow himself such passion."

"Honour? Passion?" Edward's face hardened into a mask of royal displeasure. "And tell me, is it honour or passion that has you bedding my wife every night? What does Lady Joan think of your honour? What, pray, does my son think of it? And what does he think of his whore of a mother, that French—"

The slap resounded through the room. Adam moved forwards, hand on his sword, not sure if his intention was to defend the king or save Lord Roger from himself. To judge from Mortimer's compressed mouth and the way his nostrils dilated, Adam feared the man was about to fly into one of his memorable—though uncharacteristic—rages. With a curse, Mortimer turned his back on them. Adam counted to six, and then Lord Roger turned to face them, his features fixed in a bland expression.

"So," he said. "Will you do it?"

"Do what?" Edward gave him a puzzled look, a hand to his flaming cheek.

"Safeguard the crown for your son by abdicating." Lord Roger sounded bored.

"Do I have a choice?"

"There's always a choice, but one must abide by the consequences." Lord Roger stretched his lips into a wolfish grin. Silence stretched between them. The king and his baron glowered at each other. Finally, Lord Roger shrugged and made for the door. "Parliament has already made its decision." He threw it open and stood back, indicating Edward should precede him.

"Where are you taking me?" Edward retreated, the folds of his black robe merging with the shadows.

"To the hall—there is an entire delegation waiting for you there." Mortimer regarded his former king. "Sire," he added mockingly.

"No." Edward planted his feet wide and lowered his head.

"No?" Mortimer fingered the hilt of his sword. "And what makes you think you have a choice? Either you walk on your own or I'll have you dragged there." Mortimer leaned his shoulders against the wall and waited. Edward looked from him to Adam before he succumbed.

"Very well. Lead the way."

"Oh no. After you." Mortimer made a little bow.

The walk from the keep to the hall was short, Adam and Lord Roger flanking the king. They stepped inside, and Edward came to an abrupt stop.

"What is this?" he demanded. "Why is my peace so disrupted?" His gaze flew from his steward, Thomas le Blount, to his chief justice, Geoffrey le Scrope, his tongue darting out to wet his lips. His eyes narrowed when they found William Trussell, the man who'd presided over Despenser's mock trial, and Trussell paled and clasped his hands before him.

Adam studied the various knights and barons, then shared a nod with Orleton. He liked the Bishop of Hereford and was glad to see him here, confident that he would ensure matters were handled in an orderly fashion—well, as orderly as it was possible to handle the removal of an anointed king from his throne. Adam swallowed. A momentous occasion, to be sure. None of the men now present had any reason to love their former liege, but quite a few shifted on their feet, coughed and cleared their throats, faces averted as they attempted to avoid looking straight at the man they aimed to depose.

"Edward of Caernarvon, we are here to seek your voluntary abdication from the throne." William Trussell raised his voice but was so overcome by what he was saying that all of him shook. He had not volunteered to be the spokesman—it had been an honour thrust upon him by Mortimer. An unnecessary turning of the knife, in Adam's opinion, and he didn't know quite where to fix his gaze as Trussell continued. "This realm no longer recognises you as our king. You have failed your subjects, you have repeatedly broken your vows, you have sinned, and…" His voice tailed off, but other men took over, some loud and vociferous, such as the Earl of Surrey, others speaking in more measured tones. The message, however, was the same: Edward of Caernarvon would rule no more.

Utter silence settled on the company when Edward knelt. When he abjectly begged them for forgiveness, more than one man looked away. A king, to kneel before them—no, it wasn't right. Adam shuffled where he stood, hoping his young lord would never ask him to describe this scene or the ravaged man before them.

Edward remained on his knees as Orleton read out the formal proclamation, and then Thomas le Blount took a step forward, looked his former master in the eye, and broke the staff of office. And just like that, the man before them was no longer king; he was but a knight—and a landless one at that. Adam pursed his lips. A conundrum: How to handle a deposed king?

Matters concluded, the man who was once their king was escorted back to his chamber by Mortimer and Adam. With a shaking hand, Edward poured himself wine—heavily sweetened, to judge from the scent—and drained the goblet before throwing it at the opposing wall.

"Curse you," he said thickly. "Curse that treacherous wife of mine. You have stolen my crown!"

"No, Edward. You lost it." Mortimer shrugged. "You were born to it, but it never fit, did it?"

Edward studied his rings. "I am what I am," he said after some moments of silence. "I could do no other than I did."

Lord Roger's mouth thinned, but he said nothing. Instead, he nodded in farewell and made for the door.

"Wait!" Edward called out. "What about me?" There was a forlorn tone to his voice, more akin to that of a child than a grown man. "What will happen to me?"

"I don't know." Lord Roger pulled on his gloves. "It is not up to me."

"Will I..." Edward swallowed audibly. "Will..." His hands rose to his neck.

"Of course not!" Lord Roger scowled. "What do you take us for? I give you my word of honour that you will not be harmed."

"Ah yes, the famous Mortimer honour," Edward said with a sneer. "God knows you set a high store on it."

"At least I have honour—you don't," Lord Roger snapped.

"For now."

Lord Roger bristled, and Adam took a careful step closer.

"My lords," he said, and both turned to look at him. Lord Roger scrubbed a hand over his face while Edward's shoulders slumped.

"My son, may I see him?"

"Not yet." Mortimer knocked on the door for the guards to let him out. "Once he is crowned, perhaps."

There was a glimmer in Edward's eyes as he turned away. Clearly, he did not believe Lord Roger. Neither did Adam.

"Did you mean it, what you said in there?" Adam asked once they were back on their horses, Kenilworth's keep already far behind them. "Would you have tried to take the crown for yourself?"

Lord Roger's mouth fell open. He blinked a couple of times, and Adam was reassured by his apparent surprise. He loosened his hold on the pommel of his sword, realising with a start that he'd been gripping it ever since Lord Roger's threat of usurpation.

"God's truth!" Lord Roger glared at him. "And do you think that woman of mine would have stood to the side while I disinherited her precious whelp?" He snorted. "Never come between a lioness and her cub, Adam. It will cost you your life. Besides, I have no right to the throne—but neither does the man we just left. He forfeited it long ago."

Amen to that, Adam thought.

Chapter 4

Kit arrived at court on the last day of February—too late to attend Edward's coronation, but she was not unduly distressed. From what she'd heard, it had been a magnificent if hasty affair, the young king an obedient puppet to his mother. Lord Roger had been most resplendent, and the entire abbey had been decorated in gold cloth, a fitting setting for their new young king, for the day in red samite—or so Egard had explained when he rode into Tresaints a week ago, carrying Adam's request that Kit join him as soon as possible.

She'd have preferred it if he had come home instead, but the king refused to consider allowing Adam to retire to his lands—not now—and so Kit had ridden the long way here, accompanied by Egard and four men-at-arms.

Egard helped her down, lifting her effortlessly to the ground. It was nice to have him back with them, she reflected as she smiled at the Welshman. As tall as Adam but considerably broader, Egard had spent the last few years serving Lord Roger but had requested to be allowed to return to serve Adam now that the matter of Despenser had been sorted.

Westminster was as Kit remembered it. Unmarked by recent conflicts, the royal palace was as bustling as always, servants scurrying back and forth between buttery and bakery, wine cellars and kitchens, while men-at-arms displaying the royal arms stood dotted about the large courtyard.

A party of young men came prancing out of the hall, gaudily coloured hose matched with equally gaudy robes and tunics, here and there a hat, a gold collar, a flashing ring. Not so much men as lads, Kit amended as they came closer; loud and vain, they wasted no attention on anyone but themselves—and the pretty little maid who was hastening by with a covered pot.

In a matter of seconds, they'd surrounded the poor girl, and Kit was considering whether to go to her aid when the group dispersed, the blushing maid running for the safety of the kitchen, her neat headscarf askew.

One of the youngsters said something complimentary about the girl's figure, another laughed, and just like that Kit stood face-to-face with Prince Edward—King Edward.

"My liege." She dropped into a deep reverence.

"Lady Kit!" His voice was deeper than when she last saw him, and fair fuzz rimmed his upper lip, though his cheeks remained as downy as before. He'd grown a couple of inches, and there was a new width to his shoulders, a sharper angle to his jaw. The man was emerging, bit by bit, but as yet their king was mostly a lad, as proven by how widely he grinned at her. "And my godson?"

Kit gestured in the direction of Mabel, and the king bounded over to study what little could be seen of infant Ned, tightly swaddled as he was.

"Does he look like me?" the king asked.

"You're his *god*father, my lord." Kit set a finger to her son's nose. "He has my hair, but in everything else he resembles his father."

"Big, then," King Edward said, handing the infant back to Mabel.

"Everywhere," Mabel muttered, smiling down at her charge.

"Mabel!" Kit hissed but was distracted by the appearance of a boy, ten or so, who came loping over the courtyard towards them.

Edward groaned. "Not him again."

"Your brother?" Kit guessed, taking in the obvious similarities between the boy-king beside her and the lad who'd now skidded to a stop beside them. She'd only met the younger prince once, some years ago, and had nothing but a vague memory of a loud lad with fair curls.

"For my sins." But Edward grinned as he said it, ruffling his brother's wavy hair. Both were fair, both were tall, but Prince John resembled his mother rather than his father. Green eyes fringed with tawny lashes regarded Kit with open curiosity.

"Maman wants you," Prince John said to his brother, who made a face.

27

"She'll have to wait. We're going to inspect my new birds."

"She said now." The prince took hold of Edward's sleeve. "Immediately."

The king's cheeks went a dull red, mouth setting in a stubborn line. "I—"

"My liege, she has need of you," Kit interrupted. "She relies on you." Not, as far as Kit could tell, the truth, but as a sop to the king's pride, it served. She moved closer. "Some things cannot be decided without the king's presence."

Edward shot her a dark look. "Most things are decided without me." He sighed and turned on his toes. "Where is she?"

"She's in the hall with Cousin Louis."

"Louis?" Edward shone up. "He's here?"

"He's here as our royal uncle's emissary. I heard of gifts for the new king." John was talking to his brother's back. "Edward! Wait for me!" The prince shot off, long legs eating the distance to his brother.

"Brave lad, isn't he?" Mabel said from beside her.

"Prince John?" Kit nodded distractedly, all the while scanning her surroundings for her husband. It had been strange to see Lord Edward without Adam—for the last year or so, Edward had not gone anywhere without being accompanied by Adam. "Not that he was in any real danger, was he?"

"A lad of ten, and all those scruffy Londoners breaking into the Tower!" Mabel crossed herself. "They could have killed him."

"That was never their intent," Kit pointed out. London had been quick to side with Queen Isabella and Lord Roger against Edward of Caernarvon, and a mob had broken into the Tower to proclaim Prince John as London's ruler.

"The laddie didn't know that, did he?" Mabel sniffed, hoisting Ned that much closer to her ample chest. Behind her hovered Rhosyn, the new nursemaid, with little Meg clutching at her skirts.

"No." Kit stroked her son's capped head. "He will wake soon." Her breasts strained against her linen chemise. She was still nursing her son despite Mabel's grumblings. Soon enough, a wet nurse would be installed, but for now Kit needed the proximity with her baby son.

"Aye," Mabel said just as Ned gave up a howl. "Like now."

She was busy with their son when Adam found her. Alone in the smaller of the rooms allotted to him, she'd undone her kirtle and chemise sufficiently to display her round breasts. Here, in private, she'd discarded her veil and was sitting curled up in the bed, rocking slightly back and forth as she sang to her suckling child—their child.

Her braid snaked down her back, and for some moments Adam remained at the door, drinking in this vision of his wife and son. The room was dark, the shutter remaining firmly closed, but two candles illuminated Kit's face, her hair. Her free hand smoothed at Ned's cap, brushed over the fine linen of his smock. She raised her face, met his eyes, and smiled, patting at the bed beside her.

"Join us."

Gladly. He kicked off his boots, shrugged off his cloak, and undid his sword belt, laying it carefully on a stool. Two hours working with Gavin had left him tired, but he suspected his squire was sore all over—being rapped by the flat of a sword repeatedly left bruises and aches.

The bed swayed with his weight, the rope frame groaning in protest when Adam settled as close as possible to his wife. She'd finished with one breast, was presently shifting Ned to the other. Adam cupped her free breast. Soft and warm, it fit snugly into his hand. His thumb brushed over her nipple, still dark and swollen after Ned's ministrations.

"Does it feel the same when he suckles as when I—" He broke off, having to laugh at how she'd gone quite pink.

"No," she replied primly.

"Ah. And do you miss it when I don't?" He slid lower in the bed, placed a soft kiss upon her breast.

"Yes." It came out breathless. Adam smiled, set his lips round her nipple and sucked. There was a responding little gasp—and a dribble of warm, sweet milk. He rose to his knees and leaned forward to kiss her mouth instead.

29

"Is he not done yet?" he murmured, poking gently at his son. In response, the babe sighed, releasing the breast with a soft *plop*. Adam lifted Ned out of Kit's arms, amazed at how much heavier he felt than last he'd held him. There was a blister on his son's mouth, his eyes slits of grey shaded with lashes as dark as his mother's.

"Your eyes," Kit said from behind him. "Lovely silver eyes."

"Your hair." He undid the cap, stroking the dark red fuzz. In his arms, Ned squirmed, stretched his legs, and farted. A distinct sour smell filled the room. Kit made as if to take him, but Adam shook his head. "Rhosyn is outside. She can change him."

Rhosyn was plump, dark, and very young. She was also Mabel's third cousin in some convoluted way, which was why she was now part of the de Guirande household. With Ned in her arms, she disappeared down the passage, saying something about clean clouts and water. Adam returned to the inner chamber and his waiting wife.

He undid her hair. She helped him out of his heavy tunic. Deft fingers on her laces and the kirtle was discarded, landing on top of his shirt. Her embroidered chemise—a new one, he noted—was thrown to the side, and there she was, in only her hose. He gestured at his braies. She smiled and ran a teasing finger round the waistband before loosening the drawstring. He didn't bother with undoing the points; he tugged braies and hose off, and when he opened his arms, she stepped into his embrace, warm skin pressing against him.

They stood like that for some time. Her hands travelled up and down his back, over his buttocks, up to his shoulders and arms before sliding back down to his waist. He inhaled her scent, nuzzled his way down her neck, traced the shell of her ear, the contours of her mouth.

She trapped his finger, biting down ever so gently. His cock swelled and lengthened. She pressed herself that much closer. Her mouth, warm and wet, opened to him, and he plunged his tongue into it. Kit gripped his shoulders and moaned. Adam swept her up in his arms and carried her over to the bed, still with his lips sealed to hers.

His cock throbbed and heated, hard like a rock after so many weeks of abstinence. But by now she'd been churched, had healed after the ordeal of birth, and from the way her hands tightened in his hair, she wanted him as much as he wanted her. Adam pressed her down on her back, and she widened her legs in invitation. He ran a finger through her curls, into her cleft—she was hot and moist, ready for him. He rolled on top, she gripped at his buttocks, and in one decisive movement he buried himself in her. Ah yes! So warm, so welcoming, so close, so his. A couple of long, hard thrusts, heat pooling in his loins, and with a grunt, he finished.

Below him, Kit giggled. "Is that it?" Her hands stroked his back, his head.

"For now." He lifted himself to the side. "I've missed you."

"Missed me or missed this?" She was in his arms, breasts pressed against his chest. She undulated, and his cock stirred.

"Both." He cupped her buttocks when she rubbed herself against his hardening member.

"Me too," she said.

This time, he took his time. She was like wax in his arms, eyes narrowing to blue slits as he pleasured her with first his fingers, then his eager cock. This time, it was her crying out his name, her nails raking his skin, before he took a firm hold of her hips and drove himself to finish.

She gave him a satisfied smile, lying sprawled half on him, half off. A strand of her hair was plastered to her cheek, her mouth soft and vulnerable. His woman. Adam tucked the tendril of hair behind her ear.

"Is my lady wife content?"

She hummed a response, turning on her side. He followed after, cradling her to his chest. Her hair tickled his face, her round bottom squished against his groin, and all in all it was quite perfect to lie like this. She nestled even closer. Adam kissed her shoulder. Somewhat fuzzily, he considered just what to say at his next confession but decided that whatever the penance for making love to his wife during Lent, it was worth it.

It was in a state of contentment Kit accompanied Adam to the hall. She glanced at him, wondering if it was as apparent to others as it was to her that her husband had but recently risen from their bed, sated after hours of lovemaking. His mouth curled into a little smile.

"Wanton," he whispered in her ear. "All of you rosy and glowing."

"So are you," she retorted, adjusting her veil so that it covered some more of her heating cheeks.

"Rosy?" he growled. "Men should not flush pink with pleasure."

"More ruddy," she told him. "But you do glow." She stood on her toes to comb her fingers through his hair. Messy and fair, it spoke of hours spent rolling in the hay. "There," she said, surveying the result of her efforts. "Much better." She brushed her fingers over his clean-shaven cheeks. Adam had never worn a beard—a habit he'd learned from Mortimer.

When they entered the hall, Kit shrank back against Adam. So many people! At the high table, the young king sat flanked by his mother and Lord Roger, with several of the young men Kit had seen earlier also at the table. Queen Isabella said something to her son, laughed, and shared a look with Mortimer. He smiled, turned to continue his conversation with Bishop Orleton, but every now and then his dark eyes flashed in the direction of the queen. Every time they did, she seemed to sense it, turning to meet his gaze.

Adam led them to a table to the right of the high table. Kit nodded greetings as she sat down, smiled at the page who filled up her cup, and went back to studying the queen and her baron. As always, Queen Isabella was the most beautiful woman in the room. Her dark hair was not entirely covered by her veil, the odd curl snaking down to caress her cheek. Attired in green and gold, sleeves snug all the way to her wrists, she sparkled—from within as much as due to the various rings she wore.

Queen Isabella placed a light hand on her son's arm, whispered something that made him laugh, and for an instant the king's fair head rested against his mother's. The queen set a hand on the backrest of her son's chair. Mortimer did the same, their fingers touching briefly while they continued with their respective conversations, she with her son, Mortimer with his favourite churchman.

Beside Kit, Adam muttered a "God help them", and belatedly Kit realised she was not the only one studying the queen. In fact, it would seem most of the assembled company was staring at Queen Isabella and her lover.

"It's a farce," Adam said, lowering his voice. "In the company of others, they act with utmost decorum, at most exchanging a look or a casual touch. But everyone knows that come night, Lord Roger visits her chambers, emerging just before dawn to hasten back to his own bed." Adam stabbed at a piece of capon on the trencher. "An upstart baron and his royal concubine," he added in a whisper.

"A concubine?" Kit leaned closer. "You cannot speak of the queen like that!"

"But that's what she is, isn't she? He's a married man—and God knows his lady deserves more from him than to be treated as a cast-off—and she is the queen, her husband languishing in captivity but very much alive." He set his lips to her ear. "They call her worse than concubine—they call her whore."

"Who?" Kit asked shakily.

"Everyone." Adam sighed and reached for her bread, raising an eyebrow. She nodded, sipping at her wine while her husband devoured most of the food.

"And what does the bishop say to all this?" she asked, nabbing a dried apricot.

"Orleton? God alone knows." Adam gestured for one of the servers to fill up his goblet.

"It must pain them both," Kit said. "In particular the queen—she's so devout."

"Ah yes." Adam pursed his lips. "She spends her nights on her knees before him, her mornings on her knees in the chapel. Sin and penance, in a vicious circle."

Kit choked. "Adam!" she gasped once she'd stopped coughing. "You can't say such things."

"It isn't me saying them, sweeting." Adam offered her a slice of cheese. "It is everyone else—well, assuming the king is nowhere within hearing distance."

"He would not stand for his mother being slandered."

"No." Adam wiped his eating knife carefully. "And he would blame it on Lord Roger."

"What are you two gossiping about?" A hand slapped Adam on the back, and moments later Kit was on her feet, greeting Earl Thomas. "As radiant as ever," Thomas said, looking Kit up and down. "What have you done to deserve her, de Guirande?" He punched Adam on the shoulder, laughed at Adam's scowl, and sat down beside him. "We both know your wife cares for me as she would care for an enervating older uncle."

Kit suppressed a smile. Thomas was far too young—and handsome—for her ever to consider him an uncle. Dark and lean, the earl regarded the world with sardonic wit and sharp intelligence, added to which he was fiercely protective of his nephew, the young king. She'd never met the earl's wife but knew for a fact that he had a son and a couple of daughters—and he had to be devoted to their mother, seeing as she was but a burgher's daughter.

Thomas helped himself to Adam's goblet. "Adam has not stopped bragging about his new son since he got here. I trust my nephew's namesake is doing well?"

"He is." A precious son, an heir—now that their firstborn was dead. Kit studied her hands in an effort to compose herself. It gnawed at her constantly, the uncertainty: she'd never seen Tom dead, nor had Mabel, and what was to say he had not survived? She knew this to be so improbable it was ludicrous, but now and then that little flame of hope flickered into life—until she remembered that even if he were, her Tom was lost, nowhere to be found.

A gentle pressure on her hand, no more, and Kit met Adam's concerned look. He knew her well, her lord husband. In response, she gripped his fingers.

"A pity you missed the coronation," Thomas said, his mouth twisting. "Adam helped carry the canopy." He shook his head. "Mortimer resplendent as an earl, his two sons first in line to be knighted by the king..."

"Not only them," Adam objected. "The king knighted a complement of others."

"True," Thomas said, "but for all that it was Edward's coronation, the spectacle danced to Mortimer's tune."

"And the queen's," Adam reminded him.

"Ah yes, our avaricious Jezebel."

"My lord!" Kit hissed, throwing a nervous look round the table.

"I am but stating the truth—ask your lord husband."

"He is, sweeting. As a coronation gift, the queen requested an annual income of twenty thousand marks—that's a third of the royal revenues."

"Not much to quibble about," Thomas said with a soft laugh. "Between them, Mortimer and the queen have the rest of the royal income under control as well." His face darkened. "In fact, Mortimer controls the entire kingdom." He drained the last of Adam's wine and turned the conversation to other matters. But Kit did not listen, her gaze fixed on Mortimer and the queen.

"Is it true, what Thomas said?" Kit asked Adam once they were alone in their chambers. "Does Mortimer control the kingdom?" Two rooms set aside for their use this time, with all but Adam and Kit bedding down in the larger room while they retired to the smaller inner chamber. Through the thick door, Kit could hear the muffled sound of Mabel talking to Rhosyn, and Gavin was probably already asleep on his pallet by the hearth, accompanied by one or two of Adam's dogs.

"He does." Adam sat down on the bed. "He does nothing without discussing it with the queen, but it is Mortimer's men, Mortimer's spies. It was Mortimer's friends who came away from the coronation carrying gold and silver plate. It is his sons who are ever put forward, his daughters who are proposed as matches to the richer nobles. And over the last few months, his land holdings have increased substantially, making him one of the richest men in the kingdom."

Kit sank down beside him. "Like Despenser."

"Not at all like Despenser!" Adam flew to his feet. "Lord Roger is a good man—an honourable man! He may be in control, but he will do nothing without the support of the queen and parliament." He whirled, bracing himself against the mantel over the hearth.

Kit refrained from saying it was a well-known fact the present parliament did Mortimer's bidding. Instead, she went to her man, slipping her arms around him and resting her cheek against his back. "You don't like it."

Adam turned in her arms. "No, my perceptive wife, I don't. And no matter that Lord Roger is no Hugh Despenser, one man should not wield so much power. And as to my lord, he likes it not at all."

"Edward is too young to rule," Kit said.

"He is. But he resents being used as a pawn, requested to set his seal to what his mother and Lord Roger lay before him. And those friends of his like it even less; Montagu regards Lord Roger as if he were a rabid wolf and Lord Edward a defenceless lamb."

"Montagu?"

"One of our young king's new shadows." Adam smiled slightly. "Will is a good man, for all that he distrusts Lord Roger."

"And you? Do you distrust him?"

Adam closed his eyes. "Sometimes." He leaned his forehead against hers. "So help me God, but sometimes I do."

Chapter 5

It took some weeks for the queen to summon Kit to her rooms. The page who came in search of her was at most eight, giving Kit a gap-toothed grin before remembering his manners and bowing instead.

"Our queen requests your presence, my lady." He beamed at her, wiped his nose with his sleeve, and scurried off as fast as he'd come.

Other than a deep reverence or two, Kit had had no interaction with the queen—the insignificant wife of a minor knight was of no major concern to a lady whose days were filled with the precarious matter of ruling her son's kingdom. And yet Kit had expected more: Had she not been one of Isabella's constant companions during the last few years?

The queen was in her bedchamber, surrounded by her ladies and her three younger children. Kit smiled a greeting at Prince John, who regarded her out of almond-shaped green eyes before excusing himself and ambling out of the room.

Queen Isabella laughed. "That one will break plenty of female hearts in some years." She beckoned for Kit to rise out of her reverence, slipped an arm under Kit's elbow, and steered her to the window seat.

New Turkish carpets adorned the floors, the tapestries on the far wall were a gift from the queen's brother, the French king Charles IV, but otherwise the room looked very much the same as when Kit had first seen it, some three years ago. The plastered walls were still decorated by the fleurs-de-lis, the bedstead was the same, gold inlays decorating the predominantly white paint. Dark red curtains framed the bed and to the side was a small table the queen used for her private writing, a crucifix hung on the wall above it, and neatly stacked to the side were a number of books, the uppermost a book of hours Kit recognised as being the one Queen Jeanne had given her sister-in-law as a parting gift last June.

"Back where I belong," the queen said, clapping her hands for wine and sweetmeats. The little page returned in an instant, an adoring look on his face as he served his queen first, then Kit.

"Thank you, Simon," the queen said, and the lad's smile widened further. The queen shared an amused look with Kit and sat back with a little sigh, eyes on her girls who were playing quietly by the bed. "A year ago, there were days when I feared I'd never see them again."

Kit studied the little princesses, both of them as fair as their brothers. Eleanor, the eldest, was some years younger than Prince John, while little Joan was no longer the chubby baby Kit recalled, but a sturdy five-year-old.

"They look well-cared for," Kit said, throwing the queen a cautious look. Queen Isabella had been incandescent when her husband had entrusted the girls to Despenser's sister and Prince John to Eleanor de Clare, Despenser's wife.

"Well enough. Fortunately, nothing came of that marriage with the Castilian king." Queen Isabella peered at her eldest daughter. "She will be wed as it benefits us. Besides, she's still very young, isn't she?"

"As young as Despenser's daughters," Kit said and wished she could have bitten her tongue off.

"What are you referring to, Lady Katherine?" The queen's voice was laden with ice. Kit swallowed a couple of times, considering whether to back down. In the end, she decided not to. Those poor Despenser girls had done nothing to merit being forcibly veiled.

"They are children, my lady."

"They are *his* children!" the queen spat. "His—and hers! And look what they did to Roger's girls! Did anyone speak up on their behalf? On your son's behalf?"

Kit bit her lip. Her son had died. Lord Roger's children remained alive. So unfair, so… She inhaled. "The girls are innocent."

"If so, they will make excellent nuns. There are worse lives than that of a nun." The queen stood. "And Eleanor was allowed to keep the baby and that ailing son of hers. She should be grateful."

"But—"

"No." The queen shook her head. "This subject is closed. You will never raise it again. Never." Narrowed eyes regarded Kit with little warmth. "I will not be judged by the bastard daughter of a salter's brat." She'd spoken loud enough for several of the assembled ladies to hear. Kit's face burned. All she wanted to do was leave, but until the queen gave her leave to do so, she couldn't. A little smirk played over Isabella's perfect mouth as she ordered Kit to help with the sewing.

"Lady Kit! Wait, my lady, Kit!"

Kit did not want to stop. After two hours of being stared at, all she wanted was the comfort of the abbey—as far away as possible from Queen Isabella's ladies and their prying eyes. But she recognised the voice and had no choice but to come to a halt, dabbing discreetly at her wet cheeks.

"You're weeping." King Edward stood beside her, as tall as she was.

"No, my lord. It's just a mote of dust."

"In both eyes?" The king frowned. "Why are you weeping?"

"I…" She looked away. "It's nothing, my lord."

For all his youth, Edward was perceptive. His brows rose into incredulous arcs, one finger brushing back and forth over his upper lip. "In my experience, Lady Kit, you do not weep for nothings."

"Women are weak creatures at times."

"Weak?" He laughed. "My lady mother would have you belted for speaking such nonsense."

Kit averted her face, but the king was quicker, his hand darting out to cup Kit's chin. "Did my mother say something?" he asked, strong fingers forcing her to face him.

"We had words, my lord." Kit inhaled, held her breath, and exhaled slowly. "I forgot my place." She moved away. He dropped his hands. "A bastard should never do that."

"Ah." King Edward shifted on his feet. "Your parentage is not your fault."

"No." She picked at her skirts. "If you'll excuse me, my liege, I was on my way to the abbey."

"So was I."

She smiled at his lie. From his attire, the king had been making for the mews.

"A blessing on your falconer's glove?"

Edward laughed. "It'll do no harm, will it?"

He accompanied her through the garden gate, across the open space that separated the abbey from the royal palace, and all the way to the northern door. "You are no longer one of my lady mother's ladies, are you?"

"Not since Vincennes." Not since the queen had found out that Kit was no true-born daughter to Thomas de Monmouth, but rather his by-blow with pretty Alaïs Courcy, daughter to a Lymington salter.

"Ah. Well, we must find you another position at court." He furrowed his brow. "I have it." He grinned. "You shall oversee all preparations for the arrival of my wife."

"Your wife?"

"My betrothed," he corrected himself, and Kit had to smile at the way his cheeks reddened. The king had developed a fondness for his future bride, and as to Lady Philippa, she was just as smitten with her intended.

"I am sure your lady mother has all those preparations in hand."

"Knowing her, I dare say you're right." He sighed. "Best not meddle in that."

"No, your lady mother would not take kindly to such attempts."

"So instead, I appoint you one of Philippa's ladies." He looked quite pleased with himself. "Philippa will have a need of someone like you."

"Your lady mother may object."

"I am the king, am I not?" His face clouded. "And as this is a matter of no importance, I am sure she'll let me have my way." With a nod, he was off, striding at speed towards the mews.

Over the coming days, Kit ensured to stay well away from the queen and her ladies. With Adam's time spent on further honing Lord Edward's fighting skills, Kit's days dragged, the long hours between Ned's feeding times whiled away either with sewing or with slow strolls round the palace garden with little Meg.

On a particularly chilly March afternoon, she stood to the side watching as Adam took the king through one sword exercise after the other, the blunted blades crashing against each other over and over again. In gambesons and vambraces, Lord Edward and Adam circled each other, sword in one hand, dagger in the other. Kit listened with half an ear as Adam explained that a knight, once unhorsed, had better regain his feet as soon as possible, switching to his one-handed sword.

"I know all that." The king sounded irritated, fair hair plastered to his forehead. Repeatedly, he'd rushed Adam, repeatedly he'd been beaten back, and now he was prowling like an angered cat, concentrating his efforts to Adam's right side, thereby forcing him to place too much weight on his damaged foot.

Adam was limping—badly—but what he lacked in mobility, he made up for in the speed of his blade, and the king cursed when he was yet again pushed back, this time slipping on the cobbles. Down he went, and Adam immediately lowered his sword and extended his hand.

"Is that what you would do to an enemy?" the king snarled, leaping back to his feet unaided. He attacked yet again, the blade glinting where it caught the sun. Adam parried, parried again, moving as little as possible. Edward ducked, jabbed at Adam's leg, Adam leapt backwards, the king came after, and in a welter of arms and legs, they fell to the ground.

Adam sat up, grinning. The king did the same, sweat and mud and faint streaks of blood decorating his face.

"You're bleeding, my lord," Kit said.

"Not me." Edward stood up. "Adam."

"A minor scrape, no more." Adam shrugged.

"I won," the king declared.

Adam snorted, getting to his feet. "Death by scraped chin?" He studied his muddied boots and hose. "A bath, I think." He slid her a look, eyes glittering like silver in the sun.

"Yes, a bath," Kit said, distracted by the rider who had just entered through the main gate. Bright red hair, a heavy beard several shades lighter, and when he saw her, he smiled.

"Richard!" Kit hurried over the muddied yard. She'd not seen her brother since well before Christmastide, when he was dispatched by Roger Mortimer to manage the restitution of the Mortimer lands—further augmented by several of Despenser's lordships.

"Sister." Richard blew her a kiss before dismounting, landing lightly on his feet. "I trust you are well?" He took hold of her arms and studied her. "You look well."

"I am." She tugged at his beard. "What's this?"

"You don't like it?"

"Not much." Kit looked closer. "There's egg in it."

"And something that resembles dried pottage," Adam put in, greeting Richard with a slap on the back.

"It will come off within the hour," Richard said.

"I am glad to hear that," someone said from behind Kit. Mortimer. She dipped into a reverence while Richard bowed deeply before his lord. "No need for that." Mortimer gripped Richard by the shoulder. "It is good to have you back. Have you news for me?"

"Plenty." Richard grinned. "The Mortimer colours fly over Wigmore again, my lord—as they do over all your castles."

"They've been doing that for some months now, lad," Mortimer replied drily. "But I am glad to have you confirm it." He looked Richard up and down. "Meet me in my chambers in an hour—clean and shaved."

"Yes, my lord." Richard reached for his saddlebags, and Kit made as to help him.

"The queen was asking for you," Mortimer told her. "She requires your sewing skills."

Such a direct request could not be ignored. Kit shared a look with Adam, who lifted his shoulders.

Mortimer looked from one to the other. "Now."

Kit dragged her feet all the way to the queen's rooms. From within came the sound of several voices, someone laughed, and Kit took a deep breath and stepped inside.

"Ah, at last!" Queen Isabella came towards her, light green skirts swirling around her. Her dark hair had been brushed to a gloss before being collected in a complex array of braids adorned by silk ribbons matching her surcoat—pink silk embroidered in emerald green and yellow. The queen took hold of Kit's arm, an affectionate gesture, and led her towards the large table in the middle of the room. "See?" she said, pointing at a darkened patch on the tapestry spread on top. "Burned."

Kit ran a hand over the damaged fabric. The warp threads were clearly visible where the weft threads had unravelled, singed at the ends.

"I am no weaver, my lady," Kit said.

"But the damage can be repaired with needle and thread, don't you think?" Queen Isabella peered at the heavy cloth.

"Not so as not to be visible."

"Pah! Typical of my dear brother: he sends me what he no longer wants." Long fingers tugged at the damaged threads. "I like it," the queen added. The tapestry depicted a pair of swans surrounded by flowers, various waterfowl, and lilies. Queen Isabella traced the graceful curve of the male swan's neck. "Fidelity," she murmured, before turning to Kit. "I am sure you'll do your best."

"Me?" Kit was adept at sewing, but no more than any other of the queen's ladies.

"It is important to me. I can't entrust it to just anyone." Isabella floated away, retrieved her delicate veil, and draped it over her head. She met Kit's eyes. "You have never let me down."

An apology? Kit managed a faint smile. "You honour me, my lady."

"Can you have it done in a week?" The queen was back to her normal brisk self.

"I can try."

"Good." In a flurry of bright colours, the queen left, accompanied by most of her ladies. Not all, though.

"She nearly choked, didn't she?" The pretty wife of Edmund of Kent smiled at Kit.

"My lady?" Kit liked Margaret Wake, a spirited woman who shared her dark colouring with her cousin, Lord Mortimer.

"She humiliated you the other day." Lady Margaret sat down, puffing loudly. She patted herself on her stomach. "Restless babe."

"Ah." Kit moved a stool closer and helped Margaret prop her feet up.

"Eleanor de Clare is a sensitive subject," Lady Margaret continued. "And as to her daughters… Too late to undo." She cleared her throat. "Shall we start working on this?" She gestured at the basket containing various skeins of coloured thread. "We could give the female swan green eyes."

Kit burst out laughing. "There's nothing wrong with the swans."

"No," Lady Margaret agreed. "Except that they are both wed elsewhere." She cast a nervous look over her shoulder. "Edmund is much aggrieved."

The Earl of Kent made no effort to hide his disapproval, Kit reflected, recalling just how the earl had scowled at Mortimer yesterday.

"Red or pink, do you think?" Kit asked, effectively putting an end to the discussion.

Adam was fast asleep when Kit returned to their little room. Naked, sprawled diagonally across their bed, he snored softly. The glow from the fire in the hearth gilded the fair fuzz that decorated his limbs and chest, and for some moments Kit remained by the door, drinking him in. Should she look closer, she knew she'd see various scars—foremost among them the damage done to his right foot by Despenser, may he rot in hell—but from where she was standing, he looked unblemished, a perfect man in repose.

She took a step towards the bed, and he woke, half sitting up before relaxing with a smile, his hand held out to her.

"At last. Come here, sweeting."

Kit undid her veil and slipped off her shoes. The bed was warm; he was warm, smelling faintly of lavender and soapwort.

"Was she kinder today?" He stroked her hair, and she nestled closer, her ear over his beating heart.

"Yes." She yawned. He rubbed her behind her ear. Kit's eyelids drooped. "The king's uncle is not much pleased with the new order of things."

"Edmund?" Adam traced her ear. "No, I dare say he isn't. Neither is his brother, although Thomas has the sense to work with the queen rather than against her." His chest rose on a deep inhalation. "And then we have Lancaster, hovering like a restless ghost."

"Oh?" Kit had only met Henry of Lancaster a handful of times, a man of sombre countenance and splendid attire.

"He doesn't like it, being forced to relinquish custody over Edward of Caernarvon." Adam laughed. "As if Lord Roger would be fool enough to leave such a weapon in the hands of a man who considers himself entitled to rule on behalf of our young lord—even less now, after those foolish Dunheved brothers attempted to break him free."

"Where is the king—er, the former king, now?"

"He is headed for Berkeley Castle. Maltravers and Berkeley will keep him safe—and comfortable." Adam pulled the pins out of her hair, one by one. "Beautiful," he murmured, running his fingers through her loosened hair. "Like conkers in autumn."

"Will they ever let him go?" Kit ran a hand over his chest.

"No." Adam eased her down on her back. "He'll live and die behind walls."

"How sad."

"No choice, sweeting. To release him is to invite strife and rebellion."

But sad nonetheless. Their former king was a vibrant man, a man accustomed to living life to the full. How would he fare confined to endless days behind walls? She was distracted from pondering this further by her husband's warm breath on her neck. Adam pillowed his head on her shoulder, humming softly.

His hand found hers, their fingers interlaced, and they lay like that, close together and silent, as what little daylight seeped in through the shutters shifted to night.

Chapter 6

"A wife?" Kit grinned at her brother. "Truly?"

"We wed just before Christmas. No point in delaying."

"Ah. And does she please you, your wife?" She handed Meg the last of the dried apricots.

"Maud comes with plenty of land." Richard adjusted the neckline of his tunic. "My lord has ensured I am well set up, a strong presence on the Marches."

"So it is only for her lands that you've wed her?" Kit felt a little twinge of pity for this unknown sister-in-law.

"We suit well enough. She is already with child."

"That," Kit told him, "only takes the once."

Richard laughed. "It took us a bit more than that." He shifted on the bench, squinting at the sun. "She is rich, but of merchant stock."

"Ah." Kit wiped Meg's hands and set her down on the ground.

"And young."

"You're young." Kit counted in her head. Her brother was two years her senior, which made him all of twenty-six, five years younger than Adam.

"She's fifteen—and an orphan. Her father was one of Despenser's men." Killed, he explained, stabbed in a skirmish after Despenser was executed. Poor girl: her father killed, and within weeks she'd been hastily wed to a man she did not know, distributed like a trophy of war.

"Did you not think to bring her to court?"

"No." He looked away. "She will remain at home. She prefers it that way."

"Will she not be lonely?"

"She has Alicia to keep her company." Richard laughed out loud when Kit made a gagging sound. "They get on— Maud is a sweet girl."

46

"In difference to Alicia, then." Kit would prefer never to clap eyes on her half-sister again, and rarely a day went by without her giving thanks to the Lord for the fact that Lady Cecily, Alicia's and Richard's mother, was no longer in the world. Unfortunately, the daughter had inherited most of her mother's temperamental qualities, among which was included a streak of cruelty.

Richard stood. "She's to wed after Easter. An older man who will be sure to keep her on a tight leash." He smiled grimly. If Alicia grew into a woman resembling her mother, Kit could but commiserate with the poor man.

By the gate, a large party was waiting for admittance, the guards inspecting every beast and rider thoroughly.

"What are you expecting? Hidden daggers?" The man on the roan palfrey adjusted his travelling cloak. "By God, man, you should know me by now!"

"Oh, I do," the captain of the guards said, "but our Lord Mortimer has made it clear all travellers are to be searched— even trusted men such as you, Bishop Burghersh."

"Hmph!" The bishop crossed his arms over his chest, looking like a sulky child.

Behind him, Kit saw the familiar figure of William, and after ensuring Meg was safe with Rhosyn, she hurried over to greet him. He'd been tonsured recently—and harshly at that, leaving but a narrow border of his thick fair hair encircling his head. As always, his fingers were smudged with ink, and when he saw Kit, he smiled.

"I thought you'd be at Tresaints."

"Adam wanted me here," Kit replied, throwing a look towards the west. Spring in Tresaints was lambs and primroses, catkins on the willows, hours in her herbal garden. Spring here was mostly dancing attendance on the queen.

"Well, he would, wouldn't he?" William dismounted carefully.

"Are you hurt?"

"No." He sounded curt.

"No? So why—"

"It is nothing." William turned away—stiffly.

The bishop had by now dismounted, dark robes being smoothed back in order.

"Bishop Burghersh." Richard bowed in greeting. "Lord Mortimer awaits you eagerly."

"He does, does he?" Bishop Burghersh smiled, eyes bright. "Well, we must not keep the mighty man waiting." He followed Richard across the busy yard, tailed by one of his clerks.

"Not you?" Kit asked William.

"Me?" William shook his head. "I am but one humble clerk amongst many." There was a tinge of bitterness in his voice.

"I thought you liked the bishop."

"I do—in many ways. He, however, does not always like me."

"What's not to like?" Kit slipped a hand under William's arm. Her brother-in-law visibly tensed. Kit released him, took a step away from him. What was the matter with him?

"I have been told I must revert to being obedient and silent." William looked away. "My adventurous past is no more, and I must reconcile myself with being but one unimportant cog in the bishop's administration."

"Ah." Kit pursed her lips. "He doesn't like that you've served Mortimer and the queen." William had spent several years carrying secret messages for Queen Isabella and her lover.

"Something like that." William sighed. "I miss it, Kit. Where before I was happy to spend my days copying and ciphering, where I would be happy to spend hours in contemplation, now I am constantly restless."

"Why don't you tell the bishop? Maybe he can put you to other use?"

"I did." William shifted his shoulders carefully.

"Did he beat you?" Kit's hand hovered just over the undyed wool of William's cloak.

"Oh no." William shook his head. "I beat myself—and am instructed to wear a hair shirt."

"And is it helping?"

"No. Sometimes, I wish I could just leave. I—"

Someone called his name, and William started. With an apologetic smile at Kit, he made for the rest of the bishop's party.

Adam was pleased to see his brother but was somewhat taken aback by how unhappy he seemed. The bishop was a man high in Mortimer's regard, and he'd have assumed this worked in William's favour. Not so, according to William.

"It is of no major importance," William said. "I have food and board; I have no cause to complain."

"Hmm." Adam had committed the mistake of giving his brother a hearty embrace, releasing him immediately upon hearing William gasp. "Why the penance?"

"For the sin of pride." William drained his mug.

Adam called for more ale and moved closer to his brother. The little inn was dark and smoky, but the ale was good, and it had the benefit of being outside the palace grounds—but close enough that one could walk there.

"There are other masters."

"There are." William made a face at his empty mug. "At times, I wonder what my life would have been like had I not taken orders."

At Lord Mortimer's request, he being the person who'd entrusted Adam's dirty and stick-thin younger brother to the resident priest in Ludlow, and several years later William had completed the education necessary to enter the Church.

"Do you regret it?"

"What would that serve?" William nodded in thanks when Adam poured him more ale. He belched discreetly. "I can't change it now, can I? And mostly, I am happy with my lot in life. It is just this bishop and I that do not quite see eye to eye."

"As I said: there are other masters."

"Bishop Burghersh would not take it well should I choose to leave." William finished his beer. "Without his recommendation, who would take me in? A lowly priest, no more."

"Lord Roger might."

"Not if the bishop asked him not to."

Once he'd bid William farewell, Adam went in search of Kit. Days of strenuous sword-play with his young lord and king had left him with a sore foot and a notable limp, and he had need of Kit's warm hands. Besides, his recent conversation with William had left him concerned.

"You could ask the king to help," Kit suggested.

"The king has little say in who joins his household." He added yet another piece of wood to the fire. "His mother has yet to forgive him for appointing you as one of his future wife's ladies without discussing it with her." The king had not backed down, and after a number of exasperated comments, Queen Isabella had told him to do as he pleased—this once.

"Why does the bishop dislike him so much?" Kit kneeled before Adam and helped him out of his boots. He brushed her head in passing.

"The bishop is one of Lord Roger's closest friends. Maybe he is jealous of the fact that William knows Lord Roger too."

"Is that not a mortal sin?" Kit enquired, smiling slightly. "Should the good bishop not do penance too?"

Adam laughed. "Maybe he does." He poured her some wine, settled himself on a stool. "Why don't we send him down to Tresaints? As our priest?"

"Would he want that?" Kit rooted about in one of their coffers, producing a small jar of ointment.

"I think so." Adam frowned. "It would not be much of a living, but he could act as my steward as well. What with our new lands, I need someone to supervise things when I'm not there." He couldn't stop himself from smiling: since some weeks back, his landholdings had more than quadrupled, the king and Mortimer settling several small manors on him—all of them in the vicinity of Worcester and Tresaints. A gift for loyal service, Lord Roger had told Adam in an aside, giving him an affectionate smile. "And he could tutor our children." He smiled at his wife, tugging at her braid as she knelt before him. "You'd like that, wouldn't you?"

"Knowing how to read and write are useful skills."

Aye, he'd come late to learning his letters, while his wife had been well-tutored by a priest she still spoke fondly of, a Father Luke.

"Will the bishop allow him to leave?" She had her hands under his tunic; a couple of swift tugs and she was rolling down his hose.

"For Tresaints? Aye." The bishop would have no reason to object. "If William accepts, we can send him down there immediately—with Mabel and the children." He cast her a cautious look. They'd had words some days ago about it being time for Ned to be wet-nursed.

Kit plucked at her girdle. "I don't like it when they're not with me."

"I know, sweeting. But this is best for them. Have you done as I asked and found Ned a wet nurse?"

"I have." She kept her eyes on her hands. "She starts tomorrow."

"Good." However much he loved his son, he preferred his nights to be uninterrupted, with his wife at his disposal. Kit did not reply. She set her hands to his foot and worked the fragrant ointment into his aching toes.

Three days since she'd seen Mabel, a happy William, and the children off, Kit was still feeling bereft. Her breasts no longer ached at the thought of Ned, but her heart did, as it did when she recalled Meg's casual farewell wave. Her little daughter had been happy to go home, prattling excitedly as Adam lifted her into the litter and Mabel's waiting arms. Kit hugged herself. Meg's world revolved around Mabel rather than Kit, and sometimes that hurt.

She spent the morning in the abbey, hours of meditative silence as she prayed for the safety of her children—all of them, including little Matilda, dead some hours after her birth, and Tom. The abbey was rarely empty, but a person desiring solitude could always step inside one of the many smaller chapels, and Kit had done just that, kneeling before the little altar as she said her prayers.

She was stiff when she finally stood, moving aside to allow three monks to enter the confined space. As always, she came to a halt once she was back in the nave, staring up at the vaulted ceiling. Where the abbey lacked the grandeur and sweeping lines of the Sacre Chapelle in Paris—one of the most beautiful spaces dedicated to God Kit had ever visited—it made up for it in sheer colour, the arches of various doorways, the pillars, decorated in red and white, gold and green. And then, of course, there was the magnificent retable.

Like a moth to a candle, Kit was incapable of ever visiting the abbey without spending some moments before the gilded depiction of Christ the Saviour tenderly holding the earth in His hands while beside him stood His mother, the Virgin. It was to the Holy Mother Kit directed most of her prayers, one woman to another, albeit Kit was a mere mortal, not the mother of God.

Once back outside, Kit blinked at the bright light. It had rained earlier, leaving behind various little puddles that glittered in the sun. From the smithy came the sounds of hammers on iron, a horse was prancing across the yard, dragging the stable boy along, and from the kitchens came the smell of fish. Always fish. Kit longed for crackling and pork, for mutton and venison. No more stockfish, no more carp and salted herring. Well, in less than a week Lent would be over, with meat aplenty on the royal table.

"Doing anything today?" Richard's voice startled her.

"No." She smiled at her brother, wayward hair standing like a fiery halo round his head.

"I am going to London on behalf of Lord Roger. Care to come along?"

"By boat?" Kit shivered.

"Yes." He gave her a curious look. "Adam says you can swim."

"I can. But I'd prefer to do it elsewhere than in the Thames." But she was tired of remaining in the palace, and Adam was in the tiltyard with the prince. Besides, she had some coin in her purse, and she needed new hose, both for her and Adam—and shoes, she reflected, studying the ones she was wearing.

"How can anyone want to live here?" Kit clung to Richard as he helped her ashore just below the walls of the Tower.

"Here?" He gestured at the Tower. "Or there?" He pointed the other way, at the warren of streets that made up London.

"Both." Kit glanced at the royal fortress.

"In general, people do not choose to live in the Tower," Richard said, something dark settling over his face.

"No." Kit placed a hand on his sleeve. "I'm sorry, I should not have reminded you." For close to two years, Richard and Mortimer had been locked up in one of the towers, taking turns to sleep so as not to be surprised by a murderous guard.

Richard made a dismissive gesture. "No matter. Besides, this is my first stop for the day."

Kit shrank back. "In there?" She'd spent several weeks here some years ago and had little fondness for the place.

"The constable is expecting me." Richard led the way, nodding curtly at the men-at-arms manning the first gatehouse. The approach to the Tower was an impressive construction— or so Adam always said, gesturing at the double portcullis and various arrow slits with as much pride as if he himself had built it. Kit might not grasp the finer points of defensive structures, but, as always, she was adequately overwhelmed as she followed her brother through first one, then towards another gatehouse. To their right, one of the lions paced its cage, a small band of apprentices yelling encouragement at it. Kit wrinkled her nose: the lion's pit stank—it always did.

Some moments of darkness as they walked through yet another arch and they were in the fortress, high walls on all sides. Richard extended his stride, Kit hastened after as well as she could, and soon enough they were in the presence of the constable, a man of an age with Mortimer who introduced himself as John de Cromwell.

Richard had private matters to discuss, and so Kit excused herself and wandered outside, sidestepping children and young men-at-arms as she made her way across the inner bailey. Tucked into the northwest corner of the curtain wall was the old chapel of St Peter, and in the narrow, open space before it was a little bench, shaded by a linden tree, its spring foliage that brittle light green that looked almost edible. Someone was sitting on the bench, contemplating the chapel, but it was big enough for two, so Kit sat down at the far end, content to study the bustle that surrounded her.

A sound from the other end had her glancing that way. The woman was weeping. At present, not all that uncommon in a reign where until recently so many men had died—either in combat or on the gallows.

The woman straightened up, and Kit could not suppress her exclamation. Eleanor de Clare, Lady Despenser, had more reason than most to weep. Gone was the haughty royal niece, gone was the woman high in favour, wife to the most powerful man in the land. At present, her husband's remains were rotting on various spikes throughout the country, and Eleanor de Clare was a widow—but a powerless widow, very much under the thumb of Queen Isabella.

She wore grey. A heavy wimple and veil reinforced the severity of her attire, but even dressed like a nun Lady Eleanor was a beautiful woman, if at present bowed with grief.

Kit was debating whether to leave when something made Lady Eleanor turn towards her.

"My…my…my lady," Kit stuttered, leaping to her feet and backing away.

"What are you doing here?"

"I am here with my brother."

Lady Eleanor's mouth tightened, and belatedly Kit recalled that much of the land bequeathed to Richard had until recently belonged to Hugh Despenser.

"I was thinking to light a candle for my son," Kit went on, mostly just to say something.

For a moment, Lady Eleanor's face crumpled, grief and agony visible in every line, every feature. She averted her face, inhaled.

"And I suppose you blame me for his death."

"You? No." Kit approached her. "Your husband, yes."

"He died of a fever." Lady Eleanor sounded weary. "Children die of fevers all the time. And he wasn't the only one to die—the entire village was affected."

"He died because he was there. My son died far away from me—because of your serpent of a husband."

Lady Eleanor flinched. "He's dead! Whatever crimes you accuse him of, he's paid for them."

Kit crossed herself. She'd been spared the obligation to attend Despenser's execution due to her swelling belly, but from what Adam had told her, it had been gruesome.

"And now my children will pay as well," Lady Eleanor continued. "My three daughters, forcibly cloistered." There were several unsteady inhalations. "Is that fair, do you think?"

"No." Kit came to crouch beside her. "To punish the children for the wrongs of the father strikes me as cruel, not fair."

"And yet the Holy Writ says that is what we should do."

"Not we, my lady. The good Lord." Kit raised her eyes to the sky and crossed herself. "It does not behove man to act in His place."

"In which case, I pray that God punishes Isabella—and Mortimer."

"As He will surely punish your husband," Kit said.

Meeting Eleanor de Clare left Kit with a sour taste in her mouth, even more so when the poor woman had been joined by the two children that remained to her, the sickly son named John and her youngest, still a babe in arms.

"What will happen to them?"

"What do I care?" Richard replied, spitting in the dust.

"They are children—and she's a cousin to the king."

"She is first and foremost Despenser's widow, and those are his get. Best for everyone if the Despenser bloodline is stamped out once and for all."

London was as intimidating as ever, with Kit clinging to her brother's arm while negotiating the thronged streets. She'd worn her pattens and had cause to repeatedly applaud herself at the foresight, manoeuvring through streets covered in waste of all kinds. Houses stood cheek to jowl, the upper storeys jutting out above the lower so as to almost enclose the streets in permanent dusk, the sky a mere ribbon of blue.

Some streets sported fine houses with glazed windows and armed servants at the door. Ladies, as elegant as any of those at court, were visible in doorways or as they stepped out of lavish litters, their male companions as richly dressed, with robes edged in fur and gold and jewels decorating hands and chests. Other streets were a sequence of humbler abodes, here and there deteriorating into hovels.

People were everywhere. Trollops displayed their wares with uncovered hair and generous necklines; a band of minstrels sang their way up a street; lads hauled carts laden with goods. In the distance rang church bells. A group of greyfriars hastened by, ignoring the outstretched hands of the many beggars.

"How do they live?" Kit asked, pressing herself closer to Richard. These human wrecks wrung her heart, but she had heard too many stories of beggars who presented themselves as lame or blind while being neither to be willing to part with as much as a farthing.

"They beg." He grinned at her. "And now and then they do a spot of thieving."

Not only the beggars: urchins ran about, swift bands of miniature predators that would easily cut your purse and disappear with all your coins before you'd even noticed they were there. Richard shoved a couple of lads out of the way, dagger prominently displayed.

From somewhere came the scents of baking bread, and everywhere were men and women, busy with their trade. A widow hauled an apprentice along by his ear; by the conduit, women stood in groups and gossiped as they waited their turn; hawkers wove their ways through the crowds, selling everything from warm pies to almond fritters.

Richard guided her down Cheapside, waited patiently while she made her purchases, and spent a considerable amount of time haggling with one of the goldsmiths before returning with a satisfied smile.

"For your wife?" Kit asked. Richard didn't reply, suggesting instead that they find somewhere to eat.

Kit sank down on the bench, relieved to be out of the press of people. Richard called for ale, bread, and cheese, and the innkeeper complied, adding an onion and a couple of wrinkled apples to the feast.

She'd finished her meal when the door banged open. In came a group of men, loud and swaggering. Armed men, Kit noted, swords visible beneath their cloaks. No arms on their tabards, nothing to show who they might be serving, but it took but a glance for Kit to recognise one of them. She muttered a curse and shrank further into her corner. Richard frowned and followed her gaze, stopping mid-chew as he studied the newcomers.

"Swords for hire, or worse."

"Yes." Kit's hands tightened round her mug. "And one of them is Godfrey of Broseley." The scar slashing across his face was distinctive, and Kit had been in far too close proximity to Godfrey of Broseley on a number of occasions for her to ever forget him. She'd thought him dead, and here he was, alive and hale, lording it over his companions. Not a tall man, Broseley made up for lack of height in width, powerful shoulders outlined by his tunic. Dark hair, dark beard—grey around the scar—and deep-set eyes under heavy brows, he heaved with menace—or so it felt to Kit.

"Broseley?" Richard gripped his dagger.

Kit shook her head. "They're four, you're one." She pursed her lips, studying the man who had once abducted her—and who she'd stabbed in return. "What is he doing here? With Despenser gone, he should stay well away." Broseley had been a Despenser man, had come close to murdering Mortimer and the queen last year, and as to the slashed face, that was courtesy of Adam's blade, damage inflicted when he defended himself against Godfrey some years back.

"Despenser may be gone, but the former king is still very much alive, isn't he?" Richard shoved the cup away from him. "We must talk to Lord Roger."

"Why? You think he poses a threat?"

"Not him. But those he serves." Richard made as if to stand, but Kit pulled him down.

"He'll recognise you—and me. Best we wait until he's gone."

Chapter 7

The king was in a foul mood. So was Lord Roger, and at present they were glaring at each other over the table.

"We must," Lord Roger repeated.

"Why? Those Scottish dogs are not to be trusted."

Adam sighed. His lord and master had quite the thorn up his side when it came to the Scots, cheeks going a dull red whenever someone mentioned the devastating defeat his father had suffered at their hands well over a decade ago.

"Neither are several of your barons," Lord Roger snapped. "We turn our back on them to crush the Scots, and who knows what may happen."

King Edward snorted. "Are you saying I have barons that would rise against me?"

"In the name of your sire, yes." Lord Roger scrubbed at his face. "Not everyone is content with how matters have ended."

"I wonder why," Edward muttered, staring down at the table. Adam glanced at Lord Roger. He'd obviously heard the king, his jaw clenching, but chose instead to return to the subject at hand.

"The truce will not hold unless we offer them a treaty."

"Then let them break it. Let them, and we will pound them to the ground." Edward banged his fist on the table.

Fool. Adam shared a look with Lord Roger. Their fiery young king knew nothing of war—and even less about fighting the Scots.

"I shall discuss it with your lady mother," Mortimer said, making Edward scowl.

"I will not—" Whatever the king was about to refuse to do, they would never know. Richard de Monmouth entered the hall as if his shoes were on fire, making directly for the dais. Behind him came Kit, at a more controlled pace.

"My liege," he said, bowing deeply before the king.

"What is the matter?" Edward asked.

"We've seen Godfrey of Broseley."

What? Adam whipped round to face Kit. She nodded, hands clasped tightly in front of her.

"Godfrey who?" Edward stretched for a walnut.

"One of Despenser's men," Lord Roger explained. "The man charged with murdering me and your lady mother."

"And he's here?" Edward half stood. "What are you waiting for? Find him!"

"The more relevant question is *why* is he here," Lord Roger said just as the queen entered.

"Who is here?" Queen Isabella smiled at her son, smoothed at his dark blue tunic, and kissed his cheek. "You look quite regal, my son."

Edward shrugged off her hand. "Godfrey someone."

"Broseley?" Queen Isabella looked at Richard. "Is he here?"

"We saw him, my lady," Kit said. "In an inn just off Cheapside."

Cheapside? Adam raised his brows and looked at her. He couldn't recall having been informed of his wife's excursion to London, and he was less than pleased at the thought of her braving those vermin-infested streets without him. Kit dropped her gaze.

"Why would he risk coming here?" the queen asked.

"Maybe he has nowhere else to go," Kit offered.

"If that is the case, he'd have been better off staying on the Continent." Lord Roger cracked his knuckles. "Here, it is but a matter of time before he adorns a gibbet. No, if Broseley is here, it is at the request of someone else." For an instant, his teeth flashed. "One of your loyal barons, my liege?"

"Find him," Edward said. "Let us have the truth from him."

"I have sent out men already," Richard said. "If he's still in London, they'll find him."

Adam was not as certain; one man in London was like a needle in a haystack. Godfrey of Broseley, here! He set a hand on the hilt of his dagger. The man should have died for what he did to Kit in Valenciennes.

"Good." With a curt nod, the king strode off, calling for Adam to come along.

"Do you think he's right?" Edward asked once they were outside.

"My lord?"

"Mortimer. Must I treat with the Scots because I have rebellious barons who may stab me in the back?"

"Aye, I think you must." Not that the lad would be anywhere close to the negotiation table. Such matters would be handled by his mother and Lord Roger.

"God's blood!" A stone went sailing. "Why would they want to harm me?"

"Not you, my lord."

"No, of course not." Edward sounded bitter. "I am but the puppet, am I not?"

There was nothing Adam could say to that.

They'd not found Broseley. Adam and his men had turned London upside down, but they had found nothing—not even a trail worth pursuing. The damned man had come and gone like a ghost.

"Gone like the wind," Richard commented, gritting his teeth.

"More like a rat." Adam served himself some more ale.

"Why so anxious to find him?" Will Montagu joined them. Adam shared a hasty look with Richard. This the eldest of the king's new boon companions, was ever asking questions, dark eyes revealing little of what he thought.

"Broseley attempted to murder the queen." Adam decided it was best to not mention Mortimer had also been an intended victim.

"Ah." Montagu's face revealed nothing. "Not entirely surprising—if you happen to have pledged your loyalty to our former king. Had he succeeded, he'd have been a baron by now."

Adam had a firm hold of Richard's thigh under the table, pinning him to his seat. "But he failed."

"Yes." Montagu studied his nails. "And so the king is incarcerated like a felon."

"Hush," Adam warned. "Such talk can have you joining him."

"Besides, he's king no more," Richard put in. "Your king, the lord you've pledged yourself to, is there." He nodded at the king, sprawled on the floor with his brother and his dog.

Montagu nodded, his mouth curving into a little smile. "Fortunately, he will not forever remain a lad." The smile broke free, revealing a lot of teeth. "And then we'll see."

"See what?" Richard demanded, half out of his chair.

"What happens next." Montagu sauntered off to join his comrades.

Adam studied them thoughtfully, the knot of noble youths that these days were the king's closest companions— at the king's insistence rather than his mother's, saying it was his obligation to heal the rifts caused by the last few years of constant strife. Wise lad, in more ways than one. The loud youths presently laughing and jostling each other would, in time, grow up to be the most influential men in England, bar Lord Roger.

One of the more recent arrivals was a thin lad called Robert—Robert de Langon, from somewhere near Bordeaux. For some reason, he'd taken an instant dislike to Adam, taking every opportunity to point out that some—like Robert himself—came of ancient lineage, while others were mere upstarts. Not that de Langon's lineage was all that remarkable: his grandfather a merchant made knight in connection with de Montfort's rebellion, his father a somewhat wealthier lord, but if anything, his lack of antecedents made Robert all the more sensitive as to his family.

At present, Robert was hovering on the outside of the group round the king, laughing loudly at Stafford's jests while trying to push his way closer to the king. He turned, caught Adam looking, and scowled. Adam merely smiled.

"He's right, you know." Adam poured Richard some more ale

"I know." Richard frowned at the table. "He's not helping, is he?"

"Who?"

Richard lowered his voice. "Lord Roger. He's amassing land and offices, distributing them to his men, his family. Good men, competent men, mostly—not like those insufferable lackeys Despenser surrounded himself with—but still." He gave Adam a glum look.

"It's not only him." Adam nodded discreetly in the direction of the queen. "She is as much a power behind the throne as he is."

Richard snorted. "Yes, of course she is. But for some odd reason, most men fail to recognise a she-wolf as long as she disguises herself behind a soft voice and fluttering veils." He fiddled with the cuff of his sleeve. "A woman like that requires a strong man to keep her in her place."

Adam smiled into his ale. Easy to say if your woman was a mere child.

"Do you truly think he's planning something?" Richard asked. Adam scratched his head. His brother-in-law had a most irritating tendency to leap from one subject to the other.

"Broseley? I don't know. But just the thought of him being nearby has me gagging."

"Well, he'd be a fool if he tried anything with Kit, what with Egard trailing her like a shadow."

"Useful man, Egard." Adam rubbed at a stain on the table. He owed Egard his life and trusted him implicitly with that of his wife. He was, however, quite convinced that if Broseley was here for a reason, it was not to exact revenge on him or Kit. Not only.

"Lady Kit!"

Kit wheeled, smiling at the young man who came bounding towards her, a flurry of purple wool and bright red silk. Dark curls fell unhindered to his shoulders and an elegant little beard adorned his features but did little to harden the soft, pouting mouth, the large dark eyes.

"My lord," she said, "I've scarcely seen you since you arrived." Louis of Valois had ridden in with great fanfare some days earlier, bringing with him greetings from his cousin, the French king, to his much younger cousin, the English king.

"Pff! Being an emissary is hard work. An endless succession of meetings." Count Louis flapped his hat before his face. "Hot, eh?"

"Very." Kit went back to surveying her packed belongings. The court was moving to Windsor, and for days Westminster had been a beehive of activity. "Will you be joining the king at Windsor, or must you hasten back to King Charles?"

"He can wait." Count Louis shrugged. "Three times this year, I've crossed that infernal narrow sea. Every time, there has been a storm. I need to rest before I brave it again."

"Yes, you do look rather careworn," Kit said, tongue-in-cheek.

"Late night." Count Louis grinned. "My royal cousin and I partook of the more delicate of English fruits."

"I know. Adam came back just before dawn." Smelling of wine and rose water, but stone sober and in a foul mood after having yet another night's sleep disrupted on account of the French whelp and his predilection for wenches and wine.

"I can assure you he did no partaking," Count Louis said.

"Why, thank you, my lord."

"Not for want of opportunity. Men like your lord husband, they attract a certain kind of woman."

"Really?"

Count Louis grinned. "My kind." He mimed a voluptuous female body. He cocked his head. "Not at all like you, my lady. You are… Ah yes, you are like a graceful reed, supple and…"

"Green?" Kit suggested.

"Green?" Count Louis grinned. "Oh, I think not, my lady. Red, I think. Cool on the outside, but hot and passionate inside, as juicy as a pomegranate." He winked and licked his lips.

"My lord!" But she couldn't stop herself from laughing. A pomegranate indeed.

Adam was not as amused when she shared the little incident with him, muttering that he preferred it if that French troubadour stayed well away from his wife.

"A pomegranate? Cheeky little thing, isn't he?" He slapped Raven on his broad rump and moved towards her, the straw rustling under his boots. The stables were close to empty, most of the horses presently out in the yard, saddled and ready to go.

"And you are no reed," he added, his hand following the contour of her hip. "There are far more curves here than he can see."

"As it should be. I have no intention of disrobing before him."

"I am right glad to hear that," Adam growled, his hand tightening possessively on her buttocks.

"What do you do while the king and his cousin engage in bed-sport?" Kit asked, leaning into his touch.

"Wait." He scowled. "Beat off whores who want me to sample their wares."

"Ah." She brushed at his jaw. "And are you never tempted to…"

"Me?" He looked down his nose at her. "Why would I go elsewhere for what I can get from my wife?"

"I gather my wares are somewhat less generous than those of the ladies of the stews. Maybe you enjoy variety."

Adam blinked. "Your wares? You are my wife, not a trollop. You have no wares."

"I don't?"

"No." He nibbled at her ear. "You have hidden delights that belong only to me." A grin flashed across his face. "Are you jealous?"

"Of the whores? No. Of the king and his cousin, yes. They see far more of you than I do." She ran a light finger up and down his forearm. "But should you ever come home smelling of another woman, I would likely use a knife on you."

"Many men bed with whores—or other women than their wives."

"Not you." She captured his eyes. "I could not bear it."

He ran a thumb over her lower lip. "Not me."

Edward was proud as a peacock as he rode towards the massive gatehouses of the castle. "Welcome to Windsor, Cousin," he said, standing in his stirrups to gesture at the towering walls. "Quite something, isn't it?"

For once, Count Louis was at loss for words. Adam smiled to himself as he followed the king and the count through the gate, smiled even wider at Count Louis' reaction upon entering the lower ward and seeing the next set of gates, those leading to the middle ward.

They dismounted, and Adam was considering whether to wait for his wife when Edward set off, gesturing for Adam to come with him. With a little sigh, he fell in behind his king, listening with half an ear as Edward pointed out St Edward's chapel to his cousin, thereby initiating a heated discussion as to the merits of this English saint versus those of St Denis.

They hastened through the gatehouse and entered the middle ward, and for an instant Count Louis stopped, staring at the large motte just ahead. A squat keep sat atop it, and a deep, dry ditch surrounded it, making it near on impregnable, no matter that someone was using the bottom of the ditch as some sort of flower garden.

Edward pulled Louis along, leading him through the small postern gate inserted in the northern wall and out on the natural terrace beyond.

"See?" He opened his arms wide. "What enemy can ever breach this?"

The castle was built upon an escarpment, the cliff falling away into a sheer drop impossible to climb—at least on horseback. Below them, the Thames glinted in the sunlight, a natural moat, yet another barrier for anyone attempting to take the castle from the north.

"Beautiful," Count Louis said, staring at the landscape before them. "Almost as beautiful as France." He grinned slyly. "Not as rich, of course. Or as cultured."

Edward punched his arm, making Count Louis laugh.

"When I am king of France…" Edward began, and Louis laughed even harder.

"You? No, no, my dear cousin that will never happen. My brother was more than delighted when Queen Jeanne presented her husband with yet another daughter. It seems

65

Cousin Charles is not to be blessed with sons, but fortunately for France, the Counts of Valois are ready to take over."

Edward set his jaw. "I am Charles' closest male relative."

"Yes, but through his sister." Louis made a dismissive gesture. "Women don't count—not when there are male heirs through the male line."

"My mother would not agree with you," Edward said.

"What would she know? She's a woman." Count Louis ducked Edward's punch, grinned like a gargoyle, and raced back towards the postern gate with Edward in loud pursuit. Adam followed more slowly. Count Louis was right: the French would never countenance an English king on their throne, not when there were other male heirs. Unfortunately, Queen Isabella shared her son's conviction that the only true heir to King Charles was Edward of Windsor.

With the keep and the royal apartments filled to bursting, Adam had been allocated a room in the lower ward, above the stables and just across from the chapel. Not that Kit minded, but the room was dark and fusty, and the bedframe itself was too narrow for her precious feather bed. Rhosyn complained about everything: the horses smelled, the floor was dirty, there was no hearth, and the shutters squeaked. Exasperated, Kit sent her off to find herself a pallet in the great hall—once she'd replaced the straw in the mattress.

It was late before Adam came to find his quarters. She heard his limping footsteps, careful on the ancient stairs, slow along the narrow, darkened passage. There was a muttered exclamation—no doubt he'd cracked his head on the low rafters—some moments of conversation with Gavin, and then the door opened.

She'd left the shutters open, and a breeze tinged with the scents of new grass, dog roses, and elderflowers wafted through the room. Adam moved towards the bed, sitting down with a sigh.

"Your foot?"

"Aye."

Kit helped him off with his boots—since Despenser had driven that red-hot stake through his foot, Adam rarely wore shoes. He lay back, and she stripped him of his hose before retrieving a small pot from one of their chests. Adam groaned when she rubbed the ointment over his foot, releasing the scents of St John's wort, lavender, and comfrey into the night air.

Kit took her time, humming softly under her breath as she worked her way up and down his foot and calf a number of times. Under her hands, she felt his muscles relax, the toes uncurling from their crooked state.

"Better?" She set the pot aside. When he nodded, she turned her attention to his thighs instead, her fingers tracing small, uneven circles as she moved slowly upwards. Adam's hand rested on her head, stroking her softly over her unbound hair.

"Undress me, sweeting," he ordered in a husky voice. The bed dipped and swayed as she rid him of his braies and tunic, of his shirt. The weak light of the candle danced over his naked body, reflected in his eyes. She fondled his member, and it grew hot and hard. Kit met Adam's gaze before lowering her head. He inhaled, loudly, and held his breath. She kissed her way up his heavy cock, and when she took him in her mouth, he exhaled, a breathless "Kit" escaping him.

She released him, buried her nose in his groin, and drew in the scent of him, that most intimate smell of hot skin and arousal. His wiry curls tickled her, and she sneezed, making him jerk.

"Lie still," she told him, running her tongue up the length of him. There was a strangled sound, and when she kissed the head of his cock, his fingers tightened in her hair.

"Dearest God," he groaned, making Kit intensify her efforts. His thighs tensed, his balls tightened and shifted in her hold, and Adam had his head thrown back, hips moving in time with her mouth. He gripped her shoulders.

"No." A hoarse sound. "No, Kit, I don't want to…"

In response, she flicked her tongue, and he sucked in air, his buttocks rising off the bed for an instant.

"No, my lady." His fingers sank into the fine linen of her new chemise. "My turn."

Moments later, she was on her back, her shift pulled over her head, still tangled with her arms. The heat of his mouth on her nipples, the strength of his leg as he used it to widen her thighs, the softness of his lips, the scraping sensation of his bristles on the tender skin of her belly—Kit clutched at him, strangling a little cry when a strong finger slid into her.

The straw in the mattress rustled. That thick thatch of fair hair tickled her skin and his hands slid under her and lifted her up, towards his warm mouth and skilled tongue. Kit groped for something to hold on to, found one of the bedposts. Warmth shot through her loins, and in her ears she heard her heartbeat, pounding at her temples.

"Adam," she gasped. Beneath her skin her blood boiled while her body twisted under his mouth. She tugged at his hair. No more. She was falling apart, her limbs shivering, her skin tingling. That tongue…Kit banged her hand against the bedpost, arching her back off the bed. Adam. Her Adam. Her toes curled. She needed him. Now. Here, at last, he came, and she tasted herself on his lips, drowned in his wide-open eyes as he thrust himself inside of her.

Kit clutched at him. He eased out, captured her eyes, and surged into her, skin slapping against skin. So big, and she groaned but wanted—needed—more. Again, and he was so deep inside of her it made her quiver helplessly. His breath came in gusts, he drove hard into her, and Kit was surrounded by his warmth, by his strength and his scent, while he impaled himself deeper and deeper into her.

"Ad—"

He kissed her, sucking the words into his mouth. Kit's body exploded. Vaguely, she heard him exclaim her name, all of him going rigid before he collapsed on top of her.

His weight was squashing her. His mouth was wet against her neck, his breathing tickled her. Kit closed her eyes and rubbed a foot up and down his hairy calf. Adam lifted himself up on an elbow, brushing the back of his fingers down her cheek.

"Not a pomegranate. A furnace," he said before slumping down beside her. He yawned and pulled her close, legs still entwined. "My furnace."

Chapter 8

"I told him, didn't I?" King Edward turned to grin at Adam. "One cannot trust those Scottish mongrels." He didn't wait for a reply, galloping off to the head of the column. He cut a fine figure in hauberk and greaves, new gauntlets and boots. The Spanish stallion was as temperamental as its master and just as flamboyant, long tail flowing in the wind like a pennon.

Adam held in Raven and waited for Kit, riding farther down the line. They'd been on the road for several days, a slow march in the direction of York. The king had insisted it was time to teach the Scots a lesson, and Mortimer had finally acquiesced, this after months of continuous Scottish raiding.

Waiting in York were Lord Percy and Henry of Lancaster, and Adam had little hope for an amicable meeting between Lord Roger and the disgruntled Lancaster.

"Beautiful, isn't it?" Kit said when she drew her horse to a halt beside him.

"Aye." The land folded softly, copses of trees separating narrow fields of growing crops and meadows. Poppies dotted the grassy verges, the wheat already shifting from green to gold. Less than seven weeks to Lammas Day, but this year it seemed the harvest would be good—assuming the weather held. Further to the northeast, the walls and spires of York were faintly visible, and come vespers they would all be installed in the town—or so Adam hoped, longing for a bed and some privacy, hours alone with his wife.

"Do you think there will be war?" Kit asked in a casual tone as they ambled along.

"Outright battle?" Adam shook his head. "That old fox, King Robert, has far too much to lose. But skirmishes? Aye."

"Oh." She rode closer.

69

"It will not amount to much." Adam gave her a reassuring smile. "And neither Lord Roger nor the queen intend risking the king, so I dare say I'll be safely away from action."

"What? Will you not be joining our glorious campaign?" Thomas of Norfolk grinned at them and wiped his face. "Lady Kit, as radiant as ever—and a capable rider at that."

"I thought you were riding at the front, my lord," Adam said, watching with some irritation as Kit blushed and adjusted her floating veil. Not, Adam noted, to cover, but rather to frame her face and dark red hair.

"So did I. But handsome here had other plans." Thomas slapped his horse on the neck. "Back to being docile now, aren't you?" In response, the large horse snorted, chestnut tail swishing back and forth.

"I had taken you for an experienced horseman, my lord," Kit teased.

"I am. Had I not been, I'd have been lying in pig-shit by now." He shook his head. "One could think Merlin has never seen a sow before."

"Maybe he hasn't," Kit said. "Or maybe he disliked the smell—it was somewhat overpowering." They'd passed a herd of pigs some miles back, spotted things the size of a calf.

Thomas smiled at her before directing himself to Adam. "Edward will never allow Mortimer to set off without him."

"Mortimer? I thought it was Lancaster, Norfolk, and Kent that were to lead the assembled men." Not that any of the royal earls had the experience required to lead a campaign, but Adam chose not to say that. Instead, he winked, causing Thomas to huff.

"And Norfolk says Mortimer will ride, as will the king. Our young king wishes to heap himself with glory on the battlefield."

Adam snorted. "There will be no battlefield—not against the Scots. If our king desires glory, better he seeks it at the lists."

"Ah yes, I heard he unhorsed you last week." Thomas laughed. Adam did not. Kit muffled something that sounded like a giggle.

"Luck," Adam muttered, rubbing at his chest. He guided Raven around a puddle. "Do you truly think King Edward will convince his lady mother to allow him to go?"

"It is a wise mother who knows what battles she cannot win. In this, our Ned will not back down."

Adam pressed his lips together. He should have insisted Kit return home when they turned north, but instead he'd allowed her to ride with them, confident that this little adventure would end before it began. He studied her from under his lashes: the fresh air brought out roses on her cheeks, but the glow on her face came from within. His practised eye slid over her bosom, and he cursed inwardly. His wife was carrying, and had she told him a week ago, she'd have been safe and sound in Tresaints by now instead of sitting astride her horse while bantering with Thomas.

"Something has to be done," Thomas said, recalling Adam to the conversation. "Those Scottish rogues have raided and pillaged the north for months."

"Impossible to catch," Adam said. "They come at night, wreak destruction, and disappear like morning fog when the sun rises."

"Douglas is riding with five hundred knights and uncounted foot soldiers." Thomas set his jaw. "And so far he shows no sign of dissipating into thin air with the coming dawn."

"Five hundred knights do not sound like much." Kit shaded her eyes, studying the men around them. "We must be many more."

"Aye, but in difference to this lot, Douglas has battle-hardened men." The earl tapped his nose. "One thing my sainted father always said was that the wise general never underestimates his foe." He set spurs to his horse. "Best I share that little nugget of wisdom with my royal nephew."

"Best of luck with that," Adam said to his back. In response, the earl waved.

"It's interesting how two brothers can be so different," Kit commented.

"Aye." Edmund of Kent never as much as glanced at Kit, while Thomas took every opportunity to compliment her, leaving her with glittering eyes and pink skin.

"I'd hazard it is Thomas that most resembles his royal sire," Kit continued. "Both in wits and looks."

Adam grunted, no more. Edmund was an inflated popinjay, so handsome men never saw much further than his pretty face, but Adam found him devious and cunning, not at all as sunny and innocent as the countenance he turned upon the world. As to Thomas, he liked and respected the man—a lot—but it irked him that his wife was so fond of him.

"Do you think he is right?" Kit asked. "Will the king prevail upon his mother?"

He shrugged, no more. Kit gave him a sidelong look. Adam stared straight ahead.

"What's the matter?" she asked.

"The matter?" He turned her way. "Why, surely you know the answer to that, Wife." She looked away and he suppressed a little smile. A lad, he hoped. "Well? Even Thomas commented on how radiant you look."

Kit collected the reins and urged her palfrey into a trot. Adam followed suit. She rose in the saddle, and the palfrey set off at full gallop over the nearby field. Raven easily kept up, and Adam leaned across and snatched the reins out of her hands, bringing both animals to a halt.

"Well?" he repeated.

"I'm sorry," she mumbled. "I should have told you before."

"You should. Had you done so, you'd have been in Tresaints by now."

"I…" Thick lashes shielded her eyes. "I didn't want you to go without me."

"Sweeting." He reached over to cup her chin, thereby forcing her to meet his eyes. "There will always be times when I must leave you."

"I could ride with you. Plenty of women do."

"To war?" He shook his head. Aye, an army rode with women, from the mandatory camp whores to the washerwomen who kept them in clean linen. "It is not a life for a lady."

"And yet Lady Joan accompanied Lord Roger on various campaigns."

"Lady Joan is a formidable lady." He smiled, recalling just how she'd berated her husband for trying to stop her from riding with him. His Kit, thank the Lord, was not as forceful—albeit she could be as stubborn as a mule.

"And I am not?" She sounded hurt.

"Of course you are. But you're with child."

"And she never was?" Kit made a disbelieving sound. "She gave Lord Roger a dozen children. Had she stayed at home all the time she was carrying, she'd never have seen him."

He chose not to reply. Instead, he took her hand. "What Lady Joan did or didn't do is neither here nor there. You are far too precious to me to risk your well-being—and that of our babe." He kissed her fingers, one by one. "I shall arrange for an escort with Egard in charge. You will be home within the fortnight."

She made as if to protest, but he set a finger to her mouth. "Don't, sweeting. I hate it as much as you do when we are apart, but I will not take you with me to war."

"You hate it? Truly?"

"You know I do." He rode closer, his leg brushing against hers. "Were it up to me, we would never leave Tresaints."

"Or our bed," she replied, sending him a blue look.

"That too." He smiled at her. "And I am very glad about the babe."

"So am I." Her face broke into a radiant smile. "So am I."

They entered York through the Mickelgate Bar, riding through narrow cobbled streets thronged with people. Sturdy cross-timbered houses lined the street, most of them with some sort of trade being plied out of the ground-floor rooms. Higher up, the houses sported latticed windows and whitewashed daub and wattle, and at times the upper storeys hung so far out over the street it would have been a simple matter to leap across from one to the other. They passed dark crooked alleys that had Adam riding as close as he could to the king's left side, hand resting on the hilt of his sword as he peered into the dark, wondering just how many armed men could be hiding in the shadows. It made his skin crawl, however fanciful.

Someone had spread herbs on the streets, but the scent of trampled mint and rosemary did little to cover the prevalent stench of urine and shit, of constantly damp wool and smoky fires. Through the marketplace, and right in front rose what would be the cathedral, at present covered in scaffolding. The king held in his horse as if considering whether to ride over to inspect the building work but decided not to, turning instead to his right.

The horses clattered over the ancient stone bridge that spanned the Ouse, turned right, and there before them rose the huge and impressive keep of York Castle, atop a conical motte. The people of York trailed after them, some shouting blessings to the young king, most ominously silent. Most of them were men, with flat eyes and unsmiling mouths, and here and there Adam spotted the gleam of a blade, the contour of a hidden crossbow. Adam's scalp itched, and it was with some relief he allowed the king to precede him through the gatehouse separating the castle from the town of York.

Inside was a large bailey, on the other side of which stood a giant gatehouse guarding the southern approach to the castle, further defended by the expanse of the River Foss. At present, the enclosed space was full of men and horses, an assortment of buildings lining the inner circumference of the walls. Smoke rose from various fires, there was linen hanging to dry, a sour tang of overfull latrines, and opposite to the main gatehouse was a smaller gate, leading to the separately enclosed keep.

Thick walls, vigilant sentries—Adam nodded in approval before dismounting and throwing the reins to Gavin. "Take my wife's horse as well," Adam instructed, lifting Kit to the ground. "Ask Stephen to help you," he added, referring to his new page.

"That tadpole?" Gavin scoffed. "He's more of a nuisance than anything else."

"Oh? Not that long ago, so were you." Adam cuffed him. "I expect you to teach him how to groom a horse and polish armour."

"I already know how to groom a horse, my lord," Stephen informed them. A heavy, dark fringe all but hid his eyes, the sleeves of his tunic not quite covering his knobbly wrists. The lad sprouted like a leek, Adam grumbled to Kit, any day now he'd overtop Gavin despite being three years his junior.

"Gavin won't like that," Kit said, watching the lads out of sight.

"I dare say he'll hold his own." Adam took her hand as they negotiated the bailey. "Where's Rhosyn?"

"There." Kit pointed at her maid, who was slowly getting down from one of the carts. "She'll make my ears sore with all her complaining—our Rhosyn would have preferred a litter, she says."

"She's a maid, not a lady." Adam bowed in greeting when a man he recognised as Lord Percy came striding towards them. With a blank look on his face, Percy pushed by them, not bothering to return the greeting.

"That was rude," Kit said, lifting her skirts as they skipped across a pile of horse dung.

"Northerner—what can you expect?" He frowned. Why were so many of the men making for the gate that led to the town? And what was that noise?

Kit came to a halt, tilting her head. "Can you hear that?"

He could. He took hold of her shoulders. "Go straight to the keep," he ordered. "Now."

"What…" Her voice tailed off. Loud, angry voices—many, many voices. A mob in the making, Adam concluded, shoving her gently towards the keep.

"Go." He swivelled on his feet, near on barging into Earl Thomas and the king.

"What is that noise?" the king demanded.

"Your subjects," Thomas replied. "And from the sound of it, they're none too happy." He slapped Edward on the shoulder. "Probably think you spend far too much on shiny armour, far too little on food for them."

The king scowled at his uncle and insisted on seeing for himself. Together, Thomas and Adam pushed their way through, creating sufficient room for the king to enter the gatehouse and make for the ramparts. The stairwell was dark, slippery, and mercifully short, and once outside, Adam gaped.

The silent crowd was no more. Before him was a sea of angry men, as if every man within the walls of York were on the road below, armed with whatever they'd had at hand. Amongst them were scores of English archers, and surrounded by all these men was a tight knot of soldiers—Hainault men, Adam concluded after peering at their colours, men loaned to Mortimer by the Count of Hainault prior to last year's return to England.

"They don't seem to like foreigners here," Thomas commented.

"Those Hainaulters have themselves to blame, casting aspersions on our English archers," Percy said. "It's been like this since they arrived some days ago. They've been brawling in inns and whorehouses, and God alone knows how many men have been injured—or killed."

"More to come," Adam said just as the crowd got hold of one of the Hainaulters and dragged him away from his beleaguered fellows. The following screams had him wanting to cover his ears, and then there were no screams. Instead, various body parts flew up into the air under loud cheering.

"God," Adam muttered, all of him tensing when the mob threw itself forward, intent on new prey. "They're going to kill them—all of them." And the Hainaulters were going to sell themselves dear, pikes and swords flashing in the air as the mercenaries yelled their defiance.

"What is happening here?" Mortimer pushed his way through. "Damnation! We need those men! All of them."

"I'm not risking any of my men to save those Flemish bastards," Lord Percy said, and beside him Henry of Lancaster muttered an agreement.

"Why are they so aggrieved?" the king asked, staring at the crowd.

"Why? Because for two months the people for the north have suffered the rampage of those accursed, misbegotten Scots, and not once have those equally misbegotten Flemish bastards been on hand to save them." Percy's voice shook with anger. "Your people bleed and starve, my liege, and all the while you've sat in London doing nothing."

There was a moment of utter silence.

"They think I have failed them?" Edward shot Mortimer a venomous look. "Me? No, that I will not have!"

Before anyone could stop him, he was gone, leaping down the stairs. "My horse," Adam heard him yell.

"Shit," Thomas said.

"Aye." Adam was hurrying as well as he could down the narrow stairs. At one point, his damaged foot gave way, and he'd have fallen had not the earl reached out and grabbed his arm.

The king was already riding towards the gate. Adam shoved a man aside and mounted a sturdy grey, with Thomas vaulting atop Percy's stallion.

"To me!" Adam yelled, and the knights of the royal household came running, mounting whatever horses they could find.

"You heard him! Protect your king!" Mortimer appeared beside them, astride the queen's palfrey. He charged off, and by the time the gate was opened, Mortimer was riding just behind the king, paired with Thomas.

"Move!" Henry of Lancaster crowded past Adam, with Edmund of Kent hot on his heels. He allowed them to pass before ordering the king's knights to take up a protective formation—hard to do when the king made straight for the roaring mob.

"I'm going to belt the fool," Adam muttered once he'd caught up with Mortimer and Thomas.

"Believe you me, that will not be necessary. Not once his lady mother has finished with him." Mortimer spat out the words. "Dear God, if he gets himself killed…" A tremor rushed through him. He spurred his mount forward.

"No boy-king, no Mortimer," Thomas said in an undertone, eyes boring into Lord Roger's back.

Adam grunted. Should his lord perish, there was the young John of Eltham, safe in Windsor

"My people!" Edward rose in his stirrups, his sword pointing at the sky. "Too long have you suffered the savaging of the Scottish dogs, but I tell you—I swear to you—it will stop. I will crush them and rid your fair lands of this vermin, once and for all."

"Has a flair to him, doesn't he?" Thomas commented.

He was magnificent. Young and handsome, his fair hair gleaming in the sun, Edward looked a martial archangel, sword raised, cloak fluttering in the wind. And the people responded.

"God save you, our liege," someone yelled, and thousands took up the cry, some even falling to their knees. Pitchforks and cudgels were lowered, men shuffled to the side, allowing the mercenaries to escape their death trap. Too late for some— for very many. The trampled ground was stained with blood, and there were dead men everywhere, men-at-arms lying side by side with common men.

Edward's sword wavered, and Adam could see the lad clenching his teeth, eyes on anything but the corpses. As the mob fell back, Adam urged his men forward—slowly, so as not to create panic. Only once the king was safe did Adam relax, loosening his grip on his sword.

"Adam!" Thomas' voice rose to a shout. "Behind you!"

He turned his mount. One man, standing up. One man cradling a crossbow—aimed at Lord Roger. Adam clapped his heels into the horse. It surged forward, towards the hooded shooter.

"My lord Mortimer!" he yelled in warning, just as the bolt whizzed by him. Adam roared and pulled his sword. The man flung the crossbow at the horse, causing it to veer to the side. The rogue darted off through the crowds with Adam in pursuit. Narrow cobbled streets filled with people made it hard going for a man on a horse, but Adam had his eyes on the dark red hood, bobbing rapidly in the direction of the Ouse.

"There!" Thomas appeared beside him, using his sword to point down a dark and winding alley. It ended in a wall. Their quarry slid to a stop so abruptly the hood became dislodged. He threw a glance over his shoulders, and for an instant he met Adam's eyes. Godfrey of Broseley.

"You!" Adam pulled his mount to a brutal halt.

"Indeed; me." Broseley sneered and clambered up the wall, verily like the rat he was. "And next time, I'll aim at you." One moment here, the next he was gone, disappearing out of sight into the yard beyond. Adam was already dismounting.

"No! No point." Thomas gestured at their silent spectators. "We'd best return to the king—and Mortimer."

Chapter 9

"It was nothing," Mortimer said.

"He could have killed you." Queen Isabella's hand hovered over Lord Roger's arm, at present neatly bandaged.

"A graze, no more." For an instant, Lord Roger's fingers gripped the queen's. "A graze, my lady—which you have seen properly doctored." They shared a look, and Adam averted his gaze, uncomfortable with the heat, the tenderness, that passed between them. She smoothed a strand of dark hair off Mortimer's brow. His face softened, mouth curving into a gentle smile.

The queen cleared her throat and straightened up, distancing herself a foot or so from Lord Roger. "Broseley, you say?"

"Yes, my lady." Adam balled his hand into a fist.

"And he got away?" The queen's tone cut straight through him.

"He scaled a wall. Difficult to do on a horse," Thomas said.

"He tried to murder Roger!" The queen whirled, her kirtle swirling. She held up her hand, thumb and index finger a couple of inches apart. "This close! Somewhat more to the right, and he'd have..." She inhaled, lowered her hand. "He'd have been dead," she finished dully. She looked at Lord Roger. "And I would not know how to bear it."

"My lady." Lord Roger jerked his head in the direction of the door, and the few men assembled fell over their feet in their haste to allow him and his queen some privacy. Just as Adam ducked out of the door, he saw Lord Roger enfold the queen, her long fingers clinging to his broad shoulders as she hid her face against his chest.

"Well." Thomas sounded shaken. "She does love him, doesn't she?" He led the way down the circular stairs.

"Aye." Adam felt an itch in his throat, an urgent desire to

find Kit and hold her like Lord Roger held Queen Isabella, protected within the curve of his arms.

"Sad," Thomas reflected. "An illicit love always leads to hell, no matter how pure."

"Maybe God makes an exception now and then."

Thomas laughed. "Maybe." He sobered. "I hope so. One does not deserve to burn for loving."

From behind them came a loud snort. Henry of Lancaster stepped out of an embrasure in the wall.

"Love? That is not love; that is adultery. But even if our Lord should forgive him for that, He will never forgive him for his greed." He tugged at the sleeves of his robes, deep blue velvet adorned with an embroidered border of lions and prancing bears.

"Greed?" Thomas looked at his cousin. "Are you suggesting Lord Roger is greedier than you are, dear Henry?"

Lancaster paled. "What is that supposed to mean?"

"Well, ever since February, you've been on and on about the lands your brother lost." Thomas smirked. "My namesake's erstwhile domains were by far the largest in England—and you want them, don't you, Henry?"

"They should be mine! They were my father's, granted to him by my royal uncle." The earl's eyes narrowed. "By blood, it is I that should act for the king, not that upstart!"

"Really?" Thomas purred. "By blood, you say?" He took a step towards Lancaster. "I would argue I carry more of the royal blood than you do, Cousin."

Lancaster lifted his chin. Several years older than Lord Roger, Lancaster was lean like a greyhound, if somewhat grey around the muzzle. Where his beard was completely grey, his hair retained streaks of its original dark colour and was carefully combed and oiled, further adorned by a hat in the same blue velvet as his clothes.

"I am the elder," he said. "I am best placed to guide our young king."

"Ned has all the guidance he needs," Thomas said. "If anything, he'd resent any more hands on the reins that curb him."

81

"Wrong hands." Lancaster pushed by them and swished off, elegant shoes visible under the hem of his robe.

"Far more dangerous than Broseley," Thomas commented as they followed Lancaster down the stairs.

"Aye." Adam pulled a face. "Should I tell Kit? About Broseley being here?"

"What would it serve beyond frightening her? Besides, she'll be riding south soon—far from our dear Godfrey."

Wise advice, Adam decided, but he was not entirely sure how to avoid telling her. Unless, of course, he avoided her.

York was abuzz with men eager to set off and teach those perfidious Scots a lesson. As a consequence, Kit saw little of her husband, always occupied with one preparation or the other, and after several days of having him dart off with an apology as soon as she approached him, she chose to find company elsewhere, hurt by his distance. Having him spend his days at the castle while she remained with most of the court at the friary Queen Isabella had appropriated for her lodgings did not improve things. The only time they had together were the few hours when he slept beside her, but he complained he was too tired to talk, drifting off into heavy sleep the moment his head touched the pillow.

Fortunately, Lady Margaret was there, welcomed back among the queen's companions now that she'd been churched after the birth of her daughter, a pretty enough infant who spent most of her time fast asleep in her wet nurse's arms.

"I like having her close," Lady Margaret said with a little smile. "And as to her father, well, he is utterly besotted."

One of Earl Edmund's more endearing qualities, that angel face of his bent in adoring contemplation of his baby daughter. Not only was he an attentive father, but he was just as conscientious a husband, spending as much time as he could with his wife. Not at all like Adam, Kit reflected. The moment they woke, he was gone, hastening off to see to his horses or his weapons, or his men, or the king's armour, or…

"It is my experience all men are like that when war is in the making," Lady Margaret said. "We become distractions when all they want to do is ride out and cover themselves in glory."

Kit moved one of her bishops. "Adam sees little glory in war."

"No? Strange man." Margaret peered at the board. "You've got me trapped, haven't you?"

"Yes, I do. Only fair, seeing as you always win when we play draughts."

"I don't like losing," Lady Margaret stated. "Something I have in common with my dear cousin, I believe."

"Yes," Kit agreed. "Lord Mortimer does not take it well when he emerges as anything but the victor."

"Which is why he rarely lowers himself to pastimes such as these." Margaret sat back. "Have you displeased him?"

"Who? Lord Mortimer?"

"Your husband."

"No." Kit nibbled at her lower lip. He'd been annoyed with her for not telling him about the coming child, but it was not like Adam to hold grudges. "His thoughts are elsewhere—all the time."

"Ah." Margaret helped herself to a strawberry. "Another woman?"

"What?" Kit sat up straight.

Margaret laughed. "No, I don't think so either. That man of yours is oblivious to all other ladies."

Kit managed to stop herself from breaking out in a wide smile. "As it is, he's oblivious to me too."

"Time to do something different." Lady Margaret grinned. "And I know just what that might be."

Some hours later, Kit was not so certain Lady Margaret's suggestion had been a good one. She felt denuded entering the great hall with nothing covering her head. Yet again, her hands fluttered up to ensure her thick hair was adequately constrained by the golden net, held in place with a ribbon as dark blue as her fitted kirtle and its tight sleeves, recently stitched into place by Rhosyn. She raised her chin. It was the latest fashion in France for well-born ladies to expose their hair, and Queen Isabella herself had adopted the fashion—at least for tonight. Kit walked slowly in the direction of her husband, aware of interested looks from many of the men she passed.

With each step, the coil of hair grew heavier, and when one of the older ladies gave her a long look accompanied by a pursed mouth and raised brows, Kit regretted having followed Lady Margaret's advice. Too late. She swallowed. Adam was saying something but stopped mid-sentence when he saw her, and Kit felt her cheeks heat. Would he deem it inappropriate? Chide her? She made a reverence; his hand shot out to close around her elbow, steadying her as she straightened up.

"Sweeting." He sounded hoarse.

"I…" She licked her lips. "Do you like it?"

"Like it?" He traced the golden net with a finger. "It is most becoming."

Her shoulders relaxed.

"But I'll not have my wife walk about unveiled," he continued, guiding her back towards the door.

"But the queen—"

A firm finger on Kit's mouth hushed her. "The queen is not my wife. You are." He picked at a tendril of hair, tugging ever so gently. "This is for me to see, my lady. Only for me." He ran a finger down the side of her neck. "I like how you've coiled it, and I will greatly enjoy undoing all of this to tumble round your shoulders later. But for now, Wife, fetch a veil."

Mortified, she did as he asked, returning some time later to find him still at the door, waiting for her. The sheer veil floated round her face, held in place by a thin circlet. He nodded his approval, offered her his arm, and led her in to rejoin the company.

On the dais, Queen Isabella's dark hair gleamed in the candlelight, adorned by jewels and gold. To her side sat Lady Margaret, equally unveiled. Kit turned a chilly look on her husband, only to be met by the slightest of smiles.

"They're not mine. You are." He helped her sit, nodding a greeting at Earl Thomas.

Kit sniffed. "Would you mind?" she asked, turning to the earl who looked confused.

"Mind what?"

She pretended not to see Adam's scowl. "If your wife were to display her hair as the Countess of Kent does, would you mind?"

Thomas pursed his lips, regarding his sister-in-law. "If my wife had hair as beautiful as yours, Lady Kit, no, I wouldn't mind." He grinned at Adam. "On the other hand, maybe I would. Such glorious hair should be for the eyes of the husband only."

"Men," Kit muttered. "It's only hair."

Adam leaned towards her. "My wife, my hair. The matter is closed, Kit."

"Hmph!" But she smiled at him all the same, oddly proud that her husband should find her too precious to display her to the world. Her cheeks heated when she felt his hand on her thigh, a soft but insistent caress that had her thinking of other things than the food on their trencher.

The moment was disrupted when Queen Isabella beckoned for Kit to join her and the other ladies. With a rueful look at Adam, Kit made for the assembled ladies.

No sooner had Kit excused herself than Adam turned to Thomas.

"You court her, my lord."

Thomas' dark eyebrows rose. "Court her? She asked me a question, and I replied. And yes, I complimented her, which she richly deserves." His gaze flitted in the direction of the ladies, a collection of brightly coloured silk and velvet. Adam tightened his grip on his eating knife.

"She's my wife."

Thomas laughed. "And you think I don't know that? Damn it, your wife is an admirable woman, but leaving aside the fact that she sees no other men but you, I would never push my courting beyond this playful teasing." He smiled. "I like it when she blushes, when her eyes sparkle—can you blame me for that?"

"She's my lady, not yours!"

"More importantly, you're my friend, Adam de Guirande. I would never do anything to dishonour a friend."

"Friend?" Adam could have kicked himself. What had possessed him to speak thus to the earl, a man he knew to be honourable? A man who counted him a friend…Here at court, he had at most a handful, even less now that Sir Henry Beaumont had remained behind in Windsor, entrusted with Prince John.

"Brothers-in-arms," Thomas said solemnly, extending his hand. Adam grasped it.

"Brothers. I am honoured, my lord."

"Thomas." The earl cuffed him on the shoulder.

"Thomas." Adam nodded. "Friend." He grinned.

"Does this mean you will not mind when next I word-fence with your comely wife?" the earl—Thomas—teased.

Adam glowered. "No. But seeing as we're friends, there's nothing to stop me from kicking you if you do."

Thomas laughed and raised his goblet. "To friendship."

"Friendship."

Later that night, Adam took Kit for a walk through the scented gardens, helped her up the steep steps to the city walls themselves. All was quiet, the sentries greeting him in hushed tones as he moved along the battlements, his wife's hand held firmly in his. They stood for a moment at the point which offered a view over the waters of the Ouse, glittering under the pale moonlight.

"Why did you do it?" He draped his cloak over them both.

"Hmm?" She kept her gaze on the dark shape of a bird outlined against the waxing half-moon, low enough to brush the distant treetops. A nightjar, its distinctive churning vibrating through the night.

"Your hair. You knew I would not approve."

"I was merely trying to be fashionable."

He bumped his hip against hers. "But you knew."

"I did." She slipped in between him and the parapet; he hugged her from behind. "I just wanted you to notice me."

"Notice you?" He brushed her veil to the side, planted a soft kiss just below her ear.

"I have been like air to you lately. It's as if you've been avoiding me." She turned in his arms, hands floating up to touch his face, his hair.

"No," he lied, nipping her ear. "I've just been too busy." And he didn't want to tell her about Broseley. He slid his hands round her waist and inhaled her warmth. "You're leaving tomorrow."

"Tomorrow? And you choose to tell me now?" Kit tore free.

"It'll not take Rhosyn long to pack, will it?"

In reply, she turned and ran away from him, darting like a swallow between the sentries.

"Kit, wait!" He ran after, but, slowed by his foot, he couldn't catch up. "Wait!" He heard her leap down the stairs, watched her run across the darkened gardens, her veil a fluttering point of light as she wove her way through roses and fruit trees. "Damnation." One moment she was warm and pliant in his arms, the next she was fleeing him. Women.

By the time he'd made it to their room, she was in bed. The candles had been doused, and she was on her side. Of Rhosyn there was no sign—the Welsh maid preferred the pallets and the company in the hall to their cramped quarters.

"I don't understand." He sat down on the bed. "It cannot have come as a surprise that you were going home."

She did not reply.

"I have to see you safe. How am I to ride off to war and not know you are safely at home?"

"I could stay here with the queen."

"I want you at home. And Tresaints needs its mistress, don't you think?"

"It needs its master as well." Her voice was thick with tears. "For the first time in days, you find time for me, but only to tell me you are sending me home."

"That isn't all I want to do tonight." He lowered his voice and stretched out beside her. Her back was stiff and unyielding. "Sweeting," he murmured, dropping a series of kisses on her nape and shoulder. "Come here, my heart."

"I don't want to go," she whispered, still with her back to him. "What if…" She cleared her throat, and he knew she was thinking of the last time he rode to war, back in 1321, where her bravery and wit saved his life. Reflexively, he bent the toes of his damaged foot, spikes of pain darting through his calf. All in all, a small price to pay for remaining alive, but the memories of what Despenser had done to him still plagued him.

"This is no great matter. I'll be back by St Bartholomew at the latest."

"Two months from now." She turned to face him. "Anything can happen in two months."

"Aye." He kissed her nose. "But nothing will. Lord Roger will never risk the king, neither will Kent nor Norfolk. So while our young and eager king sets out intending to do battle, his commanders have only one objective: to keep him as far away from Scottish steel as possible."

Kit smiled. "He won't like that, will he?"

"No." He dropped yet another kiss on her nose. "But hopefully it can all be blamed on those cowardly Scots, as ephemeral as wood smoke when faced with the splendid English host."

"Maybe the Scots want to fight."

Adam shook his head. "They can't afford to—not in the long run." He touched his lips to hers, a chaste caress, no more. "Can we stop talking about this?"

She nodded, her eyes luminous pools of darkness.

"Good." This time, he kissed her until there was no air left in his lungs, until his blood pounded through his veins and all he could think of was her.

Chapter 10

"I could have stayed," she grumbled to Egard once they were safely on their way. She set a finger to her lips, attempting to trap the recollection of Adam's tender farewell. Ignoring the fact that the forecourt was crowded, he'd kissed her deeply and lifted her up on her horse. And then, just as she'd been about to set the palfrey in motion, he'd stepped back, set his hand over his heart and bowed. As ever, this, his special little gesture, had her eyes clouding with tears.

"Sir Adam needs to know that you are safe, my lady." Egard replied. "Having you in Worcestershire places you safely out of harm's way." He clucked his horse into a trot. "Far enough from that accursed Broseley, at any rate."

"Broseley?" Kit asked. "What do you mean, Broseley?"

It was entertaining to watch the huge man squirm—or would have been if she hadn't been so hurt by Adam's decision not to confide in her.

"He didn't want you frightened," Egard said. "And it was Mortimer Broseley tried to kill, not your lord husband."

"Mmm." Should Godfrey of Broseley get the opportunity, he would gladly kill her Adam. Kit made as if to turn her horse, but Egard stopped her.

"No, my lady. I am to take you home. Sir Adam can take care of himself—even as we speak, men-at-arms are searching for that rat. The queen has offered a fat purse for his capture, has expressed she wants to see the miscreant boiled alive."

"Boiled?" She stared at Egard.

"Words, my lady. If Godfrey of Broseley is found, he'll be hanged by his neck until he stops twitching."

They made good speed south, the horses ambling steadily for long hours every day. Egard kept a tight control over their little party, allowing no laggards, no complaints, and after some days of moping at having left Adam behind, Kit began to enjoy the ride, face firmly turned to the south and her waiting home. But Egard had been entrusted with more than her safety. Five days from York, he informed her they would be riding to Wigmore first.

"I have letters, my lady."

"To Lady Joan?"

"Aye." He looked away. "He tries."

"Tries?" Kit pulled the folds of her mantle closer.

"Lord Mortimer." Egard's face clouded. "It's not his fault the queen refuses him to leave, is it?"

In Kit's opinion, Mortimer would no more leave his lady love than pluck out one of his fine dark eyes, but knowing Mortimer, she suspected Egard was right: Mortimer cared far too much for his wife not to try and establish a cordial relationship. Sadly, Lady Joan was not interested in scraps.

It had been five years and more since Kit last saw Wigmore. As they approached, she drew her horse to a stand, regarding the imposing castle that rose before her. The Mortimer colours snapped in the wind, the gates to the huge outer bailey stood open, and a steady stream of people were coming and going. Almost like the first time she'd seen it, a symbol of the mighty Mortimers, the walls clinging to the oblong escarpment on which it was built. Not at all as it had been the last time, when she'd ridden off in haste, leaving behind a grim-faced garrison and a distraught Lady Joan, the inner drawbridge raised, the gate beyond closed and barred.

The sentries nodded as they rode over the bridge, a couple of seconds in the dark of the gatehouse, and then they were in the lower bailey. The scaffolding that had surrounded the hall five years ago was still there, testament to years when nothing had been done. Now, however, masons were everywhere, the steady *tap-tap* of chisels on stone one sound among many. A couple of dogs barked, children yelled and laughed, men-at-arms hastened by at a trot, and to one side stood one of Lady Joan's clerks, face red as he harangued a merchant.

"Like old times, eh?" Egard landed lightly on his feet and came to help Kit down. Rhosyn slipped down from her perch behind one of their men, voice raised in a Welsh greeting. Kit nodded at a familiar face, shooed away a curious dog, and made for the keep. Three young girls appeared from the little garden Kit remembered from her last visit, and although she had no idea who they were, they were all remarkably alike. Cautious dark eyes regarded her from under dark brows, and there was something about the set of their shoulders, how tightly they clung to each other, that had Kit blinking away tears. Mortimer's daughters—girls who'd been locked up for several years.

"My lady." One of the girls dipped her a reverence.

"Agnes?" Kit guessed.

A shy smile appeared. "Catherine, my lady." She gestured at the younger girls. "Agnes and Beatrice."

"I am Kit." She smiled at them. "Last I saw you, you were all much, much smaller." She looked about. "And Blanche?"

The youngest Mortimer child, Kit remembered Blanche as a babe in arms—and Beatrice as a loud and happy little girl, her father's special favourite. This Beatrice was silent and wary, a constant crease between her brows that had Kit wanting to embrace her and kiss it away.

"With Mama." Catherine pointed in the direction of the next gate. "My lady mother is in her solar."

As Kit ascended the path that led to the inner bailey and the lord's chambers within yet another protective wall, she couldn't help thinking that things were much different than when she'd been here last. Then, Wigmore had appeared impregnable, not only because of its massive walls, but just as much because of Lord Mortimer and his lady wife, two people who stood united and faced the world together.

At the entrance to the inner bailey, Kit ran into Geoffrey Mortimer.

"My lord." She bowed to this youthful copy of his father, a lad she'd last seen some weeks ago at Westminster.

"Lady Kit!" Geoffrey's face shone up. "Do you bring us news? Are the Scots adequately defeated?"

"As yet, the Scots have not been sighted, let alone compelled to do battle." Kit gave him a curious look. "Shouldn't you be in York?"

Geoffrey scowled. "My father felt it sufficient to risk two of his sons, my lady." He twitched his tunic into place. "Allow me to escort you to my lady mother."

"I do know the way," Kit teased, making for the last, very steep stretch leading towards Lady Joan's rooms. "Is it nice to be back here?"

"Here?" Geoffrey shrugged. "This will never be mine, my lady. I do homage to the French king for my estates."

"But this is still home, isn't it?" At his invitation, she preceded him up the narrow inner stairs, blinking at the sudden loss of daylight.

"Not anymore, not now that…" He broke off and looked away. "It is no longer the same. My lady mother rarely smiles or laughs."

Kit did not know what to say, so they walked the last few treads in silence. Geoffrey opened the door for her and bowed.

"Lady Kit to see you, Mother."

Kit took a hesitant step into the room. The large window, set with precious glass, allowed the brightness of the day to illuminate the chamber, at present filled with several women. On the floor was a rich carpet in red and blue, the bed had new hangings, there was an elegantly wrought armchair by the hearth, a couple of large chests stood to the side, and a dog slept in the sunlight. Standing very alone in the centre of the room was Lady Joan, straight like a candle and just as thin.

Kit made a deep reverence. Lady Joan motioned for her to rise and led her over to the window seat. A wave of her hand and her ladies left, taking two little girls with them.

"My lady," Kit began, not knowing quite what to say to the woman in front of her. To say she looked well would be to lie, the recent years having stripped everything that was soft from Lady Joan's face, leaving her a collection of sharp angles, no more. The Lady Joan Kit recalled had not been beautiful, but she'd been vivacious and pleasing to the eye. This woman had hardened, something dark lingering in her eyes. Her eyebrows rose, her mouth quirking as she returned Kit's open inspection.

"Do you find me much changed?"

Kit could not lie—not when those intelligent eyes met hers. "I do, my lady." She clasped Lady Joan's hand. "I am so sorry for what you've had to live through."

Lady Joan looked away. "At least I remain alive. May the dear Lord grant me many more years of life—my children need me."

"They do, my lady. Your sons…" She cleared her throat. "Have they recovered?"

"My sons?" Lady Joan looked at her as if she were a half-wit. "You've seen them, haven't you? They've emerged relatively unscathed. Edmund and Roger were lodged in Windsor, a comfortable captivity to begin with. John joined them some years ago, and Geoffrey, thank the Lord, was spared all this, safe as he was in France. But my daughters…" Her voice shook. "Nuns make grim gaolers. I can't say it saddens me to hear the three Despenser girls have been veiled and cloistered—apt retribution for what their father did to my girls."

"They're children," Kit protested.

"As were mine." Lady Joan held out her arm, an impossibly thin arm, the bones at her wrist clearly visible, the fashionably narrow sleeve hanging loose around it. "It has marked them—just as it has marked me."

The door creaked open, and a page appeared, followed by a couple of maids. Wine, cheese, and bread, and Lady Joan gestured for Kit to partake.

"And you my lady?"

"Later, perhaps." She smiled crookedly. "Years on restricted rations have dulled my appetite permanently."

Kit handed her the letters Egard had given her. Written by Mortimer himself, to judge from the handwriting. Most unusual, but then everything about Mortimer and his wife was irregular. Lady Joan glanced at the missives and set them aside.

"Will you not read them?"

"I will." She set a finger to the seal of the closest. "He is a conscientious letter-writer. Would that he was as conscientious a husband."

"Which is why you never write back," Kit said, wishing immediately she never had.

"How would you know that?" Lady Joan nudged at the closest letter.

"I see it in his face." Kit wasn't sure how to describe the avid look on Mortimer's countenance when a messenger strode in with letters for him, how he would rifle through them, scanning each and every one of them before throwing them to his clerks.

"He wants absolution." Lady Joan sipped at her wine. "But I cannot forgive him—not for this." She gave Kit a long look. "I deserve his loyalty after all those years. Instead, I am subjected to the humiliation of watching him dance to the queen's pipe—verily like a trained bear."

If Lord Mortimer was the queen's tame beast, then the queen was his falcon, as dependent on him as he was on her. But Lady Joan would not want to hear that.

"Have you seen him, my lady?"

"Once." She smiled slightly. "With Adam. He did not quite dare to come alone. How is he?" she added in a casual tone, her finger caressing her lord husband's letters.

"Well enough." Mortimer had looked careworn of late. "He works too much, sleeps too little."

"As always, then." Lady Joan nodded. "That man..." She shook her head, her mouth drooping at the corners. "Unless someone tells him to, he can even forget to eat." Her voice quavered. Kit pretended a coughing attack to allow Lady Joan to regain her composure.

"I will not embarrass you with my tears. I have shed enough of those." Lady Joan stood, indicating the meeting was over. "Will you be staying overnight?"

"If we may."

"Of course you may." Lady Joan patted Kit's cheek. "It was good to see you, Kit."

"And you, my lady." Kit made for the door, remembering there was one more thing she had to ask. "My lady, what do you want us to do with the treasure?"

"Treasure?" Lady Joan's brow wrinkled. "What treasure?"

94

"The gold you entrusted me just after Mortimer's submission to the late king." A couple of small chests filled to the brim with what coin and portable treasure Lady Joan could find.

"Is there anything left?"

"A third or so." Most of it had been smuggled out of England to the exiled baron.

"Then leave it where it is. God knows we may need it again."

"God give that we don't," Kit muttered to herself as she made her way down the stairs.

Three days later, they turned down the long lane that led to Tresaints. The hornbeam hedge had been recently cut, the wheat and barley was well above waist height, a rippling sea of various shades of green and gold. To the west, the evening sun hung like a burnished orb in the sky, causing the manor buildings to cast long shadows up the lane. Home. A bell began to chime, they were back in time for vespers. She cocked her head, a thrill running through her—they had a bell for their chapel!—and the closer she got, the more she saw of all the other improvements.

The wooden palisade had been replaced by a stone wall, the gate a massive thing in wood that was wide enough to allow entry to a cart, but not much more. Inside, the little bailey was a beehive of activity. Adam had decided to enlarge the ancient manor house to include modern kitchens just off the hall and a new set of rooms on top.

"Separate kitchens are a thing of the past," he'd told her, and Kit had smiled at his officious tone. What did Adam know of kitchens? "We must embrace these new times," Adam had continued before explaining that the two new rooms would serve for guests and for their growing brood of children. There was a smell of wet mortar, of newly spliced wood, of sundried thatch and hot iron—Kit inhaled, hoping to make out the smell of something edible as well.

"Kit!" William waved and loped towards her. The William approaching her was restored to his normal self. The tonsure

95

was somewhat haphazard, he hadn't shaved for days, and his face displayed a peeling sunburn and a wide smile. "In time for prayers," he said, helping her off the horse.

"A bell," she replied, and he nodded and grinned.

"Indeed, a bell."

The little chapel was full—men on one side, women on the other—and Kit took her place to the front, squeezing in between Mabel and Mall. The chapel was older than anything else in Tresaints, and consisted of plain walls, an elongated eastern window with precious glass, the altar with its triptych—a thing so ancient William thought it had been made in the distant Byzantium—and behind the altar was a secret crypt in which rested what remained of Lady Joan's treasure. Kit shuffled on her feet, releasing the scents of beeswax from the tiles beneath.

She took her time leaving the chapel. A candle for Tom, one for her dead infant daughter, one for her long-dead mother, Alaïs, and one for Adam, to keep him safe and guide him home. She crossed herself before each of the three little statues just inside the door. St Winefride the chaste was so old she no longer retained any features but a slight protuberance that might be her nose, St Wulfstan was still visibly a man, although his foot had been worn smooth from repeated kisses, and St Odo looked much the same as he always had—not so much a good man as an ambitious man, Alaïs had always said, viewing their French saint with little fondness.

She exited to a bailey sunk in the soft light of a summer evening—and the demanding wail of Meg, who came rushing towards her, arms extended. After Meg, there was Ned to inspect and kiss, and then she had to find John and hand him the new tabard she'd made him before finally allowing Mall, the cook, to show her to the new kitchens.

"Look!" Mall's broad face was bright with excitement. "Two hearths, my lady—and an oven! And over here…" She pulled Kit along to inspect new larders and storage space, repeating over and over again that never in her life had she hoped to be mistress over such a fine kitchen. Kit nodded, moving hopefully in the direction of the large table and the pies that sat atop it. Her stomach growled, and Mall laughed, shooing her off while promising she'd send one of the kitchen maids in with food and drink.

"Good to be home?" William's voice startled her from her silent reverie. Kit moved aside to allow him to join her on the little bench in the herbal garden. Someone had taken good care of it, the various plants standing neat and well tended. In the southern corner, Alaïs' precious rose was heavy with blooms, splashes of white against the darkness of the surrounding foliage.

"It is." She popped the last piece of pie in her mouth. "Ned is twice the size of when I saw him last." And very much his own little person despite those beautiful grey eyes of his reminding her of his father.

"Meg has missed you," William said. "Has talked about her mama from dawn to sunset."

"She has?" Kit smoothed at the as-yet-invisible bump that contained her new child.

"A right active little lass. Time to set a spindle in her hands to calm her down somewhat."

"It never worked on me," Kit replied. "Besides, she's just two."

William smiled at her. "Idle hands make mischief, Kit." But he winked, and she laughed, promising she would ensure her daughter was suitably occupied. They sat in the gloaming as he told her of the crops and the beasts—the lambing had been good, most of the little creatures surviving their first few months, and she could see for herself the fields were already bowing with the promise of a rich harvest.

"And you?" she interrupted him halfway through an account of the recent shearing. "Are you content?"

William just smiled and nodded.

In the third week of July, the peace of Tresaints was disrupted. Three riders came galloping down the lane, and Kit's heart was in her mouth, her skirts held high as she rushed from the orchard to receive them.

"William de Guirande," the lead rider snapped. "Is he here?"

97

"Who is asking?" Kit said.

"We are here on behalf of the queen," the tall man said, driving his restive horse round in a couple of tight turns. "Is he here?" The queen? Belatedly, Kit had recognised the arms on his tabard. This was one of Thomas Berkeley's men.

"I am." William stepped out of the stables, and there was a light in his eyes, a spring to his step that had Kit sighing inside. Her brother-in-law was like an eager alaunt about to spring to the chase.

"Your help is needed. We leave instantly."

"Surely, you have time for some food?" Kit asked. They looked as if they'd been riding for hours, all three of them covered in a thin layer of dust that had mingled with sweat to form dark streaks on their faces and necks.

"No."

"No?" William said. "That urgent?"

"You can say that again." One of the other men spat to the side. "Time is of the essence."

Kit clapped her hands together. "Some ale while you wait?" she asked, already sending Rhosyn off.

"Much appreciated," the leader said, his face sagging into utter exhaustion.

"What has happened?" Kit asked in a low voice.

The man shook his head. "I can't tell you, my lady." He crossed himself, mumbling that God help them all if they didn't sort this quickly. His gaze fixed on Egard. "You! We will need you as well."

Without a word, Egard trotted off to the stables.

A whirlwind of activity later and William was astride Goliath, a sword by his side. Kit stroked Adam's old stallion over his soft nose. Even the horse had picked up on the general urgency, small ears pricked, hind legs bunched in expectation.

"Be careful," Kit said, shading her face to look up at William. "And bring back Goliath whole," she added. "You know Adam loves that horse."

"More than he loves his brother?" William called back, already halfway through the gate.

"Almost," she muttered, watching the party of five set off at a canter. She turned to Mabel and John. "We'd best see to our own defences. I fear something very bad has happened."

John nodded, no more. "Aye." He wiped at his face. "One could almost think they're looking for an escaped lion." He met Kit's eyes. Dear God: the old man was right. Somehow, their former king had fled his prison.

Chapter 11

They were ready. Adam surveyed the carts, the packhorses, he personally inspected each and every man-at-arms under his command. An impressive force, to be led jointly by the earls of Kent, Lancaster and Norfolk—something that did not inspire Adam with much confidence. He was even more surprised when he heard Mortimer would not be riding out with them, citing urgent matters that required his attention.

"I'll catch up," he said dismissively, but there were bags under his eyes, a set to his jaw that had Adam wondering just what these other matters might be. And when he saw the queen, something tightened in his belly. Only once before had he seen the queen so lacking in composure, and that had been when her husband deprived her of her dower. Her brow was furrowed, green eyes shot with red, resting repeatedly on Lord Roger while her teeth gnawed at her lower lip.

Distractedly, she listened to her son's enthusiastic promises that soon he'd have the Scots at bay, cutting him off mid-sentence with a vague smile and a "God bless" before floating over to join Lord Roger, standing very alone on the stairs to the keep, staring south.

"Something's wrong." Adam rode up beside Richard de Monmouth. His brother-in-law avoided Adam's eyes, fiddling instead with his horse's mane.

"Wrong? How so?"

"Why is Lord Roger not riding with us?"

"Maybe he is displeased at not having been given command," Richard said.

Adam just looked at him. "Had he wanted command, he'd been given it. We both know that. So why?"

Richard sighed. "News from the south. Bad news."

"From the south?" Adam tightened his hold on his reins. "Have the Welsh risen in revolt?"

"No, no, nothing like that." Richard gave him a fleeting smile. "Kit is in no danger."

"So then what?"

"I…" Richard wet his lips. "The king."

"What of him?" Adam's gaze flew to Edward, for the day in gleaming armour, the cross of St George adorning his tabard.

"Not that one." Richard gave him a crooked smile. "It's confusing at times, isn't it? Two kings in the same country." He lowered his voice. "He has escaped!"

"What?" Adam's hands shook, that initial tightening in his belly twisting his innards into painful knots. He looked at Lord Roger, for the day in stark black. Apt, as death—a painful, extended death ending with evisceration and decapitation—awaited him should their former king regain his throne. And as to Queen Isabella…Not death—oh no, the king would immure her in a convent, there to live out her days in silence and solitude.

"Maltravers and Berkeley are scouring the countryside for him," Richard continued, his voice no more than a whisper. "But word must not get out, Adam. Least of all to his son."

"No, of course not. How?"

"Those damned Dunhaven brothers again." Richard shook his head. "While he remains alive, this is what will happen."

Adam reared back, pulling so hard on the reins Raven snorted in protest. "He's an anointed king," he hissed, struggling to keep his voice down.

"Unfortunately." Richard nodded in the direction of Lord Roger. "If it comes to him or Edward of Caernarvon, I know who I will choose—no matter what that may require of me. I thought you would do the same."

Adam frowned. "I serve Edward of Windsor." Even to him, it sounded stilted.

"So does Lord Roger," Richard reminded him.

Lord Roger caught up with them well before they reached Durham.

"Any news of the Scots?" Thomas asked in lieu of greeting.

"There's a whole lot of them in Carlisle, but Douglas and his men remain in the vicinity." Lord Roger rode over to the king and bowed as well as he could while on horseback. "My liege, I trust you are well?"

"As you can see." Edward studied him through narrowed eyes. "But what ails you, my lord? You look as if you've seen a ghost."

"A ghost?" Lord Roger laughed. "Oh no, my lord. I spend little time worrying about dead men. Once dead, always dead in my experience." He shot a glance at Adam, held his gaze for a moment before looking at Richard. Adam's redheaded brother-in-law went an unbecoming shade of madder, and Lord Roger's mouth set into a line so thin Adam felt quite sorry for Richard.

"What is this?" Lord Roger asked, gesturing at the forest of banners and pennons that surrounded them, all of them displaying the red cross of St George.

"We fight under St George," the king said. "A warrior saint for a warrior king."

There was a muffled sound from Thomas.

"Ah," Lord Roger said, giving his young king an indulgent look. Fortunately, Edward was too busy studying his pennons to notice.

"He slayed a dragon. I will slay Scots—both are vile creatures."

"I dare say you'll find the Scots are mostly like us, my lord," Mortimer put in. "They eat, they shit, they swive, they fight and bleed, they die."

"They are savages!"

"There are men of honour among them—their king for one, and Black Douglas is another true knight." Mortimer pointed at one of the banners. "St George is a fine saint to follow into battle, but do not commit the mistake of underestimating your enemy—or denigrating him. And St George wasn't English to begin with, was he?"

"As good as," the king retorted. "England breeds the finest soldiers in the world."

Thomas laughed. "Really, Ned, what nonsense is that? England is a land of sheep farmers and wool merchants."

Lord Roger and the king looked equally displeased, making Adam bite back a smile. They were far more similar than they realised, those two—ambitious and innovative. In fact, the king and Mortimer together had decided to carry those newfangled devices with them, heavy things that looked like large buckets and sounded like God's own thunder when deployed. Cannon, Lord Roger had explained proudly. Not that Adam saw much use for them—beyond striking the fear of God into the enemy.

"I will turn those shepherds and merchants into soldiers, riding to glory under the cross of St George." The king gestured at the many flags. "England will be more than it is, and we will start with Scotland."

With something that sounded as a cross between a curse and a guffaw, Mortimer took his place behind the king.

Adam waited until they were safely installed just north of Durham for the night before approaching Lord Roger.

"Any news from the south?" he asked in an undertone, ducking to enter Lord Roger's tent.

Lord Roger's mouth quirked. "News from the south? There is always news from the south." He threw his gauntlets on a table. "What news might you be referring to?"

"You know which, my lord. And Berkeley Castle is not that far from Tresaints."

"Damn Monmouth for not keeping his mouth shut," Lord Roger muttered. He sighed. "You must excuse me if my first concern is not for your little non-descript manor, Adam. Besides, he'd be a fool to go that way, wouldn't he?" Lord Roger turned around. "No, there is no news. But he'll not get far." He gestured at his back. "Help me with the straps."

Adam did as he asked, unbuckling the Italian coat of plates. Beneath, Lord Roger was wearing a hauberk, and Adam acted the squire, lifting it off.

"Like old times," Lord Roger said, twisting his head to catch Adam's eyes.

"Aye, my lord. Should we not be going south instead?"

"And alert the country he has escaped?" Lord Roger shook his head. "Besides, we have this matter of the Scots to settle." He smiled thinly. "Our king wishes to prove his valour and heap us all with glory."

"Not much glory here. There never is on a battlefield."

"But he doesn't know that yet, does he?" Lord Roger called for one of his pages, ordered him to fetch wine and victuals. "Fetch the earls for me," he told Adam. "We need to consider our next steps."

"Not the king?"

"It is him we need to consider." His brows rose. "And yes, you may stay. God forbid that you should fear we plot against your precious whelp." He laughed softly, something dark moving in the depth of his eyes. "Your loyalty to your new lord is commendable, but it breaks my heart to see you looking at me as if you suspect me of wishing our king ill."

"I don't…" Adam began.

"Fetch the earls," Mortimer interrupted.

Only Thomas of Norfolk, Earl Marshal of the realm, was at his ease in Lord Roger's presence. His brother remained on his feet, as if wishing to spring away at a moment's notice, while Lancaster immediately appropriated Lord Roger's chair, sitting stiff and tense in it. Lord Roger shared a quick look with Adam, shrugged, and found a stool instead.

"What now?" Lancaster said.

"We must walk a thin line, my lords," Lord Roger said bluntly. "The Scots must be encouraged to depart but be allowed to do so with as little loss as possible."

"We aim to hammer them into the ground," Lancaster said.

"Really? You personally?" Lord Roger smirked. "I think not." He studied the earls one by one. "England would not benefit from full-out war with Scotland."

"Says the man who has all his estates to the south," Lancaster said. "I stand to lose a great deal if that proposed treaty goes through."

"Except that you have never set foot on those Scottish lands of yours, have you?" Thomas said. He directed himself to Mortimer, "What exactly are you saying here?"

"We should avoid a pitched battle."

"You fear death?" Lancaster sneered.

"I fear the king's death," Lord Roger retorted. "That royal lad of ours will gladly ride at the head of any sally, convinced of his own invincibility—as all youths are. But we all know a battle bears little resemblance to a chivalric joust, and the Scots will have no compunction in shooting our Ned full of arrows, no matter that he is still a youngster, not yet fifteen."

Earl Edmund nodded. "We must keep him safe. At all cost."

"Amen to that," Lord Roger said. "That young lad has the makings of a great king. It is up to us to ensure he survives long enough to become one."

Lancaster sat back. "They are harrying my lands. Mine! The lands of my father, of my loyal vassals, infested with Scots. Are you saying I am to allow that to go on?"

"No, of course not. We haven't mustered the army just to have them kick their heels here at York, have we? We will ride north, and we will drive Douglas and Randolph back over the border. But it must be done with stealth, my lords. Enough force to ensure they know we are serious, not so much as to have them feel cornered. One never knows just what a cornered dog will do." Mortimer speared a dried fig with his eating knife, sliced it in two, and popped one of the pieces in his mouth, chewing slowly as he looked from one to the other. "Are we in agreement? No pitched battle if we can avoid it, and the king is to be kept safe at all times."

Edmund nodded, as did Thomas. Lancaster took his time.

"Very well," he finally said. "But you will have to tell him."

"Tell him?" Thomas threw his head back and laughed. "We can't tell him, Cousin. We must just ensure things happen as we want them to. No pitched battle—unless those foolish Scots come charging down a hillside at us."

"Which they won't," Lord Roger said. "James Douglas has no death wish."

By the end of July, Adam was sick of this cat-and-mouse game. The men were getting tired, the supplies were dwindling, and to make matters worse, the last few weeks had been uncommonly wet. This evening, however, the skies had cleared sufficiently for Adam to see the thin veils of dark smoke rising towards the heavens.

"They're burning as they ride." Mortimer gritted his teeth.

"Dogs," King Edward said, eyes on the smudgy horizon. "Cowardly curs, harrying defenceless peasants rather than meet us full on."

"They're doing it to taunt us." Adam threw a look to the south. "Behind our backs, no less. We ride to meet them, they sneak around us."

"Raiders," Edward said scornfully. "They have no discipline, no backbone to meet us in battle."

"Really?" Mortimer gave him a sour look. "Tell that to the English who died at Bannockburn."

Edward bristled. "One single battle, Lord Mortimer. One. My grandfather, on the other hand—"

"Lost at Stirling Bridge," Thomas filled in. "Irked him no end, it did, even if he blamed it on de Warenne." He frowned, staring at the wisps of smoke. "Could they have brought in French reinforcements?"

"Maybe," Adam said. "They've renewed that unholy alliance, haven't they?"

Edward snorted. "That won't help them."

"Oh, it would," Mortimer told him. "But no, we've had no news of a French fleet—and we would, had there been one."

"So it is only Douglas, is it?" Edward slapped his gloves against his thigh. "Well, best we find him, then. That upstart Scottish bastard is due a lesson or two." He turned on his toes, a slow circle as he surveyed his army. "Time to bring him to battle, my lords. We set out in the morning."

It was fruitless. Through woods and swamps, through hills and glens, they marched in as good an order as possible. An impressive array, bristling with swords and spears, their banners snapping overhead—the English army in all its glory, led by its young and eager warrior-king. But their enemy was ever one step ahead—or behind—and the only thing they achieved was to be that much closer to the burning hamlets. After days of this, the king called for a council, and well after compline the three earls, Mortimer, and the king settled down before the fire in the king's lodgings.

106

Adam dismissed the pages and squires, bowed his thanks to the layman who appeared with wine and victuals, and closed the door. The little monastery was all agog at hosting their king, although Adam suspected it was with relief the thin prior would see them leave on the morrow.

"We will never catch them like this." The king looked from one earl to the other, pointedly ignoring Mortimer, who was leaning against one of the walls, sunk in thoughts of his own. Dark thoughts, to judge from the look on his face.

"They have the advantage of speed." Thomas used a poker to stir at the fire. "We have the advantage of numbers. Douglas would be a fool to stand and meet us in open battle."

"Ever the cowards, those Scots," Lancaster muttered, and Adam was tempted to smack him over his elegantly coiffed head. Wily as snakes, aye, but cowards?

The king stood. "We will hunt them on horseback. Mounted knights only."

"But my lord," Adam objected, "men need food—as do horses."

"We can't drag our entire baggage train around! It slows us down to have us resemble snails. Besides, all it will take is a day or two—those sorry Scottish bastards will never know what hit them until it is too late." King Edward clapped Adam on the shoulder. "Have the men carry a loaf or two. That should suffice." He grinned. "And as to the horses, I do believe they eat grass."

Well before dawn, the knights were ready. Harnesses jangled, leather creaked as the men settled in their saddles. Adam did one last inspection and walked over to where the king was breaking his fast, surrounded by his three commanders and Mortimer.

"They're ready, my liege," Adam said, accepting a cup of hot cider.

"Good." The king bit into a pasty, inhaled a couple of times. "Hot," he said. He nabbed a second pasty and grinned at Adam. "Best eat, Adam. God knows when next you will see food." He laughed. Adam did not.

Just as they were preparing to mount, a messenger came charging up the slope towards them. Mud-spattered and wet, he brought the horse to a halt before Mortimer, bowed deeply to the king, and handed Mortimer a letter, the parchment tightly folded and sealed.

"From our lady queen," he said.

Mortimer nodded, retreated a couple of steps, and broke the wax, scanning the few lines quickly. His fingers tightened on the parchment, and when he met Adam's eyes, Lord Roger shook his head infinitesimally.

"What does she say?" The king made as if to take the parchment.

"She's a woman, my lord." Lord Roger fed the parchment into a nearby fire. He grinned at the king. "She worries you have no clean hose left."

"Neither do you—and she should be worrying more about your smelly feet than mine," the king spat back. A hush descended on the assembled men, and the king's cheeks went a dull red.

"I worry about yours, Ned," Thomas drawled. "These last few nights, I've had them right in my face." He punched his nephew's arm. "I have some clean hose if you want to borrow them. Now, are we going to stand around discussing apparel all day?" He gestured at their horses. "I thought we were going to hunt Scots."

With the king at their head, the knights set off, an interminable line of men and horses riding neatly in their units. Hooves pounded into the wet ground, horns squealed, and behind them the foot soldiers cheered. Earl Edmund stood in his stirrups and waved his hat, Lancaster and Percy were at the front with the king, and Mortimer rode in a cloud of silence.

"Bad news?" Thomas inclined his head in the direction of Mortimer.

"Hmm?" Adam pretended confusion.

"Something is gnawing at our baron," Thomas said.

"Aye. His lack of hose, apparently."

Chapter 12

"A bloody disaster." Thomas kicked at a stone and sent it skidding through the wet grass.

"Aye." Adam went back to what he was doing, carefully rubbing Raven as dry as he could. He shivered in the wind, wishing he'd had something else but his cloak to use on his horse. A week of cold and rain, of little food and even less sleep. A week of riding up and down the northern shores of the Tyne, hoping to waylay the Scots as they crossed the swollen river.

The men were sick and hungry, fights broke out over what bread they could find, and after days of living in full armour, several of the men complained of chafing sores on their shoulders and backs. Adam moved his arms gingerly. So far, he was spared such rotting sores, but it was but a matter of time, what with the damp. He coughed, a deep rattling sound that had Thomas giving him a concerned look.

"You're poorly."

"Me and every other man here." Adam bent down to inspect Raven's hooves, ignoring the pressure in his chest as he did so. No rot, thank the Lord. In difference to many of the men here, Adam could not afford to lose his horse— Goliath was too old, and the colts he had back home too young.

"Here." Thomas draped his cloak over Adam's shoulders.

"You need it," Adam protested, but with little heat. It was blissful to be encased in something warm and dry.

"Not as much as you do."

They both turned at the sound of commotion to the west of the camp. A squire, riding hell for leather towards the king.

"Now what?" Thomas said, leading the way towards the king and the kneeling man at his feet. The king gesticulated and pointed, the man nodded eagerly, and for the first time in days, King Edward smiled.

"At last!" he yelled. "We have found them." He beckoned for the squire to rise. "Well done."

"Mischance, my king," the squire said, blushing all the way to his ears.

"Or Providence," the king said.

"Providence?" Thomas snickered. "Well, we haven't seen much of her around, have we? How did you avoid detection?"

"My lord?" The squire turned to face him. "No, no—they captured me!"

"Ah, you escaped." Thomas nodded approvingly.

"No," the squire mumbled. "I was set free and told to find the king and tell him where they were." He squirmed. "Douglas said it was right annoying to have to sit in the rain and wait for the cowardly English to show."

Edward's face tightened. In the rain and with his hair plastered to his head by a combination of sweat, rain, and grime, he no longer looked quite as much the youthful hero as when they'd ridden north a week ago, but in difference to his commanders, he remained as determined as ever to find the Scots.

"Cowardly? Us?" He clapped his hands. "Make ready to ride. Now!"

"It could be a trap," Adam said to Thomas.

"It could." Thomas beckoned to one of their scouts. "Best make sure it isn't."

Crossing the Tyne a week ago had been bad. Contemplating crossing it again today was terrifying. The river was in full spate after days of incessant rain, and Adam knew from experience the water would be cold enough to have his balls scurrying up to hide in his belly. He coughed.

"Are you ill?" Lord Roger asked.

"Snivels and cough, no more. Nothing that a warm bed wouldn't cure." And a warm bath, preferably with Kit washing him. He scratched at his groin. Lice everywhere, he reckoned.

Raven was big enough and strong enough to make it across the river safely. Other men were not as lucky, watching with despair as their horses were taken by the waters and swept downstream.

"We'll reimburse them," the king said with a shrug. "Later. Now we must make haste."

"Whatever for?" Thomas frowned at the king. "To hear your eager squire, the Scots have found an excellent position. They'll be in no hurry to leave it."

"I am sick of this!" the king hissed. "Sick of being cold and hungry and wet, of seeing men cough themselves to death, of doing nothing but wait and wait. This brings no glory, this is just…"

"War," Adam filled in.

The king scowled at him. "War? We've not crossed swords with the enemy once."

"And yet this is what campaigning is about," Mortimer said. "Waiting, riding, waiting. Boring and muddy most of the time. Requires patience rather than courage, my lord."

They rode in tight formation over the moors, the king insisting on moving at speed.

"We make for Blanchland," Mortimer suggested. "An opportunity to rest and sleep dry before we take on Douglas." The king gave him a grim look but nodded. The Scottish raiders had set part of the abbey lands on fire some weeks back, making Adam wonder if the hapless monks would be all that pleased to have the king descend upon them. But the abbey was a good choice and reasonably close, for which Adam gave silent thanks.

"Have someone find the baggage train and order them there," was all King Edward said. "I could do with some clean hose." A brief smile flashed across his features.

"So could I, my lord," Mortimer replied. "And preferably dry."

By the time they got to the abbey, Adam was shaking with fever. Despite his protests, Thomas insisted he be transferred to the infirmary.

"I'll look after your precious horse," Thomas promised. "And that flea-bitten squire of yours." He patted Adam's arm. "I'll send your page for clean clothes." Adam attempted yet again to protest. Midway through, he gave up.

When next he woke, it was dark. He was clean and dry—and naked. He sat up, and a monk came hurrying over.

"Thirsty?" he asked, holding out a wooden mug. Adam drained it in three gulps.

"Hungry," he said, his voice oddly hoarse. He cleared his throat. "My clothes?"

"The ones you came in? Gone. But there are clean ones there." The little monk smiled. "It was hard enough undressing you, big man that you are."

"The king?" Adam stretched for his braies.

"Sleeping." The monk crossed himself. "They all are, preparing themselves for tomorrow."

"Tomorrow?" Adam tied the braies into place. There was a faint whiff of vinegar from his genital area—and from his hair. The lice, it would seem, were no more.

"They ride out to do battle."

"God's blood!" Adam tugged his hose up his legs. "How long have I been sleeping?"

"A night and a day—and most of this night." The monk knelt and helped untangle the right leg of his hose. "You were tossing with fever well into terce. You should stay in bed." But it was said in a resigned tone.

"I must ride with the king."

"To kill?" The monk made a face and crossed himself.

"To keep him alive." Adam crossed himself too. "God willing." He stood too quickly, and the darkened room tilted around him.

The monk grabbed at him. "You must eat."

"Aye." Adam allowed the monk to lead him to the hearth and sat down on one of the stools. Moments later, he was handed a bowl, its contents hot and rich, with meat and broth and parsnips.

"Rabbit," the monk said. "And wine." He handed Adam some bread. "You really should stay in bed. Coughs like that require tender nursing."

"Can't," Adam said through his food. He scraped the bowl clean, and the monk shook his head and refilled it from the earthenware pot on the hearth. Adam smiled, recalling how his mother had done all her cooking in such a pot, balanced so as to heat evenly throughout.

He left the infirmary with two small stoppered bottles and a little pot of something that smelled like the devil but that the monk had insisted he rub into his chest.

"Elderberry cordial in one, willow bark in the other," the monk had told him, handing him the bottles. "One for the cough, the other for the fever."

"Yes, Mother," Adam said, and the monk had rolled his eyes.

After mass and confession, the king was ready to ride out. So was Adam, much restored after yet another meal, washed down with a sizeable quantity of ale. Clean clothes, polished armour—even Raven was his old self, bobbing his head up and down while moving restlessly back and forth.

"Are you sure you should ride with us?" Lord Roger asked, looking Adam up and down.

"Aye, my lord."

Mortimer left it at that, guiding his horse over to where his two eldest sons were already astride.

"Is this really wise?" Thomas asked a mere heartbeat or so later. "Should you not remain here?"

"No," Adam replied, giving his friend an irritated look.

The king came trotting over, resplendent in new armour and a bright red cloak. His helmet hung from the pommel of his saddle, a new thing adorned with a rampant golden lion.

"Adam! So glad to see you on your feet again." The lad furrowed his brow. "But should you really be coming with us?"

"Aye!" Adam scowled. "What is this? Am I surrounded by mother-hens?"

"Hens?" The king laughed. "I think not." He stood in his stirrups. "Behold the force that will crush Black Douglas and grind his bones into the ground."

It was a sight to gladden a warrior's heart. Foot soldiers marched by in orderly files, accompanied by mounted knights. And at the back came the baggage train, guarded by Adam's own men.

"No more riding without your supplies, my lord?" Adam teased.

"I never commit the same error twice, Adam."

"Good to know, my lord." Adam gave the king a cheeky grin, returned in full. He was in high spirits today, their royal lad, all of him a-quiver at the thought of having his quarry at hand.

"God save us," Thomas said some hours later.

"Indeed." Adam had to hand it to Douglas: the man had chosen his position with utmost care, the Scotsmen sitting high atop a hill—and on the far side of the Wear. In the evening breeze, a large banner flapped lazily, three stars argent against a bright blue background. Douglas' arms, shouting to the world that at present the hillock in front of them was Scottish land, no matter that they were miles and miles from the Scottish border.

"And now what?" Thomas nodded in the direction of the king, sitting motionless atop his horse.

"Well, we won't be riding back, will we?" Adam leaned forward over Raven's neck. "He's sending them a herald."

"Probably to ask them politely to ride down and fight us on the even ground," Thomas jested. They shared a chuckle, Thomas leading the way as they rode over to join the king.

Some moments later, Adam was hard put not to guffaw out loud. Thomas made a strangled sound, and the king's head whipped round.

"You find this amusing, Uncle?"

"No, no." Thomas slapped himself on the chest. "A congestion of sorts." A hasty look at Adam, who had the wits to turn slightly in his saddle, thereby hiding his face from the king. Douglas must be laughing his arse off, Adam reflected. He would if someone had sent him a herald inviting him to relinquish such an excellent position.

The herald came galloping back.

"Well?" the king demanded.

"Sir James Douglas thanks you for your kind invitation to do battle on the ground of your choosing but must, he says, decline," the herald said. Adam's lips quivered with contained laughter. "He also says that he will be happy to continue marauding and pillaging your kingdom—unless you force him to retreat," the herald continued. Whatever mirth the incident had caused Adam was now wiped away. Bastard, to throw a challenge like that in the face of a young hawk like their king.

The herald wiped at his neck. "First the river, then it's hard uphill, my liege. They'll have us looking like hedgehogs before we reach the ridge."

"So what are we to do? Wait?" The king scowled at the distant banner. "I've had enough of waiting."

Half an hour later, the army began to move. Several groups of men marched towards the river while right at the front swarmed hundreds of archers who were to cover the advance up the hill.

"He'll be expecting that," Thomas said to Adam. He'd said that several times already, mostly directed at his nephew, but the king had refused to back down from his planned attack. "I sent out a few scouts, just in case."

"So did I," Adam said. "As did Mortimer." He frowned. So far, Lord Roger had been unusually quiet. Maybe he was still smarting from Lancaster's acid remark that, as far as he knew, Mortimer had no position of command in this expedition.

The archers had reached the river and were wading over it to the other side and the scant cover offered by some scraggly shrubs. A first group reached the opposite shore and started up the hill. More archers entered the water, holding their precious bows aloft. Adam held his breath, watching as one group of archers after the other made it safely across. What were the Scots waiting for? A loud war cry split the air. Horns bellowed, and out of every shrub rose a Scot, sword or axe in hand. The archers didn't stand a chance. They screamed as they were hewn down, some of them toppling down the hill to land, dead, in the water.

"Retreat!" someone yelled.

"No!" the king raised his voice. "Kill the Scots bastards! Shoot, damn it!" Except that the remaining archers couldn't, trapped as they were in the water. The air darkened with

Scottish arrows—all of them aimed at the English archers, most of whom were still in the river. More screams, and the archers turned and fled, a goodly number of them falling as they ran.

"Shit," Mortimer said, loud enough to carry to the king. "This nonsense stops now."

"We will regroup and try again," the king insisted.

"No, we will not." Mortimer stripped off his gauntlets. "We will never take that hill by force. I know that, you know that, and I can assure you Douglas knows that."

"We must try!" the king yelled. "We can't turn tail and run."

"Turn tail and run?" Mortimer's normally low voice rose. "How many men do you want to see bobbing lifeless in the water, my liege?" He stabbed his finger in the direction of the river and the various floating corpses. "Those men are dead, you fool! Dead because of you."

Edward looked away. "I didn't—"

"Think," Mortimer finished. "Neither did your three commanders."

"We will try again, my lord," Lancaster said, shoving Mortimer out of the way. "We throw sufficient men at them and we will win the day."

"No," Mortimer said.

"Why not?" Edward demanded. "I second Lancaster's motion." He straightened up. "My men will fight for me, Mortimer, even if you won't."

"Fight and die, my lord," Adam put in, wincing at the look the king threw him.

"Mortimer is right," Thomas said. "Only a fool would try again."

"Cowards!" Edward scowled. "All of you—cowards. I'm ordering you to attack!"

"No." Mortimer shook his head. "I will not allow it."

"Allow it? What are you, a traitor?"

"Me?" Mortimer laughed. "I am the unfortunate man taxed with keeping you and this realm safe, my liege. Else your mother will have me gelded and thrown into a pit of vipers." He looked at Thomas. "You will not attack, Earl Marshal—not today."

"Not today," Thomas echoed. With a curt nod, he set his horse into a slow canter, off to recall the vanguard.

The following night was hell. Constantly, the Scottish horns blew the attack, and every time they did, men stumbled from their sleep, rushing to prepare for battle. The Scots howled and yelled, laughed and sang, and from the noise they were making they had to be beating their shields with the flat of their swords, making it impossible to sleep or even think.

King Edward and Mortimer had words in the king's tent, loud and angry from the king, low and measured from Lord Roger. At some point, the tone in the conversation changed, and come dawn they emerged together, the king looking substantially happier than last Adam had seen him.

"We ambush them," the king explained, drawing a large circle in the dirt. "A thousand knights to fall on their backs while we distract them with a frontal attack."

Mortimer nodded, no more, pausing to clasp his oldest son's shoulder before calling for his squire.

"You aim to ride, my lord?" Adam asked.

"Me?" Mortimer gave him a crooked smile. "No. Such ventures are best left to the young and brave."

"The king?"

"God spare us!" Mortimer nodded at his son. "Edmund will ride. The king remains here, a general supervising his forces." He winked. "Or so I told him."

The ambush failed. The following night was just as bad, and on Lammas Day the weather turned surly and cold—very much in keeping with King Edward's mood. Yet another day of useless posturing, a night of blowing horns and howling Scots. Just before dawn, the Scots decided they had had enough—they needed sleep as well, Adam reckoned—and for some hours it was blissfully quiet.

"Gone!" Thomas shook Adam awake. "Douglas is gone."

"Hopefully to hell," Adam groaned, sitting up.

"No such luck. He has found himself another hill."

"God curse him. What is he playing at?" Adam gave the earl a bleary look.

"I think he is enjoying himself." Thomas inspected Adam. "You look awful."

"Tired." The cough was back—or rather, the cordial was gone.

They broke camp, only to set it all up again some few miles away. Adam rode with Will Montagu, in charge of doing something—anything—to bother the Scots while scouting out their new position.

"An even better hill," Montagu concluded, looking up the wooded slopes.

"Aye, but somewhat smaller." Adam pursed his lips. "Here, we could maybe starve him out. Maybe."

They returned to camp flushed after a recent skirmish with a Scottish foraging party. No casualties, but at least one of the Scotsmen would not be moving much tonight, having had his thigh pierced by an English arrow.

"That Douglas, he's doing all the right things," Adam commented to Montagu. He inspected Raven's legs and hooves, patted his big horse on the rump, and told Gavin to make sure he was properly rubbed down. "This campaign is turning into an utter failure."

Montagu's teeth gleamed white in the dusk. "Mortimer is not as infallible as he thinks he is."

"Or the Scotsmen are wilier." Adam scrubbed at his face. "Besides, it's not Mortimer who commands this venture."

"No? Seeing as the other three jump like eager hounds to do his bidding, I would say he does."

"Aye, there is that." Adam massaged his aching chest. "Well, at least tonight we'll get some sleep." He nodded up the hill. "They've been up and about all night. Other than their sentries, they will sleep like logs."

"Thank the Lord for small mercies," Montagu said.

"Amen to that."

Montagu suggested they eat together, and as the king was entertaining the earls and Mortimer in the privacy of his tent, Adam agreed, spending an agreeable evening with Montagu and a further few of the king's favoured companions. He already knew the de Bohun twins, was comfortable in their presence, seeing as their father had been Lord Roger's closest friend. A warrior of the old school, Humphrey de Bohun had died at Boroughbridge, impaled on a pike, and the two lads were forever begging Adam for further anecdotes about their brave and famous father.

Where the twins were of an age with the king, Ralph Stafford was about Montagu's age, some years younger than Adam, as was the man Adam had never met before, John Neville. A northerner like Percy, he gathered, even if there seemed to be little love lost between the Nevilles and the Percys.

Unfortunately, Robert de Langon made an appearance halfway through.

"Ah, the guard dog," he sneered when he saw Adam. "Imagine finding you here—I'd have thought you'd either sleep at the king's feet or lick Mortimer's arse."

"What?" Adam said, dropping his voice into the lower registers.

"You heard." Robert de Langon grinned. "Here we are, all lords—you are what? An upstart man-at-arms?"

"Robert," Montagu cut in, "that is quite enough. Adam is a trusted king's man—"

"Adam de Guirande is a weathervane. Once he served Mortimer, now he serves the king. Who knows where his true loyalty lies."

Adam rose. Slowly. Just as slowly, he advanced upon Robert. "Take that back, and best be quick about it."

"Or else?" Robert set his hands at his hips. "What can you do to me?"

"I can start by belting you until your arse glows," Adam snarled, and just like that he had Robert by the nape of his neck.

"You wouldn't dare!"

"Oh, I think he would," Montagu drawled. "And rightly so, given how you've provoked him."

"Provoked him?" Robert spluttered, struggling like a hooked worm. "He should know his place!"

"As should you," one of the de Bohun twins said. "If Adam is an upstart knight, what are you? A glorified merchant?"

There were snickers all around.

"Apologise," Adam said. "Loudly."

"No." Robert aimed a kick at Adam's shin.

"Fine."

Amidst loud hoots and cheers, Adam threw Robert over a bench, planted a knee in his lower back to keep him still, and undid his belt.

"Stop this! I'm telling you, de Guirande, you'll pay, you hear?"

"Pay for what? You insulted me." Adam slapped him once on his arse—hard. Robert howled. By the time Adam was done, his audience was silent. He shoved Robert to the ground. "Next time you question my loyalty, I'll come after you with my sword instead."

De Langon had long since stopped yelling. He raised a pale face and spat at Adam's feet. Adam raised his hand, Robert de Langon cringed, and Montagu stepped between them.

"Enough. As it is, de Langon won't be sitting much the coming days. Now, more wine?"

It was late when Adam made it back to the tent Thomas had invited him to share. Gavin and Stephen were already fast asleep, as were Norfolk's two squires, but Thomas was sitting outside on an upturned bucket, head cocked to the side.

"Listen," he said.

Adam did. "Nothing."

"Precisely." Thomas grinned. "Wonderful, isn't it?"

"It is." Adam lowered himself to the ground and smothered a yawn. For the first time in weeks, the night was warm. No rain, no wind, just the scents of the surrounding forest and the various fires. Some tents down, someone was singing. A couple of men stumbled by, both the worse for drink. Thomas hummed something under his breath, and Adam was considering crawling to bed when he heard the distinctive sound of horses—many horses—coming at a gallop.

"Damn!" Thomas was already on his feet. Adam ducked his head into his tent and grabbed his sword. A horn sounded to his right. Not a taunting little blast—no, this was an order to attack, and out of the dark surged a group of mounted men, swords held high as they charged through the English camp.

They swept by him, close enough that Adam could smell the sweaty hide of the horses, hear the creak of harness, and then they were gone, ploughing through the camp towards the central pavilion.

"The king! They're making for the king!" Adam was already making for Edward's tent. He crashed into Montagu, appearing tousle-haired from his tent.

"Your sword!" Adam barked, leaping over the guy rope. "Arm up, man!" A Scotsman charged by, his sword flashing in the light of the fire. The blade sang through the air, Adam pushed Montagu aside, managed to parry the blow, and then the Scotsman was gone, galloping towards the closest tent with his companions.

The few men who stood to meet them were mowed down, helpless in their near nudity when faced with the armed and mounted Scottish knights. The swords rose and fell. A scream ended in a gargle; men staggered this way and that. One man fell to his knees, clutching at the bleeding stump where his hand had been. Another toppled forward, landing facedown in the mud. The back of his head was gone, spilling brains and blood down his back.

"They're cutting the guy ropes," Thomas yelled. Adam stumbled over a body, going down on one knee in the blood and mud before Thomas hauled him upright.

Everywhere, tents were collapsing like pricked pigs' bladders. Men screamed, struggling to free themselves of the heavy canvas.

"Dear God," Montagu groaned, as yet another group of Scotsmen appeared, armed with heavy spears and burning torches. The ground shook at their approach, and Adam counted at least two score of the bastards. Firelight gleamed on the long, evil spearheads. They roared and cheered as they charged through the camp. The screams of the men trapped in the tents became shrieks, high-pitched sounds that ended in gurgles and whimpers. Skewered, poor bastards, unable to flee.

Some of the tents caught fire. Acrid smoke stung Adam's eyes, made it difficult to breathe.

"The king!" Adam gasped. The tent was down, the royal banner trampled into the mud. From within came Edward's voice, screaming for help. Adam ran, limped, and jumped side by side with Montagu and Thomas. Mortimer came running from the other direction in boots and shirt, no more. But he had his sword, and behind him came his squires.

Men ran like witless hens, screaming in terror as they dodged the Scottish spears and swords. A horse squealed and went down in a flurry of kicking legs. Five Scotsmen charged towards the king's tent, and Adam skidded to a stop beside Lord Roger, sword held high.

"Is he alive?" Mortimer asked.

"I am," Edward yelled back. "If only this infernal priest would get off my back—"

"Stay where you are," Adam shouted. "Don't—ah!" He ducked a vicious thrust, swiped at the horse's legs, and when the poor beast went down, Adam threw himself at the Scottish whoreson, his sword sinking into the man's face. A spray of blood, and the man went still.

On the other side of the collapsed tent, one of Mortimer's men was swinging a club, screaming as he fought off one Scotsman after the other.

"Help him!" Mortimer snapped, stamping at the flames that licked the corner of the king's tent. "If they get past him…" Thomas and Adam leapt to do so. Too late. Before their eyes, the man went down, a swarming heap of Scotsmen ensuring he would never breathe again.

Adam tightened his grip on his bloody hilt and roared, using his heavy sword as a scythe. The attackers fell back, watching him warily.

"Douglas!" Montagu pointed in the direction of one of the mounted men. "That's Douglas!"

"Get him!" Mortimer hollered, just as someone struck the Scottish leader in the back, effectively toppling him off his horse. Someone cheered. Adam ducked an axe, swung his sword, and the man before him collapsed, clutching at his belly. A horn sounded. Like trained alaunts, the Scotsmen flew towards the sound. Douglas calling for help? Adam couldn't see, too busy fighting off two men while Mortimer tackled a third.

And then, just as quickly as they had come, the Scots were gone, carrying with them their wounded leader and leaving a trail of carnage behind. Adam braced his hands on his knees, contemplating the scene before him. So many dead, even more wounded. The ground was a churned mess of mud and blood; men limped and coughed and retched. Adam straightened up. The king. Already, Montagu and Stafford were propping up the tent, and moments later Edward crawled out, spitting like an angered cat.

"Are you unhurt, my lord?" Adam's hands flew over the king's arms, his head.

"Leave me alone!" Edward shook him off, but not before Adam felt the tremors running through him. As undressed as Mortimer, Edward's face was streaked with mud and dominated by wide eyes. His hair was a mess, the fine linen of his shirt torn and dirty.

"What are you waiting for?" the king asked, eyes darting from one dead man to the other. "Sit up and ride. Ride, damn it, and kill every single one of them."

"They have the advantage." Mortimer handed his sword to one of his squires. "We ride against them, they slaughter us."

"I did not take you for craven," Edward said. There was a collective intake of breath. Mortimer took one long step towards the king, who sidled away from him.

"What did you say?" Lord Roger's voice dropped dangerously low.

"I called you craven." Edward straightened up.

"No man has ever called me that and lived. Count yourself fortunate you're nothing but an untried lad." Mortimer nudged at the closest corpse. "He died for you, my liege. So did tens of others. And you would waste more lives just to soothe your wounded pride?" He spat to the side. "Get these men buried," he commanded. "Adam, double the sentries." He turned to the king. "You, my liege, had best retire to bed."

"You do not tell me what to do," Edward tried. "I am your king."

"Then act as one." Mortimer gestured at the destruction that surrounded them, at the wounded and the dead. "They should be your first concern."

Chapter 13

Some days after the surprise raid, Douglas and his men left, riding north under the cover of the night. And so the English host turned south, making slow progress over muddied roads.

"Humiliated by a band of ruffians." King Edward cast a long look in the direction of Mortimer.

"Sir James would resent that," Adam said. "He is considered one of the most valiant knights in Scotland."

"Hmph!" The king scowled. "He serves his king well," he admitted some while later.

"He does." Adam slid him a look. "He loves him, I think."

"Douglas loves his king?" Edward smiled. "And does the king love him back?"

"I would imagine so. No James, no crown."

A shadow flitted over Edward's face. "A king should not be beholden to anyone." For a moment, the king fixed his gaze on Mortimer's back, several yards ahead of them.

"It is difficult to live your life without becoming beholden to someone," Adam pointed out. It had been difficult riding back with the king and Mortimer. One was unfailingly polite, condescending, almost. The other smouldered with rage. And the closer they got to York, the tenser Lord Roger became, his gaze never leaving the road to the south. Hoping, no doubt, for a message telling him Edward of Caernarvon had been apprehended.

"We should never have left our baggage train behind," the king said abruptly. Adam suppressed a little groan. Every day, they went through the recent events, the king attempting to identify just why things had gone as they did. "An army is never as good as its supply lines," Edward continued, nodding to himself. He flashed Adam a smile. "Maman always says one must look for the lesson in each failure."

"Very wise of her."

"Mmm." Yet again, Edward looked at Mortimer. "Does she love him, do you think?"

Adam was taken aback. But the expression on his young lord's face was earnest, as if he truly wanted to know.

"I do, my lord. What do you think?"

Edward nodded, chewing his lip. With a wry little smile, he set his horse to canter, yelling for Will Montagu to wait for him.

The moment Adam saw the queen, his shoulders relaxed. She came towards them, face shining, her voice serene and collected as she welcomed home first her son, then her baron.

"I gather the former king is back in his cage," Adam muttered to Richard. They'd been riding together for the last few days, thrown together when Thomas announced his decision to continue to Suffolk and his waiting countess, while Richard's boon companion, Edmund Mortimer, was sent off to Ludlow with messages for his mother and several of Lord Roger's retainers.

"It would seem so. For now, at least." Richard kicked his horse into a trot. "Coming? I could do with a bath."

The friary was full, and the castle was crammed to the rafters with men, so Richard and Adam spent several hours looking for an inn, neither of them relishing the idea of bedding down among the men-at-arms in the hall of the friary. The inn they found was just beside the city wall, so embedded in woodbine it was as if the plant was holding the house up rather than the reverse.

"Baths?" The innkeeper looked them up and down. "There's a bathhouse up the street, and they serve a good meal as well." He winked. "Other services are also available."

"Oh?" Richard brightened, and rather reluctantly Adam followed him up the narrow, cobbled street. He had no interest in whores. All he wanted was a hot bath and a soft bed.

Some hours later, Adam left Richard to his pastimes and took a slow stroll back to the inn. The hot water had done him good, sore muscles adequately relaxed. Only one extremity was at present a source of discomfort, and that was more due to the featherlight touch of one of the whores than any ailment. Adam adjusted his braies and detoured through the gardens of the Dominican friary presently hosting the queen.

He nodded to the sentries and slipped further into the perfumed greenery. This late in the summer, dark came early, but a heavy harvest moon was visible above a bank of clouds, making Adam think of Kit—as if he needed more reminders of his wife, what with the way his member remained somewhat stiff. He sat down gingerly on a bench, realising belatedly that he'd ended up very close to the queen's rooms.

Soft candlelight spilled from the open windows, the queen walking back and forth while talking to someone inside. Her veil came off, deft hands undid her braids, and when the queen shook out her hair, Adam inhaled, mesmerised by the fall of dark hair.

"It's the only way," she said. A responding murmur from within, and the queen nodded. Yet another little turn, her hands lifting and falling in time with her voice, and now she was working the buttons of her cotehardie. If she was undressing alone, that could only mean one thing: whoever she was talking to was Lord Roger, as otherwise her rooms would have been full of her ladies, helping her out of her garments.

She shrugged off the dark cotehardie and came to stand by the window, laughing at something her companion was saying.

"Of course it will work," she said. "Besides, there's no choice. We have to do something to ensure it never happens again."

Lord Roger appeared beside her, swept her hair aside, and kissed her neck, and Adam held his breath and wished he'd never entered the garden or sat down on the bench. That long white neck, the way the queen's eyes closed, dark lashes fluttering against her cheeks. He'd always considered her the most beautiful woman alive—but cold. This woman, however, this creature with dark hair who swayed in Lord Roger's arms, who moaned and cupped her lover's cheek with infinite tenderness, she was smouldering with heat.

Lord Roger drew off his shirt, his broad chest covered with a mat of dark hair. He undid her laces, and the kirtle dropped out of sight. A soft laugh, a murmured "Roger", and ever so slowly the queen leaned back against the window arch, a provocative posture that had Adam sinking lower on his bench.

Lord Roger came after. One inch at a time, his hands slid up her waist to cup her breasts. Two people made one, her hair shielding them both as Lord Roger finally kissed her. Fortunately, at that point Lord Roger swept her up in his arms. After counting to a hundred, Adam slipped away. What, he wondered as he made his way through the fragrant garden, was it that the queen wanted to stop from ever happening again?

Next morning, Adam entered the friary church just before prime. He'd woken far too early, a consequence of Richard's snoring, and had avenged himself by kicking Richard awake as he left.

"What?" Richard had asked, sitting up abruptly.

"You snore."

"And you wake me up to tell me that?" Richard had collapsed. "I need my sleep."

"So do I. Didn't get much, did I?"

"Not my fault you won't scratch the itch that's keeping you awake." Richard had stretched languorously. "Although I suppose I should be pleased for my sister." He'd peered at Adam. "Why don't you go back to Tresaints? The king would surely let you go now that the Scottish venture has been so happily closed." He'd snickered, ducking as Adam threw a cushion at him.

The queen looked surprised to find Adam in church but bid him a quiet good morning as she swept by him, followed by her ladies. Moments later, a grumpy king joined them, trailed by the de Bohun twins and Lord Roger, looking as fit and fresh as if he'd started the day rolling about in the dewy grass. Newly shaved, sporting a new tunic in purple, embroidered with flowers and butterflies, he looked happy, his eyes lingering far more often on the queen's svelte figure than was appropriate while listening to a priest.

Once the service was concluded, Adam made straight for the king's chamber, only to discover he was not first in line—Lord Roger was already there, explaining he had urgent matters to take care of in southern Wales.

"What matters?" the king asked suspiciously.

"Matters regarding the safety of the realm." Lord Roger plucked at his sleeve. "Do you want to come along, my lord?"

"No." Edward grimaced. "Very well, you may go." He sighed when Adam approached next. "You want to go home," he stated, sounding irritated.

"Is that so strange?" Adam asked. "My lady wife is breeding, and I—"

"Go," the king interrupted. "And when you come back, bring Lady Kit. I miss her."

When Lord Roger suggested they ride together, Adam readily agreed. Riding in the company of Lord Roger held far more appeal than a week and more in the sole company of Gavin and Stephen and his men-at-arms. He said as much, making Lord Roger laugh.

It was the longest Adam had spent alone with Lord Roger since that failed campaign back in 1321. Come evening, he and Lord Roger shared a room—now and then, even a bed—and during the days they rode mostly side by side, away from Lord Roger's retainers. At times, it felt as if the intervening years had not happened, and the further west they rode, the lighter Mortimer's mood, his eyes regaining their normal sparkle, his shoulders relaxing as if a yoke had been lifted off him.

"It is no easy matter to rule a country," Lord Roger said when Adam carefully shared his observations. His mouth twisted. "Endless work, little gratitude."

"And unlimited power," Adam added.

"Ah yes, power." Lord Roger's hand tightened on the reins, the sun catching his jewelled rings. "But with power comes responsibility, and the need to do things no one else dares to do. Necessary things." He stared straight ahead. "You know, there are instances when I find myself sympathising with Despenser. Even he must have had days when he was obliged to do things that stuck in his craw."

Adam spat to the side. "Sympathise? Never." His foot twitched just at the mention of Despenser.

Mortimer eased his horse into a walk. "Walking in your enemy's shoes can be quite an elucidating experience," he said after a while.

They arrived in Ludlow a week or so later.

"Eat, rest, and then be on your way. I insist." Lord Roger grinned. "It's been years since you've been back."

"Aye." Truth be told, Adam preferred avoiding Ludlow, home to far too many disturbing childhood memories. He followed Lord Roger through the dark arch of the gatehouse and into the outer bailey. The stone wall encircled a huge space with stables and other buildings to the left, a defensive tower straight ahead, a small orchard to the right, and a bevy of masons and workers busy along the southern side of the curtain wall, where a new chapel was slowly taking shape.

"He's dead," Lord Roger said perceptively. "And you are in no way his son. Walter de Guirande was a snivelling bully, a vicious coward. You, on the other hand..." Lord Roger broke off, mouth falling open for an instant before he collected himself. "My lady," he said, his voice shaking. "I did not expect to find you here."

"No?" Lady Joan said. "My lord, where else would I be? This, after all, was my father's favourite home."

Lord Roger tugged a hand through his hair. "Yes, yes, of course."

Lady Joan's mouth twitched, her eyes meeting Adam's. They both recognised the gesture: Lord Roger was uncomfortable.

"My lady." Adam was off his horse, bowing deeply over Lady Joan's hand.

"Adam. Always a pleasure." She squinted up at him. "I saw your wife some weeks ago. She was blooming—yet another little de Guirande on its way?"

"Aye."

By now, Lord Roger had dismounted, standing a foot or two to the side. "You look well."

"You mean I look better," she retorted, a hand fluttering up to her neck, scrawny and thin.

"No." He smiled at her. "I said what I meant, Joanie."

Lady Joan gave him a scathing look, on the verge of saying something, but she was interrupted by the appearance of her daughters. Little bodies to be hugged, cheeks to be kissed, and for a moment it was as it used to be, Lord Roger surrounded by his large family, including his wife. The illusion was shattered when Lady Joan moved to the side. Her daughters stilled, returning like a flock of goslings to the mother goose.

For an instant, Lord Roger looked abandoned, so alone Adam took a step towards him. Lady Joan arrested him with a pre-emptive movement of her hand.

"Shall we walk, my lord?" she suggested. "You have as yet not seen the new gardens, have you?"

"No." Lord Roger gestured in the direction of the low garden wall. "After you, my lady."

They walked side by side, him with his hands clasped behind his back, she with her arms folded across her chest—but at least they were talking, and it made Adam glad to see them thus.

Someone called his name, and Adam turned to nod a greeting to Geoffrey. His favourite among the Mortimer sons smiled in return, eyes on his parents.

"Do you think he'll return to her?"

"I'm not sure the queen would let him." He squeezed Geoffrey's shoulder. "She depends on him."

"So does Mama."

Adam laughed. "Your lady mother is much stronger than you think. If it ever came to a battle between her and our lady queen—and may God spare us such a horrible event—it would not be Queen Isabella who walked away unscathed." He nodded in the direction of where Lord Roger and his wife had disappeared. "Lady Joan is an admirable woman, and no one knows that better than Lord Roger."

"And yet he betrays her," Geoffrey said, turning away.

Yes, Adam thought, so he does.

"Men are utter fools at times," Kit scolded. "Even those in holy orders."

"It is no great matter." William studied his bandaged arm with pride.

"No great matter?" She shook her head. "You're a man of God, not some sort of errant knight."

"I was called to serve." A bright smile lit up his face. "Haven't had this much fun in years."

"Fun?" Kit wrung out the bloodied rag she'd used to clean his shallow wound. "I don't think Edward of Caernarvon thought it much fun, do you?"

"No." He cleared his throat, a guarded look in his eyes.

"What?"

"Nothing." William stood up. "Well, at least the former king is back where he belongs, safe and sound at Berkeley." He chewed his lip. "Kit, I—"

"What?" She busied herself at the hearth, filling an earthenware mug with heated wine.

"The king, one of the men with him…"

He was making no sense, but his tone made her uneasy. William sighed. Deeply. "When we found him—and God knows he seemed most relieved we did—he was with a band of ruffians." William made a face. "Men with little scruples, intent on feathering their own nests."

"In my experience, that comprises most of England's barons. Go on," she added when he remained silent.

"We caught some of them. Not all of them." William shifted his injured arm. "And one of those who got away had a badly slashed face."

The earthenware mug shattered on the hearth. "How clumsy of me!" Kit crouched, picking up the pieces. "Godfrey of Broseley?"

"The same."

"But he was in York. Adam saw him there."

"He was?" William struggled with the heavy cloth of his dark tunic, his head disappearing in its folds. "I dare say he can ride."

"I don't like it." Kit sat down on a stool, the broken pottery in her hands. "Godfrey has a score to settle—with Mortimer and with Adam."

"And with you, as I hear it."

"And with me." She closed her hand round one of the shards. It had been self-defence, but she doubted Godfrey would see it that way. "He won't come here, will he?"

"Here? To Tresaints?" William shook his head. "Last I saw him, he was fleeing northwest." He ran a hand over his recently shaven cheeks. "Time for mass." He made for the door, standing ajar to allow the sunlight entry. "Coming?"

Kit presided over dinner in the hall before finding an opportunity to slip away. The August day was hot, a distant edge of dark clouds promising thunder by the evening. Not as much as a whiff of wind, and by the time Kit had reached her favourite spot, she was damp with sweat.

Everyone knew better than to disturb the lady of the manor when she disappeared behind the great alder, so Kit undid her veil and released her heavy hair before slipping out of her green kirtle. No hose—not today—and the shoes were old and well-worn, the original blue leather faded to the softest of greys.

Barefoot, in only her chemise, she approached the water. The little stream that meandered through the upper pastures of Tresaints widened into a pool, deep enough in places for the water to reach above her waist. Not at all like swimming in the sea, Kit reflected as she waded out until the water lapped at her hem. She smiled, recalling how her mother had taught her to swim in the Solent, insisting one never knew when such unusual skills could come in useful.

The water was cool. Kit floated for a while, eyes on the endless expanse of sky above. Her chemise billowed around her, and she moved her head from side to side, relishing the sensation of her hair swirling in the water.

At long last, she stood. The linen of her garment clung to her, outlining the soft curve of her breasts, of her belly. Kit retreated to sit on a rock, collecting her hair in a damp tail to lie over one of her shoulders. A couple of robins chirped in the nearby shrubs; a thrush hopped across the ground, its speckled chest shimmering in the light. A wren whirred by, a dragonfly hovered over the sunlit waters, and Kit raised her face to the sun and closed her eyes.

Grass swished. She opened her eyes. A twig cracked, and she twisted sufficiently to see who was approaching. As yet not fully visible, screened by the foliage of saplings and shrubs, she recognised him all the same, her fingers tingling with the memory of his skin, his sleek muscles. He ducked under a trailing branch, halted just to look at her.

His shaggy thatch of hair had lightened after weeks of summer sun, and there was golden stubble on his cheeks. The fuzz on his bare forearms gilded his tanned skin, and the way he smiled had butterflies fluttering in her chest, her blood igniting.

"My lady." He tugged his tunic off, discarding his shirt as he came towards her. "You," he said, bending down to kiss her, "look like a mermaid." She was in his arms, and he was splashing through the shallows, laughing as he threw her to land in a cascade of water. Moments later, he was beside her, drawing her towards him. Cold, wet linen on her skin, scorching lips on her mouth, on her eyes. He hefted her closer, lifted her slightly, and thrust inside.

"God in heaven, but I've missed you," he groaned, resting his forehead against hers.

"And I you."

Small, small movements at first, and she clung like a limpet to his shoulders, legs hooked round his waist. A kiss, a hungry ravenous kiss that left her with no air. Hands sliding down to cup her buttocks, lifting her that much closer. She felt him widen his stance, threw her head back to offer him her throat. His arm round her waist, banding her in iron, holding her still. Hot, moist exhalations tickling her ear, teeth nipping hard enough to make her gasp.

She slid her hands into his hair and tugged. He groaned and flexed his hips. It was an odd sensation: the cool water, his hot, hard member. When he eased out, water rushed in. When he plunged back in, the water was forced out. The sun on her back, causing sweat to spring forth. She was hot all over, a dull ache throbbing through her lower back, her womb. When he kissed her, she bit him, and he growled her name, already wading to the shore.

They were on the ground. She was on her knees, hands gripping at the grass as he pounded into her. Strong hands on her hips, pulling her back to meet his thrusts. So deep, so strong, so hers. Kit groaned and fell forward. He choked out her name as he found his release.

They remained in the little clearing for the rest of the afternoon. A long, cooling soak was followed by a gentle session in the grass, this time on a bed of discarded clothing. But mostly they talked, she lying as close to him as she could as he told her of the Weardale failure, when she shared what William had said about Godfrey of Broseley. He stilled at that, his arms tightening around her.

The sun dipped behind a screen of trees.

"We should get back," he said, stroking her belly.

"We should." But she made no move to do so, content to lie here in his arms, surrounded by the scents of drying grass and cool, clear water.

"We really should get back," he said much later.

"We should." She smiled. They really should. Maybe later.

Chapter 14

There were so many horses, carts, and litters making their way north they could have been on a crowded London street. Or so Kit thought, sharing this with Adam as they yet again picked their way round a company of merchants, sitting at their ease on the broad verge.

"No smell," Adam replied. "No Thames, no urchins hoping to cut your purse."

"No. Instead, we have the outlaws of the forest, eager to steal anything they can get their hands on." Kit rode her horse closer to Raven, making Adam laugh.

"It would be a foolish outlaw who chooses to attack when the road is brimming with knights such as myself. Besides, there's not much cover here, is there?"

"Not here, no." They were presently riding through a field of coppiced trees, the odd oak left standing like a sentinel over stands of hazel and ash. Little cover for any would-be outlaws unless they were hiding in the high grass, pressed flat to the ground. They passed yet another group of eating men before regaining the road, now disappearing into the darker shadows of the forest proper.

Under the rustling trees, the travellers grew silent, small groups forming larger groups, armed men gripping the hilt of their swords. Adam nodded at his men-at-arms, and they spread out around them, vigilant eyes on the surrounding wooded slopes.

"Are all these men aimed for parliament?" If so, half of England planned on attending—accompanied by the other half.

"Most of them." Adam nodded discreetly in the direction of a well-dressed merchant astride a roan palfrey. "He is—and he has chosen to ride accompanied."

"Who is he?" Kit nodded briefly at the man as they rode by him and his servants, most of them armed with cudgels.

"That is Hamo de Chigwell," Adam said, spitting to the side. "One of the men who condemned Lord Roger to death back in 1322."

"Oh." She twisted in her saddle to get a better look at the man, but other than the rich velvets of his robes, she saw little but his eyes and a high, domed forehead. "Maybe he was coerced to do so."

"Maybe." Adam sounded unconvinced. "As I hear it, Hamo is no friend of our baron."

"One could say that of very many men."

"Aye." There was a soft sigh, indicating this was all Adam had to say on the subject.

They arrived on the outskirts of Lincoln just as the sun broke through a bank of clouds, bathing the town in golden autumn light. Kit drew her horse to a halt and just stared.

"It's…"

"Tall?" Adam teased, leaning over to take her reins. He set their horses in motion.

"Magnificent," Kit corrected. The jumble of streets and houses that made up the town of Lincoln clambered up a steep hill to huddle at the base of the minster, its impressive central tower pointing directly to the sky. "Like a castle for God," she added, awed by the sheer size of it.

"The castle is the somewhat humbler building to its left," Adam said with a laugh. She could just make out a massive tower and a segment of the walls, but beyond a quick glance, she returned to gazing at the minster.

The road narrowed markedly as they approached the bridge over the Witham and the travellers came to a standstill. Houses lined both sides of the road, to the right was a chapel clinging to the banks of the river. Carts jostled with riders, and voices rose in irritation.

"Out of our way!" From behind came a large group of riders, and despite the throng, they did not slacken their pace. People leapt aside, intimidated by the men in armour, the flying pennons.

"Lancaster," Adam muttered, using heels and thighs to back Raven out of the way. "Gavin, see to the packhorses."

137

Kit followed suit, but her palfrey was unused to so many people, so much noise, and threw her head, dancing awkwardly over the cobbles. With a whinny, the mare leapt to the side, barging into the mount of the knight leading the Lancaster party.

Moments later, it was utter confusion. Horses, people, yelling men and screaming women. Kit's horse stomped and shied, and it was all Kit could do to remain astride, buffeted this way and that. The palfrey reared. Kit felt herself slipping backwards. The palfrey came down, the resulting jarring causing her to bite her lip.

"Kit!" Adam appeared beside her on foot. A horse came charging through, and the palfrey sidestepped, throwing Adam against the wall. He was down, beneath all those hooves and panicked feet.

"Adam!" Kit yanked hard on the reins, bringing the palfrey to a shuddering stop. "Adam?"

"Here, sweeting." He scowled at the horse as he regained his feet. "I swear, I'll…" Whatever he intended to say was drowned in the blaring of horns. Henry of Lancaster was coming through, his men in a tight knot around him, his banner held overhead. A flash of scarlet, of matching trappings on a handsome bay, and then he was gone, one hand clapped to his headwear.

It took Adam some time to get them across the crowded bridge. In the aftermath of the earl's passing, everyone was in a hurry to get across, and by the time they'd made it through the gate to the city, the sun was setting.

The ground rose steeply towards the minster and the adjoining castle. The main thoroughfare was bordered by sturdy houses in stone, here and there in timber, all of them symbols of relative wealth.

"Wool," Adam explained. He pointed back the way they'd come, towards the marshier land that abutted the busy little harbour. "And there'll be plenty of hovels that way. There always are."

The queen and her son were not at the castle. Instead, they were directed to the bishop's palace, right beside the massive minster. They entered the minster ward through double gatehouses, and Kit just had to stop and turn her face heavenward, incapable of dragging her eyes away from the soaring golden stone and the huge arches that decorated the western front of the minster. Never in her life had she seen anything as magnificent, her gaze leaping from the statues atop the pinnacles to the carved arches to the row of kings seated above the main door and back to the central spire, tall enough to scratch at the sky.

"This way." Adam rode first, leading them down the south side of the minster before taking a sharp turn to the right. Yet another gatehouse, and they drew rein before the stables. Before them rose a building almost as magnificent as the minster, the entire ward full of people rushing back and forth. Adam helped her dismount and led her to the inner gatehouse, this one with a brightly painted ceiling.

"A bishop?" she whispered to Adam. "This should belong to a king."

"While our queen agrees entirely, I don't think Bishop Burghersh does," Adam said before disappearing into a nearby room to inquire about their lodgings. Kit stood very still, intimidated by the amount of men in priestly robes, the servants, and the surrounding buildings. Arched windows set with glass, elegantly carved doorways, covered passageways running from one house to the other—all of it in stone, all of it decorated with statues and friezes.

"Very grand, my lady," Rhosyn offered.

"Very." She smiled at her maid and got a reluctant smile in return. Rhosyn had not wanted to leave Tresaints, but Mabel had been poorly, and there had been no time to find someone else.

Adam reappeared, accompanied by a young clerk who gave Kit a cursory nod before pointing in the direction of a narrow passage. "There. Beyond the East Hall. Last door to the left – a bit of a walk." With that, he swept off.

"Well, at least we have a room to ourselves," Adam said.

"A bit of a walk?" Gavin groaned, looking at their various chests and bundles.

"Do you good, lad," Adam told him. "And Stephen is here to help, isn't he?" He offered Kit his hand. "You and I are requested to present ourselves to the queen." He burst out laughing when Kit groaned as loudly as Gavin had done.

A week later, Adam banged into their room. "Dearest God," he croaked, bracing himself against his knees while inhaling repeatedly. "He's dead."

"Who? Lord Mortimer?" Kit set her embroidery aside. That would explain why the queen's beloved baron had yet to arrive.

Adam shook his head. "Richard just told me: the king— the former king." He straightened up, dragging a shaking hand through his hair.

"He's dead? How?"

"How?" Adam paced up and down their little chamber. "I don't know." He threw her a look out of eyes as dark as pewter. "I only pray he died of natural causes."

"Natural…" Kit stood up. "What are you saying?"

"Two kings in one land make for an uncomfortable fit, sweeting." Adam took her hand, his fingers tight round hers. "And there are plenty of men who'd rise to do battle on the former king's behalf, disgruntled at being excluded from government by the queen and Lord Roger."

"Men like Henry of Lancaster." The earl was growing louder by the day in his opposition to the queen and baron.

"And that popinjay, Earl Edmund." Adam snorted, releasing her hand. "That man was born with plenty of intelligence but the constancy of a weathervane, and even worse, he is afflicted by guilt every time he changes his colours."

"Like when he deserted his half-brother." Earl Edmund had been an early convert to Queen Isabella's cause, very much due to the former king's preference for Hugh Despenser— and his annoying tendency of showering his favourite with whatever he wanted, even if it belonged to someone else, such as Earl Edmund.

Adam was back to pacing. "The fool thought we'd rid ourselves of Despenser and slap Edward over the wrists, no more. How he ever came to that conclusion is a right mystery. Edward of Caernarvon was not fit to rule."

"And now he's dead." Kit crossed herself, uttering a *requiscat in pace* under her breath.

"Aye. I must go to my lord." With a nod in her direction, he exited the room, looking verily like a man about to purge his bowels.

Kit returned to her sewing. A king dead—well, a deposed, imprisoned king. Maybe laying him to rest would finally put an end to the unrest in the country. She stabbed the needle through the fabric and set her work aside. Their present king was indisputably king now that his predecessor was dead. Poor Edward, she sighed, somewhat embarrassed to think thus familiarly about her young liege. Any opportunity of reconciling with his father was now gone.

Adam found his lord in the bishop's orchard, the half-grown Lancelot at his heels. The dog raised its head, dark eyes regarding Adam as he approached.

"My lord?"

Edward presented him with his back. "Go away."

"How can I? You may have need of me."

"Need?" The king wheeled, and there were tear-streaks down his cheeks, but his eyes were like cut glass; bright and sharp, they bored into Adam. "Can you bring him back to life? Can you…" He spluttered. "A king, to die shut away from the sun and light, to die like a felon in a damp and draughty dungeon."

"Your lord father has not been so constrained." The queen had insisted on her husband being accorded adequate comforts, which included everything from the best of silks and linen with which to clothe him, to books to amuse him.

"So she says—so *he* says." Lord Edward bit his lip. "But I do not know, do I? I was never allowed to see him." He shifted his shoulders, straightened up, no more than a head shorter than Adam. Their young liege was growing into a most impressive man, a living reminder of his famous grandfather, who, to hear it, had been as tall.

141

"My lord, your father—"

"Edward?" The queen's voice interrupted. She came floating down the incline towards them, an apparition in red, her cotehardie adorned with buttons down the front, tight sleeves clinging to her shapely arms. A dark cloak billowed in the wind, her veil and wimple were in the sheerest of linen, skirts raised sufficiently to allow a glimpse of white hose as she hastened towards them. Green eyes under a creased brow, her mouth set in a little pout. "My son, we must talk."

"We must?" Edward scowled. "Should you not be distressed? Torn asunder by grief?" He laughed. "But no, of course not—the news that grieves me must gladden you."

Queen Isabella flinched. "Don't be a fool!" She took hold of her son's arm, hard enough for the lad to inhale. "I said, we must talk. Now."

Adam kicked his heels for a while, but when it became apparent neither the queen nor the king were returning, he went in search of Thomas of Norfolk. The earl was in his chamber, turning bleary eyes Adam's way when he entered. There was a huge stain on one of the whitewashed walls, the floor beneath sticky with spilled sweetened wine. A dented silver goblet lay by the wall, and there was more wine on the table, down the front of Thomas' bright green tunic. Even his hair was sticky with it, his lips stained purple.

"Adam." Thomas braced his hands on the table, rose, swayed alarmingly, and collapsed back down. "I..." He burped. "I..." He blinked and grabbed at one of the apples adorning a large platter. "Dead." Thomas sliced the apple with clumsy movements that had Adam fearing he might cut off a finger. "How convenient."

"How so?" Adam asked, even if he agreed with Thomas. So soon upon the former king's recapture—and where was Lord Mortimer, why had he not returned to court, why had he ignored the summons to parliament?

Thomas used his knife to convert the slices into dices, his face hidden by his fall of hair. "My brother." He stabbed at the core of the apple, missed, did it again. "Dead. And I, God help me, helped in his undoing." With a curse, he swept the platter off the table, sending apples flying through the room. "What have I done?"

"He died of sudden illness."

"So they say." Thomas wiped the blade on his sleeve. "Edward was a remarkably healthy man." His mouth twisted, corners dropping. "My brother," he groaned, covering his face with his hands. "My foolish, high-handed brother, my king, damn it. My king!"

"Thomas…" Adam began, placing an arm round his shoulders.

"Leave me alone!" Thomas snarled, shoving Adam hard. "Just go, Adam."

"Devastated," Adam told Kit some while later. He poured some wine, noted with some surprise that his hand was shaking. "And drunk." Adam drained the cup, sloshed some more wine in it, and joined Kit in the window seat. Too narrow to fit them both, but she accommodated him by crossing her legs.

"Do you think…" Adam's throat thickened. He tried again. "Would Lord Roger…"

"Lord Roger?" Kit sat up straight. "Are you asking what I think you're asking? Dear God, why would you even think that?"

Adam shrugged. He placed a hand on her belly, caressing the little life within. "It makes things easier, doesn't it? For Lord Roger, but also for the king."

"No." Kit took the cup from him and settled herself in his lap. "No, Adam, never." She cupped his face. "Mortimer may have changed, but he would never lower himself to something that heinous."

"How can you be so certain?" He rested his head against the wall and closed his eyes.

"How?" Kit stroked his face. "Because my lord husband has been moulded into the man he is by Mortimer, and you would never do something so dishonourable."

Adam took some comfort in that. Some.

Next day, the queen requested Adam's presence—immediately. He made his excuses to the king, wiped the sweat from his brow, and took his time making it to the queen's apartments. Not entirely out of choice as he was limping badly after his recent session in the tiltyard.

"How is he?" the queen asked without preamble.

"Angry," Adam replied, carefully shifting his sore shoulder. And when his lord was angered, he had the unfortunate tendency of taking it out on Adam, which was why he was covered in grime and sweat, why his damaged foot felt as if it had been caught in a bear-trap, and why there was a taste of blood in his mouth.

"It is for the best," the queen said, moving over to stand before her little altar. She crossed herself, long fingers tracing the outline of her ivory Madonna. "For the best," she repeated before moving over to twitch one of the expensive tapestries into place. She sat down on the bed draped with an embroidered silk coverlet, the matching hangings in pale green and pink pulled back to reveal several pillows and one of the queen's dogs.

"Did…" Adam had to ask. "Did he die in pain?" He kept his voice low, one eye on the three ladies sitting in a corner.

"Isn't it always painful to die?"

An elegant sidestep, the queen fixing him with a wide, green look. Lord Roger had once told him that only people who are consciously lying will look at you like that. Adam's innards twisted.

"Had he been ill for long?" he pushed on.

"For long? I don't know." The queen picked at an embroidered lily. "I am sure Lord Berkeley will fill us in on all the details soon enough."

"Yes, my lady." He shifted on his feet, wincing at the responding pain.

"Your foot?" Isabella smiled sadly. "He must have been truly angry to cause you such discomfort."

"Angry and confused." Adam met her eyes. "He doesn't understand how this could happen." And neither could he.

"It is God's will." The queen nodded a couple of times. "God's will."

On one of the last days of September, King Edward III announced to the assembled parliament that his father was dead. A hush fell in the room, men looking from one to the other. Mostly, though, they stared at the dais and the young king, standing straight before them with his lady mother at his side. Lord Roger was still not back. Adam suspected he was not the only one to wonder why.

Chapter 15

They tilted. They worked with their swords. Adam walked about covered in bruises, as did his lord and master, but any suggestions that they do something else fell on deaf ears, the king venting all his grief, all his frustration, in the tiltyard.

"Let him," Lord Roger said when Adam came to him. "It does him no harm, does it?"

Mortimer had come back well after the conclusion of parliament, saying only that he'd been detained by personal business. He'd presented himself to the king, clad in black from head to toe as he offered his condolences, further sweetened by the gift of a new peregrine falcon.

The king had been pleased with the bird but sullen in all other matters, and for now both his mother and Lord Roger left him mostly alone, encouraging Edward to drown his sorrows in whatever pastimes he preferred while they managed the kingdom and the preparations for the upcoming funeral.

Since some weeks, Lord Roger was yet again absent. The court ambulated from one location to the other, and it was while in Leicester that Adam saw Godfrey of Broseley again. This time, the man was not skulking about. Instead, de Broseley was strolling among the market stalls, laughing loudly with his two companions, both of them sporting tabards adorned with the arms of Lancaster. Adam tucked the ribbons he'd just bought for Kit into his pouch and fell in step behind him. All he needed was one opportunity, one deserted alley, to finish Broseley off once and for all.

The men talked for a while. After an intense discussion, punctuated by several nods, the two Lancaster men moved off. Godfrey went the other way with Adam on his tail.

At long last, Broseley turned up one of the narrow streets leading to the High Street. Still too many people, Adam hung back, eyes never leaving his quarry. They passed an inn or two, a goldsmith, and there before them was a church. Broseley cut in front of it, and Adam took his chance.

He caught up with Broseley just as he ducked through the gate leading to the churchyard. A hissed inhalation, eyes that widened, and Broseley went for his dagger. Adam did the same, lunged, and had the pleasure of hearing Broseley squeal as he scrambled backwards. He had the wall at his back, that ugly scarred face of his pulled into a snarl.

Adam feinted, whirled, and struck. Broseley's right arm hung useless, and he transferred the dagger to his left hand. Blood stained the sleeve of his tunic. He backed away, licking at his lips.

"Kill me and you'll hang for murder." Broseley's left hand was clenched so tightly round the hilt of the dagger his knuckles looked about to burst.

"I don't think so. You're the murderer, not me. Except you failed—repeatedly."

"Murderer?" Godfrey sneered. "Me? You have it wrong, don't you? It's not me who has murdered the king!"

"He died—of grief, they say."

"Yes, of course," Godfrey said. "Try the one about the princess and the unicorn while you're at it." He laughed. "Your precious baron, murdering his former liege."

"No! He would never do that. Never!"

"You protest too much, de Guirande." Godfrey leaned forward. "And I bet the royal whelp was in on it too."

Adam went for him, slammed him against the wall, and wrested the dagger from him. Broseley attempted to scream, but Adam's forearm, pressed against his throat, muted the sound to a gargle. He increased the pressure. Godfrey's eyes widened, his nostrils flared, mouth wide open as he tried to suck in air. He clawed at Adam's face, nails tearing at his skin.

"Kill me…no son…" he hissed. Son? Adam released his hold somewhat. Broseley gasped, breathed like a winded horse.

"You kill me, and you'll never see your precious son again," he croaked.

"What?"

"You heard." Godfrey licked his lips. "Maybe he isn't dead after all."

Adam's chest constricted. "Not dead?" He took a step back, his blade wavering. Broseley didn't hesitate. With a roar he shoved Adam to the ground, vaulted over the wall, and disappeared.

Adam returned to the castle in a foul mood. He should have killed the rat, or at least apprehended him and dragged him back to face justice. Instead, he'd been utterly thrown by Broseley's comment about Tom. He needed to talk to someone—not Kit, not about their Tom—and so he ended up at Earl Thomas' chambers instead.

"Do you believe him?" Thomas sprawled in his chair, legs extended before him. Back to his normal self, Adam reflected.

"I don't know." Adam beckoned for one of the pages to fill up his goblet. "What do I tell Kit?"

"Nothing." Thomas shook his head slowly. "Unless you think he speaks the truth. Do you?"

"No." Adam turned the goblet round and round, staring at the swirling wine. Tom, alive? His breath hitched. No, he reminded himself, William had been to fetch the sad remains. "Godfrey of Broseley is capable of lying about anything—even a dead child."

"It served him, didn't it?"

Adam scowled at the contents of his goblet. Played like a fool—it rankled. "Won't help him next time." He shook himself. "And what was he doing with those Lancaster men? Do you think he's working for the earl?"

Thomas laughed. "Knowing Cousin Henry, any man who professes an abiding hatred for Mortimer is more than welcome in his household."

Kit had the distinct impression Adam was holding something back as he told her about his recent sighting of Godfrey of Broseley. Knowing her husband, she knew it would not serve to push—and besides, she had news of her own.

"Here?" Adam looked so astonished Kit had to smile. "With the queen?"

"With the Countess of Kent." Kit rolled her eyes. "Apparently, she came warmly recommended—by Lady Joan."

"Lady Joan has never met her!"

"But maybe she felt she was doing her a favour. After all, she doesn't know Alicia, does she?"

"And what does the queen say?"

Kit laughed. It had been entertaining, to say the least. Lady Margaret had swept in, hastening over to greet Queen Isabella, and in her wake had come her ladies, one of them being dear sister Alicia. If looks could kill, Alicia would at present have been lying still and shrouded in a coffin somewhere. Instead, she'd sagged like a wet beanpole, trying desperately to hide from eyes as brittle as emeralds.

"So now Alicia will not be accompanying Lady Margaret anymore—at least not when she is with the queen."

"And you? What did she say to you?" His fingers brushed over the old scar that decorated her face.

"Nothing."

Alicia had looked straight through her, and Kit had returned the favour. It was a small mercy that they were so different, Kit reflected. Where everyone commented how alike she and her brother were, no one seeing Alicia with Richard—or with Kit—would ever think they were related. Well, beyond the red hair, of course, but even here the similarity was superficial, Kit's hair a deep, dark red while Alicia, poor thing, had been afflicted with tresses the colour of dirty rust.

"She's changed." It was well over a year since Kit had last seen her half-sister, and the intervening months had served to fill out her previously stick-like form into something resembling womanly curves. Nothing, however, could ever be done to soften her face, a collection of so many sharp lines Kit was reminded of an axe, sharp and lethal. "And she's with child."

"Oh." Adam shrugged. "Why would Lady Margaret take her in among her ladies?"

"I don't know." Kit gnawed her lip. "Maybe Richard does."

They found Richard in the hall, standing with a group of other Mortimer men. They looked somewhat isolated, an

149

island of quiet, serious men in a sea of prancing peacocks. In the absence of Roger Mortimer himself, men such as Lancaster took the opportunity to hold court, one careful eye on the queen, who spent most of her attention on her son.

"She's here?" Richard looked perplexed. "How?"

"She serves in Lady Margaret's household," Kit explained. "You didn't know she was here?"

"Me?" Richard laughed. "I was more than happy to turn her over to her husband back in May. A dowry paid, a sister gone—and thank the Lord for that."

"And your wife? Doesn't she miss her?"

"Not anymore." Richard grinned. "She has a son to care for."

"Ah yes, the impossibly handsome baby Roger," Adam teased. "Has the infant learned to speak yet?"

"No." Richard gave him a cool look. "I suppose it has to do with her husband's business. Alicia," he clarified. "Her husband, Henry, is a wealthy merchant, and Edmund of Kent is one of his patrons, has granted him several favours."

"Well, if she's going to be here, I prefer to go home," Kit said.

"Do that," a voice said. "Spare us all the embarrassment of having to deal with the bastard get of my father."

Kit turned, rearing back when she more or less bumped into Alicia. In a surcoat the exact icy blue of her eyes, the sleeves trimmed with fur, she looked rich, the folds of her clothes straining over her rounded belly.

"Slander my wife and be prepared to take the consequences," Adam said.

"Slander? Since when is the truth slander?" Alicia asked.

"Behave," Richard warned. "If you don't—"

"Then what, dear brother? You have no authority over me, not any longer." Her tone hardened. "I belong to Henry Luytens now."

"How unfortunate—for him," Kit said.

"For him?" Alicia gave her an incredulous look. "He's a merchant, a commoner!" She shuddered. "You stole my life," she went on, glaring at Kit.

"Your life?" Kit glared right back. "I was coerced into impersonating your sister—not you." She glanced at Adam, feeling the familiar tingle of shame she always felt when she recalled how she'd been blackmailed into duping him, having him believe he was marrying Katherine de Monmouth rather than Katherine Coucy. "After all, your mother could not have passed you off as your sister, could she? You're too…" She broke off. She'd intended to say 'ugly' but there was something very vulnerable about Alicia despite a personality that mostly resembled jagged glass.

"Too what?" Alicia demanded.

"Tall," Kit retorted, and out of the corner of her eye, she saw Adam smiling.

Alicia gave her a venomous look. "I would have made him a better wife! Me, raised to be the wife of a lord."

Adam snorted. "You? Never in a month of Sundays would I have considered wedding you. God spare me—you remind me far too much of your late mother."

Alicia laughed, a high, braying sound. "Of course you would—had the dowry been high enough." She moved closer. "That's the difference been lowborn sluts and trueborn ladies, you see. Some come with more lands than the other."

"As I recall, some trueborn ladies dabble in poison," Adam said coldly, making blotches of red appear on Alicia's neck and face.

"I…" She snapped her mouth shut, lashes swooping down to hide her eyes.

"Alicia?" A richly garbed man shoved past Adam. "I told you to wait for me by the door, did I not?" Not a loving relationship, to judge from the tone of his voice. He took hold of her arm, pudgy fingers tightening around it.

"Yes, Husband," Alicia replied meekly. "I saw my brother."

"Your brother?" The man peered at Richard. "Ah yes. Monmouth—congratulations on your son."

"Thank you, Henry." Richard gave him a little smile. "May you be equally blessed."

"Yes," Henry said, studying his wife. "Well, if it's not a boy, one must simply keep on trying." He winked, fingers tightening

151

yet again on Alicia's arm. "Isn't that right, my sweet?" Alicia winced but managed a smile.

"Yes, Henry."

"Allow me to introduce my other sister," Richard said. "Lady Katherine de Guirande."

"Ah." Henry Luytens looked Kit up and down. "A pleasure, I am sure." He smirked. "I have heard a lot about you."

"Have you?" Adam fixed the merchant with a steely gaze. "I trust nothing uncomplimentary. I dislike when people speak ill of my lady wife."

Henry's face sagged. "No, no, of course not." He retreated a couple of steps. "And now if you'll excuse me, I have business to conduct." With Alicia in tow, he made for the far end of the hall.

Adam rose on his toes. "Dancing round Lancaster. The earl seems to be cultivating everyone at present."

"Scotland." Richard rolled his eyes. "Henry of Lancaster will not be budged: peace with Scotland at the expense of his lands is, according to him, too dear."

"The king is none too pleased either," Kit ventured.

"The king doesn't want peace with Scotland. Fool," Richard said, "he insists the Scottish crown belongs to him and is incensed at having his sister wed to a northern barbarian." He snickered. "I do not think the Scottish prince is old enough to have acquired any barbarous habits."

"As I hear it, Lancaster is blaming the failed campaign on Mortimer." Adam frowned. "Little words of poison, dripped steadily into the royal ear."

Richard nodded. "The man is a snake."

"I dare say he says exactly the same thing about Mortimer," Kit said.

"The difference being that Lord Roger rarely slithers with his belly in the mud," Richard told her—rather curtly, in Kit's opinion.

Adam took Kit's hand as they made their way up to their room and bed.

"I wish we were home." He was tired of endless days at the receiving end of his young lord's indefatigable energy, and he resented the constant lack of privacy. At present, their little room had three pallets plus the bed, and Adam longed for their solar at Tresaints, for an hour or two with his wife in a scented bath. And then there was this whole matter with Tom. Dear God, what if Broseley wasn't lying? What if Tom was still alive? He sighed deeply, and Kit drew him to a stop.

"What is it?"

He shook himself. "Nothing," he tried, smiling ruefully. He inhaled in preparation of sharing what Godfrey had said about Tom, but at the last moment he found that he couldn't. His Kit would not survive having her hope rekindled and then squashed yet again. This was a burden he would have to carry on his own.

"You're lying." She squeezed his hand.

"It's all this talk about murder," he said—he had to say something. "Everywhere we go, I hear the whispered accusations that maybe the king did not die of a broken heart, but was helped along."

"Maybe he was." Kit drew him to a halt. "But that is not your main concern, is it?"

"No." He pulled her close, dropping a kiss on her veiled head. "I do not want to discover that Lord Roger is a snake."

"Silly man." She stood on her toes and kissed him. "Ask him, Adam. If anyone can assess his answer, is it you."

"How do I ask him something like that?"

"I think he'll prefer that you ask him outright."

"Assuming he hasn't ordered the smiler with his knife to make a visit to Sir Edward."

Kit took his hand again. "He hasn't. I may not always like him, but Mortimer does not lower himself to assassination."

Their empty room smelled of damp wool and young men—a pungent combination of sweat and flatulence and… Adam sniffed, raised a brow, and looked at Kit. She inhaled, her mouth setting in a displeased little line.

"For shame," she muttered, moving close enough to press her entire body against his. "Gavin and Rhosyn?"

"Well, let us hope it isn't Stephen—with either of them."

She gave a horrified little gasp, making Adam laugh. He nibbled her ear. "It isn't uncommon, sweeting."

"He's a child!"

"True. And he is utterly besotted by one of the kitchen maids." He frowned down at Gavin's pallet. "I will talk to them."

Chapter 16

It had been decided that the former king was to be buried at St Peter's Abbey in Gloucester. Some days into December, the court was slowly making its way across a sodden and gloomy England, the king preferring to ride apart with his young companions.

They arrived in Worcester in a squall of rain and sleet. Kit had never entered Worcester from the east before, having always approached from the west and over the bridge spanning the Severn, but once through the gate, the town was very much as she remembered it—albeit surprisingly empty of people, which she took to be due to the freezing weather. They made their way towards the river and the huge whitewashed church of the priory of St Mary's, stark against the grey skies beyond. By the time they were ushered inside the priory's guest hall, they were muddy and cold to the bone.

Kit settled herself in a corner, waiting for the bustle to settle. The queen insisted on private accommodation, and the little prior bowed and scraped, hands twisting nervously as he assured his lady queen he would do everything to fulfil her wishes.

Kit pulled her damp cloak closer and suppressed a shiver.

"Cold?" King Edward sat down beside her.

"And wet."

So was he, his hair plastered to his head. A day of constant wind and rain had left him with windburn, he had a streak of mud under his right eye, and his boots squelched when he moved. And yet it wasn't that which moved her to place a hand on his face—it was the shadows under his eyes, the uncertain set to his mouth.

"It will be over soon, my lord."

"Will it?" He pulled off his gloves, rubbing his hands. "I am not so sure, Lady Kit." He scraped at a scab on his hand, studying the little beads of blood intently.

"Once he is laid at rest, things will be easier." She used her sleeve to wipe his hand clean of blood.

Edward grunted, no more, sinking into a heavy silence. Kit cast about for a somewhat cheerier subject.

"Looking forward to your wedding, my lord?"

The king blinked. "My wedding?" His mouth curved into a soft smile, and he nodded. "She will be on her way soon." He gnawed his lip, throwing Kit a look from under long, fair lashes. "I hope she is as pleased as I am."

"Oh, I am sure she is."

"Truly?" He smiled again, briefly. He made as if to say something, broke off. Kit waited. "I..." He turned troubled eyes on Kit. "I have never...er...deflowered a maid."

"I am glad to hear that," Kit said, laughing silently at his discomfited expression.

"Will I hurt her? I don't want to, but Montagu says it always hurts the first time for a woman." He leaned back against the wall, long legs extended before him.

"It doesn't have to." Kit recalled her own wedding night. It had been uncomfortable as Adam had been convinced she was no virgin. But he had made amends, loving her with far more tenderness the second time around.

"Lady Philippa will have been told two things: that it may hurt, and that she must lay back and bear it—as any good wife must." She rubbed at her belly. In response, the child within kicked. "If you want a happy marriage, you don't want her to lay back and bear it, my lord. You want her to enjoy it." From the amused look in the king's eyes and the heat in her cheeks, Kit suspected she was presently the bright red of rowan berries, but she pushed on. "You must...well, I suppose you have to..." She glared at him. "Why don't you ask Adam instead?"

"He's not a woman." The king studied his hands. "I have to touch her, don't I?" He cleared his throat. "Everywhere."

"Yes." Kit fiddled with the clasps of her cloak. "Touch her and kiss her until she strains towards you."

"What if she doesn't?"

"Then you're not touching her boldly enough."

The king grinned. "Can I hope for some demonstrations, Lady Kit?"

"Most certainly not!" She stood. "If you want further guidance, I suggest you ask someone else."

"Like Adam." Yet again that broad grin. "He must do everything right, to judge from your bright face, my lady."

Kit grinned back, patting her belly. "As a matter of fact, my lord, he does."

"Why here?" Kit asked Adam as they joined the throngs assembled to pay their last respects to Edward of Caernarvon. "Why not in Westminster, with his father?" They'd arrived in Gloucester late the day before and had spent the night sharing a pallet in a cold hall, accommodation being hard to find what with every single grandee in England being in town to attend the funeral.

"Convenient, I suppose. Berkeley Castle is just up the road." He smiled tightly. "And I don't think Lord Roger—or the queen—wanted to parade him in London."

"No, I suppose not." The Londoners were fickle people, one day supporting Mortimer, the next his adversaries. At present, it was mostly the adversaries. She stood on her toes to catch a glimpse of the hearse. No expense had been spared, Richard had told her, describing statues of the evangelists, painted lions, and a marvellously lifelike effigy. All Kit could see was the closest statue and the tail end of one of the lions.

Queen Isabella was standing with her children, face locked in a mild smile. The two little princesses were silent and still beside their mother, Prince John was holding Queen Isabella's hand, and King Edward stood in a pool of solitude. Just behind him were his uncles, resplendent in sombre robes and golden collars, and on the other side of Queen Isabella was Lord Roger, for the day in black velvet. Otherwise unadorned, the starkness of his attire served to highlight his strong features, the light from the thousands upon thousands of candles reflected in his dark eyes.

"Well, at least he is at rest now," Kit said some hours later. She was in a haste to exit the church, collect their belongings and set off for home. She said as much, her heart sinking when Adam grunted, no more. "We're not going home?"

"I'm not. I am ordered to return to Worcester and celebrate Christmastide with my lord."

"Worcester?" So close to home and yet so far away. "Will the prior be happy to receive us back?" It was a weak jest, but it made him smile.

"I don't think he has been given much choice in the matter, sweeting. But as I hear it, we'll be lodging in what remains of the castle."

That did not sound comforting.

No sooner had they installed themselves in Worcester—some in the dilapidated keep, most of them in the priory's guest lodgings—but the queen demanded a private audience with her son.

"But we are going hawking," Edward protested.

"Later." Queen Isabella made for her chamber, beckoning for him to come with her.

"Maman," he groaned, dragging his feet as he followed her. "I don't—"

The queen whirled. "Now!"

Adam shared a look with Montagu, received a shrug in reply.

"Draughts?" Montagu offered, gesturing at the table. "One never knows how long this will take." He threw a worried look at the closed door.

"Is he in trouble?" William de Bohun looked up from where he was sprawled on a carpet with Lancelot curled up beside him.

"When are sons not in trouble?" his twin replied. He yawned. "My head hurts."

"Too much wine," Montagu said without turning around. "Come to think of it, that's probably why Ned is facing the dowager queen right now."

Nervous laughter erupted among the lads. Adam gave Montagu a warning look. Their lady queen had made it quite clear she would not tolerate being addressed thus.

"What?" Montagu moved a piece. "Her husband is dead and buried—murdered, some say—and in a month or so her son will be wed to his Philippa—our queen. Surely, there cannot be two queens? Besides—"

The door crashed open. Their king stumbled out.

"Edward, wait!" The queen appeared behind him.

He did not listen, crossing the large room at speed. Lancelot leapt up and padded after him, the closest de Bohun twin stood up and held out his hand, but Edward walked straight by him, pushed open the heavy oak door, and left.

"Ned!" Montagu was on his feet, as was Adam.

"Leave him alone." The queen's voice was like a whiplash. "If he won't talk to me, he will not talk to anyone else either." Her door banged close.

"Not the wine, I think," Adam commented drily.

"He looked as if he'd seen a ghost," Montagu said, sitting down slowly.

"I'm going after him." Adam was already halfway to the door.

"But the queen said—"

"Aye, I heard. But I am the king's man, not the queen's." And she had sounded bitter and angry, while her son had looked as if she'd eviscerated him.

He found Edward in the church, kneeling by the tomb of his great-great-grandfather.

"Go away."

"My lord, I—"

"I said, go away!" the king yelled, turning to glare at him. Tears and snot, narrowed eyes, and a mouth that hung open in a half wail—Adam covered the distance between them in two strides and pulled the lad into his arms. At first, Edward struggled, but halfway through an angry rant that he'd have Adam flogged if he didn't let him go, Edward inhaled, sobbed, and fell into Adam's arms, crying his eyes out against Adam's shoulder.

There was no point in asking what she'd said. Adam just held him, crooning as he would to a restive horse. At long last, Edward disengaged his fingers from Adam's tunic and straightened up. He wiped his face on his sleeve, cleared his throat, and turned his back on Adam.

"Thank you."

"I am always here for you, my lord."

King Edward nodded, no more. "I'd like to be alone," he said politely.

"Is that wise?"

"You heard me, Adam. Alone." There was steel in the voice.

"Yes, my lord."

"Could it be something about Philippa?" Kit asked as they were getting ready for bed.

"Like what?" Adam pummelled his pillow into shape. Thank the Lord, here they had a chamber to themselves—squires, maids, and pages bedded down in the hall.

"Dear God!" Kit sat up straight. "You do not think she's died?"

"If the future queen was dead, we would have heard. Lie down, sweeting."

"Then what?"

Adam rolled over on his back. "I don't know. But I've never seen him so distraught—well, except for when he heard his father had died." He'd spent most of the afternoon mulling it over, and he had a frightful headache, compounded by the fact that Egard had returned and told him he'd found no trace of Godfrey of Broseley, neither in Leicester nor among the Earl of Lancaster's retinue at Gloucester.

And then, of course, there was the matter of the recently buried king. Will Montagu was not the only one openly discussing the rumour that Edward of Caernarvon had been murdered. Just after compline, Adam had found Gavin with a bloodied nose, and all because he'd loudly proclaimed Lord Roger was no killer. Adam sighed: there was no choice—he had to speak to Lord Roger.

"How many times must I say this?" Lord Roger slammed his hand down on the table. "I did not murder Edward." He glared at Adam. "But I am already judged and found guilty."

160

"He died most opportunely, my lord. Of course everyone suspects foul play. And then there is the matter that no one saw him dead."

"Lord Berkeley did. He sent the letter, did he not?"

Adam did not deign to answer that: Berkeley and Maltravers would die for Mortimer.

"He died. He was embalmed. He wasn't murdered." Lord Roger scowled. "I can assure you that had Isabella suspected as much, she'd have torn Berkeley Castle apart looking for his murderer. For some odd reason, she still cares—cared—for the man."

"Sending gifts of clean linen to your imprisoned husband speaks more of charity than love," Adam said. Or guilt.

"She shouldn't send him anything. Why should she, given how he treated her?" Lord Roger cleared his throat. "It's nothing but evil gossip, set about by men like Lancaster. Besides, would his son tolerate my presence if he thought I had murdered his sire?" Lord Roger laughed, a harsh sound having little to do with mirth. "He may be young, but Edward is not without deviousness. Had he thought me guilty of such a crime, I would..." He dragged a finger across his throat.

"And yet every second word I hear at court is a muttered accusation of murder, elegant fingers pointing at you, my lord."

"God's blood! I did not murder him!" Lord Roger scrubbed at his hair. "Surely, you believe me, Adam?"

"You've changed, my lord," Adam replied, sidestepping Lord Roger's question. "Power has seeped into your veins and corroded you."

With a crash, Lord Roger upended the table, sending quills and inkpots flying. "Corroded me? It wearies me, it weighs on me, but corrosion? Are you saying you find me a lesser man?"

"I am saying no one would have suspected the Lord Mortimer of old of any underhand actions, but now it is a different matter."

"Power comes with responsibilities." Lord Roger crouched and retrieved one of the inkpots, still unbroken. "It also inspires jealousy in others." When he straightened up, he glanced at Adam, and Adam's heart tightened in pity at the ravaged look on his face. This was a man burdened, a man who lived every day in the awareness that others wanted nothing so much as his failure. "But I don't deserve having my honour besmirched. My enemies whisper, and even my friends and former vassals listen and believe."

"My lord, I…" Adam fell silent. Lord Roger merely nodded.

"I didn't kill him," he finally said. "But just because he wasn't murdered doesn't mean there aren't other secrets that need to be kept."

Adam didn't follow. "Other secrets?"

Lord Roger exhaled deeply. "Practising for the role of the king's jester, are you? Use your wits, man! A dead king—a man who auspiciously dies so as to make his son's claim on the throne irreversible. A man whose purported corpse has remained unseen throughout, embalmed at speed, and laid out before the prelates already covered by the cerecloth. So it follows that…" Lord Roger raised his brows and waited. Adam frowned. Purported?

"He isn't dead!"

Lord Roger gave him a sarcastic smile. "I bow to your powers of deduction, Sir Adam."

"Does the king know?"

"Since yesterday." Lord Roger smiled thinly. "I gather he did not take it well. Accused his mother of making him an unwitting accomplice in keeping his father imprisoned for life." He shrugged before giving Adam a warning look. "No one must know. No one, you hear?"

Adam stiffened. "I won't tell." Beyond Kit, of course, but no need to tell Lord Roger that. It was hard enough keeping one secret from his wife; two would break him.

"Good." Lord Roger went back to his disordered papers. "Send in Richard, will you?"

Kit listened in silence, hands busy with her hair.

"Poor man," she said once Adam had finished. "His crown and now his life." A deft twist, and her hair was piled atop her hair. Her hands fluttered like sparrows, inserting one long pin there, one long pin here.

"He's not dead—I just told you that."

"Not dead? And remaining imprisoned, invisible, for the rest of your life—is that not being dead?" She shivered. "Better kill him and be done with it."

Adam crossed himself. "May it never come to that." He adjusted his new robe—a gift from the king—and twirled slowly.

"Most handsome," Kit said, settling her veil on top of her head. "It may."

"May what? Oh." Adam adjusted his belt, ensured he had dagger and eating knife, and looked about for the new embroidered pouch Kit had given him. There. "Lord Roger would never lower himself to something like that."

"It isn't only Lord Roger who has a vested interest in ensuring Edward of Caernarvon never returns from the dead."

Adam met her eyes, dark and glittering in the candlelight, and nodded. The thought had crossed his mind too.

"He's a lad," he tried. "A good and honourable lad."

Kit interrupted him with a light kiss. "I know. But lads grow into men, and a crown is quite the prize." She kissed him again. "He won't forgive them for this, duping him into believing his father is dead."

"Who would?" Adam said.

Chapter 17

"Shouldn't you be in confinement?" Alicia looked at Kit as if she were a farrowing sow. "Any wellborn woman would have retired to her chambers by now."

"The babe is not due until Candlemas." Kit struggled to sound calm. "And as Adam must be here…" Once the Christmas festivities were concluded, she'd be on her way to Tresaints, while Adam would accompany the king north to York.

"Adam must be here," Alicia mimicked, rolling her eyes. "Maybe he'd prefer it if you weren't. A man like that needs…" She made a rude gesture. "Something he won't be getting much of with his bloated wife."

"Are you always so crude, Alicia?" Lady Margaret's voice had Alicia leaping to her feet.

"M-M-My lady," Alicia stuttered, shoulders rounding under her mistress' disapproving eyes.

"I'll not have it," Lady Margaret said. "You will apologise to your sister, and then you'd best get back to your sewing."

"Yes, my lady." Alicia bobbed a little reverence and fled—without apologising. Lady Margaret made as if to call her back, but Kit shook her head. No need. An insincere apology from Alicia she could do without.

"I'd hazard there is little lovemaking in her life," Lady Margaret said, frowning as Alicia ducked into the distant stairwell. "Clearly, she and her husband find little pleasure with each other now that she is breeding."

"Clearly." Kit did not think there was much pleasure at all involved when it came to Henry Luytens and his much younger wife. That marital bed had more than its fair share of thorns—and very few blooms in between.

"Not like us, then," Lady Margaret continued with a sly smile. She elbowed Kit—none too gently. "I find I am constantly in heat while breeding."

"Um…" Kit smoothed at a wrinkle on her new silk surcoat. In response, the babe within kicked.

Any further conversation on the matter was interrupted by the queen. She came from outside, face bright red with cold, and a bevy of younger ladies rushed towards her, offering everything from mulled wine to dry shoes.

"Ah, Margaret." The queen took the armchair closest to the hearth. "I did not think to see you here—or our Edmund." She laughed jarringly. "I thought it likelier that you would celebrate the festive season with dear cousin Henry."

Lady Margaret's dark eyes disappeared behind a screen of lashes. Long fingers played with the tassels that decorated her elaborately embroidered cotehardie. "Why so, my lady?"

"They are close, your husband and dear Henry," the queen said, smiling widely. "Close enough that what one does will tar the other."

Lady Margaret paled, hand closing round one of the tassels. "I don't understand, my lady."

"Of course you do." Queen Isabella leaned towards her. "Best beware: I will not tolerate traitors—ever."

Lady Margaret's head came up. "My lord husband would rather kill himself than betray his nephew or his nephew's interests."

"Good. Keep it that way." The queen rose. "After all, it would be unfortunate if your precious children were to grow up without that handsome father of theirs."

"Not very subtle," Lady Margaret commented once the queen was out of earshot. Her voice shook. "How dare she insinuate my husband is dabbling in treason?" Her gaze locked on the queen's shapely back. "And with what right do she and Mortimer rule in our young king's stead?"

"She is his mother," Kit objected.

"A young king needs men to guide him. Men like his uncles and cousins, not that upstart of a Marcher lord."

"Your cousin," Kit reminded her. Lady Margaret flushed.

"Yes," she said, "my cousin. It's not that I don't think him capable—the Lord knows Roger can move mountains when he sets his mind to it—but he aims too high. To bed openly with the queen, to take open control of the offices of the king, to exclude the royal earls from government—Lancaster will not stand for it."

"And what will Lancaster do?"

Lady Margaret's face shuttered close. "God alone knows," she replied blandly. Her tone sent a shiver of alarm up Kit's spine.

"I'm not sure if she told me to have me warn Mortimer, or have me warn the king." Kit twisted her hands together.

"Maybe it just slipped out?" Adam suggested.

"A woman like Lady Margaret does not allow things to slip out." Kit did another turn round their little room. "I think she likes me, and so it could be she was simply warning me—us."

Adam pursed his lips. "But she would know you'd come to me."

"And what will you do?" Kit joined him on the bed, nestling into him. Adam studied his boots, deep in thought.

"I must talk to Lord Roger. At present, King Edward cannot rule on his own, and God knows England will fare far worse under Lancaster than under Mortimer."

He insisted Kit accompany him, one firm hand on her elbow guiding her through the freezing cloisters to the rooms Lord Roger had appropriated for himself and his various officers. A couple of braziers heated a room cluttered with tables and clerks, there was a smell of parchment and ink, hot wax and mulled wine, and in a smaller room beyond, Lord Roger was seated in deep conversation with some of his men.

Lord Roger looked up when Adam entered, dark brows rising at the sight of Kit, and with a snap of his fingers he cleared the room of any others but the three of them.

"Not precisely news," he said when Adam had finished explaining why they were there. "More of a confirmation than anything else." His mouth quirked. "Margaret is having qualms, I gather. She may not always love me, but she cares enough for me not to want to see my head adorn a pike."

"A pike?" Kit's eyes widened in alarm.

"If Lancaster succeeds, he can't very well keep me alive."
Lord Roger shrugged. "So we must make sure he doesn't succeed, mustn't we?" He levelled a dark look at Adam. "You had best sound out your friend."

"My friend?"

"Norfolk." Lord Roger reached for a quill. "I dare say he's as disgruntled as the others—he just hides it better."

"Earl Thomas would never—" Kit began, and Adam was annoyed by the heated tone of her voice.

"What?" Lord Roger interrupted. "Conspire to remove me and my lady queen from the confidence of the king? Of course he would—assuming he was allowed to step into my shoes." He twirled the quill around. "Not, I believe, what Lancaster has in mind."

"Earl Thomas loves the king," Kit tried again.

"He does." Lord Roger gave her an amused smile. "So does the queen, I can assure you. And I."

"Thomas is not like his brother, my lord," Adam said. "And he and Lancaster are not at all close."

Lord Roger nodded. "I know. But ambition makes strange bedmates." He settled back in his chair. "We have had Lancaster under surveillance for some months. He aims to finance this venture through disgruntled London merchants..." He broke off, saying something uncomplimentary about false friends. "Which is why we are keeping an eye on them—all of them." He tapped his nose with the feather end of the quill. "And as to Lancaster..." The quill snapped.

"Have you any idea why our Ned is walking about like a wolf with a toothache?" Thomas leaned across Raven's broad back and clasped Adam's hand briefly in greeting. "And don't you have other things to do but curry your own horse?"

"It soothes me."

"Ah. And what is it that requires soothing?"

Adam concentrated on Raven's hind quarters. "Godfrey of Broseley, for one."

"I gather Egard hasn't found him?"

167

"Nowhere." Adam straightened up. "What if he does have Tom? What if…" He placed a hand on Raven's smooth coat. If Tom was alive—and in Broseley's hands—Kit would never forgive him for not telling her, for not doing everything he could to find him.

"It is most unlikely. Besides, as you tell it, he was badly wounded in France. How was he to make it back in time to get hold of Tom?"

The logic was sound. In fact, the more Adam thought about it, the more impossible it was. Mabel had seen Tom at death's door before she'd fled with Meg—at a time when that accursed Godfrey should still have been nursing that wound to his groin. He gave Thomas a rueful smile.

"I tell myself the same all the time. But…" He shrugged.

"Hope is a dangerous thing." Thomas tugged at Raven's mane. "Are you planning to braid it and decorate it with ribbons?" In response, Adam threw the brush at him.

"So, Ned," Thomas said, leading the way to the hall and the promising scents of roast meat. He was still in the clothes he'd ridden in in, the boots spattered with mud, as was the heavy cloak.

"This matter with his father has left him troubled," Adam replied. Not a lie, he told himself, but he kept his eyes on the ground.

"He's had three months to come to terms with it." Thomas pulled off his gloves, unclasped his cloak, and handed it to one of his pages. A couple of brisk movements and the dark green of his robe was arranged as it should, offsetting his heavy gold collar. With his dark hair and matching beard, eyes a shade somewhere between green and brown, the earl turned several heads as they walked down the hall. Not that the man seemed to notice, his gaze riveted on his nephew, sitting side by side with Queen Isabella.

"Aye, he has. But all these rumours about foul death…" Adam left the rest unsaid.

"Ah yes: it is either Mortimer, the queen, or our young king himself who plunged the dagger in Edward's chest." Thomas leaned closer. "My gold is on Mortimer."

"This is not a jesting matter!" Adam was hard put not to shove Thomas away.

"And yet it *was* a jest." Thomas eyed Adam. "Or are you saying there is truth to the rumours?"

"No, of course not." Once again, Adam had to avert his face. This secret was a veritable millstone, dragging at his soul. "Did you enjoy your time with Lancaster?" he asked in an attempt to change the subject. Thomas came to a halt.

"Lancaster? Why would I have been with Lancaster?"

"That's what I heard," Adam muttered.

Thomas stilled. "You did? From whom?"

Adam grinned. "Rumours?"

Thomas frowned. "Not funny, Adam. Whoever is linking me with Lancaster is doing me a disfavour. I am not Edm—" He bit off, jaw clenching.

"In which case, you have a lot in common with Mortimer." Adam gestured discreetly in the direction of Lord Roger. "He is the victim of rumours too."

It was as if the recent funeral had caused all the suppressed suspicions to bubble to the surface. Days of cold and wet did not help, with the people presently at Worcester growing bored and restless. Mortimer submerged himself in work, the queen sat with her ladies—endless hours of sewing—and the king was the centre of a rowdy group of young men, men who made increasingly more insinuating comments about adulterers in general, murderous ones in particular, without ever being foolish enough to name the queen or Mortimer.

While Adam was obliged to spend most of his time with the king, Kit kept to herself as much as she could, uncomfortable with all the hushed speculations, the hooded glances thrown at Mortimer—but just as much at the queen. A choked giggle here, a strangled whisper there, and one would think no one had anything else to do but to wallow in poisonous gossip.

The queen presided over every meal, her son on one side, Lord Roger on the other. Unruffled and constantly smiling, the queen conversed with her son about horses and hawks, with her lover about France and Scotland. Rarely did she touch her son, even more rarely Lord Roger, but now and then a finger would, as if by chance, come to rest atop his hand or brush against his sleeve. Where his lady looked serene and calm, Mortimer was twitchy and tense, his normally controlled temper flaring frequently and viciously.

Fortunately, on the day of the Holy Innocents, the weather cleared. The king and his companions rode out after breaking their fast, and with them went most of the other lords and ladies presently in attendance. Frisky horses, gaudy clothes, here and there a hooded hawk astride its handler's arm—people laughed, dogs barked, and then someone blew a horn, and they were off, a rippling tide of colour.

It was blissfully quiet. Kit took a slow stroll round the cloisters, sharing a polite smile or two with the few monks she encountered. The priory would take months to recover from the extended royal visit, and she could only imagine the state of their larders. Lent this year would be harsher than usual for the poor monks.

A weak sun lit up the straggly roses in the central garden. A neatly trimmed boxwood sheltered a little bench, and Kit sat down on the edge, nose turned up to catch what little warmth there was. She was still sitting there when she heard the footsteps—a man's heavier, slower tread accompanied by the patter of female feet.

"I don't understand why you are so bothered by it."

The queen. Kit considered standing up but chose instead to pull up her hood and remain where she was.

"I'm the one labelled a murderer, not you," Lord Roger said, his voice harsh. "It is at me they stare, me they hate."

"Hate?" Queen Isabella laughed softly. "And since when do you care what others think of you, my hawk? It was a necessary ruse—you know that as well as I do. A living, captive king is a dangerous king, and my son's grasp on the crown is as yet too fragile."

Kit risked a hasty peek. They were walking along the cloisters, hands linked together.

"It is my honour, Isabella. And all of this has handed my enemies the blade with which to destroy me."

"Destroy you? They wouldn't dare. Besides, now Edward knows the truth—he knows his father is still alive."

Lord Roger exhaled. "At times, you're quite the fool. There will come a time when your son will prefer it if his father is dead—and in me he has the perfect scapegoat. Accusing me of his father's death will give him the perfect excuse to get rid of me—permanently."

"Never." There was a sound of someone biting into an apple. "My son would never do that to me."

"Of course he would. That son of yours has a ruthless streak in him—all strong kings do."

"He will not harm you." The queen's voice faded as they reached the far end. "I will not…"

Let him, Kit filled in silently.

"She sounds so unconcerned," Kit said to Adam later, having recounted what she'd overheard. "But he is plagued by this stain on his honour."

"Aye." Adam settled his head in her lap and kissed her swelling belly. "And it may well come back to haunt them."

"Not her." She smoothed his thick hair off his forehead. "It is Lord Roger who stands with a tarnished reputation." She frowned. "And how do they aim to keep this secret?"

"That he's not dead?" Adam kissed her again, leaving a moist impression on her linen shift. "I dare say only a very small number of men know the truth."

"Men talk. Their tongues can be loosened by gold or by wine." Kit reclined against the pillows. "Such a secret can be sold at quite the price."

He sat up, hair tousled. "It is not our concern, sweeting." He moved closer, lips travelling up her neck to her mouth. "Your concern should be me," he growled. "Your husband demands your attention, fair wife."

"A sin," she murmured against his lips. "My husband leads me to sin repeatedly."

"Aye. But it is your fault, temptress." He nuzzled her, nibbled at her ear, while slowly tugging her shift up to reveal her belly and her breasts. Together, they rid her of the garment.

His shirt was discarded, his braies and hose ended up in a pile on the floor.

"So beautiful," he said, resting his hand on the distended skin of her stomach. "So mine." He laughed when her belly rippled with life. "Mine," he repeated. "You, my child, just borrow her."

The bedding rustled as he moved on top of her, his weight suspended on his arms. Slowly, he slid inside, sinking into her bit by bit. A gentle joining, his voice lowered to a rumble as he told her just how much he loved her.

"As I love you," she whispered back, closing her eyes for an instant. He stilled, making her smile.

"Sweeting." His nose brushed hers, his voice hoarse.

"I know." She opened her eyes, staring into his, so close, so dark, the thick, fair lashes gilded by the soft light from the glowing embers. "Your wife loves you with her eyes wide open."

"Always."

Such soft lips. Kit smiled into his kiss. Her man, as much hers as she was his.

Chapter 18

"It's like spending time with two aggravated bears," Will Montague said one morning, looking pointedly from King Edward to Adam. "See?" he continued, addressing the younger lads. "This is what women do to us—reduce us to emotional wrecks." He ducked the cushion the king threw at him. "One is pining for his bride, the other for his wife." He fluttered his lashes.

"Shut it," Adam warned but couldn't quite stop himself from smiling. After the briefest of visits to Tresaints, Adam had kissed Kit farewell and hastened after his young lord, catching up with the court south of Northampton—a bedraggled collection of wet men plodding north.

"Fortunately, our royal bride approaches daily." Montagu stood up, set a hand over his heart. "As fragrant as a rose, her tresses as soft and silky as sable fur, and her eyes, oh, her eyes, like pools of water under a rising moon."

"She has brown eyes," the king objected, making his companions fall over laughing. With a loud sniff, the king stalked out of the room, Lancelot padding at his heels.

"What got into him?" Edward de Bohun sat up.

"Wedding nerves." Montagu flashed Adam a smile. "Mounting a virgin requires nerves of steel."

"For shame," Adam said. "You are talking about your future queen, not a broodmare."

"Not much difference, is there?" Montagu sounded bitter. "Look at your own wife, about to whelp for—what is it, the fifth time?" Seconds later, he was flat on his back.

"Don't you ever talk about my lady wife like that." Adam sucked at his broken knuckles. "It isn't her fault your wife has not presented you with a son." Montagu's wife was of an age with Kit, and so far only a mother of one. Not, according to Montagu, for lack of trying.

"My apologies." Montagu accepted Adam's extended hand. He tried out a smile. "But he has himself in a right knot, our king, doesn't he? About the bedding, I mean."

"Aye." Adam shrugged. "Such things sort themselves."

"One would hope." Montagu sighed. "We'd best find him. Coming?"

The king, it seemed, had vanished in thin air. No matter where they looked, they could not find him, and after ascertaining from the sentries that the king had not ridden off on some harebrained excursion or other, Adam tramped off to fetch his fleece-lined cloak.

They were back in York, this time staying in the castle. Space was limited, what with Lord Roger having transferred the Exchequer to York to properly keep an eye on it, and without his wife to accord him the privilege of a separate room, Adam was sharing his lodgings with Montagu and Stafford.

The small chamber showed the lack of female organisation. Clothes and footwear were strewn everywhere, chests stood wide open, spilling everything from hose to hats and the odd book. Stafford's, Adam thought with a smile, carefully replacing the precious book among Stafford's clothes. That man was as often to be found reading as in the tiltyard.

He ran into Gavin on is way out.

"They're coming," his squire told him, "they've been sighted, my lord. Stephen reckons they'll be here by terce, but I made him a wager it will not be until vespers—the count rides slowly these days."

Gout, coupled with advancing years and an expanding girth, had reduced the formerly forceful Count Guillaume of Hainaut to a cripple. Of an age with Lord Roger, as Adam recalled, but no matter that Lord Roger was over forty, the man remained as energetic as ever, striding at his customary speed from early morn to sunset.

"She's here!" King Edward near on barged into Adam. He dragged a hand through his hair, tugged at the heavy wool of his tunic.

"Not yet, my lord," Adam said.

"No, no, of course not." The king scuffed at the ground, a slight frown marring his features. "I want her to like me. Me, for myself."

"And why wouldn't she?" Adam cocked his head. "You're still somewhat puny over the arms, but with time you'll fill out and…" The rest was lost in his laughter, the king pummelling him.

"Puny?" the king demanded, landing a blow that had Adam wincing. "Me?"

"My lord." Adam made a grab for his hands, held him still. "I was jesting."

Edward reclaimed his hands. "I know you were," he said stiffly. "Do you think she will?"

"I think she already does." Adam dusted off his sleeves. "Don't her letters indicate as much?"

"Letters? Anyone can write a letter!" The king stomped his feet. "God's blood, but it's freezing out here."

"We can always go inside," Adam suggested, but the king wasn't listening. He was staring to the south.

"Montagu says wives hate the bedding. A refined lady is not as hot-blooded as a tavern wench."

"Then Montagu is a fool—or not doing it right." It was Adam's considered opinion that Montagu and his wife did not suit—not truly. "A young girl such as your lady, she requires gentle wooing, my lord. Tender kisses, soft caresses."

"I know, Lady Kit already told me."

"She did?" Adam had to suppress a grin. His wife, counselling the king?

"Aye, she—"

"Edward?" The queen's voice carried across the bailey. She came ploughing towards them through the snow, skirts raised. "They'll be here before the evening." The cold had brought out roses in her cheeks, and with the sparkle in her eyes and the few dark curls of her hair that peeped out from under her hood, she looked happy. She slipped an arm under her son's, towing him in the direction of her apartments. "I think it is time we have a little talk, Son."

"Talk?" Edward's cheeks went bright red. "Talk about what?"

175

"This and that." The queen gave her son a sly look. "Birds and bees, Son."

"Maman," he groaned. "I don't need this."

"Now, Edward."

Adam was watching Stephen ride his new mount when Edward stormed out of his mother's chambers, his cloak billowing like a raven's wing behind him.

"My lord?" Adam easily caught up with him.

"She says I must not consummate my marriage." Edward scowled. "For Lady Philippa's sake."

"Ah." Adam drew the king to a halt. "She is young, your bride."

"But older than my mother when she wed my father."

"True enough." At the time, the queen's new husband had been enthralled by Piers Gaveston, and from what Adam had heard, it had taken the former king some time to bed his bride—maybe out of consideration, maybe out of lack of interest. "But she'd been wed for quite some years before she gave birth to you, my lord."

Edward nodded, no more. "I want..." He broke off. "Philippa, I care for her. I must ensure the marriage is made irrevocable."

Adam raised his brows. "No one is going to annul it without your approval."

"A lot is done without my approval." He sounded so young, and without really knowing how, Adam had placed an arm round his shoulders.

"Your lady mother is right. Childbirth is a great strain on a very young mother." He tightened his hold on Edward's shoulders. "But a bloodstain is easy to arrange."

"A bloodstain?" Edward disengaged himself, turning to stare at Adam. "They bleed?"

"Some do." What in the name of God was he doing, talking to his lord about such matters? Adam cleared his throat. "As I said, an easy thing to sort." He mimed slashing at his thumb. "Not too much, mind you."

"No, no." Edward looked at anything but Adam. "What do I tell her?"

"That you're doing it out of consideration."

"She...Couldn't you tell her?"

"No." Adam shook his head. "This is between man and wife."

Edward flushed. "What if I want to? What if she wants to?"

Adam smiled. "It will do you no harm to wait, my lord. But while you're waiting, there's nothing stopping you from exploring, is there?"

"Exploring." Edward studied his hands. "Yes, quite: exploring." He glanced at Adam. "Do you truly think she said it out of consideration for Philippa?"

"I do. She is merely offering advice. Had your father been here—"

"But he's not—he's dead." There was a challenge in Edward's voice, his vivid blue eyes sharpening as they studied Adam.

"Aye," Adam agreed, ducking his head to avoid that penetrating look.

There was silence. Adam pretended great interest in his boots.

"Look at me, Adam."

"My lord?" Adam raised his face, tried out a little smile.

"You know, don't you?"

"Know what?"

"No." The king held up his hand. "You will not lie to me, Sir Adam. Never again, remember?"

Chastened, Adam nodded. Once, he had fooled his lord, and he had given his word he would never do it again.

"Aye," he said reluctantly. "I know."

"Since when?"

"Since Christmas." Adam lowered his voice to a whisper. "I confronted Lord Mortimer—accused him of murder, almost."

There was a muffled sound Adam chose to interpret as a chuckle.

"Murder? Mortimer? How ludicrous." Edward's mouth twitched. "He did not take that well, I gather."

"No." Adam half closed his eyes. "He was insulted." And hurt.

177

Edward nodded. "I can imagine." He pursed his lips. "No one must know. No one." He whirled on his toes. "Make sure our horses are saddled. I want to ride out to meet her."

The wedding day dawned anything but auspiciously, heavy showers alternating with freezing sleet. And yet despite the weather, despite the unfinished minster—most of the western roof was still missing—it was a heartwarming sight to see Edward of Windsor wed his bride.

The radiance of their smiles, the way her fingers braided with his, large eyes turned to gaze in admiration at her handsome, royal bridegroom—Edward glowed as he guided his wife from the minster to the waiting wedding feast.

"Touching," Thomas murmured much later, nodding at the high table, where the king was presently offering his goblet to his wife. The earl had ridden in with the bride's party, complaining loudly about chilblains and saddle sores until Adam had suggested a bath—and a pitcher or two of Lord Roger's excellent wine. Now, two days later, he was as resplendent as the king, his earl's robes swirling round him as he moved.

"She'll do him good," Adam said. "Though at present, she is very much a child." Seeing the king's intended in the flesh, all dark hair and dimples, shy smiles and lustrous eyes, Adam was prone to agree with the queen—Philippa of Hainaut was too young to be bedded.

"So is he – at times." Thomas smiled fondly at his nephew. "But then, he's only fifteen—not exactly an adult man." He grinned. "I hear there will be jousting—plenty of it—over the coming days."

"God spare us all," Adam muttered. "I'll be leaving it to the younger lads."

"Aye, decrepit ancients like you had best stay clear of the lists." Thomas laughed. "I, on the other hand, will ride and shine."

"Braggart." Adam nodded in the direction of Count Guillaume. "He won't take part."

"No, that would probably kill him." Thomas frowned. "Was he like this when last you saw him?"

"No." The count who'd entertained the queen at Valenciennes in 1326 had been as energetic as Lord Roger. Not quite two years ago, but to judge from the change in Count Guillaume, it could have been ten years hence.

"They're of an age, aren't they?" Thomas asked.

"A year or so apart. But Lord Roger carries his years with ease."

"Pity," Thomas said, making Adam scowl.

There was no getting out of the jousting. The king insisted all his men take part, and at one point Adam found himself facing Robert de Langon. Since that evening in Scotland, de Langon had gone out of his way to avoid Adam, but that had not stopped his poisonous tongue, even if by now most of what he said fell on deaf ears. Montagu had distanced himself from the sullen Gascon, and where Montagu led, most of the king's companions followed, leaving Robert de Langon very much on the outside—yet another thing he blamed Adam for.

De Langon attacked without any warning. Not entirely unexpected, nor was it a breach against the rules, not while the melee was ongoing. He was astride a new mount, a well-built stallion adorned by a caparison in green, further decorated by de Langon's coat of arms. Not only his horse was new: de Langon had new armour, new weapons, and even a new helmet, sporting one of those newfangled crests. None of it helped—Adam sent him flying in their first encounter. He turned Raven neatly and trotted over to where Robert was getting to his feet.

"I trust you are unharmed?"

"One day…" Robert vowed.

Adam looked him up and down. "I think not, de Langon. I could beat you with one hand tied behind my back—my right hand, even." He tipped his lance and returned to the ongoing fight. Out of the corner of his eye, he saw de Langon pick himself up and leave the field.

"He'll not forgive you for all these repeated humiliations," Montagu said, riding over to join him.

"Repeated?"

"Well, there's Scotland, there's today, and then there are all those times when you best him at swords without even trying." He grinned. "He hated it when you had him landing flat on his face in Worcester."

Adam chuckled. It had been a restless king who'd ordered them all out to practise with their swords despite the rain and the cold.

"He slipped," Adam said. "Nothing to do with me." And it had not helped that de Langon had recently returned to court after some months at home, bragging about the numerous hours he'd spent perfecting his sword-work with his French master-at-arms.

"As far as Robert de Langon is concerned, everything is your fault." Montagu adjusted his helmet. "Easier to blame you for remaining invisible to the king than blaming the king himself." He nodded in the direction of the knights, presently going at it. "Shall we?"

After three days, the wedding festivities were over. A markedly pale little queen bid her father farewell, waved the count and his party off, and managed a smile at her husband before fleeing indoors.

"Leave her," Adam said when Edward made as if to follow her. "Give her time to regain her composure."

"But…"

"Comfort her later, my lord. Allow her the privacy she requires to weep."

Edward frowned, clearly torn between wanting to hurry after his wife and heeding Adam's advice.

"How about we ride against each other?" Adam asked, knowing full well this would distract his lord.

"Me against you?" Edward grinned. "I'll have you spitting mud, Adam."

"We'll see," Adam replied. "Pride often goes before a fall, my lord."

"Practice runs only," the king decided, lifting his face to smile at the sun. "I can't be bothered to put on full armour."

Adam nodded, no more. "A gambeson and a coat of plates will do, my lord. We'll use the blunted lances."

They rode a couple of times, lances jarring into their shields. Not enough force to unhorse, but sufficient to drive home who was the victor.

"I am still bruised after yesterday," the king said, scowling at Adam when he won yet another point.

"Of course, my lord." Adam grinned. "A good line to use when you're facing the enemy, isn't it?"

"Hmph! Again!"

This time, Edward knocked Adam backwards, whooping like a raiding Scot afterwards.

"Again," Adam said, wiping at his sweaty face before putting his helmet back on.

"May I have a go?" Lord Roger sauntered over. Behind him, Queen Isabella settled herself on a bench.

"Of course, my lord." Adam made as if to dismount.

"Against you, Adam." Lord Roger bowed to the king. "Edward here is far too dangerous an opponent."

The king grinned. "See?" He tapped his lance against Adam's shield. "You're losing it, old man."

"Old man? I'll have you know I'm not yet thirty-two."

The king laughed and trotted off.

"Are you sure you want to do this, my lord?" Adam asked.

Lord Roger squinted up at him. "Why? You think I am past it?" He handed his cloak to a squire and proceeded to undo his robe. Moments later, he was standing in only shirt and hose, broad shoulders causing the fine linen to tighten and strain. He stretched this way and that, and it struck Adam that Lord Roger was posturing, exposing his trim physique to whoever was watching.

One of his squires came running with his gambeson, another buckled Lord Roger's breastplate into place. Queen Isabella shielded her eyes with her hand, watching as Lord Roger pulled on worn boots and heavy gauntlets. He mounted his horse, tightened his coif, and put on his helmet.

"Ready?" he asked, his voice muffled.

"Aye." Adam rode closer. "For real or for show?"

"For real, of course." Lord Roger's eyes were barely visible. "I'll send you sprawling, dear Adam."

"I think not, my lord." Adam tightened his hold on his reins. "But you can try."

A long charge, a jarring impact, down to the other end of the list, and Adam turned Raven round. His shield arm throbbed. Again, and they both hit each other's shields full on. Out of the corner of his eye, Adam saw Lord Roger hanging halfway out of the saddle before he righted himself.

The next time round, Lord Roger came thundering towards him before Adam had fully turned, lance held at an angle. No more play, Adam concluded, tightening his hold on his own lance. At the last moment, he managed to bring his shield up, cursing loudly as Lord Roger's lance near on drove him off his horse. Lord Roger laughed, set his stallion to prancing before the queen, who applauded.

"New lance," Adam said, throwing the one he'd just used to the ground. Someone handed him one, he brought Raven under control, settled the lance in the crook of his arm, and charged. Sun glinted off the tip of his lance. Sun did not glint on wood—not like that. Someone yelled. Lord Roger was galloping towards him, his lance as firm as a rock. Raven snorted, lowered his head, and set off. Adam was carried towards Lord Roger, transfixed by the glittering metal tip of his weapon. Yet another scream. A metal point? Adam raised his lance, tried to swerve aside. Lord Roger caught him full on his shoulder, and this time Adam knew who it was that screamed. It was him.

"Adam?" Someone shook him. He coughed, tried to sit up, but desisted.

"God's blood," he croaked. His mouth was full of mud, his shoulder felt as if Raven had stamped on it, and there was a taste of blood in his mouth. He licked his lip. It had burst. There was a scraping sensation as someone pulled his helmet off.

"Sweetest Lord," Lord Roger said. Adam blinked. "Don't move," Lord Roger ordered.

Adam wheezed with laughter. Move?

"What happened?" The lance. Someone had handed him a real lance. He clutched at Lord Roger's arm. "My lord, I would never—"

"Shush, don't you think I know that?" Lord Roger smoothed at his hair. "Kit is going to kill me," he muttered. "Assuming, of course, that dear Edward doesn't do so first."

"Wasn't your fault."

"You raised your lance. I should have done the same." Lord Roger shrugged. "It all happened too fast. Best have the monks see to you." Lord Roger called for help.

"I can walk." Adam attempted yet again to sit up. Everything around him tilted.

"Walk?" Lord Roger said. "You lie still, you hear? You're bleeding like a pig."

"I am?" Adam slumped back down. Lie still. Aye, he could do that.

Lord Roger insisted on carrying Adam himself—with the help of Richard. A long walk across the bailey, and Adam closed his eyes to avoid seeing the concerned faces. Up some stairs, Adam wincing when the stretcher banged against the wall, and they were in the little infirmary. It smelled of honey and herbs—yarrow, predominantly.

Richard puffed loudly, setting down his end of the stretcher carefully. "You've not grown any lighter with the years."

"Brawn," Adam replied, trying to smile. His face was on fire. His left arm he couldn't feel.

"Dislocated," the monk said.

Adam could have told him that himself.

"It will hurt."

Adam nodded. He was placed facedown on a bench, his injured arm hanging straight down. For a man the size of a mouse, the monk had substantial strength in those hands. Adam gritted his teeth, gasped all the same, and fell into a void.

He came to, and the same monk was busy stitching up the wound to his chest, just below his left shoulder. There was a stinging sensation as his face was washed. He protested loudly when the monk stitched up his nose—his nose?—a long gash along his hairline, and an ugly cut below his ear. Lord Roger was right, Kit would kill him. The thought made him smile, but that hurt.

"Here." The monk handed him a mug. Wine, nice and sweet and laced with milk of the poppy.

When he next woke, it was dark. Someone moved out of the shadows. Lord Roger. He took Adam's right hand, holding it, no more. They didn't talk. They just held hands while Adam dozed.

The monk shook him awake to the sound of the prime bells, insisting that he had to piss. Adam staggered to his feet, making big eyes at the black bruise that covered most of his left torso.

"Fool of a man, to play at war without full armour," the monk said.

There was nothing to say to that, so Adam concentrated on aiming his cock at the piss pot instead.

After a thorough inspection of Adam's various wounds, the monk called for gruel and watered wine, watching as a hawk while Adam ate it all.

"Good," he said once Adam was done. "If there's no fever, you can return to your own bed tonight."

"God grant me that there isn't." The pallet Adam was on was hard and narrow, what went for a mattress so thin he could feel the poles beneath.

An hour or so later, Thomas entered, coming to an abrupt stop at the sight of him.

"That bad?" Adam asked carefully, not wanting his lip to burst open again.

"Bad enough. Kit won't like it."

"Kit won't see it." For the first time in weeks, Adam was delighted his wife was far away. No. His hand went to the little pouch he always carried round his neck, containing a lock of her hair. He'd have given anything to have her sitting beside him—even if she'd be scolding him.

The door opened. Lord Roger again, with Richard at his heels.

"Feeling better?"

"I have pissed, so apparently I am," Adam replied, making them all laugh. A heavy silence fell.

"Who handed you the lance?" Lord Roger asked at long last.

"I don't know." Adam frowned. Gavin had been on the other side, of that he was sure. "They wanted me to kill you." His mouth dried up.

"Had you not raised your lance, Lord Roger here would have been lying neatly shrouded," Thomas said. "That lance came with an evil tip." He used his hands to indicate something close to a foot long.

"Narrow and sharp like the devil. Italian work," Richard put in.

"One of the king's new toys." Thomas pressed his mouth into a tight line. "A king's lance to kill a baron."

"Thank the Lord it didn't work," Richard said—needlessly, in Adam's opinion.

"So who?" Adam asked.

"Who?" Lord Roger shook his head. "I have many enemies." Dark eyes in dark hollows regarded Adam. He hadn't shaved, his cheeks sporting a dark bristle.

"Creative enemies, even." Thomas shifted in his seat. "Whoever handed Adam that lance acted on the spur of the moment. Shows initiative, doesn't it?"

"One could almost think you'd be willing to commend the man," Richard said.

"I don't hold with murder," Thomas snapped. The temperature in the room dropped into the frigid range.

"Neither do I," Lord Roger said after a long silence. "Nor do I commit it."

Chapter 19

She'd said farewell to Adam just after Epiphany, standing at the gate to watch him ride up the lane, a dark shape on his black horse. As always, he'd halted his horse right at the top. As always, she'd come running—although given the state of her, it had been more of a sedate trot. As always, he had dismounted and come to meet her, sweeping her into one more lingering embrace.

"The day you stop doing that is the day you no longer love me," he'd said, setting her down gently.

"That day will never come." She'd brushed a hand over his new tabard, a dark red adorned with the king's arms.

And so, after one more kiss, he'd sat up, set his hand to his heart and bowed, and ridden off.

Since then, Kit had submerged herself in managing their various manors. She'd overseen the distribution of new clothes to the household servants, had spent hours with Mall ensuring they had enough food to see them through the winter.

William had ridden all the way down to Bristol, returning with barrels of salted herring, precious packets of exotic spices, and a bedraggled ball of fur that turned out to be a kitten. Meg took one look at it and claimed it as her own, and so, in addition to her daughter and her year-old son, Kit now had a ferocious little cat to handle.

"Poor mite," Mabel said, bending over ponderously to stroke the little beast. Moments later, she straightened up, sucking at her thumb.

"He only likes me," Meg told her. It seemed to be true. Where Flea—so named after Kit discovered a multitude on him—scratched and bit all others, with Meg he was constantly docile, resigning himself to being lifted and cradled and sung to.

At present, the solar was a beehive of activity. Other than the smocks and swaddling for the coming baby, Meg and Ned needed new clothes, as did Kit herself. Not entirely true, but upon seeing the ells of light blue worsted that William brought back from Bristol, she'd decided she needed a new kirtle.

"My lady?" Egard appeared in the doorway. "There are some men coming down the lane."

"How many?" On a bleak January day, travellers were an anomaly.

"Half a dozen or so," Egard said. "Not sure I like the look of them."

"Brigands?"

"Could be. I've closed the gate, my lady."

"Good." Kit looked about for her cloak. "Let's see what they want."

Weak sun filtered through the cloud cover, glittering on puddles and wet cobbles. Kit inhaled, and there was a tinge to the air that had her thinking of spring and cossets. There was a week and more to Candlemas, so winter was nowhere close to being done, but the wind had a softer edge to it, the occasional muddy patch soft and squelchy rather than frozen solid.

She puffed her way across the yard. The child was heavy now, a slight mauling in her back indicating the birth was not far away. Egard steadied her up the ladder that led to the small platform above the gate.

"Sweetest Mother!" She clutched at her belly.

"Should you be here, my lady?" Egard shifted from foot to foot. "Should you not be inside?"

"It's not coming yet. This is just the babe settling itself." She gripped the wooden railing and straightened up. Her head cleared the top of the wall, and there, on the other side, was a man she'd hoped never to see again.

"Lady Katherine." Godfrey of Broseley was dishevelled, wet and muddy, his cloak held together by a large circular brooch embossed with a lion. "I have matters to discuss with your husband." His eyes travelled the newly erected walls, the massive gate, a displeased set to his mouth.

"My husband has no matters to discuss with you." Godfrey was armed to the teeth, as were his men, and Kit gave silent thanks to Adam for having insisted on protecting their home.

"No?" Godfrey smirked, and the ugly scar across his face tightened. "Oh, I think he does, Lady Katherine." He rode his horse closer, gesturing for the other men to remain where they were. "It is about the king, you see." His unkempt dark hair hung to his shoulders, lank with grease and dirt.

"The king? What would you know about him?" She threw a hasty look at Egard, who nodded, pointing discreetly at John and his grandsons, crouched with their crossbows at the ready. They'd never miss at this range, and Kit's shoulders relaxed somewhat.

"More than you think. I come from Berkeley Castle." He gave her an expectant look, scratching at his heavy beard.

"The king is at York," Kit told him. "Everyone knows that."

"Depends on which king, doesn't it?" Yet again, that avid look.

"Is there more than one?" Kit was glad of her hood, shielding most of her face. "I know only of Edward, third of that name."

"And what of his father, my lady?"

"His father is dead—and buried at Gloucester." She blew on her hands. "I see no point in this discussion, so I bid you good day."

"What, you won't invite us in?"

"I would rather open my doors to the four riders of Armageddon."

Godfrey's ugly face screwed up into a scowl. "One day, you may well eat those words, my lady." He rested his hand on his sword, his gaze sweeping the gate, the wall. This was when Egard chose to step into sight. Massive like a mountain, he held his axe in his hands, hefting it lightly up and down.

"Mama?" Meg tugged at her skirts. "Who's that, Mama?" Like a ferret, she clambered up to balance on the railing, thin ankles visible under her hem as she leaned over the stone parapet.

"Meg!" Kit grabbed her.

"Ah, the brat that survived," Godfrey said. "Not like the brother—Tom, was it?" There a gleam in his eyes, a taunting tone to his voice.

"Just go," Kit said, wanting him and his mocking smile gone. "If you want words with my husband, he's in York with the king—the one and only king."

Godfrey held his ground. There was a speculative look in his eyes, as if he was considering whether to say something more. His horse snorted; Godfrey shook himself free of whatever he'd been thinking.

"Until we meet again, my lady."

"Pray God we never do."

"Oh, I think we will." Godfrey looked her up and down. "We have matters to settle, you and I."

She raised her chin and stiffened her spine. Show no fear. In silence, she watched him out of sight.

"My lady?" Egard touched her arm. "Best get you inside."

"But what if they come back?"

"They won't." Egard sounded unruffled. "They'd hoped to find it as it was, I reckon, that old wooden fence, no more. This—" he broke off to pat at the stone, "it will keep such vermin out."

William was not pleased to hear Godfrey of Broseley had made an appearance. "For now, we keep the gate shut," he instructed. "And John, ensure there are sentries at all hours. First it is war, then it is brigands. When will this ever end?"

"He knew Tom was dead," Kit said, interrupting William midway through a little speech about evil men like Broseley and what they deserved.

"Is that so strange? He was one of Despenser's most trusted captains."

"But Despenser didn't know. So how could Godfrey know?" She had no idea why it mattered, why it made her feel discomfited that Godfrey should know about her son—or rather, be interested enough to inform himself.

"He may have run into some of Despenser's other men," William suggested. "Been back to Tewkesbury, even."

"Maybe." Kit decided it didn't matter. Instead, she went to light a candle for her little boy.

That same night, her waters broke. Mabel went from snoring heavily on her pallet to bustling about in a matter of heartbeats, keeping up a soothing chatter as she helped Kit to stand, ordering Rhosyn to strip the bed of the wet sheets. Clean but old sheets, a posset of dried raspberry leaves, and Kit was ordered to walk.

"I've done it before," Kit protested, but she did as she was told, waddling carefully from one side of the solar to the other. A rush of pain, and she fell forward, spilling the hot posset down the front of her shift.

"Dearest Virgin," she croaked. "See to me, your servant, and help me through this."

Yet another contraction—like iron bands tightening around her belly, making it impossible to breathe, to think, to do anything but stand and bear it.

"This should be over quickly," Mabel said with an encouraging smile. Kit grimaced. In her experience, childbirth rarely was.

By the time dawn tinted the sky, Kit was exhausted. A sequence of labour pains, each of them like having her womb gripped by a giant fist and wrung until ripped apart, and still the child was far from crowning.

"A big child." Mabel handed her yet another posset. Honey and more raspberry leaves.

"I have to walk," Kit gasped some hours later. The shift clung to her sweaty skin, her legs trembled and shook, yet the pain in her back made it unbearable to sit or lie down. So she stood propped against a bedpost, but even that didn't help. She had to move, stop this constant mauling.

With Mabel's help, she shuffled round the room.

"I want Adam," she admitted in a whisper. Mabel smiled and nodded, telling her that other than the fact that Lord Adam was in York, she, Mabel, would never allow a man to enter the birthing room. "It's not done, m'lady."

Kit knew that. But still, she wished he was here to hold her hand.

It was gone compline when Mabel rose from her inspection and told her the baby had crowned. Kit gave a weary nod. Since some time back, she'd been in bed, incapable of walking, all of her body concentrating on expulsing the child within her.

"Push, m'lady." Mabel gripped her hand. "At the next contraction, push."

There was that moment—there always was—when the child's head was almost out, when it felt as if everything between her legs was being torn apart.

"I…" Kit panted. "I can't."

"Of course you can, m'lady." Mabel's eyes were very close. "None of that, my Kit. None of it. Next time round, push and scream with it."

She did, and her legs and the bed beneath her were drenched with yet more water as Kit's child entered the world. Her head fell back. Kit held her breath, listening for the squalling sounds of a healthy infant. Nothing. Dearest God in heaven, please don't…A slap, a loud protesting wail.

"Thank you," Kit said, "thank you."

"A son, m'lady." Mabel beamed at her.

"A son." Kit licked her lips, dragged herself up to sit. "Never again." But she smiled and held out her arms to receive her newborn. "Never again," she crooned, holding him close enough to inhale his scent.

Mabel snorted. "It is woman's lot to birth her children in pain and blood—that is the way things are ordered. And as to more babies, well, they're difficult to avoid, aren't they?"

Kit didn't reply, already utterly in love with this the new addition to her family. A son. She stroked him over his fair fuzz, gazed into eyes that still held the depth and wisdom of every newborn babe—as if they'd gazed into eternity while they rested in the womb.

"He looks just like Tom did," she said, her breath catching in her throat.

"He does." Mabel sat down beside her. "The image of his sire."

Kit nodded, cradling her boy. A son. "Henry." She placed a kiss on his brow. "But I will call him Harry."

Despite the monk's best efforts, Adam had been gripped by a raging fever. For days, he lived in an existence of dark and fiery red, moments of lucidity before being plunged back into the restful bliss of near unconsciousness. His dreams were of Kit, and her hands were soft, her eyes so blue, and she held him in her arms. And then he woke, and he was on fire, he was cold, he shivered and sweated while the healing wounds in his face throbbed.

A week or so later, he was sitting up in bed, feeding himself for a change. Chicken broth, and he'd just bit into a peppercorn when Thomas entered. Adam smiled. The earl had been his most constant visitor, albeit he never stayed for long. The upcoming parliament had everyone rushing this way and that, the city of York thronged with the various participants— or so Adam heard.

"Better?" Thomas sat down on the single stool.

"Aye." Adam moved his left arm carefully. Heavily bandaged and in a sling, it still ached, and his hand remained clumsy and uncoordinated. "But I am sick to the bone of broths and soppy bread."

"Invalid's fare for our invalid." Thomas grinned. Adam managed to strike him with his spoon.

"And the king? Is he well?" It rankled that Edward had not visited him—and neither had the queen. An indication of his relative unimportance, Adam supposed, but he'd always assumed the king cared for him.

"Never better." Thomas produced a wedge of cheese and handed it to Adam. "His pretty wife keeps him most entertained. The dowager queen is less than pleased at how much of their time—and nights—they spend together."

Adam nodded, no more. The Lord knew his young master needed a loving wife, and maybe He had ensured Edward got one.

"It's not because he doesn't care," Thomas blurted. "Daily, he asks about you. It is just that he is young, and that incident in the tiltyard brought home just how fragile life can be. Young men prefer not to be reminded of that—they want the glory, but not the blood and mud."

Adam fixed his eyes on the frayed edge of the bed hangings. A weak excuse, in his opinion.

"Once you're more yourself, he'll come."

"What, you don't find me my normal handsome self with these?" Adam jested, gesturing at his face. It irked him to admit it, but he'd been shocked at the sight of himself, most of the damage caused by the dented helmet. He traced the line of stitches along his nose. They itched, as per Friar Anthony a good thing, indicating the body was healing as it should.

"Handsome?" Thomas laughed. "Those scars will add rather than detract—at least where the ladies are concerned."

"Not all ladies," Adam mumbled.

"No, Kit won't like it. But that's because she loves you and therefore cannot bear the thought of seeing you hurt. Not all men are as fortunate in their wives." Thomas stood. "I must go. I've promised Ned a long ride."

Adam was up and about when parliament started but was ordered to rest and stay out of trouble.

"If you can," Friar Anthony said in a snappish tone.

"I can do my best," Adam replied, struggling to dress one-handed.

"Here." The friar helped him. "Time to start using that hand. I'll have you out of the bandage by tomorrow."

"Use my hand," Adam muttered to himself some hours later, clenching and unclenching his hand round the hilt of his dagger while his eyes never left Alicia, a surprising presence in the queen's chambers. He'd been ordered to present himself well before vespers, so here he was, sitting to the side while the queen's pages lit candles and coaxed the fire back into flames.

"My lady." Adam bowed as the queen entered.

"Adam, how nice to see you back on your feet." The queen gestured for him to sit. "I have not had the opportunity to thank you. Mind you, for a moment, I thought you were planning on skewering him." Her voice hardened. "Had you done so, I would have hanged you."

"Someone handed me the lance, my lady. That's the one you should hang."

"Oh, I will—once I find him." She frowned. "You don't remember who handed it to you?"

"No." A gloved hand, a dark green sleeve—that was all he recalled.

"My son worries it was meant for him."

"For him? But who—"

The queen waved him silent. "Of course it wasn't. Whoever handed you that lance wanted to see Lord Roger dead—or permanently maimed." She crossed her arms over her chest and gave him a wavering smile. "You must forgive me for not finding that much of a relief. My son spared, my trusted Roger dead."

"It didn't happen, my lady."

"Not this time." Queen Isabella cast a covert look at Alicia, sitting among her ladies. "But just in case, I've decided to keep our enemies close."

"Alicia did not hand me that lance."

"No. But she goes markedly pale whenever it is mentioned." The queen lowered her voice to the extent that Adam had to lean forward, close enough to have her exhalations warm his skin. "I saw her talking to one of Lancaster's men."

"Ah." He studied his sister-in-law, stick-thin beyond her bloated belly. "Would she truly dare?"

"Does she have a choice?" The queen sighed. "I take it her husband is not the gentlest of men." Something akin to pity flashed across her face.

"Neither is she the kindest of ladies," Adam reminded her.

The queen pursed her lips. "She is too much like her mother, I fear." She slid Adam a look. "That salter's daughter who birthed your wife must have been of a sweeter disposition."

"That, my lady, is not saying much," Adam replied, choosing to ignore the barb about Kit's mother. He had never met Alaïs Coucy, but from what John and Mabel had told him, she'd been a good woman for all that she was of common stock.

The queen laughed. "I dare say you're right, Adam."

From what Adam heard, the parliament was not going Lord Roger's way. After some minor matters, such as finally releasing Eleanor de Clare from the Tower, the brunt of the time was spent on discussing Scotland. Lancaster, supported by Neville and Percy, refused to accept a treaty which required them to renounce their lands in Scotland. While the king said little during the heated discussions in parliament, in private he was just as adamant, repeating over and over again that he would never affix his seal to a treaty that so humbled England.

"Fool," Lord Roger said, serving himself some more of the lampreys. "The treaty will be signed and sealed—it has to be." He held out his hand for the salt. "Scotland must be appeased—for now." A week after Candlemas, they were sitting in Lord Roger's chambers: Adam, Richard, Bishop Burghersh, and Lord Roger himself. Adam was there mostly by mistake, having bumped into Lord Roger earlier, but he was enjoying the company and the wine, even more the conversation.

When the bishop moved on to discuss the state of the royal coffers, Adam reclined against the wall. The heavy weave of the tapestry brushed his shoulder, and he craned his head back, smiling at the motif. A knight in armour and a dragon, locked in deadly combat. St George, it seemed, was not only a favourite with the king.

There were two other tapestries—one of St Sebastian pierced with multiple arrows, the other of St Eustace in full hunt. Dark hangings enclosed the bed, the silk of the bedding shimmering in the soft light. Red silk. Adam brushed his hand over the wool of his tunic, wondering what it would feel like to love his Kit in a bed of silk. He fidgeted. He'd not had word from home, and by now the babe should have arrived—hale and hearty, he hoped, although his prime concern was his wife.

"Lancaster may protest as much as he likes," Lord Roger said, dragging Adam back to the conversation. "Our king will do as instructed. It is best for all that he does."

"One does not instruct a king, my lord," Adam objected.

"One does as long as the king is a child." Lord Roger made a dismissive sound. "And for now, that is what he is."

"Not much longer, though." Bishop Burghersh shoved his plate aside. "Soon enough, Edward of Windsor will rule in his own name."

"Of course," Lord Roger said smoothly. "But not yet, my friend, not yet. For now, our young king remains firmly under the control of his lady mother."

And you, Adam added silently. It was no secret the queen and Lord Roger travelled nowhere without the Great Seal. He studied Lord Roger over the rim of his goblet, trying to make sense of the conflicting sensations within. On the one side, he loved Lord Roger. On the other, he feared his former lord was overreaching, so confident that with the queen by his side he was untouchable. And this matter with the former king, officially dead, unofficially not…Adam sipped at the wine. He didn't like it.

The day after, William rode in, and Adam only had to see his brother to know the news was good. William, however, clouded at the sight of Adam.

"What in God's name happened to your face?"

"A jousting accident," Adam said.

"Hmm." William had the most penetrating gaze when he wanted it so.

"I'll tell you later, but first, what news from home?"

"You have a son," William said, hugging him. "A healthy, bawling son."

Adam disengaged himself. "And Kit?"

"Recovering." Something flitted over William's face. "It was a hard birth."

"But she is well?" Adam's hand tightened round William's forearm.

"She is. I would not have left her otherwise."

"You shouldn't have left her anyway. I've entrusted her to you, not to Mabel and John."

"Egard remains at Tresaints," William said. "And I think Kit realised I needed a change."

"Are you unhappy at Tresaints?"

"Unhappy? Not at all. But at times, the fact that I have more sheep than men in my flock makes me restless."

"What, you preach to the beasts?"

William rolled his eyes. "No. I was merely making a point."

"A son, eh?" Adam slapped his brother on his back. "And properly baptised, I hope."

"As you wished, he's been baptised Henry." William smiled. "Harry, Kit calls him. And he's big and lusty, as fair as his sire—

and just as hairy, or so Mabel says." He pursed his lips. "He looks just like Tom. And I'm not sure that is a good thing." He handed Adam a carefully folded and sealed letter. "From Kit."

"He can't help how he looks." Adam sighed, uncomfortable with the idea of a replica of Tom.

"No, he can't. And his eyes may yet shift to something other than blue." William eyed him from under his brows. "There's something else."

"Yes?" Adam looked up from his wife's writing—so much neater than his own.

"Tresaints had visitors." William's tone had Adam lowering the letter. "Godfrey of Broseley rode by, and I do not think he came with good intentions."

"That man..." Adam said once William had finished recounting the events.

"Aye, well, chances are he'll be in York. Best beware, Adam."

Chapter 20

Alicia took to hovering round Adam. Not so that she'd simper and send him come-hither looks—God forbid—more in that she was constantly on the fringe of things. Where Adam was, there was Alicia. At times, she attempted to melt out of sight. At others, she was conspicuously present.

"As a spy, she lacks in subtlety," Adam commented to William.

"She's not even trying to be subtle." William glanced at Alicia, for the day standing behind a convenient pillar, eyes fixed on Adam. "Right disconcerting to have someone staring at you like that."

"Aye." Adam shifted his left shoulder and winced.

Just after mass one Sunday, Alicia bumped into Adam on the way out. Her hand found his, pressed something into it, and then she was gone. His first reaction was to discard whatever it was she had given him. Instead, he closed his hand around it.

"A love token?" Richard teased, watching his sister hurry away.

"God forbid," William muttered from behind them.

"Amen to that." Adam led the way to the nearest guard room, tersely told the two guards loitering before the hearth to disappear for some moments, and unrolled the tightly rolled scrap of parchment.

"I knew it!" Adam tossed the crumpled missive into the hearth. "She's not to be trusted—no one who runs errands for Godfrey of Broseley is."

"Maybe he just asked her to pass it on," Richard suggested.

"Or she is in regular contact with him." Adam scowled. "You'd best find out, hadn't you?"

"Me?"

"She's your sister! And if she's working with Broseley, we can be sure of one thing: whatever they're planning, it will not be to Lord Roger's benefit."

"Unless we bluff them." Richard nodded in the direction of the hearth. "You're not planning on going, are you?"

"How can I not?" Adam scrubbed at his hair. "He says he has my son." A trap. It smelled of a nasty ambush.

"How many times must I tell you this?" William sounded exasperated. "Tom is dead, Adam."

"I must make sure. Damn!" Adam kicked at one of the stools. "The one bait he knows I can't ignore, and he dangles it before me."

"The question, of course, is why." Richard rocked back on his chair.

"I dare say I'll find out soon enough." Broseley would gladly slit Adam's throat should he get the opportunity. Adam swallowed, a hand to his neck. On the other hand, if all Broseley wanted was to see Adam dead, why set up an assignation? Something did not smell right.

"You can't go!" William stood to block the door.

"I have no choice. But if it makes you feel better, you can come with me." Adam pushed by him. "We leave after sunset."

Richard came running after. "I'm coming with you as well." He draped an arm round Adam's shoulders. "But I'll get there on my own." He winked and hurried off. The knot in Adam's belly softened somewhat.

Adam spent most of the day working with his longsword. His left arm shook and protested, but Adam gritted his teeth and pushed on, careful to keep the movements smooth and unhurried. Like a dance, he reflected, grinning to himself. In the chaos of a real battle, there was no time for dancing or twirling, it was chop, stab, chop, chop—which was why he preferred the shorter war sword.

"Recovered, I see."

"My lord?" Adam turned towards the voice. The king was standing some way off, most of him in the shadow of the nearby wall.

"I'm sorry." Edward beckoned for Adam to join him.

"Sorry for what?" Adam asked once he'd handed over his sword to Gavin.

199

"I should have come to see you." Thick lashes shielded his eyes. "I…" The tip of his tongue darted out.

"You were busy with your new bride," Adam offered.

The king shone up. "Yes, yes, I was." He sidled closer, put a hand on Adam's shoulder. "Is it mending as it should?"

"Well enough." Adam lifted the shoulder a couple of times. "But it is a relief you're not planning to ride to war tomorrow."

Edward scowled. "I wish I was! Those Scots…" His eyes narrowed. "Not only do they want me to recognise that upstart Bruce as rightful king, but I must return that sacred stone of theirs." He spat to the side. "A stone, Adam! Shows you just how wild and uncivilised they are, that they venerate a slab of rock."

Adam chose not to say anything, hemming at adequate intervals as the king went on to moan about his poor sister, soon to be wed to one of those redheaded bastards, and—

"Um…" the king brought himself up short. "Not that I have anything against people with red hair—well, not all of them, at any rate."

"I am sure my lady wife will be most pleased to hear that." Adam laughed silently at Edward's evident discomfort. "And your own wife, is she faring well?"

"Philippa?" King Edward flushed. "Yes, I think she is. And she likes me, I believe. A lot."

"A loving wife is a priceless treasure," Adam said, not even trying to suppress his grin. The king gave him a shy smile back.

"She is," he mumbled.

"My lord!" Will Montague stood at the gatehouse that led to the keep. "Your lady mother…"

"Requests my presence," the king filled in. "She always does these days," he added acidly. "One could almost think she resents the time I spend with my wife."

She most probably did, Adam reflected as he watched his lord hurry off. He wondered idly how long it would take before the new little queen was crowned. Something told him it would take some time—Queen Isabella did not have it in her to retire gracefully to the role of dowager queen.

It was dark by the time Adam and William set out. The sentry at the gate waved them through, told them to beware of the foul mist rising off the marshy ground that abutted the road, and went back to lounging against the wall.

Their lantern spread a weak glow—sufficient to see the road just ahead, no more.

"Cudgel?" Adam asked, nodding at William.

"And sword. You?"

"Sword."

Once in York proper, the darkness was less absolute. Light spilled from windows and doorways; here and there hung a lantern. They picked their way through the shambles, the air pungent with the stench of rotting offal and drying blood, crossed the silent marketplace, made their way down to Stonegate, and took a right towards the cathedral close. Halfway down there was an alley, and standing at its entrance was Broseley.

"I said alone," Godfrey snarled, shifting his shoulders. The man was almost as wide as he was tall, overlong arms bulging with muscle.

"I'm not a fool." Adam held out his arm, ensuring he and William came to a halt a good distance from Broseley. There was a tense silence. Broseley glowered at William, at Adam. A scruffy beard covered most of his face, his cloak was ragged and dirty, but from what little Adam could see, the clothes beneath were of good quality—as were his boots.

"So." Adam crossed his arms. "What do you want?"

Broseley hawked and spat, wiped his mouth, and burped into his sleeve before replying. "I propose a trade."

"A trade?" Adam held out his hands. "I have nothing to trade with you."

"Oh yes, you do." Broseley sneered. "Information can be worth its weight in gold."

Adam merely raised his brows.

"I get information about the king, you get the brat."

"The king?" Adam bristled. "I would never betray my lord."

"I'm not talking about the whelp Mortimer controls. I am talking about his living sire, our true anointed king!"

Adam was glad of the murky light, hopefully sufficient to conceal his features. How could Broseley know? But he managed to laugh—loudly.

"That king is dead, you fool."

"Is he?" Broseley moved his head slowly from side to side. "Little birds whisper differently, de Guirande."

"What nonsense is this?" Adam said. "Edward of Caernarvon was buried last December."

"So you say," Broseley smirked. "I, on the other hand, hear otherwise. I hear of a man being moved like a ghost from one castle to the other, a man travelling swathed in cloaks and hoods."

"Edward is dead," Adam repeated firmly, cursing silently. It would seem this supposed secret was not so secret after all.

"King Edward to you!" Godfrey spat. "King Edward to all of us, including that arrogant baron of yours and that whore of a queen."

"What does it matter? The man is dead."

"I think not. Neither do others." A sly smile played on Godfrey's lips. "Soon enough, we'll find a way to free him, and when we do, Mortimer will die, the adulterous queen will be immured in a convent, and the son…" He slashed a finger over his throat.

"You speak treason," Adam warned, drawing his sword.

"Come closer and I slit your brat's throat."

"My brat? He's dead too."

"Or not." Godfrey smirked. "But unless you give me what I want, I'll not give you your son."

"The former king is dead," Adam said. "And even if he weren't, why should I take your word that my son is alive?"

Godfrey called out an order. A man appeared from the shadows, holding a boy in one hand, a torch in the other. At Godfrey's instructions, the torch was held over the lad. All Adam could properly see was a shock of fair hair and a pinched little face.

"I can't see him."

Yet another barked instruction, and the boy tilted his head back, light playing over grimy features. Tom? Adam had no idea, and it filled him with despair that he did not immediately know if this was his son, yes or no.

"So," Broseley said, and the man holding the lad tightened his hold, causing the child to whimper. "Your son for a king—a fair trade."

"There is no king to trade," Adam said, eyes never leaving the laddie. "Tom?" he asked hoarsely. "Is that you, Tom?" There was no answer.

"You'll never know now. He's as good as dead," Godfrey sneered. "As are you." He moved closer, his blade held aloft. "Unless you tell me where the king is."

"There is but one king in this realm, and he is here in York." Adam lifted his sword, keeping a careful eye on the alley and the shadows he could see moving within.

"Him? A traitorous pup, a whingeing mama's boy," Godfrey hissed.

"That's the only king we have," Adam said.

"If that is how you want to play things…" Godfrey raised his left arm. Out of the alley spilled several armed men. "Can't say I'm sorry. I've always looked forward to seeing you die, de Guirande, preferably drowning in your own blood."

William stepped forward. "That won't happen."

"The priest?" Godfrey laughed. "What, you aim to fight us with your prayers?"

"No." William produced the cudgel he'd held concealed behind his back and pulled his sword. There was a mutter from one of Godfrey's men.

"Two?" someone piped up. "You said this was going to be easy."

"We're nine, and they're two." Godfrey waved his men forward. "Besides, only one of them is a true fighting man— and he is not entirely whole at present, is he?"

"Two actually." Thomas of Norfolk dropped down from a nearby roof.

"Three." Montagu followed suit.

"I took precautions," William muttered. "I hope you don't mind."

"Mind?" Adam half laughed. "How can I?"

"Four," someone yelled, and Richard stepped out from a nearby doorway.

For cutthroats, they put up a good fight. Several of them had seen battle, to judge by how well they handled the sword, and as to Broseley, he was an excellent swordsman. The blade whirled and sliced, parried and stabbed.

One man turned and fled. A second followed suit. William exclaimed and dropped the cudgel, cradling his arm. Godfrey and his men retreated, a tight knot bristling with blades.

"Him again?" Thomas held his sword at the ready, eyes never leaving Godfrey. "I seem to recall saving you from him once before."

"Like a rotten apple," Adam said, staunching a shallow cut with his sleeve. "Verily like his former lord."

"My lord Despenser is dead. Dead!" Godfrey bared his teeth, gripping his sword.

"Aye. But you're not. Yet." Adam moved towards him. "The lad. I want to see him properly."

Godfrey sneered. "Too late, isn't it?" He backed away, sword held aloft.

"And should I care? A street urchin, no more, a lad you've picked up because he has a passing resemblance to my Tom."

"Ah, but you don't know that, do you?" Godfrey slid a further few steps backwards. Adam lunged. With a yelp, Godfrey fell back, stumbled, and Adam pressed his advantage, the edge of his sword at Godfrey's exposed throat. Like a snake, Godfrey struck back. A kick to Adam's bad leg, his blade hissing through the air, uncomfortably close to Adam's groin. Adam retreated. Godfrey ran into the dark and narrow alley.

Adam made as if to follow him but was held back by the earl.

"Follow him in there and you follow him to your death," Thomas said, nodding in the direction of the dark alley. "Something tells me our Godfrey has more friends there than you do."

"Friends? More like vermin!" But Adam lowered his sword. Moments later, Godfrey darted out of sight.

"What do you think?" Adam asked William, wiping his blade clean. "Was it Tom?"

"Tom is dead." William frowned. "Dead, Adam. That laddie was of an age with Tom, but he wasn't Tom."

"Are you sure?" Adam wasn't. He was almost sure, but hope surged hot and painful through his veins, and he closed his eyes, pretending their Tom was indeed the snivelling lad he'd but glimpsed, noting little beyond that thick mop of fair hair.

"I am." William crossed himself. "That was not Tom—not unless the laddie's blue eyes have suddenly darkened into brown."

"Brown?" Adam couldn't recall anything but the hair. He cleared his throat. "Not a word to Kit. It would just break the wound wide open again."

William gave him a doubtful look. "Surely, you should tell her."

"No," Thomas interrupted, "Adam is right. To do so would be cruel." He threw a look over his shoulder. "I think it's best if we retreat while we can."

"You live an exciting life," Montagu commented as they hurried through the dark streets.

"You can have it," Adam told him, making Montagu laugh.

"What exactly what he talking about?" he asked. "The old king alive?"

"Yes," Thomas said silkily, "what was that all about?"

"I have no idea." Adam picked up pace. "The ravings of a desperate man?"

"What else could it be?" Richard said. "We all saw him buried, didn't we?"

"Yes," Thomas repeated, "we most certainly did."

But Adam could feel the weight of Thomas' eyes on his back all the way to the castle.

It was somewhat complicated getting back into the castle, but after a heated discussion between an aggravated Earl of Norfolk and the sullen sentry, they were allowed entrance.

"Thank you," Adam said, smiling at Richard, at Montagu, and at Thomas in turn. "I owe you for tonight."

Montagu departed with a cheery wave, William and Richard went looking for some wine, leaving Adam alone with Thomas.

"So." Thomas gestured for Adam to follow him. "I am all ears, Adam."

"Ears?"

The earl, not Thomas, his friend—no, this was a royal earl, and an angry one at that—whirled. "What exactly was he talking about?"

"I don't know," Adam lied.

"He said my brother was alive. Alive! Is that true?"

"Sounds like gibberish to me."

"Don't." Thomas warned. "You may fool Montagu and Monmouth—even your brother—but I know you too well by now. You were lying through your teeth when you insisted my brother was dead. I could hear it in your voice."

Adam gave him a considering look; it was not his secret to tell—he'd been sworn to silence by Lord Roger and the king.

"He's my brother," Thomas said. "He may not have been the best of kings, but he was always a good brother."

"I—"

"Damn it, Adam! I deserve to know!" He gripped Adam by the shoulder and shook him. "Tell me!" His eyes bored into Adam's. At long last, Adam sighed.

"I don't know much."

"But you know something."

"I do. But I won't tell you anything unless you swear an oath never to tell."

"Fair enough." Thomas set his hand to his heart. "I swear, Adam. Whatever you tell me, I will tell no other. I promise you this on my honour." He smiled crookedly. "And just so you know, your behaviour alone has confirmed what Broseley was saying. He is alive, isn't he?"

"He is. But I have no idea where he is."

Thomas took him by the arm. "You'd best tell me all you know, Adam. But in my rooms, I think. Just you and I and a pitcher or two of wine."

"It will not even require a mouthful," Adam told him. "As I said, I know very little."

Chapter 21

Adam groaned. "Now what?" His head ached, his mouth tinder-dry. The evening had been long and wet, Thomas insisting they celebrate his brother's return to life by finishing all the wine. Someone shoved at him. Adam squished his eyes shut, angry at whoever it was that had stomped into his room and thrown the shutters wide open, allowing sun and an icy wind to sweep through the little room.

"Up," Lord Roger snapped.

"My lord?" Adam swung his legs over the edge of the bed, scrubbed at his face, and made it over to the pitcher. The water was ice-cold, banishing the last vestiges of sleep.

"Broseley," Mortimer said, perching on the narrow windowsill. His green tunic rode up, allowing a glimpse of black silk hose.

"What of him?" Adam rinsed his mouth, found a sprig of dried mint, and chewed it meticulously.

"He knows!" Mortimer hissed. "Or so I gather after listening to Richard's account of last night."

"He suspects," Adam corrected. "But how?"

"A very good question." Mortimer fiddled with his various rings. "A very small group of men know, and I trust them all with my life. All of them. So how?" He gave Adam a long look.

"It wasn't me!"

"If I thought it was, you'd have been in one of the dungeons by now." Mortimer stood, moved restlessly around the room. "I've sent word to Berkeley and Maltravers. They must find the leak and silence him."

"And Broseley?"

"I have two score men looking for him. They're under orders to kill him on sight." Mortimer did yet another little turn. "If Lancaster finds out…" He came to a halt. "Norfolk!" he rounded on Adam. "Have you told Norfolk?"

Adam was tempted to lie. He even opened his mouth to do so, but instead all he did was nod. Once. The punch sent him staggering back against the wall.

"You were told to keep it a secret!"

"He was there last night. I couldn't lie him straight in the face." Adam touched his tender cheek.

"You tell one royal earl, it is but a matter of days before they all know. I'd hazard Norfolk has already told his brother."

"As a matter of fact, I haven't." Thomas stood in the doorway, looking from Lord Roger to Adam. "Nor do I intend to. I promised Adam I wouldn't."

"Yet another worthless promise?" Mortimer sneered. "Like the one Adam gave me?"

"I'm not your biggest problem, Mortimer." Thomas dipped a rag in the water and handed it to Adam. "Your lip." He turned back to Lord Roger. "Broseley is."

"And you think I don't know that?" Lord Roger glanced at Adam. "My apologies, I shouldn't have hit you like that."

Adam nodded, no more, holding the rag to his lip. "He's heard something. But not enough to know for sure."

"Men like that are like ratters," Mortimer said. "Give them half a bone and they'll not rest until they've found the other half."

"I suppose you'll move Edward from Berkeley," Thomas said casually.

"Suppose whatever you wish, my lord." Mortimer gave them both a cold look. "Not a word. Can I hope you'll hold to that this time, Adam?" He stalked out.

"Best not tell him Kit knows," Thomas said with a grin.

After this disruptive start to his morning, Adam spent some fruitless hours trying to locate Alicia. The silly goose was somehow involved in all this, and if it took using his belt, Adam intended to have the truth out of her. Well, maybe not his belt. A man who hit a woman was a cowardly worm, best stamped out of existence.

He saw her on the other side of the hall and set off towards her. She caught sight of him when he was halfway across and fled. By the time he'd reached the door that led to the inner bailey, she was gone. Adam was persistent. He followed her to the chapel, hastened after her as she rushed back to the queen's apartments, but on each of those occasions she managed to evade him.

She was not at dinner. The queen entered, accompanied by her ladies, and nowhere was Alicia's distinctive height. Adam wolfed down bread and stew, grabbed a leg of chicken, and set out to find his elusive quarry.

She was alone in the queen's solar. The page at the door squeaked in protest when Adam shoved by him. Alicia leapt to her feet and rushed to the window, and for a moment Adam feared she might jump. He lunged, got hold of her sleeve, and pulled her back. The fabric ripped, she cried out, Adam let go. With a thud, Alicia landed on her knees.

"Explain," Adam said, hoisting her to her feet.

"Explain what?" She sniffed, giving him a haughty look. "Unhand me, sir."

"You almost got me killed last night," Adam snarled. Not the truth, not precisely an untruth.

"Me? I did nothing." Alicia backed away from him, holding her embroidery needle like a miniature dagger before her.

"You handed me the note!"

"I did as I was told." She clutched at her ripped sleeve, the bright red fabric doing little to complement her looks.

"Did as you were told? Is that why you have been following me around like a little dog?"

Alicia retreated further. "I was told to do so."

"By whom?" He loomed over her, and she flinched, her arms coming up to protect her head. Her ruined sleeve fell back, revealing a collection of dark bruises. Adam took a step back.

"By whom?" Her voice quavered. "Who has the right to order my life, my lord? Who must I obey at all times?" She pulled up her sleeve, and it wasn't only bruises, it was half-healed gashes and odd bumps. "My husband demands my obedience." She snivelled. "I hate him." A choked sob and Adam looked away. "Just as I hate my brother," she added, and now she was crying in earnest. "Like a cow," she wailed. "He sold me like a beast to whoever would accept the lowest dowry."

"Richard did that?"

Alicia wiped at her face. "The lower the dowry, the more for him." She shot him an angry look. "Even Kit had more in dowry than I did." Her lip curled. "But of course she did: she was pretending to be the precious eldest daughter, not the lowborn bastard she really is."

Adam chose to ignore that.

"Henry Luytens is a traitor?"

Alicia cackled and sank down to sit. "Henry serves whoever best advances his interests."

"And who is that?"

Alicia looked away.

"Who?" He took a step towards her; she cowered. Damnation! Adam retreated; she relaxed. "I need answers. If you'll not tell me, I can assure you the queen will not hesitate to use a switch to make you talk."

Alicia blanched, cradling her belly protectively. "He is Lancaster's man—and Kent's. Mostly Kent's."

"Kent's? Earl Edmund is involved in this as well?" Adam cursed inwardly, recalling Richard had mentioned Luytens had business dealings with Kent.

"He is. And Broseley is working for Kent—I think." She shivered.

"God's teeth!" Kent and Broseley? He'd have taken Edmund for a better judge of character. Alicia did not seem to have heard.

"I hate Broseley—look what he did to my mother." She glared at Adam. "But it was you who killed her."

"Rather her than Kit." Lady Cecily had died with his sword buried in her brain, still clutching the knife she'd aimed at Kit's heart.

"Kit, Kit, Kit! I am sick of Kit, you hear? Sick of all this, sick of being wed to a fat bully of a man, sick of my brother, sick of…" She broke off to inhale. "It's not fair. Why me? Why not…" She hid her face in her hands. Her shoulders shook, all of her bowing as if under a great weight.

Carefully, Adam sidled closer. He sat down beside her, placed a hand on her shoulder. To his surprise, she threw her arms around him and buried her face against his chest. He patted her back, wrinkling his nose at the somewhat sour smell from her veil.

"Shush now," he said. "All these tears do your babe no good." In response, she tightened her hold on him. "No, Alicia." He took hold of her hands, disengaging himself as gently as he could. Which was when the queen walked in, with Mortimer at her side and a bevy of ladies at her heels.

"What have we here?" The queen looked from Alicia to Adam. "I would not have thought her your type, Adam."

A flurry of giggles from the women at her back, and Adam stood up abruptly.

"A jest," the queen said. "It takes a man with guts of steel to love someone like Alicia. Who knows what she may mix in the wine, eh?"

Unnecessarily cruel, Adam thought, watching Alicia sag. "She is distraught, my lady," he therefore said, pointing discreetly at Alicia's bared arm. The queen's elegant brows pulled together at the sight of the bruises.

"Leave us," she ordered, and everyone but Lord Roger fled the room. "Now," she continued, directing herself to Alicia. "You'd best explain exactly what is going on."

Out it came, Alicia describing how Lancaster had approached Henry Luytens—and several others of the London burghers—promising them concessions and expanded trading rights as long as they helped Lancaster get rid of that cruel oppressor, Roger Mortimer.

"Ingrates," Lord Roger said, but the queen waved him silent.

"Go on," the queen said, and Alicia snivelled and sobbed, saying she'd had no choice, no choice at all, because if she didn't do as he said, Henry would beat her—again. So here she was, instructed to at all times while parliament was sitting to keep Lancaster apprised of what the queen was doing and saying, of who she met for secret meetings, and where she spent her nights.

"And have you done so?" The queen shared a quick look with Mortimer, a smile touching her mouth. Adam felt a twinge of pity for Alicia: she was being used by both sides, and anything she had told Lancaster would have been carefully planted by the queen.

Alicia blushed vividly and nodded. "My husband wishes it so."

"Ah yes, he is here as well, isn't he?" Mortimer asked. "False toad of a man!"

"An awful, awful man," Alicia agreed. "Please order me to stay with you when parliament is done, my lady. I promise I will serve you loyally, do anything for you."

"If your husband orders you to return with him, then that is what you must do," Mortimer said. "Besides, you serve us best by being by his side, eyes and ears wide open."

"No! I cannot." Alicia's light blue eyes bulged. She fell to her knees. "Let me stay here with you."

"I must insist," Lord Roger said. "You are of no use to us here."

"Lord Mortimer is right," the queen interjected. "You must go back to your husband, bear it for the greater good." The smile she gave Alicia was akin to a gust of icy air.

"My lady," Alicia crawled forward on her knees. Adam had to avert his eyes from this spectacle of streaming eyes, tangled hair, and swollen face. "One day, he will kill me."

"How you exaggerate," the queen said with a sigh. "The secret of handling a husband is never to displease him—openly. I am sure you're capable of such subterfuge."

Alicia slumped. Alone on the floor, she looked broken and forlorn. "Very well," she said after a while. "And what will you have me do?"

"Follow the gold," Lord Roger said. "The moment you hear of your husband doing anything for Lancaster, you let us know."

Alicia wiped her face with her sleeve. "And what is in it for me, my lord?"

"Our undying gratitude," the queen replied. "A permanent place at court. And maybe a new husband."

"A new husband?" Alicia's head snapped up, her face brightening. "Will you have him killed?"

"Killed?" Mortimer laughed. "That would be taking things a bit too far. Murder is a crime, Alicia. We don't lower ourselves to such."

Parliament ended in a stalemate. The king was tired and grumpy, complaining loudly that close to a month with all these chattering fools had left him with a permanent headache and bruises in his ears—and a stubborn case of the sniffles. February in York had been cold.

"Waste of time," he said to Adam while gesturing for Montagu to hand him his cloak.

"The peers of the realm will always demand a voice, my lord."

"The peers of this realm seem more interested in tearing each other apart." The king sighed. "I wish…" He broke off, jumped to his feet. "Maman?"

"He's dead!" Queen Isabella set a hand to the wall as if to support herself. "Dead," she repeated and raised a tear-streaked face to her son. Her hair was dishevelled, her clothes had been thrown on in haste—a simple kirtle, no more, gaping unlaced over her chemise. No rings, no precious jewels to decorate her hair, no floating veils—not even one of her embroidered girdles.

"Who?" Edward asked, already at her side. He slipped a supportive arm around her waist. "Is it Mortimer?"

Lord Roger? Adam swallowed. Surely not Lord Roger— he'd seemed hale enough last night.

"Roger?" The queen's mouth wobbled. "My Roger?" She shook her head. "Had it been him, I'd not have found the strength to stand, I think."

The king studied his shoes intently. "So then who?"

Queen Isabella drew in a shuddering breath. "My brother."

"Charles?" The king's head snapped up.

"He's the only brother I have—had." The queen's face crumpled together. "All three of them dead, and none of them with a son." She grimaced. "Unless Queen Jeanne's unborn child is a son, the Capets are no more. The Valois have already advanced their claim."

"What?" Edward's voice squeaked. He cleared his throat. "What?" he repeated, sounding more like a man than a lad.

"You heard; my dear cousin Philippe of Valois is, as we speak, hovering round the pregnant queen. A son, and he will be regent. A daughter, and he will be king—or so he hopes." The queen tossed the crumpled letter in her hand to her son. "Poor Jeanne, surrounded by people who pray openly that the child she carries may be yet another girl."

Edward looked up from the letter. "What about my claim?" Adam suppressed a sigh. The French would no more countenance an English king than they would be ruled by a woman.

Queen Isabella retrieved the letter, smoothed it as well as she could, and tucked it into her sleeve. "We shall have to think about it, my lion. For now, we must both pray for the safe delivery of Jeanne's child. May it be a son—and if it is not, we shall see." She looked down at herself, seemingly startled at the state of her clothes. "I look a fright."

"You had distressing news, Maman—and you never look a fright."

Queen Isabella cupped is cheek. "Such a gallant son."

"Maman." He twisted out of reach, cheeks bright red. Queen Isabella laughed, back to her normal controlled self. Deftly, she twisted her hair into something resembling a heavy plait. She adjusted her clothes, picked up the king's cloak, and draped it over her shoulders.

"I must see Roger," she said, moving with the grace of a hind towards the door. "And Valois had best remember that Philippe le Bel has a grandson."

Adam shared a look with Montagu. Their young king was staring after his mother, a determined look on his face. Montagu shook his head, eyes heavenward. Adam could but agree: the French crown was an impossible dream.

Chapter 22

There'd been no explanation. Queen Isabella had simply informed her son that she and Lord Mortimer had matters to attend to—on their own—which was why the king and his extensive following were making for Woodstock while Mortimer and the queen were God knows where. Not that the king minded. In fact, ever since they'd left York behind, he'd been in great spirits, which was why Adam approached him one morning and requested the king's permission to go home.

"Home?" The king swung himself up in the saddle, grasped the reins firmly, and waited as Adam sat up. "Now?"

"Aye, my lord." It was over two months since he'd seen his family and his home, and even if he'd dispatched William back home immediately after their encounter with Godfrey, he wanted to ensure they were all safe.

"You miss her." Edward reined in his horse to bring it abreast with Raven. "I can see it in your face, how you dream of home—and Lady Kit, I presume."

"I always miss her when she's not with me."

"And here was I thinking it was the wife who yearned and sighed, not the husband," Edward said in a teasing tone.

"It works both ways, my lord. With Kit, I feel whole. She allows me to be the man that I am, warts and all." And why on earth was he sharing this with a lad young enough to be his son? Maybe precisely because of that, Adam thought, smiling good-naturedly when the king laughed long and hard. Soon enough, he'd learn the truth in that statement.

"Warts? You have no warts that I can see. Scars, aye, but no warts." The king wiped his eyes, mouth still quivering with mirth.

"All of us have warts, my lord. Most of them are invisible."

"Hmm." Edward cocked his head. "You love her—Lady Kit, I mean."

"I do." Adam's hand rose of its own accord to touch the little pouch through the folds of his tunic. The king followed the movement, brows rising. "I would do anything for her, my lord. I would even die for her—but she would never forgive me if I did."

"And she?" King Edward twisted in the saddle to look at the litter that contained his queen. "Would she do the same?"

Adam laughed. "I take it I've never told you of how she saved my life in 1322, my lord."

"She did?" The king rode closer. "What did she do?"

"Well, for a start she went swimming in the Severn—in March. And then she somehow convinced Despenser to reprieve my life." Adam shook his head. "Had she not found me when she did, I'd have been dead, my lord." The memory had his foot throbbing: that red-hot stake slamming through the brittle bones of his foot, the stench of scorched flesh, the pain…

"What did she do to have him reprieve you?"

"She shamed Pembroke. Mind you, Despenser only pardoned me because he was convinced I was going to die." He gave the king a crooked smile. "His tender care had left me very close to doing so."

The king looked away. "And yet here you are, while Despenser is no more."

"As God has ordained, my lord."

There was no reply. The king set spurs to his horse and yelled it on.

Five days after seeing the king and his young queen installed at Woodstock, Adam turned up the long lane at Tresaints. He'd sent Gavin ahead with some of the men-at-arms and was therefore not surprised when he saw a flurry of light blue by the gate. She'd been waiting for him, and he halted the horse just to have the pleasure of seeing her running towards him, as light-footed as a young girl.

She wore no veil—she rarely did when at Tresaints—and her heavy braid bounced back and forth in time with her strides. Adam flexed his fingers. Soon enough, he'd have his hands buried in that hair, soon enough, he'd have her weight in his arms, her arms round his neck. He kicked free of his stirrups and vaulted off the horse before opening his arms wide.

And there she was, warm and soft, her hair tickling his nose, her bosom pressed against his chest. Two hands on his cheeks, blue eyes he'd gladly have drowned in, and he gripped her gently by the nape, holding her perfectly still as he kissed her.

"More," she murmured when he at last let her go, seemingly oblivious to their little audience, consisting of a gaping Stephen and two of the men-at-arms. Adam smiled, slid his hands down to her waist, tightened his hold, and lifted her in a slow twirl.

He released her, gestured for the men to ride on, and stood for a while, surveying his lands. The fields had already been ploughed, long narrow strips bordered by ditches and stunted shrubs. Some were already planted, or so Kit told him as they walked down the lane together.

"Wheat, barley, peas, and oats," she recited. "And William thinks we should grow more cabbage." She made a face, making him laugh. She went on to tell him there were ten new piglets, and most of the sheep flocks had been brought into the closer pastures for the lambing.

"Good thick fleece on them, this year," she commented, and as she knew far more about sheep than he did, he just nodded. Many of the ewes had already dropped their lambs, but more were to come, and knowing Kit, this would mean she'd spend a lot of time out in the pastures helping John and the shepherds ensure they lost as few as possible.

"And the mares?" he asked. Two precious Spanish horses of ancient Barbary stock—last time he'd seen them, they'd been big with foal.

"One colt, one filly." She grinned. "They both look like their sire—but it is as yet uncertain if they've inherited his disposition."

"Goliath was not born mean," Adam said. "Few animals are."

217

"Do you think men are?" She crouched by a stand of coltsfoot, snapping off the flower heads and most of the leaves.

"No." On the other hand, it was difficult to imagine men like Godfrey of Broseley or Hugh Despenser as young and innocent. "Is someone ailing?" he asked as she stopped to harvest yet another stand of coltsfoot.

"John has a bad cough. He's getting old but refuses to admit it. And he doesn't like it when Mabel fusses over him— or maybe he does but pretends not to."

"A true big sister, isn't she?" If John was old like the hills, then Mabel was older than them, but she bore her three score years easily, for all that she reminded Adam of a barrel, stout and short as she was.

"She is. And speaking of which, here comes another." Kit smiled at their daughter, approaching at a brisk trot. Two braids bounced and hopped, the dark skirts short enough to display bright blue hose and muddy shoes, and in her arms was a bundle of white-and-black fur. "Beware of the cat," Kit told him with a laugh. "Flea has appointed himself Meg's protector." She took hold of Raven's reins just below the bridle ring. "I'll take him to the stable."

It was well after nightfall before Kit could claim her husband for herself. Once Meg had been properly greeted, once he'd held both Ned and Harry, he'd done the rounds in the household, spent hours with William reviewing the state of his property, and had then presided over dinner, a loud affair in the main hall that had only ended when the afternoon seeped into dusk.

William had insisted they all attend chapel, but when he suggested that Adam and he repair yet again to review the accounts, Kit put her foot down.

"Not tonight." She held out her hand to Adam. "I have a bath prepared for you." Besides, she wanted to do a thorough inspection, disconcerted by the new scars on his face.

Stephen added the last of the hot water to the tub just as they entered the solar. Steam rose in wisps, filling the room with the scents of lavender and roses. Kit shooed the page out, closed and barred the door, and turned to look at her husband, already disrobing in front of the hearth. She moved towards him, couldn't resist the urge to touch him, to splay her fingers wide as she set her hands to his chest, just over his heart. Beneath her palm, she felt his heartbeat, above her fingers was a new scar, pink and hairless.

"What's this?"

"A lance." He sounded offhand, undoing his braies.

"A lance?"

Adam sighed. "I was jousting against Lord Roger." She listened in silence as he told her about the steel-tipped lance and how he was convinced the intention had been to kill Lord Roger. William had already told her some of it, but clearly Adam had not shared everything with his brother.

"Kill him? By your hand?" She slid an arm up to his shoulder, followed the contours of his muscled arm downwards. "And this?" She set her other hand to his face, tracing the scar along his nose, the other below his ear.

"Same incident." He hooked a finger into her neckline. "Aren't you joining me?"

"It's the small tub."

"We will fit, sweeting." Deft hands on her laces, and soon enough they were in the tub, she enfolded in his arms and legs. She could feel him stirring behind her, his hands sliding up to cup her breasts.

"William said it was a difficult birth."

"It was." Kit's stomach tightened in recollection. She craned her head back to look at him. "But it was worth it." This her third son was an easy child, eating like a horse at regular intervals, in between which he either slept or regarded the world around him with wide-open eyes—grey eyes.

"A beautiful son." He kissed the top of her head. "Thank you."

The warm water was lulling. His hands were soft on her skin, travelling leisurely up and down her arms, over her belly, her breasts. She nestled that much closer, and he groaned, his member thick and hard against the upper slope of her buttocks. He slid his arms round her waist.

"Should we do this?" He cleared his throat. "Do you truly want to, after…"

"Don't you?" She pressed her backside against him. He inhaled – loudly.

"Sweeting, need you ask?" He nipped her nape, one hand sliding in between her thighs. "But I can wait, if you think it better."

"Wait?" Kit laughed softly. "I have been dreaming of you for weeks, Adam." She stood, water sloshing this way and that. "Take me to bed, Husband."

He left wet footprints on the floor as he carried her, damp and giggling, to the bed.

"Such a long time," he groaned as he sank into her. "So many weeks without you."

He was gentle, he was careful, moving with excruciating slowness until Kit began moving with him, her eyes locked onto his as they came and went, came and went. Heat—flowing through her veins, drying up her mouth. His breath in her ear, his hands tight round her wrists, his member buried inside her. Adam gasped, covered her mouth with his, and there was no air, there was only the loud thudding of her pulse, his tongue, his lips, the way he moved inside of her.

Afterwards, he held her close. She nuzzled his neck, inhaling his scent. Damp sheets clung to her skin, making her shiver, and he pulled up bedclothes and blankets as high as they could go, burying them in a cocoon of fabrics.

"It's nice to be home," he told her, snuggling up to her. Just like that, he dropped into sleep. Beside him, she rose on her elbow, tracing the shape of his ear, his nose, his mouth.

"It's nice to have you home," she said, kissing his brow before sliding out of bed without disturbing him. She had a son to feed.

Over the coming days, Adam transformed from courtier and knight—although he protested at the word 'courtier', reminding Kit he was nothing but a glorified man-at-arms—to lord of the manor. His fine tunics and robes were cleaned and folded away, and Stephen was set to go through his various pieces of armour, including the heavy hauberk that had to be sanded, wiped, and then greased with goose fat before being stored together with the collar piece.

Adam, in the meantime, reverted to thick hose and tunics soft with wear and age. He put away his fine boots adorned with red leather and reverted to using an old downtrodden pair, reaching only just above the ankle, and with Meg in tow he spent his days inspecting his beasts, his fields, and his accounts.

"Your own little shadow," Kit teased when Adam yet again came in at nightfall, carrying a half-asleep Meg.

"She and her cat," he replied with a grin, producing Flea from a fold in his tunic.

"She's in love with you," Kit said, placing a bowl of hot broth before him. She relieved him of their daughter, all pink flushed skin and unruly locks of dark hair, and handed her over to Rhosyn. Meg protested sleepily, but Rhosyn's promise of milk and bread had her tightening her arms round Rhosyn's neck.

"Intrigued, rather." Adam sat back, sighing when Kit undid his boot and lifted his damaged foot onto her lap.

"And in love." Kit set her fingers to the tight muscles in his foot. "She and all the rest of our womenfolk."

He chuckled. "Jealous, my lady?"

"Of our daughter? No." She concentrated on his foot. "She has blossomed since you came home, our Meg."

"She reminds me of you." He smiled at her. "It's her eyes, I think."

"And her fondness of horses." Meg was generally to be found in the stables, oddly enough mostly in Goliath's stall. There had been times when Kit had found her fast asleep there, Flea in her arms and Goliath watching over them both.

Adam grunted, no more. Kit eased up on his foot. "Where do you think Godfrey is now?" It caused her considerable disquiet to have Godfrey first come to Tresaints, then approach Adam in York. From what she'd gathered, it had been a strange meeting, Godfrey attempting to threaten Adam into revealing the whereabouts of the former king. Leaving aside the fact that Adam didn't know, this left Kit concerned for various reasons: First of all, how could Godfrey know the former king was still alive? Secondly, what had he threatened Adam with? Her husband was reticent on the matter, which only made Kit all the more curious.

"In hell, preferably." Adam sounded as if he'd swallowed a worm. "But the unfortunate truth is that he's probably in Kent's service—or Lancaster's."

"Do you think he'll come back here?"

"Here?" Adam spooned some more broth into his mouth before replying. "We are too far away from everywhere for him to make a habit of it."

"Not that far away. Worcester is only half a day's ride away."

"With you in the saddle, dear wife—and on a good horse. For those that are not born centaurs, it takes twice as long." He tore off a piece of bread and sopped up the last of the broth. "I'm thinking Tristan and Iseult." He beckoned Mabel over and held out his arms for Harry, settling the swaddled infant in the crook of his arm.

"Tristan?"

"For the foals." He hefted Harry closer. "Such a big, handsome lad," he crooned.

"Ah." She recognised a distraction when she saw it but was happy enough to go along with it. After all, the thought of the foals did not have her hands itching, while thinking of Broseley most certainly did.

Some days into April, Adam suggested Kit accompany him to Worcester. As Harry was no longer nursing at her breasts— the wet nurse had been installed since a week or so—she readily agreed. There was business to conclude with some of the wool merchants, and this close to Easter there'd be a busy market, offering everything from exotic spices to fine leather goods.

To Meg's delight, Adam insisted she should come along despite Kit's halfhearted protests. When he also chose to set his daughter in front of him on Raven, Meg was struck speechless, remaining mute for about an hour before she reverted to her normal prattling, a monologue mostly directed at Raven.

"I thought you'd be gone by now," Kit said, eyes stuck on a hovering lark.

"So did I." Adam shrugged. "Not that I mind, but I am surprised the king hasn't sent for me."

"Maybe he remains at Woodstock with his bride." Kit smiled. "Time for themselves, without Lord Mortimer and Queen Isabella in attendance." Together, she and Adam had speculated about where Mortimer and his royal mistress might have gone, Kit suggesting they might have felt the need of time on their own, some weeks to expend only on each other. It made her sad, somehow. Whatever other faults Mortimer and Isabella had, Kit did not doubt they loved each other deeply. And yet it was an illicit love—and there was always a price to pay for such sins.

Adam shook his head. "The king must be at Northampton—Queen Isabella will insist. No king, no parliament." He shifted in the saddle. "It will all be about Scotland."

"Peace or war?" Kit asked. He gave her a fleeting smile.

"No war. The queen and Lord Roger want peace, and so it will be peace, no matter what parliament may say. And as to the king, if his lady mother has to sit on him, he'll affix his seal to the treaty."

"He won't like that."

"No. He considers himself rightful king of Scotland—an opinion he shares with Lancaster, if with none of the Scottish nobility. But his mother is right: at present, England does not benefit from war."

When was there ever a benefit from war? Kit pulled her mantle tight, hoping she would never again have to watch her husband ride out to do battle in earnest.

"Every man and his dog seem to be here," Adam grumbled as Worcester's walls rose before them.

"And their women," Kit teased, slowing her horse to a walk. Before her, the Severn glittered in the sun, the banks edged with the bright green of new reeds. Just beyond, the priory church shimmered, its whiteness dazzling. Meg had fallen silent some miles back, staring at all the people and animals that were making their way to the little market town.

"Them too." He smiled at her. "Foolish men, to bring their wives along, eh?"

In response, she sniffed, leading the way across the bridge towards the city gate.

Theirs was a big party, but as Gavin had been sent ahead, they were soon installed in an inn just beside Greyfriars. The horses were stabled, Kit inspected the room she was to share with her husband, Meg, and their closest retainers, and after haranguing the landlady about the state of the sheets, she followed Adam outside.

"If she doesn't change the linen, we're not paying," Kit told Adam, still overheated after her recent discussion. As if she wouldn't know the difference between dirty sheet and old sheets! Pshaw!

"She'll change it." Adam lifted Meg up. "Now let's go and sell our wool."

The wool merchant was Flemish—and, according to Adam, safely in the pocket of the Hanseatic League.

"They all are," Kit said. "But Louis is a fair man." She folded away their copy of the contract, the merchant having offered to buy all their wool at a good price, with delivery to occur some days after St John's Eve.

"Louis? Not Master Befritz?" Adam frowned at the back of the departing merchant.

"I've known him since I was ten," Kit said with a little laugh. Louis Befritz was a handsome man, if somewhat long in the tooth.

"Hmph!" Adam tugged at his grey tunic, still scowling in the direction of the impeccably dressed Master Befritz. "Speaking of Louis, did you know Louis de Valois is dead?"

"He is?" Kit came to a halt. She'd heard about the French king, but the young, vivacious count? "How?"

"I don't know. But our king was very saddened by the news." Adam took a firm grip of Meg, at present squirming like an eel in his arms. "Either you sit still or I'll have you back in the inn with Egard."

"Egard!" Meg shone up, extended her arms in the direction of the large man-at-arms. But she protested when Adam handed her over, seemed about to cry until Egard distracted her by pointing at a goose.

"I liked him." Kit crossed herself, sending up a hasty prayer for Count Louis' soul. "No matter that he was too fond of wine and wenches."

"Aye, he was a good lad—and the only Valois our Ned cared about." Adam's face tightened. "With him gone, why should he not pursue his claim to the French crown?"

"The French crown?" Kit slipped her arm round his. "The French don't want an English king."

"Neither do the Scots, sweeting. But this young king of ours has an eye on both those realms."

At the market, they went their different ways. Adam and Egard made for the stalls selling weaponry. Kit insisted on looking at the fabrics, a sulking Gavin in tow.

"Some of it is for you," she reminded the squire, running a careful hand over some nicely dyed worsted. "You need a new tunic, don't you?"

"Aye, my lady," Gavin replied, eyes on the pretty girl who was selling ribbons and buttons some stalls away.

Kit had concluded most of her shopping and was just about to return to the inn when she got the distinct impression that someone was watching her. She turned, scanning the crowds among the stalls. Nothing. A flurry of movement to her right—an indistinct impression of someone large and in a cloak ducking out of sight—and Kit's eyes alighted on a boy. Small and scruffy, standing very much in the shade, all she could properly see was his hair. Thick, fair hair that reminded her of Adam's thatch.

Her windpipe clogged. Tom? No, of course not Tom! But maybe…She took a hesitant step towards him. The boy disappeared like a greased pig down the alley.

"My lady?" Gavin stood in front of her. "Is everything all right?"

Kit blinked, looked again in the direction of where the boy had been. She cleared her throat. "Of course. I just thought I saw—"

"What, my lady?"

"Nothing." She patted his arm. "Just fancies."

She didn't tell Adam about the lad. It would serve for nothing. Adam was adamant Tom was dead, and for the most

225

part, so was she. But for the rest of their short stay in Worcester, she kept on looking for that head of bright hair.

She saw him again just as they were leaving. Adam was on Raven, some yards ahead of her, and from behind the inn's privy, the boy stepped forth, eyes glued to Adam's back. An instant, no more, a shock of fair hair, a man gruffly calling the boy back, and just like that he was gone. Not Tom, she told herself sternly. Just a dirty little lad with hair as fair as that of her son.

Chapter 23

It was mid-May by the time a messenger came riding down their lane. A short note, in which the king berated Adam for not having returned as requested to Northampton, and demanding that Sir Adam and his wife make for Ludlow, there to rejoin the royal household in the beginning of June.

"Ludlow? The king and Queen Isabella are going to Ludlow?" Kit wasn't sure whether to laugh or cry.

"So it seems, and our presence is requested." Adam sighed and folded the note together.

"But what about Lady Joan? Will she be there?"

"She lives there. This promises to be interesting, at any rate." But he looked glum. Kit sat down beside him.

"Is he displeased?"

"The king? Aye, I'd say so." Adam pursed his lips. "But I never had a message, did I?"

"No. You think someone intercepted it?"

"I think there are those in the king's presence that do not mind my absence." Adam shrugged, going on to read the much longer missive from Richard.

"Parliament was a disaster," he summarised afterwards. "Lancaster and Mortimer at each other's throats, this matter with Scotland…" He sighed. "But now it seems there is a treaty with the Scots, duly signed and sealed by the king."

"And are they still at Northampton?" Kit asked.

"They're on their way to Hereford. Two Mortimer daughters to wed two future earls—an occasion for Lord Roger to entertain the king in style, complete with several days of jousting. Richard is looking forward to it, he says."

"Oh." Somehow, it made Kit feel belittled. Her brother would be there, but she would not.

"Did you expect to be?" Adam asked when she shared this with him. "I am but a minor knight."

"But a knight that has been unfailingly loyal to Mortimer for years—and now you serve the king as diligently."

"Sweeting, in the grander scheme of things, we are unimportant. Not, necessarily, a bad thing." He made a sweeping motion with his hand, encompassing the manor house, the chapel, the bailey, the orchard, and the garden in which they were sitting, surrounded by droning bees and fragrant herbs. "This is what I want: a life here, with you. I have no need of the court—I didn't think you did either."

"I don't. But it feels unfair, somehow."

Adam chuckled. "Life is unfair. What are we to do about it?" He lay down on the bench, his head in her lap. "A week. Then we have to leave." He lifted his hand, fingers grazing the swell of her breast. "Will you mind leaving the children behind?"

"No choice, is there? Besides, it is either them or you," she replied. "And I don't like it when you and I are apart."

In response, she got one of those heart-stopping smiles that only Adam could give her, a soft curving of the mouth, no more, his eyes like silver in the sunlight.

Ludlow had been enlarged. Not quite a year since Adam had seen it last, and somehow the castle had swelled, the hall now flanked by elegant solars on both sides. The kitchen had been expanded, and even the chapel of St Mary Magdalene had been recently whitewashed. A veritable army of servants were polishing and sweeping, rushing back and forth with featherbeds and blankets, barrels and baskets. In the midst of all this chaos stood Lady Joan, as unruffled and calm as ever.

Or not so unruffled, Adam amended when he approached her. His favourite lady—bar his wife—had a strained set to her mouth, narrow hands picking continuously at her beautifully tooled belt. Adam swept her a low bow before turning round to help Kit down.

"How can she stand it?" Kit asked in an undertone. "All these preparations to welcome the woman everyone knows is bedding her husband. He's even built a new solar to house Queen Isabella!"

"What choice does she have?"

"She could have left!" Kit shook out her skirts.

"Too much pride—besides, it is her home." Adam released his wife to go and greet Lady Joan while he busied himself with their horses.

It was, said Lady Joan, fortunate that they arrived before the royal party. "For all Lord Mortimer's building efforts, space will be an issue. I have, however, arranged a room for you in the new buildings." She gestured in the direction of the timbered houses that hugged the northern curtain wall. "Once you've installed yourself, meet me in the hall. There is still plenty to do."

The room smelled of newly sanded wood and contained one stool and two small pallets. If Adam spread his arms, he touched both walls, but the space was clean and had a window, covered by a heavy curtain that left the room in dusk.

"Well," said Mabel, studying the cramped space, "I shall find myself a bed in the hall, I think."

"Aye, you're not sleeping here." Adam gestured for Gavin to set down the chest. "Neither are you, lad."

"No, m'lord." Gavin grinned. "More fun in the hall."

"Stay away from the wenches," Adam warned. "Next time I find you bedding one, I'll have you dragged before a priest to wed her."

A bright red Gavin scurried away with Mabel following at a more sedate pace.

"Rhosyn didn't want him," Kit reminded Adam. No, Rhosyn had her eyes set on one of John's grandsons, which was why she was reluctant to leave Tresaints – especially since Mall's comely niece had joined the household.

"Had there been a child, I'd not have given her a choice," Adam said, already propelling her towards the stairs. "Lady Joan awaits us."

The hall had been transformed, starting with the broad steps that led up to it. Gone was the worn grey stone Adam recalled from before, replaced by smooth treads that gleamed white in the sunlight. Adam came to a halt in the doorway and gawked. He'd never seen anything like it before, a gigantic white arras tapestry in multiple sections covering the wall behind the dais.

"Butterflies!" Kit exclaimed in a hushed tone. Aye, Adam had to smile. Shimmering butterflies of all sizes, all colours, thronged the tapestry.

"Beautiful, are they not?" Lady Joan asked, coming to stand beside them.

"Very," Adam agreed. And ostentatious, he added silently, taking in silverware that adorned the high table, the statues that lined the walls. Dragons, unicorns, wolves and lions – a true bestiary, the various creatures painted and adorned with gold and red.

The three windows that gave on the bailey had recently been glazed, a border of Mortimer azure and or glass painting the floor with splashes of bright blue and yellow light. The central hearth was heaped with logs, the rushmats that adorned the floor were new, and every chair around the high table was adorned with an embroidered cushion.

"The king will stay in the new chambers," Lady Joan told them, pointing at a door in the far wall. "I myself will stay in my old rooms."

No mention of Queen Isabella, Adam noted—or Lord Roger.

The royal visitors arrived some hours before sunset. Horses, carts, and litters soon thronged Ludlow's wards, people alighting to stretch and look about before proceeding through the inner gatehouse to the bailey within and the hall. The king entered first, holding his wife by the hand, and Lady Joan sank into a deep reverence, her entire household following suit.

With no more than a churlish grunt, the king sank down to sit in his appointed chair, his face clouding as he took in the grandeur of his surroundings. Queen Philippa settled herself beside him, all sunny smiles and soft laughs. She said something to the king, and his mouth twitched. She leaned even closer and whispered in his ear, and he grinned, his dark mood dispelled.

There was no opportunity for Adam to approach his lord. From the moment the king had sat down, it was one endless progression of dishes and wines, the king surrounded by the accompanying barons and their wives. Not all wives. Lady Joan had retired to sit somewhat to the side. Not all barons. Lord Roger was stuck in the no-man's-land between his silent wife and his brightly dressed guests, as if uncertain just how to handle the situation.

"Poor man," Kit murmured with little true sympathy in her voice. She nodded discreetly in the direction of Queen Isabella. "And she is not making things easier for him, is she?"

Resplendent in green silk, the fitted cut of her surcoat and kirtle displaying her elegant figure, Queen Isabella dominated the room. Her uncovered hair had been dressed with jewels, her lips so darkly red Adam suspected she had painted them.

"Of course she has," Kit told him drily when he said as much.

In contrast, Lady Joan was in the soft colours she had always favoured, various shades of cream and the palest of greens. Her veil had been elegantly draped to frame her face, but there was no paint, no jewels—nothing but that pleasing aroma of calendula and lavender balm that always accompanied her.

The meal ended, Lord Roger invited the king to inspect his mews, and half the hall emptied in their wake.

"I'd best greet my little mistress," Kit said, standing up fluidly. She brushed Adam's hair off his forehead. "And you have to present yourself to the king."

Adam grunted, finished the last of his wine, and stood up with a sigh. He'd seen Will Montagu and Stafford at dinner, near on glued to the king, and he suspected they'd resent his return—as would Robert de Langon, who'd had the honour to stand behind the king throughout the meal.

He caught up with the royal party just as they were entering the kennels. Adam smiled a greeting at Earl Thomas, who smiled back before returning to his conversation with Mortimer. Lord Roger's hunting dogs stood on their hind legs and barked excitedly at Lancelot, who did not as much as glance at them. Further on, two old wolfhounds were standing silent in their pen, and the king stopped to scratch one of them behind its ears, talking casually with Montagu and de Langon. He caught sight of Adam and beckoned him forward.

"Where have you been?" he demanded, waving Adam up from his deep bow. "I requested your return well over a month ago."

"That message never reached me, my lord," Adam replied, noting how de Langon hastily averted his face.

"It didn't?" King Edward scowled. "Are you saying someone intercepted it?"

"Or it was lost." Adam shrugged. "One message among the many you send, my lord. Not so strange, is it?"

"Hmm." The king studied de Langon, who was still sunk in contemplation of his feet. He glanced at Adam, at de Langon, back at Adam. "I'd be most displeased were I to know someone intentionally tampered with my orders."

De Langon's ears went bright red.

"Most displeased," the king repeated, and his voice was heavy with censure. De Langon shuffled on his feet. The king whirled. "Your birds, Lord Mortimer, best see them while there is still some daylight left." When de Langon made as if to follow, the king shook his head. "Not you, Robert. You can oversee the preparation of my chambers." Edward walked on, deep in discussion with Lord Roger. De Langon scowled.

"Tut, tut." Montagu snickered, elbowing Adam. "Dismissed as if he were a lowly squire. De Langon won't like that."

"Not my doing." But Montagu was right: Robert de Langon threw Adam a look laced with venom before he slouched off.

The early June evening was too fine to spend indoors, so after the mews Mortimer suggested they take a walk along the walls. To the west, a faint line of light lingered, while above the summer skies were draped in wisps of sheerest cloud. King Edward leaned against the parapet and craned his head back, studying the faintly glimmering stars.

"A mess," he said.

"My lord?" Adam moved closer, not entirely sure who the king was talking to. Mortimer and Montagu were well ahead, strolling side by side along the wall walk while Lord Roger was demonstrating the finer points of Ludlow's defences. Thomas was some yards away, and Sir Henry Beaumont was standing just beside the king. Adam gave the king's former guardian a wide smile. It was good to see him, recovered from his recent ailment.

"You heard." The king turned his way. "That parliament in Northampton was a mess. My lady mother and Mortimer arguing for that accursed treaty with the Scots, Lancaster holding out, insisting the proposed treaty was not to his liking…" He laughed, mouth twisting into a grimace. "It is not to my liking either, and yet there I was, obliged to sign it." Edward shook himself. "So now our little Joan will be sent off to wed the future Scottish king."

"Surely not yet, my lord. She's but a child of five," Sir Henry protested.

"Surely yes," Thomas drawled, having joined them. "Little Joan Makepeace has a role to fulfil."

Edward glared at his uncle. "Don't call her that!" He cleared his throat. "The wedding will take place at Berwick in a month. They'll turn her over to be raised by those…those… flea-bitten and complacent curs!" He fisted his hand. "But one day, I'll go north to teach those Scots a lesson. One day, I'll bring Joan home, and Scotland will bend before me—or break. They will bend to me. Me. Not Mortimer." He banged his hand against the stonework, cursed, and ended up sucking his little finger.

Adam shared a quick look with Thomas. This treaty with Scotland was yet another black mark against Queen Isabella and Lord Roger, the king angered at having been forced to sign a treaty he did not want. For now, Queen Isabella could bend her son to her will, but God alone knew what would happen once this caged falcon of a king found his wings. Because one day he would—men like Montagu and Stafford, like his royal uncles, like Adam himself, would not allow their lord to remain fettered forever to his mother's side.

"She is as sweet as I remember her." Kit was already undressed, her hair brushed to a deep shine.

"Sweetness is always a good quality in a wife." Adam dismissed Gavin and Mabel, bidding them both a good night.

"As is astuteness," Kit countered. "She is no fool, this young queen of ours. Behind those wide and innocent eyes ticks an inquisitive mind."

"Yet another good quality—if it is used to her husband's benefit." Adam discarded tunic and shirt to land in a heap on the floor.

"Oh, I think she is quite besotted with her young king." Kit retrieved his clothes, shook them, and hung them from the set of pegs. "He not only has a wife, he has an ally—someone he can talk to about everything."

"And do you think he does?" He hung up his hose and braies.

"I think Queen Philippa is a good listener. Such people always inspire confidences." She settled herself on the narrower of the pallets, plumping up the sorry thing that went for a pillow.

"What are you doing over there?" Adam asked. "I want you close, sweeting."

"We won't fit," she protested as he scooped her up and deposited her on his pallet.

"Aye, we will."

"And it will be too hot."

"Shush, Wife." He pulled off her chemise, leaving her entirely naked. She giggled when he tickled her flank.

Aye, the pallet was narrow, but soon enough they were moulded together, him on his back, her on her side, her head pillowed on his shoulder. He'd left the window uncovered, the summer night beyond alive with the rustling of the wind. No moon, only a twinkling canopy of stars. Beside him, she raised her head and kissed his collarbone.

Her hand slid down his front, cupped his balls, fondled his standing cock. Soft lips on his jawline, the fall of her unbound hair caressing his chest.

"My Kit," he whispered.

"Yours." Her inhalation tickled him, a wet mouth nibbling at his earlobe. From his ear, across his cheek to his mouth, and he cupped her head, holding her still as they kissed and kissed, soft little things at first, but soon enough she was moaning his name, her mouth demanding and hot. Adam took his time, his tongue tracing the outline of her lips, exploring the welcoming warmth of her mouth, and in his arms she undulated, sinuous strength held captive by his arm round her waist.

His hands slid over the curve of her buttocks, the graceful shape of her back. Skin as soft as silk, warm beneath his fingers. The swell of her hips, the muscles in her thighs as she settled herself astride him, and his hands slid up to her waist, lifting her slightly to allow him entrance.

"Don't move," he said once he was fully inside. He tensed his buttocks, and she tightened around him in response. "I could stay like this all night," he told her, one hand caressing her breast. "Buried inside of you."

In response, she began to move, back and forth. With her head thrown back, her mouth open, she looked the picture of carnal desire, and he sat up abruptly, causing the pallet to creak and shift in protest beneath them.

His change of position pushed him even deeper inside of her. His cock was on fire, encased in her warmth. He gripped her by the waist, urged her to move faster, harder.

"Look at me," he gasped, and when she did, he locked eyes with her. "At me, sweeting, at me, at me, at me," he said, in time with his thrusts, her thrusts. Flesh slapped against flesh. She had him by the shoulders, eyes impossibly wide, impossibly dark, when, with a guttural sound, she found her release, shaking like an aspen leaf in his arms. Moments later, he followed, hips jerking as he poured his seed into her.

They sank down, still joined, to lie on their pallet. She nestled into him, her mouth wet and warm against his neck, where his pulse still leapt and pounded. He managed to find a sheet, pulled it up around them both, but when she made as if to move, he shook his head.

"No." He tightened his hold on her. "I want you here, like this."

"All night?" She laughed, her fingers threading through his hair.

"Aye." Adam smiled when she relaxed against him. "Best way to sleep on a narrow pallet, don't you think?"

Chapter 24

Kit woke feeling sticky, sweaty, and somewhat sore. Two nights sharing a pallet, of lovemaking and sleeping close together. Now Adam was fast asleep, sprawled on his back, and his only reaction when Kit slid out of his embrace was a soft grunt.

It was very early, the pale light of dawn washing everything in various hues of grey—well, not her husband, whose skin glowed in the returning light. Kit stroked him over his face and was rewarded by a flicker of a smile. She rose, stretching like a cat, and padded over to the chamber pot.

Some while later and Kit was washed and dressed. She slipped out of the room, one hand on the wall of the darkened passage outside as she made for the stairwell.

The kitchens were already busy. Freshly baked bread lay on one of the large tables, and one of the cooks cut her a slice before shooing her out of the way. So instead, Kit wandered outside, passed through the inner gatehouse, and made for Lady Joan's garden, situated in the outer bailey. Heavy dew had the grass glittering. It also soaked through Kit's thin soles, but she didn't mind—the day promised to be warm and sunny.

Other than a neat herbal garden and some large rosebushes, the garden also had three trees—a linden tree Lady Joan had told her had been planted on the day of her wedding, and two apple trees planted by her grandfather. Beneath the apple trees was a little bench, and it was for this Kit was making when someone else entered the garden, light feet dancing across the gravel paths that bordered the flowerbeds.

"Lady Kit," Queen Philippa said, hastening towards her. "You couldn't sleep either?"

"Too light, my lady." Kit made a little reverence, and Philippa blushed.

"No, no, none of that, Lady Kit." She had a pleasant voice—dark and soft, further enhanced by her quaint Flemish accent.

All of her was pleasant; this little queen of theirs was no great beauty—except for her eyes, almond-shaped and the colour of ripe hazelnuts and fringed with the longest lashes Kit had ever seen. But in her presence, dogs slept and people relaxed, and as to the young king, he would happily spend entire days sprawled at her feet, talking of this and that while she listened and commented.

"You're my queen," Kit said. "I must greet you as befits your station."

Philippa made a sound that conveyed just how uninteresting she found that aspect of things. Kit smiled to herself; it was easy to disparage what you took for granted.

"We're leaving today, and thank the Lord for that—these last few days have been quite a strain." Philippa grinned. "Especially for Lord Mortimer."

Kit chuckled. With each passing hour, Mortimer had grown tenser, and she and Adam had spent quite some time attempting to work out where he had spent the last two nights. Not, Adam assured her, with Isabella—the king's mother had but one room at her disposal, and unless Lord Roger was prepared to clamber up the outside wall, he'd have to pass through the king's room to reach it.

"Lady Joan's revenge," Adam had said with a crooked smile.

Neither was Mortimer welcome in Lady Joan's solar—and Queen Isabella would have put his eyes out if he'd slept there—which left the old keep, adjacent to the inner gatehouse. Good enough rooms, according to Adam, but nowhere near the opulence of the two solars which now graced Ludlow.

"It must be terrible for her," Queen Philippa caressed the gnarled trunk of one of the trees, eyeing it as if considering whether to climb it. "Imagine having to welcome your husband's mistress to your home."

"She's also the queen," Kit reminded her.

Philippa darted her a look. "I am the queen. She is the dowager queen. Except she doesn't like to be called that, does she? It makes her sound old." Queen Philippa took hold of one of the branches. "She is old."

"Not that old." Kit took a firm hold of Philippa when it seemed she intended to swing herself upwards to sit astride the branch. "No, my lady. Queens do not climb trees." They shared a smile. The first time Kit had seen Philippa, the girl had been up a tree.

"She's older than you." Philippa tilted her head. "But Lady Joan is even older, isn't she?"

"She is." Not that much older, but those years of imprisonment had taken a toll on Lady Joan.

"She is very gracious, Lady Joan." Philippa sat down on the bench. "Gracious but sad." She fiddled with the heavy ring that adorned one of her fingers. "I pray it never happens to me."

"What?"

"To have my husband's mistress under my roof."

"Why would it? Your husband adores you."

Queen Philippa's plump little mouth curved into a wide smile. "Yes, he does. But that may not last. Did not Lord Mortimer once love his wife?"

"Oh, I believe he still does, my lady."

"He loves them both?"

"I think so."

Queen Philippa mulled this over. "Poor him. Poor her."

"Queen Isabella?"

"No." Philippa's voice was quite cool. "Lady Joan. Queen Isabella is verily like a cat. She will always land on her feet."

Clever girl. Kit hid a little smile.

"My lady?" A shrill voice carried over the little garden. Philippa grimaced.

"Must she always yell?"

"She is responsible for your well-being," Kit remonstrated as Mathilde, the queen's former nurse, huffed into view, accompanied by an assortment of younger ladies. Most of them Kit had met over the last two days, but this morning there was a new addition, a little thing whose skirts dragged on the ground. "Who is that, my lady?" she asked in an undertone.

"That?" Queen Philippa's brows rose. "Surely, you know your own sister-in-law."

"As a matter of fact, I do not."

"But she was at Hereford and…" Philippa's voice tailed off. "You weren't at Hereford."

"No, my lady." Kit gave her a fleeting smile. "We were not invited."

Philippa blushed again—a vivid pink. "I didn't know."

"It is as it should be. Adam is but a minor knight—we do not belong among the high and mighty barons." Kit sneaked her unknown sister-in-law a look. Neither, she thought, did the daughter of a wool merchant, but she felt immediately ashamed for thinking thus.

Maud de Monmouth reminded Kit of a mouse. Inquisitive brown eyes, a twitching little nose, and a wide smile in which two overlarge front teeth drew the eye. But she greeted Kit with enthusiasm, expressing how happy she was to at last meet the sister Richard spoke so much about. She was with child, an obvious bulge contrasting with her fine-boned build, and she confided that she hoped this too would be a son—as fine and healthy as her little Roger.

On the subject of her husband, Maud grew tedious, making Kit grin when Maud insisted Richard was the finest knight in all Christendom. It seemed Richard had done well at the jousts in Hereford—until he'd been unhorsed by Norfolk. All of Maud shivered with delight as she went on to describe just how handsome Earl Thomas was.

"I know," Kit interrupted her. "The earl and I have known each other many years."

"Oh." Maud looked put out. After a deep breath, she went on to inform Kit she now had a little niece as well, Alicia having been brought to bed of a daughter just before Whitsun. On and on, Maud talked, so Kit was more than relieved when Thomas made his way towards them. She had as yet not done more than greet him at a distance, Thomas having been at his nephew's side throughout the stay at Ludlow.

"Lady Kit!" Thomas bowed. "I trust you are well?" He nodded, no more, at Maud, who sent Kit a scathing look before moving away.

"I heard you distinguished yourself at the tournament, my lord." Kit grinned at the earl.

"Oh, I did, despite not having your colours on my lance." He winked at her. "Truth be told, I survived that ordeal through experience alone. Such sport is best left to hot-blooded youths."

"Like our king."

"Yes, like Ned. He does Adam proud, our young liege. Give him some years and he will be impossible to best." He laughed. "Every time he spurred his mount forward, our little queen closed her eyes and prayed."

"They are well-suited, are they not?"

"Yes." The earl smiled. "I foresee a long and happy marriage."

Kit laughed. "A seer, my lord?"

"No. But Philippa is in love and wise beyond her years, and Ned is besotted. Good foundations to build on." He straightened up. "I shall be leaving today—I am needed at home. You, on the other hand, are bound for Worcester— by way of one of the king's manors. There is a particularly fine bull he wants to inspect." He grinned. "Maybe he needs inspiration."

"My lord!" Kit hissed, looking about. "And she is too young to carry a child—just fourteen."

"For now." Thomas nodded his head in the direction of King Edward, standing very close to his wife. "But soon enough, she'll give him a son—and a reason to challenge those who rule in his stead."

Kit's eyes flew to Mortimer, halfway up the stairs that led to his hall.

"Like him," Thomas agreed. "And the queen mother." Someone called for him, and the earl turned. "Ah, my brother." He bowed. "I hope to see you soon, Lady Kit."

Kit nodded, no more, watching Mortimer—and the man beside him, her Adam.

Adam had woken to an empty bed and the presence of Mabel, already busy with the packing. The old woman looked at the other pallet—so evidently unslept in—and made a rather lewd joke about stallions and mares that had her cackling and Adam barking that he preferred getting dressed without an audience.

"I've seen naked men before, m'lord," Mabel had replied. "Many, many times, in fact."

"Out!"

She'd hustled outside, returning the moment he had his shirt on, which had him suspecting she'd been gawking at him on the sly. Mabel winked and went back to the packing. Adam pulled on tunic and boots and left, buckling his belt as he went. He retrieved his dagger and stuck it into his belt and went in search of his wife—and food.

No Kit, but instead he ran into Lord Roger, dark eyes shadowed after days of constantly being on his guard. Having his two women under the same roof was apparently worse than facing the hounds from hell.

"Adam!" Lord Roger brightened. "Ready to go?"

"Aye, my lord." He smiled at Lord Roger's sons—all four of them, for once. "I hear congratulations are in order, Sir Edmund," Adam added, and Edmund straightened up, proud as a peacock now that his wife was with child.

"A grandson, one hopes." Lord Roger turned to his sons. "We leave in an hour—best ensure you're ready."

"I'm not leaving," Edmund told him. "I'm staying with Mother." He gave his father a cool look. "I think we all are." With that, he bowed and excused himself, his younger brothers at his heels.

"Damnation," Lord Roger muttered once his sons were gone. "They're my sons too—and all I do, all I work for, will one day end up in Edmund's hands." He led the way up the stairs to the hall, gestured for Adam to sit, and sat down in one of the ornate armchairs. A snap of his fingers and a page appeared, a brimming goblet in his hands.

"Aye." Physically, Edmund was very much his father's son: same dark eyes, same dark hair, same innate grace. He did not, however, share his father's temperament, being of a cautious disposition—or maybe this was a consequence of having spent too many years as the king's prisoner.

"Geoffrey mostly skulks in France, young John rides from joust to joust, Roger regards me as something the cat dragged in, and Edmund avoids me, as polite and distant as he would be with a stranger." Lord Roger studied his cup. "I know they suffered, locked away for years. But that was not my fault—that was Despenser's doing!"

"That's not why they avoid you, my lord." Adam glanced at the far door, the one that led to the new solar that housed Lord Roger's royal mistress. "They know who to blame for their imprisonment—just as they know who to blame for their lady mother's present distress."

"God's blood!" Lord Roger sent the cup sailing. "You go straight for the kill, don't you?"

"Would you have me speak anything else but the truth, my lord?"

Lord Roger glared at him. "No," he said after a couple of heartbeats. He slumped in his chair. "I never meant to hurt Joanie."

"She's your wife, my lord. Your loyal wife, who has suffered as much—if not more—as you on your behalf. She deserves to be treated as a wife."

"And you think I don't know that?" Lord Roger laughed—a jarring sound. "I care for my wife. I wish her a good life, years of contentment. But..." He stopped, pinching his full lips together.

"Yes?"

"It is my lady queen who holds my heart." He gave Adam a rueful look. "A man past forty, speaking follies like that—but it is the truth." He rubbed at one of his rings. "I can no more leave Isabella than I can chop off my own leg." He called for more wine, insisted Adam have some as well, and sat staring into the empty hearth.

The silence was only broken when Lady Joan entered, accompanied by her daughters and her few ladies.

"Roger?" She squinted. "Why are you still here? The king has just set off."

"I dare say he can ride six miles on his own," Lord Roger retorted, gulping down his wine.

"Oh, he can do much more than that." Lady Joan waved her female companions out of the room and came over to join them. "He is, after all, our king." She sat down. "Our king,

Roger. The man you will have to learn to obey rather than lead."

"Man?" Lord Roger laughed. "He's an untried lad." He offered Lady Joan his goblet.

"For now." Lady Joan took a careful sip before setting down the cup. "But what happens in three years? In five?" She leaned forward, brushing at Lord Roger's dark hair. "What then, Roger? Have you considered that?"

Lord Roger jerked his head away. Adam made as if to stand.

"No, you stay," Lady Joan commanded, and Adam sank back down. "Tell him," she continued. "Help me explain to this stubborn husband of mine that he who flies too close to the sun inevitably gets his wings singed."

"You're being dramatic," Lord Roger said. "The queen and I—"

"The queen?" Lady Joan glared at him. "You mean the dowager queen, Roger. The has-been queen."

Lord Roger stiffened. "There is nothing has-been about Isabella." He flushed at the look Lady Joan sent him. "I know this is hard for you, Joanie, but—"

"Don't Joanie me! You've lost the right to do so, my lord." She inhaled loudly. "She will lead you to your destruction."

"She loves me," Lord Roger protested.

"As much as she can," Lady Joan replied. At Lord Roger's thunderous expression, she held up her hand. "Of course she loves you," she said in a low voice. "Don't you think I know precisely why she does?"

"God's blood, Joanie," Lord Roger groaned, and just like that he'd dragged Lady Joan into his arms.

Adam was out of his chair. This was not for him to hear—or see. Just as he was at the door, he heard Lady Joan's voice, muffled against her husband's chest

"I fear for you, Roger. One day, that young king of yours will tear himself free of all the chains that hold him—including you."

Chapter 25

Not until they were installed in Worcester—the poor prior of St Mary looking as if the plagues of Egypt had landed on his doorstep—did Kit get an opportunity to corner her brother.

"I have to talk to you." Kit pulled Richard aside. "Is it true you gave Alicia in marriage to the man who demanded the lowest dowry?"

"Not you too." Richard scowled. "I've already had this discussion with Adam. And why should it matter to you? Alicia is no friend of yours."

"She's my sister, whether I like it or not. And it's not right to discard her like a defective toy."

"She is defective. Who would want to marry a would-be poisoner, do you think?"

"We both know that was because of Lady Cecily." Kit grimaced, a sour tang in her mouth at the thought of Richard's mother.

Richard gave her a sullen look. "I did as I thought best. This way, I saved enough on her dowry to be able to set our brother, Roger, up with a manor or two just outside Bordeaux."

"He's still there?" Kit had yet to meet her youngest half-brother.

"Where else? The lad is more French than English after all these years there. With those two manors, he has enough to find a bride."

"But Alicia—"

"Made her bed," Richard interrupted. "She is lucky not to be immured in a convent somewhere."

"Maybe she would have been happier as a nun than as an abused wife!" Kit's temper flared. "He hits her, Richard!"

"And knowing Alicia, she probably deserves it." Richard sounded unperturbed. "A disobedient wife, a scold, a harridan—I dare says she qualifies as all those, and the only way to bring such women to heel is to discipline them."

"And is that what your father did to your mother?"

"My mother?" Richard laughed. "Any man took a strap to her, she'd have disembowelled him. My father never stood up to his wife—never. I, on the other hand, will never allow a woman to rule me like she did him. And Alicia had best learn quickly that her husband is more like me than our father: he will not tolerate a misbehaving wife."

Kit crossed her arms. Richard sighed.

"I did not set out to find her an abusive husband."

"No, you set out to find her the cheapest husband you could find."

Richard tried out a smile. "If so, I'd have married her to one of the cottars. And besides, Alicia agreed to the wedding. Look, I'll talk to Luyten, have him know I'm keeping an eye on him."

"He won't," Adam informed Kit when she shared all this with him. "Lord Roger won't let him do anything that might make Luyten feel he is under surveillance. That despicable, heavy-fisted man is at present too valuable to rattle." He drew Kit close. "I told you all this, didn't I?"

"You did." She sighed. "Poor Alicia."

"Mmm." He pressed his lips to her forehead in a light kiss. "I must go. The king has his heart set on a long session with swords."

Once in the tiltyard, Adam twisted carefully from side to side. Yesterday had left him aching all over, hours of working with maces and shield. On foot, unfortunately, and today would be yet another long day. The king was like an angered bear at present, and the recent meeting with Lancaster had not improved his temper. Firstly, the haughty earl had rebuked the king on the treaty with Scotland, and then he'd refused to discuss the matter of France and their young king's claim on the French crown, insisting that a new parliament be called. It had not helped that Earl Edmund had added his voice to Lancaster's demand.

"I never wanted that damned treaty," Edward snarled, crashing his blunted blade at full force into Adam's. He grunted, took a step back, gripped the heavy blade with both hands, and came at Adam again. "I am dishonoured by it…"

Crash. Swipe. Adam's hands tingled with the force of the blows.

"Made to look a fool." A heavy swing, easily deflected by Adam.

"And Lancaster…" Edward cursed, retreated rapidly when Adam attacked. "God's blood!" He parried, leapt aside, ducked, roared, and charged. No more talk. Blades flashed in the sunlight, sweat ran in rivulets along Adam's spine, the heavy gambeson uncomfortably hot in the summer sun. Tomorrow, he'd have the king doing this in full armour, an additional thirty pounds of chain-mail to consider.

At long last, the king lowered his blade. "Enough." He pulled off his helmet, threw it to one of his squires. Adam followed suit, handing Gavin the sword and gauntlets as well. He walked carefully towards the shade, trying to minimise his limp.

"I need a swim." The king was already on his way towards the river. Adam sighed but fell in behind him. Out of the corner of his eye, he saw the de Bohun twins come running, Stafford and Montague following at a more sedate pace.

"What do you think he's doing on a day like this?" the king asked, waving at his brother, already down by the water.

"My lord?" Adam was confused.

"My father," the king clarified. "Is he lying in the dark, or is he standing on the walls of whatever castle he is being held in, staring out at the distant horizon?"

"Don't you know where he is?" Adam asked, one eye on Prince John wading through the shallows.

"No. Do you?"

Adam shook his head. "But why don't you ask them?"

"Oh, I have. But my lady mother says it fills no purpose for me to know." King Edward kicked at a stone. "And so I am plagued by images of my father, shut out of the light in the deepest, dreariest dungeons my realm can offer."

"Your mother cares too much for him to allow him to be mistreated."

The king scoffed, his throat working. "My mother would be relieved if he should die. As it is, every day she sins with Mortimer." Yet another stone went flying. "Philippa says it is wrong to keep him incarcerated, but…"

Adam came to a halt. "She knows?"

"Of course she knows! She's my wife." The king glared at him. "After all, I suppose you've told Lady Kit."

Adam chose to sidestep. "The more who know, the more dangerous it is."

"And do you truly think it is possible to keep this a secret?" The king undid his shoes and pulled off his hose. "But Philippa won't tell." He smiled. "I trust her—with my life."

"That's good, my lord."

"It is. Philippa and John—those are the only ones I truly trust."

"The only ones? Don't you trust me, my lord?"

Eyes the exact shade of a summer sky met his. "I know you'd die defending me if you had to. But to trust you with my secrets…" He shook his head, and it was as if a jagged hole opened up in Adam's chest. "There is a part of you that will always belong to Mortimer," the king continued. He studied Adam from under his hair. "You love him. I do not."

Adam cleared his throat and looked away, blinking back tears he had no intention of shedding.

"Adam?" The king set a hand on his arm. "You asked."

"Aye, so I did." He bowed. "Excuse me, my lord. I think I need to see to my foot." As he straightened up, he met the king's eyes. "And I would never betray your secrets, my lord. Aye, I love him—I always will—but you forget I love you too."

He shoved one of the de Bohun twins out of the way and strode off.

Kit finished sewing the sleeve into place and took a step back. Pink suited Queen Philippa, adding a warm glow to her skin, a sparkle to her eyes. Her dark hair was collected in an intricate combination of braids and coils, a circlet of gold keeping her veil in place.

"Will Sir Adam be joining us at mass?" the queen asked.

"Us?" Kit had the queen turn around, tweaking the heavy folds into place. "He will be standing with the men, my lady." And right at the back, if she knew her husband. Ever since that conversation by the river, he'd avoided the king, retreating into his formal role of captain of the king's guard. A role that all of a sudden required all of his time, with Adam either at the smithy or seeing to the horses, or yelling his men through one more strenuous exercise after the other.

"He took it badly." The queen bit her lip a couple of times and pinched her cheeks. "Edward never meant to hurt him."

"But he did, my lady." Fool of a lad! He'd insulted Adam by questioning his loyalty—however indirectly.

"Maybe you could…"

"No, my lady. This is between the king and my husband. I will not meddle." She handed the queen her rings, one by one. "Besides, the king does not lack companions." From the cloisters came the sound of many male voices, and among them she could make out the king's, the high voice of Prince John, and the distinctive northern accent of John Neville.

"He misses Adam. Edward needs him almost as much as he needs me. Almost." A fine flush crept up the queen's neck and cheeks, her mouth softening into a smile. Kit pursed her lips. She'd wager the king had finally claimed his marital rights, and to judge from the blushing bride, she was more than content to have him do so.

Philippa lifted her skirts and preceded Kit out of the room. A flurry of skirts, and the queen's ladies arranged themselves around her. A good mix, Kit reflected. Philippa had chosen English women of various ages and allegiances, retaining only two of her Hainault ladies—and the indomitable Mathilde. The rest of the queen's household had been chosen for her by Queen Isabella, but Kit detected Mortimer's influence in that the young queen's chaplain was English, her physician was English, her steward and various clerks were all English. Wise choices, and by now Philippa had won their hearts if not their undivided loyalty.

Kit trailed the queen's party at a distance. Adam's foul mood was nothing compared with the building tension between the king and his mother, setting the entire court a-quiver. Where the king was loud and angry, Queen Isabella was all cool reasonability, which only served to goad her son further, that infamous Angevin temper exploding far too frequently. And with Adam staying well away, there was no one to whom the king could turn but to his inexperienced wife or his boon companions, some of whom were more than eager to foment their young king's rebellious attitude.

The priory's imposing church was thronged with the various members of the court on this Sunday. After the service, clusters of courtiers remained within the shade of the cloisters while others braved the sun. Kit found a secluded spot beside one of the large stone pillars and leaned back against it. In her dark skirts, she blended nicely into the shade—or so she thought until Richard appeared beside her.

"Why is Adam avoiding the king?" Richard asked.

"Ask him."

"Whatever the reason, he'd best heal the rift quickly. Lord Roger needs him there, at the king's side."

Kit straightened up. "Adam does not serve Mortimer. He serves the king—only the king."

"The two are not mutually exclusive."

"They are if the king fears Adam's first loyalty is to Mortimer." She ran a finger along her neckline, attempting to unstick the heavy fabric from her warm and damp skin. Yet another hot day in the making. "Adam made his choice long ago."

"He did?" Richard's voice cooled substantially.

"Adam does not serve two masters. It isn't in him to do so. You know that, Mortimer knows that, but this pigheaded king of ours apparently does not." Kit sighed. "He's too young to be so distrustful."

"Young and hot-tempered," Richard muttered. "These last few days…" He shook his head. "Lancaster is making quite the determined play for power."

"Yes." Kit shook out her skirts, creating a pleasing draught round her legs, just as Adam came round the corner. He gave Richard a curt nod before holding out his hand to Kit.

"Dinner?"

"Must we?" She slid her hand into his. "We could …" Slip down to the river and splash in the shallows, or go elsewhere for food, far from the bustle of court.

"We must," he cut her off.

Adam guided Kit to their table, looking nowhere but straight ahead. A mug or two of ale later, and he began to relax, rubbing distractedly at shoulders gone stiff over the last few days. Kit pressed her thigh against his, and he returned the gesture, glad of her proximity. Of late, the king hovered in his periphery, as if inviting Adam to approach and thereby mend things, but Adam was too hurt to do so. Besides, how could something like this be mended? The king had been honest—painfully so—and how was Adam to serve a master who did not trust him?

Chicken and warm manchet bread, cheese and spinach pies—Adam ate methodically, tasting little. Now and then, he cast a covert glance at the high table, where the king was sitting side by side with his little wife. Lord Roger and Queen Isabella were conducting a conversation over their food; Lancaster was lounging on the other side of the king, talking mainly to Kent, whose fair head nodded up and down in agreement with whatever Lancaster might be saying. And as far as Adam could see, his young lord was saying little, eating even less.

Just as the meal was ending, Queen Isabella rose and glided over to her son. As slender as a sapling, as graceful as a hind, she set a hand on her son's shoulder and said something in a low voice. A heated discussion followed, voices low but intense. King Edward shook his head. Queen Isabella pitched her voice even lower, her fingers sinking into the king's shoulder.

"No!" King Edward leaped out of his chair. "I said no, Maman. I will not witness this sorry event."

Everyone still in the hall turned to face the dais. Earl Edmund smirked and elbowed Lancaster.

"Sorry event? Your sister is marrying the Scottish heir." Isabella sounded fit to burst.

"Not my doing. Those Scottish whoresons should have been brought to heel, not have my sister handed over to them as some sort of trophy."

"We have negotiated a truce," Queen Isabella began but was rudely interrupted by her son.

"You have, Maman, not me. I would never make peace with them! Never."

"Then you are a fool, my lord," Mortimer put in. "This realm of yours needs peace, not war. Your people need time to heal."

Adam nodded in silent agreement, saw several men around him do the same. Edward, however, looked as if he'd drunk vinegar.

"Besides," Mortimer continued, "Scotland will be there ten years from now as well, my liege. Ripe for the taking once Robert Bruce is dead."

"Hmph!" But for the first time in weeks, the young king offered Lord Roger a tentative smile. "We will break them."

"Oh, we most certainly will." Mortimer shifted his shoulders. "And the French." An elegant distraction, Adam conceded, watching with some amusement as his young lord brightened further, all of him quivering at the thought of war. Fool. He knew little of it, had not seen the blood, the mud, the trampled bodies, and the tattered banners. That skirmish last year which had nearly seen their liege abducted had been conveniently forgotten, and in the dark and the chaos, Edward had not seen the broken bodies of all those who died in frantic defence of their king.

"So it is decided, then," Isabella said. "We leave on the morrow."

"Not me." Edward crossed his arms over his chest.

"Don't be such a stubborn fool!" Queen Isabella snapped. "It is an insult to the Scotsmen if you stay away."

"Even better. You can lick their arses, not me."

Some instances of stunned silence. Beside him, Kit went still, not even drawing breath.

"Edward," Isabella began but was interrupted again.

"Not now, Maman." He flung himself away and came marching straight towards Adam. "The yard, de Guirande, now!" He scowled. "Swords, I think."

There was nothing Adam could do but obey.

No matter the sun, Adam insisted on chain-mail, sharply reminding the king who it was that desired this bout. So now they stood facing each other, in gambesons and hauberks, blunted swords at hand. Adam had the sun in his eyes and shifted to the left, the king following.

"Ready?" the king asked, his voice muffled by his helmet.

"Aye." Adam gripped his sword.

Edward charged.

Hours of practice, years of learning to handle his weapons, had left Edward impressively strong. Being half Adam's age, he was also faster and more agile, coming at Adam from the left, from the right—again from the right, swiping at Adam's damaged foot with the flat of his sword. Adam hopped aside, put too much weight on his permanently crushed toes, protesting pain flaring up his calf.

He stumbled, the king came after, his sword whirling back and forth. A blow to his back had him pitching forward, and he only avoided falling flat on his face by putting even more weight on his right foot. Bastard. This was not how they usually fought, the king never pressing the advantage offered by Adam's mutilated foot. Today, apparently, was different. So be it.

Adam blocked and parried, regained his stance, blocked yet another furious attack. Fool. Already, the king was breathing heavily. They circled each other, and the sand beneath their feet swirled and rose like clouds around them. Adam dipped his sword, as if tired. The king howled and lunged. One swift underhand blow and Adam's blade crashed against the king's. Another, and the king reeled. Two hands on the hilt, a swing that started low and ended high. The king parried, fell back. Adam swung again, right, left, up, down, putting every ounce of his strength into each blow.

Edward was on the defensive now. Adam did not let up. Let the pup feel what it was like to be bested in front of others. Let him realise, once and for all, that men like Adam did not grow on trees. With a grunt, he thrust his sword straight at the king's throat. A controlled movement, for sure—Adam had no intention of killing his lord—but the king bleated, leaned back, and with one last swipe Adam unarmed him, the unhanded blade clattering to the ground. Edward overbalanced, sitting down heavily on the ground.

Adam stood over him. "Do you yield, my lord?" he asked, swallowing to clear his mouth of the fine grit that coated it.

"Aye." Edward pulled off his helmet and sent it flying. Adam offered a hand, but the king batted it away, getting to his feet on his own. "I think it best if you retire from court for a while," he said as he limped off. "At present, I fear I may be tempted to tear your head off."

"You could try," Adam muttered to his back.

On the other side of the yard, Robert de Langon was grinning so widely he could have fit a whole chicken into his mouth. Beside him, Will Montagu mimed applause while Ralph Stafford rolled his eyes. Adam didn't care. They could have him, he was done with courts and kings. Or so he tried to tell himself.

Chapter 26

It should have been wonderful to spend the following week at home. Mild summer rains in the night gave way to a sequence of sunny days, long hours of daylight allowing for plenty of time to spend in the garden or the orchard. Unfortunately, Adam was in no mood to sit in the shade of a tree while quoting romances—Kit had to stifle a chuckle; her husband had never spouted love-verse—instead, he retired into heavy silences, more often than not scanning the long lane in hope of seeing a royal messenger.

"Give it time," Kit said. "He insulted you. You humiliated him. For a lad not yet sixteen, that is difficult to get over."

"He started it." Adam tugged at a nearby stand of grass. "I would have let him win—as I always do when he is in such a temper—had he not gone after my foot like that."

Kit lay down in the grass. She was still wet after her recent swim in the pond, and a sudden breeze sent shivers through her. In the distance, she could hear Meg calling for her papa, now echoed by little Ned, a determined little toddler who stuck to his sister like a burr to a donkey.

"Your children want you," she said, knowing full well that would make him smile. "Your wife wants you." She trailed a hand down his naked back. "Always," she added huskily, and he turned to look at her, eyes soft and dark as they studied her body. Such expressive eyes, she thought as he loomed over her, his head blocking out the sun. At present, they were like molten lead; recently, they'd been stormy with anger. Sometimes, they were as cold and brittle as old ice; at others, they glittered like streaks of silver.

"What are you thinking?" His lips pressed a gentle kiss to her cheek just below her old scar.

"I'm thinking of you." She traced his brows.

"Are you?" He nuzzled her. "That is good, Wife." He nipped her ear. "I wouldn't want you thinking of anyone else when you are sprawled naked in the grass."

"I shall keep that in mind, my lord husband." She wound her arms around his neck and gave herself up to kissing him.

They were still kissing when John's creaky voice interrupted them.

"My lord? There's a messenger." He was standing on the other side of the old junipers, as invisible to them as they were to him.

"There is?" Adam went from amorous to alert in a couple of heartbeats. He pulled on his shirt, retrieved his braies, and tucked himself in, winking at Kit as he did so. "Later," he promised, tying his old shoes. And just like that, he was gone, leaving Kit to dress and follow at her own pace.

The bailey was all a-bustle when she made it back. Adam was in boots and tunic, a grim look to his face as he oversaw the saddling of his horses.

"You're leaving?"

"Immediately." Adam took her by the arm and led her aside. "The former king has escaped. We are urged to ride out and search for him." He handed her a note. "Richard awaits us in Worcester, and from there we ride east."

"Richard?" Kit peered at the scrawled signature. Wasn't he on his way to Berwick there to attend Princess Joan's wedding?

"He is acting on orders of the king," Adam explained impatiently. "William! Get moving!" he yelled.

"Is he going too?"

"He is. Only him, Egard, and me, sweeting." He smiled crookedly. "After all, the man we're searching for is supposedly dead."

An hour later, Adam was gone, promising to be back as soon as he could. Kit retired to the chapel, there to pray not only for her husband but also for the former king.

She stayed longer than she'd planned in the cool interior of the chapel, at first praying, but then merely thinking, relishing the quiet that surrounded her here. Summer sun streamed through the glass window behind the altar, patterning the stone tiles with squares of light. Dust motes swirled and danced, and Kit sank into contemplation, her gaze on the central panel of the triptych. The Saviour in all his glory, returned to Earth after his resurrection. His gentle smile always filled her with peace.

The quiet was interrupted by the creaking of the door. Mabel entered, crossed herself, and came over to join Kit. "That man is here again."

"What man?"

"Godfrey of Broseley." Mabel muttered a prayer, invoking the protection of the Lord. "Luckily, John had the gate closed, but he insists on talking to you."

"Me?"

"Aye, you or Sir Adam—and he isn't here, is he?" There was an inquisitive gleam in Mabel's eyes Kit chose to ignore. Instead, she stood.

"I don't like it that he comes here."

"Who would?" Mabel grimaced. "Unfortunate that he didn't die from that wound to his groin."

Kit didn't reply, made uncomfortable by Mabel's blunt reminder of an incident she'd prefer to forget. She flexed her fingers, recalling how the blade of her eating knife had sunk into the soft flesh of Broseley's groin—not that far before she struck bone.

Godfrey of Broseley was sitting astride a large, bony nag. Alone. Kit leaned over the wooden parapet.

"What do you want?"

If he was taken aback by her rudeness, he didn't show it. "I have a child you must see."

"A child?"

"A lad. He's ailing, poor thing. Keeps on calling for his mama."

"And what is that to me?"

"He says his name is Tom. Tom de Guirande. I found him wandering round Worcester."

Mabel hissed. Kit gripped the railing while beneath her feet the world tilted and shook.

"He's dead!" Mabel yelled, her voice shrill. "Our Tom is dead."

Broseley lifted his shoulders. "I wouldn't know one Tom from the other, but this one is definitely alive—for now."

"My lady." Mabel's voice shook, gnarled hands clinging to Kit's sleeve. "He is lying, m'lady."

"Lying," Kit repeated, her tongue woolly. Her Tom, alive? Was he the lad she'd seen back in April? Her belly griped, tremors flying up and down her legs.

"Mama?" Meg tugged at her skirts. "Why is that man here?"

"Because he is a foul liar, a cruel renegade who deserves to be shot through the eye and left to die," Mabel replied.

"Shot through the eye?" Meg stood on tiptoe. "We will shoot you!" she yelled.

"Meg!" Kit pulled her away.

"But Mabel said…"

"No shooting," Kit said firmly, looking at John rather than at Meg. Reluctantly, Mabel's brother lowered the crossbow. She turned to Mabel. "And what if it is Tom?"

"It isn't, m'lady." Tears ran down Mabel's broad cheeks. "How can it be? Do you think I'd have abandoned my little lamb if there was any hope he'd live?" Slowly, she lowered herself to her knees. "Trust me, m'lady. Our Tom lies buried in the graveyard, side by side with his sister."

"But I don't know," Kit groaned. "And what if…" She cleared her throat. "I have to see this child," she whispered to Mabel.

"And why would someone like Godfrey of Broseley go out of his way to bring you news of a child he cares nothing for?" John tapped his nose. "This smells, m'lady. Like a rotting pig."

"A pig? Does he have a dead pig with him?" Meg heaved herself up on her toes again.

John was right. Kit inhaled a couple of times, and the congestion in her chest abated. She stepped forward to the parapet.

"Why?" she demanded.

"Why what?" Broseley shielded his face with his hands and squinted up at her.

"You do not strike me as a man who would take up with an ailing child out of the goodness of your heart."

"I am insulted, my lady." Godfrey bowed. "But you're right, of course. I'd no more burden myself with a brat than with a pockmarked whore. But I was thinking to sell the lad—he's comely enough."

"Bastard!"

Godfrey's face hardened. "One does as one must. Either you buy him or I'll sell him elsewhere."

"How much?"

"M'lady!" Mabel tugged at Kit's sleeve. "No, m'lady, don't." Kit shook herself free and repeated her question.

"Sufficient to see me out of the country. Ten marks?"

Kit blinked. "I don't have that much money, which you well know." But there was the hidden gold in the chapel, and surely the life of a child merited using some of it?

Godfrey pursed his lips. "Five, then."

Kit nodded. Godfrey grinned.

"You bring him here and I'll pay you for him," Kit said. Godfrey's grin disappeared.

"No. You come with me or you'll never see the brat. Besides, he's too sick to be dragged about the countryside." He sneered. "In fact, he might be dying as we speak."

No, no, no! If it was Tom… "Wait there," she told Godfrey, and then she was flying down the ladder, running helter-skelter across the bailey. Into the chapel, a "please let it be him" repeating over and over in her head as she made for the altar.

"M'lady," Mabel appeared in the door, wheezing loudly as she regained her breath. "This is folly, m'lady." She pressed a hand to her ample bosom. "Tom is dead, m'lady, and that infernal creature is but playing with you." She trotted over to where Kit was kneeling, one hand inserted beneath the altar. Kit pressed the lever, and the floor behind the altar fell away, revealing a space large enough to hold a man or two should it be necessary. In one corner were stacked several bags in oiled cloth—the last of the Mortimer treasure entrusted to Kit back in 1322.

Ignoring Mabel, Kit dropped down, opened the closest bag, and started counting.

"M'lady." Mabel sounded close to tears. "Please." She stepped down into the little space. "I don't trust him, m'lady."

"Neither do I." Kit shoved one of the bags in Mabel's direction. "But what choice do I have? If it is Tom…" She bit her lip. "I must, Mabel."

"But Master Tom is dead!"

"He is?" Kit glared at her. "Can you swear on your immortal soul that he is?"

"No." Mabel used her veil to wipe her eyes. "But I know here," she patted herself in the region of her heart, "that he is."

"But I don't, Mabel, and so I must go. But I'll take John with me."

Five marks was a lot of groats and pennies. Fortunately, there'd been some gold florins as well. The two small bags containing well over two hundred coins weighed heavily as Kit carried them to her waiting horse, hidden in the folds of her mantle. The floor behind the altar was once again back in place, the secret hiding space impossible to discover unless one knew just what to look for. Other than Adam and Kit, only William and Mabel did, even if Kit suspected John had a fair idea there was some sort of secret space somewhere in the chapel. The man might be old, but he was no fool, and his dark eyes registered far more than one would think.

"A bodyguard?" Godfrey looked John up and down. "Why, Lady Katherine, you break my heart. Do you truly think me such a rogue?"

"I do." Kit kept her horse at a fair distance from Godfrey. She gestured for him to lead on, falling in behind him with John by her side.

"That way?" Kit held in her horse. A narrow track meandered across the pasture, disappearing towards the southwest and the Malvern Hills proper. "There's nothing that way."

"There is a boy," Godfrey told her. "I hid him in a dilapidated hut." Something akin to a smile flashed over his face. Kit looked at John, who shook his head.

"No." Kit said. "I am beginning to have second thoughts about this venture." She made as if to turn her horse. "You can bring the boy to Tresaints, and if it is Tom, I'll pay you the five marks." Godfrey set spurs to his horse, and the large, ugly brute careened across the path, blocking Kit.

"I think not," he said, a cudgel appearing in his hand. John did not stand a chance. The blow sent him flying from his saddle, and Kit screamed, riding her horse forward.

"You've killed him!"

John was lying in a crumpled heap, blood staining his grey hair, his green cap. His fingers twitched. Alive! But before she could do anything more, Kit was enveloped in darkness. A cloak? "What…" The knock to her head sent her forward. Before she'd regained her wits, she'd been tied up and hauled to lie across Godfrey's horse, the pommel of his saddle chafing at her hip.

It did not take long. Kit estimated it to being at the most an hour's ride before the horse was brought to a halt. Godfrey dropped her off the horse to land on the ground, and she was still struggling to regain her feet when he pulled her upright. The cloak came off, and she blinked at the unfamiliar surroundings.

"Where am I?" she demanded.

"Shut up." He shoved her before him, forcing her into a small cottage. "So, my lady," Godfrey sneered. "Welcome to your new abode."

"My son." She whirled. "You said you had my son."

"Well, I lied." Godfrey gestured at a boy, huddled in a corner. "Not yours, is it?"

As far as she could make out, no, but when she made as if to approach the boy, Godfrey pushed her backwards.

"He never told you, did he?" Godfrey snickered. "And neither did your priest brother-in-law."

"Told me what?" Her eyes darted to the child.

"About my Tom." He laughed. "They didn't fall for it—you did." He grabbed hold of her arm.

"Let me go!"

"That depends on your husband," Godfrey said coldly. "If he delivers what I want, he can have you back." He leered. "Not necessarily unscathed, though. I have a score to settle with you."

Kit could not breathe, an ache spreading across her chest. "Score?"

"You know exactly what I refer to." He tapped the scar that adorned his face. "A gift from your husband." He cupped his privates. "And here, I have the scar you left behind. Bitch!" He backhanded her. Kit's lip burst open.

"So what do you want?" she asked, dabbing at her lip with her sleeve.

"The king."

"He isn't here," Kit said.

"Don't play the fool with me," Godfrey warned, shoving her yet again. "You know exactly what I mean. I want to know where the king is being held. A simple trade: your husband tells me where, he gets you back."

"Being held? Has something happened to our king?"

The slap sent her reeling. "He was deposed!"

"That king is dead," Kit said, steadying herself against the wall.

"Is he? Is that why your lord husband rode off in such haste?" Godfrey laughed. "I wrote the message, you fool."

"I still have no idea what you are talking about," Kit tried. "And even if it were true that the former king is alive, what makes you think Adam would know where he is?"

"You'd best hope he does." Godfrey slid a dirty finger over his throat. "If not..."

Kit lifted her chin. "You do not frighten me."

"Of course I do." He took a step towards her. He gripped her by the chin, raised her face towards the light that fell in from the little window. "He could do better than you," he commented. "A man on the make needs a rich heiress, not a scarred bastard." He made as if to touch Kit on the cheek. She spat at him. "A cat with claws?" He leaned closer. "Won't help you."

He cursed when Kit pulled her knife, was momentarily surprised, stumbled, and Kit rushed for the door. He caught her in the opening, slammed her against the jamb, and wrested the knife from her. "Like that, is it?" There was a stinging sensation down her cheek. "Well, well, look at that, marked with a cross like a repentant heretic."

"Adam will make you pay." She pressed a hand to her bleeding face. He had cut deep—blood was dripping to the floor.

Godfrey laughed. "Make me pay? No, no, you have it all wrong. It is him that must deliver to me—if he ever wants to see you again."

She kicked at him, made yet another rush for the entrance. He grabbed hold of her and pulled her towards the inner door. Every inch of the way, she fought him, but eventually she was shoved inside, landing on her knees. The door slammed shut. A bolt screeched into place, but she threw herself at the door all the same.

"Let me out!" She hammered and kicked, to no avail. On the other side of the door, there was only silence, and Kit renewed her efforts, struck by the terrifying insight that if Godfrey did not return, this is where she would die, locked in a small dark room in which a pile of straw was the only bedding.

This could not be happening. Some hours back, she'd been lying in the grass with her husband, and now she was locked in a hovel. No. Impossible. She closed her eyes, tried to convince herself this was all a dream. But when she opened them again, the floor was still of damp, stamped earth, the walls were dark unyielding stone, and the door remained as shut and bolted.

"Help me!" She kept on yelling until her voice gave out. No one came. No one.

Chapter 27

It was the next day before Godfrey returned. She heard the outer door open, heard him snarl at the boy, and then the door to her prison opened. Godfrey set down a pitcher of water and some bread and gestured for her to eat.

"Adam will come looking," she said, ignoring the bread despite her growling stomach. "And when he finds you, you're dead." She had the satisfaction of seeing something dark flash across Godfrey's face. "He'll make you suffer," she vowed, and Godfrey slapped her. The thin scab on the cut broke open, her swollen cheek throbbing in protest.

"You better hope he does as I tell him," Godfrey snarled. "He'll never find you unless he does—not before you're dead."

Kit shook her head, ignoring just how much it hurt to do so. He'd find her—he had to. She knew she was relatively close to Tresaints, and by now Mabel would have got word to Adam that she was missing. Adam would have all the men out looking, scouring the countryside for her. John. Dear God, let them have found John before it was too late.

"He will come." Yes, of course he would. Any moment now, she'd hear his voice calling her name.

Except that she didn't, and when Godfrey left, he took the bread with him.

When he came back the next day, she threw herself at the bread, which made him laugh. It hurt to chew, her cheek puffy and hot to the touch.

"He can't love you all that much," Godfrey said, settling back against the wall. "Three days, and he has as yet not done as I asked." He snickered. "Maybe he sees this as an opportunity to rid himself of his bastard wife."

"My husband cares for me."

"So you say. And yet here you are, with me, when all he has to do is give me some information for me to return you to him. It's not as if he'll have problems finding a new wife, is it? Him so big and handsome and in high favour with the puppet king."

Like poison his words were, one drop after the other leaving scorch marks on her heart. And once he'd left, she couldn't stop thinking of what he'd said, a small part of her fearing that maybe he was speaking some sort of truth—how else to explain that Adam had as yet not found her? She sat in the dark and cried.

On the fourth day of her captivity, the door crashed open. Godfrey was drunk and angry, cursing Adam to hell for not delivering.

"I'll show him what happens when he tries to trick me," he yelled, crowding Kit back against the wall. He pawed at her clothes, tried to kiss her. She bit him. A knee in her belly had her doubling over, a blow to her back had her tumbling to her knees, and he tore at her clothes, hit her over the head. She kicked him. He twisted her leg until she screamed. When he left, her breasts were bruised and tender, her skirts were torn to rags, and all she had to cover herself with was her ripped chemise. Even worse, the pitcher with water had overturned, spilling the precious liquid to the floor. Kit had no choice but to lap up what she could.

On the fifth day, he entered with a swagger, pushed her against the wall, and fondled her before forcing her hand down to his member. It stiffened and swelled somewhat. He grunted and pushed. His exhalations smelled of onion and sour wine, his breath came in loud gasps, and still he didn't harden.

"Your fault!" A fine spray of spittle covered her face. "You did this to me, and you'd better fix it or I'll kill you."

When she raked her frayed nails over his half-engorged member, he howled. By the time he left, she was a shivering, bruised mess, all of her hurting from his brutal punishment.

On the sixth day, he didn't come, and there was no bread, no new water. Kit threw herself at the door, but the bolt held firm, the boards too stout to give.

On the seventh day, he entered accompanied by the boy, carrying an apple, a pitcher of water, and some more bread. She reached for the apple. Godfrey snatched it out of her hands, biting into it. He kicked the boy out of the way before moving towards her.

"He doesn't care for you," Godfrey sneered, wiping apple juice off his chin. "If he did, he'd have done as I said." He slapped her, hard enough to have her head bounce against the wall. "Might as well have some fun with you, teach you a trick or two."

No, never. She wiped her hands on her shift—she'd been doing so repeatedly since that other day, attempting to rid herself of the sensation of his member in her hand. He laughed when she shoved at him, grinned when she bared her teeth, pressed back against the wall by his weight.

"You'll need them in the stews. Make me quite the little fortune selling you to one of the madams."

She fought him. She scratched and bit, she kicked and screamed, and nothing helped. A knife. It dug into her skin just below her chin, and Kit whimpered and lifted herself up on her toes.

"Be a good girl and do as I say," he told her. "If not..." The tip of the knife pierced her skin. Kit held herself absolutely still. Godfrey relaxed his hold, and she lunged for the blade, hanging on to his arm for dear life. Her chemise was torn off, his knife nicking her skin in the process. She screamed and cursed, was slapped and hit. She raked his face. The responding blow had her sagging, and he laughed, humping her like a dog as she hung helpless in his arms.

"Like it rough, do you?" He threw her to the ground. "I'll show you rough. And when I'm done, you'll never disobey me again." She tried to curl into a ball. He kicked her repeatedly until she did as he said, falling over on her back with her legs splayed. Her eye was swelling shut, there was something awry with her left hand, and pain walked up and down her battered body. She tried to lick her swollen lip. Blood in her mouth. In the corner, the lad cowered into the shadows, hiding his face in his hands.

"Help me," she whispered and Godfrey punched her. He was between her legs, knees spreading her open, fingers fumbling with the fastenings of his braies. Kit groped for something—anything—but the straw was wet and damp, and the broken stool was too far away. He grunted and cursed, spat in his hand, and rubbed himself forcefully. Something touched her hand. The lad placed something in it. A splinter of wood? Kit did not stop to think. With what little strength that remained to her, she rose and thrust her weapon into Godfrey's side.

Godfrey howled, gripped her by the hair, and slammed her head against the floor, hard enough that stars burst through her brain. He stood and staggered over to the door, blood staining the hand he held pressed to his flank. May he die, may he be eternally cursed. May he…It hurt—everywhere. Hurt too much to think, too much to move.

"Bitch!" Godfrey's voice came from a distance. "You'll die for this." Kit heard the door open. It banged close. "Die here," he said, and she heard the bolt shoot into place. Die? Kit smiled. Die.

She came to much later. The room was dark, from the corner came the sound of sniffling, and she sat up carefully, wincing as her body protested. It was cold, she was naked, and what little light there was spilled in from the small aperture just under the eaves. She was violently thirsty and dragged herself towards the little table. The pitcher was half-full, and she drank the lukewarm water in small swallows, enough to lubricate her dry throat.

"Godfrey?" she asked the boy.

"Gone, m'lady." The child shrank against the wall. "I heard him ride off hours ago."

Hours? Kit inspected her head. So many bumps, and when she tried to stand, the room tilted.

"He's locked us in, and he's not coming back, m'lady." The lad's voice broke. "We'll die here, m'lady, and I don't want to die, I want my Mams."

Kit inspected the room. At present, she could not muster the energy to properly absorb what the lad was saying. No, she'd think about that tomorrow. Right now, she needed to rest, to somehow heal herself. Heal? She studied her body. Godfrey's fists and feet had left her a veritable patchwork of bruises, but at least she'd been spared that final humiliation.

"What's your name?" Kit gave the boy a weak smile. "I would like to thank you properly."

The lad hid his face. "Tom."

"Tom?" Kit stared at him and began to laugh—a harsh laughter that tore at the membranes of her throat and made her chest ache. She laughed until she began to cry, and once she did, the tears wouldn't stop coming. All the while, the boy sat beside her, soft cow's eyes riveted on her. At long last, Kit calmed down.

"Sorry," she said. "It's just that my son…"

"I know. Himself told me."

"Ah." She looked at him properly. Other than the fair hair, there were no similarities between this boy and her dead son, starting with the colour of his eyes, large and dark in his pinched, dirty face. "Tom what?"

"Just Tom."

"And your parents?"

"I never knew my father. Mams said he was a good-for-nothing lout with more between his legs than between his ears."

"Oh. And your mother?"

"Mams? She's dead. Himself…" the boy cleared his throat. "He couldn't get it up, and she laughed at him, so he killed her." He drew his finger over his throat. "Like that. I couldn't let him do that to you."

"Thank you." Kit held out her hand. "You saved my life."

The boy gestured at the walls, at the stout door. "Or we die here." He gave her a bleak look. "That door won't budge, m'lady."

Kit licked her lips. Almost no water, no food beyond the crust of bread left on the plate. They'd die in a matter of days—a terrible death. She studied the little aperture just under the eaves. "Would you fit?"

Tom looked up the wall. "Maybe. But how do I get down the other side? I might break my neck."

"Or die in here." Kit sighed. "I don't think there's a choice. I wouldn't fit, and besides…" She gestured at her twisted ankle, at the bruises that blossomed up her leg, across her abdomen. Tom looked away, as if only now seeing she was naked.

"And if I get out, then what?"

"Go for help." Kit licked her lips again, tasting dried blood. "We can't be that far away from my home." She frowned, making an effort to remember. At most an hour's ride. "How long have I been here?"

Tom shrugged. "Seven days?"

Seven days with little food and with almost no water. No wonder standing felt impossible. Kit dragged herself onto her feet, supporting herself against the wall. "I'll lift you."

Tom sucked in his lower lip.

"Either we do it now or we won't have the strength to." Kit tried to look stern. She beckoned him towards her, and after some moments he came. "Tell them you know where Lady Kit is. Tell them…" She smiled. "Tell him I love him," she whispered, more to herself than the boy.

"M'lady?"

"Nothing." What if Godfrey was right? She touched her sore and swollen cheek. What if Adam would not mind if she was gone? No, she couldn't believe that—wouldn't believe that. Adam loved her—of course he did. Had loved her, she amended, yet again touching her face. But now… With a deep breath, she dispelled these thoughts.

It took them four tries before Tom managed to get hold of the little ledge and pull himself into the aperture. Kit collapsed to the ground. Her head throbbed, her vision dominated by black spots and whirling spirals. "Go on."

"But what if…" Tom's voice was muffled by the stone.

"Go!"

Tom's legs disappeared, there was a loud thump, and then there was nothing. "Tom?" No response. "Tom?"

"Tom!" she shrieked. Nothing. Dear God… Kit crawled over to the door and banged on it. "Tom!" She banged and screamed for what seemed like hours. She tore at the wood with her fingers, she wept and cursed. Midway through yet another attempt on the door, she dropped exhausted to the floor. It was no use. Tom must have landed on his head, and she would die, here, in this cold, dark room. She didn't want to die, not like this. She didn't... Adam...Ad...

Chapter 28

"We've looked everywhere," John said wearily, hoisting himself onto his horse. "Everywhere." He sported a huge bandage, but it had been impossible to stop him from riding with them.

"She's here somewhere." Adam felt as tired as John looked. Six days of riding helter-skelter over the surrounding pastures, inspecting every cave, every cottar's cottage on his land. He'd had riders in Worcester and Tewkesbury, he'd sent men off west, north, east, and south, to visit every inn along the way, but nowhere had there been a man of Godfrey's description accompanied by a woman. It was a week since Mabel's message had reached him, and no matter that he went through the motions of searching, he was beginning to fear his Kit was gone—for good.

There'd been one note, demanding to know where the former king was being held. A simple instruction, leave a note between two stones in the greyfriars' church down in Worcester, and Kit would be returned unharmed. He'd left a note—and two guards. The man who'd come to claim it had not been helpful, bleating that he knew nothing about an abducted woman—he'd been paid a groat to collect a message.

He sat up and patted Raven on the neck while urging the stallion south. Today, they'd ride to the farthest pastures, even if neither John nor Adam had any recollection of any functional buildings in the area. Surely, Godfrey would want a roof over his head.

Dawn lit up the landscape, the gorse bushes that dotted the landscape throwing disproportionately large shadows over the narrow path. It was cold enough that Adam's breath plumed, and he pulled his heavy cloak closer round his body. Beside him, John rode in grim silence, crossbow at hand, eyes scanning the horizon.

It was halfway to noon when they came upon the lad. A shadow of a boy, more bones than flesh, with a distinctive thatch of fair hair. Adam's heart lurched. Tom? No, not Tom, but this must be the lad used to entice Kit to set off with Godfrey, and he swayed in the saddle. If only he'd told her about Godfrey's little lure!

The lad raised huge brown eyes and croaked that the lady was hurt—bleeding and bruised, she was—but alive. He wiped his snotty nose with his dirty sleeve, which only resulted in smearing his face.

"Where?" Adam asked, standing in his stirrups. Nothing. The landscape was as barren as he'd expected.

"There." The lad waved vaguely in a southeasterly direction. "There's a copse of trees nearby." He looked away. "I was scared of the dark," he mumbled, "so I didn't get far last night." And he'd suffered a case of the runs, to judge from the brown streaks of dried shit decorating his bare legs.

The little stone dwelling was almost hidden beneath a cloud of brambles.

"What's this?" Adam had never seen the sturdy little house before.

"Last I saw it, this was a ruin," John muttered. "Years ago, there was a holy man living here, but he passed on when I was no more than a runt of five."

Adam was already at the door, lifting the heavy crossbar to the side. Once inside, they were in a dark little space containing no more than a hearth. Yet another door, this one bolted and locked. No sounds, no sign of life, and Adam's heart thundered as he broke the lock, pulled the bolt.

"Sir?" The laddie tugged at his sleeve. "She's naked. The lady has no clothes."

God's blood! Adam shared a look with John. The old man's jaw set, mouth all but disappearing.

"If he's harmed her, I'll kill him with my bare hands," John said.

"No." Adam cleared his throat. "That is my right." When John made as if to undo his cloak, Adam just shook his head. No cloak other than his would wrap his wife.

A heavy stench met him when he finally opened the door. Of human waste, of rotting straw, of blood and sweat and tears.

271

Kit was curled up on her side, her hair a matted mess down her back. A week—seven days which had reduced her to a collection of bruises and gashes, dark smears on her legs and arms. Her skin was hot to the touch, her lips parched and rimmed with blood. She sighed when he covered her with his cloak. One puffy eye opened—a glimmer, no more. The tip of her tongue licked at her swollen lips, and Adam swore that Godfrey would pay tenfold for every gash, every bruise.

Her hand lifted, touched his cheek. "Adam," she said, her voice a cracked, reedy thing. "Adam." With that, she was dragged back under, a heavy, unresponsive weight in his arms. For an instant, he relinquished her into John's arms, leaping astride Raven before reaching down to receive her back in his embrace. That's when he saw her cheek, the half-healed cut oozing pus and blood.

"Curse him," he said hoarsely. "May he rot as he stands and walks, may his limbs bloat and fall off, may he lose his sight and hearing, his every tooth."

"Amen," John responded grimly. "But I'd prefer to do some tearing to him first. Mark him like he's marked our lady."

Several of the men muttered an agreement. Adam set heels to his stallion and rode for home.

"Out!" Adam glared them all out of his solar. On the bed, Kit lay tightly wrapped in his cloak, he'd tracked dirt all over the floor, and before the hearth the large tub had been filled with water, the scents of rosemary and mint tickling his nose. "You too," he said to Mabel, who scowled. He merely tipped his head in the direction of the door.

He washed her. Days of dirt, dried blood—gently, he washed her clean, gritting his teeth at the damage done to his wife. Her nails were shredded, her fingertips torn away in her frantic attack on the door. There were scratches on her thighs, on her buttocks. Purple bruises on her hips, on her arms, her belly, the discolouration on her breasts—he washed and catalogued every one, promising that Godfrey of Broseley would pay for each one.

She woke midway through, but there was no recognition in her eyes, glazed as they were with fever. He kissed her brow and went on with his ministrations, and once he was done, he called for Mabel to help him, sitting beside her as she did what she could to bandage the worse of the cuts. The one on the cheek had to be opened, and Kit gasped and twisted but didn't wake.

"Why?" Mabel sobbed, studying the incision that slashed across her old scar. Like an awry crucifix, Adam reflected, the old, faded scar highlighted by this new cut.

"I don't know." He stroked Kit's face. "Can you stitch it?"

Mabel shook her head. "Too late. But I can make sure it heals." She looked him in the eye. "And you, m'lord, you must make sure he pays."

"He will." Adam set his jaw. "Once I find him, it will give me the greatest pleasure to deprive him of his dignity, slice by slice, before I finally kill him."

"Good." Mabel dabbed honey on Kit's face. "I can sit with her. You look as if you need some rest."

Adam shook his head. He wasn't moving, he told her, not until he knew his wife was healing.

"She already is." Mabel patted his cheek. "You saved her."

"Saved her?" Adam groaned. "I didn't save her. She saved herself, sending Tom off to look for help. All I did was find her, and even worse, this is my fault. I should have killed him."

Much later, Kit stirred. Adam started awake from his doze and hastened over to the bed. She was dreaming, thrashing about. He collected her in his arms and held her until she quieted, and for the coming hour he held her in his embrace. He was half-asleep when she started screaming.

"No, no!" She hit at him, tried to scratch his face. "No, let me go! No!"

"Kit, it is me, Adam."

"Adam!" she shrieked. "Dearest God, Adam help me!" She hit at him again. "Adam!" Her voice rose in terror, and the door banged open.

"M'lord?" Mabel was panting.

"She is dreaming," Adam said, still trying to hold on to Kit.

"Let her go, m'lord." Mabel helped him lay Kit down. The moment she was free of Adam's arms, she relaxed into deep sleep. Adam staggered over to the window. What had the bastard done to her? He gripped at the frame and concentrated on willing away the tears that stung at his eyes.

"Find your bed, m'lord," Mabel said from behind him.

"She didn't know me," he said hollowly. "My wife, thrashing in my arms and begging for me to save her."

"She is delirious, m'lord." She stood beside him, placing a hesitant hand on his shoulder. "She will heal. Give her time."

Mutely, he nodded and made for the door. He had never felt so wretched in his life.

The first thing she registered was that the straw was gone. She was lying in linens, and someone had piled her with blankets. Her bed? She reached for the closest bedpost, her fingers tracing the familiar wood. Her bed…She drifted back into a doze, and there were creatures lurking at the edges, evil things with bright green eyes and sharp, sharp teeth. Kit started awake. There was someone there, in the dark.

"Who's there?" she croaked.

"It's me, sweeting."

Adam. She slumped back on the pillows. And then she remembered what Godfrey had done to her, and she died with shame, hiding herself under the blankets.

"You're safe now," he continued, his voice hoarse.

Safe? She would never be safe again. She squeezed her eyes shut and clenched her jaw. The bed dipped, and his fingers brushed her face. She couldn't move, couldn't breathe. His scent, that familiar mixture of wool and ale, tinged with horses and smoke—it tickled her nose, it filled her lungs, and she should have felt safe, but all she remembered was Godfrey's breath in her face, his hands on her body, and she moaned and curled together like a shrimp.

"Sweeting, it's me," he whispered, his voice breaking.

"Go away," she said. "Please just go away."

He set a hand to her shoulder—such a warm, soft touch, and all of her recoiled.

"Don't touch me!" she shrieked.

274

He inhaled, a loud hiss. She heard him stumble to his feet, grope his way towards the door, and she wanted to yell at him to stay, wanted him to tell her that he wasn't leaving. But instead, she heard the door close. Kit hid her face in the pillow and wept.

Next day, Adam appeared in the solar just after dawn.

"How are you feeling?" he asked, remaining at some distance from the bed. He looked as if he hadn't slept for days, a thick stubble covering his cheeks.

Kit sat up, a slow leveraging of muscles that protested and shrieked. He made no move to help her, eyes as dark as thunderclouds.

"Would you..." He gestured towards the window seat. The cushions were flattened, a blanket lay in a heap on the floor, and belatedly she realised he must have spent most of the night there. He busied himself opening the heavy shutters, and Kit winced and shielded her eyes from the harsh glare of the sun. Adam plumped up the cushions, shook out the blanket and stood there, waiting.

It required substantial effort to get out of bed, stand. Kit steadied herself against the bedpost, would have wanted him to help her but had a vague recollection of screaming at him not to touch her, which presumably was why he kept his hands clasped behind his back.

One step at a time, and at one point she heard him exhale, turning his back on her. His shoulders shook.

"I swear," he said, his voice gravelly with tears, "I will find him, and I will kill him."

At long last, she was sitting at the window. Sun and fresh air played over her face. It was over. The recent nightmare was no more, and she was back home, safe and sound. Alive, she amended, studying her battered hands. Adam settled the blanket around her. She thanked him. He retreated to lean against the wall.

"Why did you go with him?" he blurted.

"How could I not? He said he had Tom," she replied defensively.

"Tom is dead. Dead!" He slammed his hand against the wall. "We've even buried him."

"But we don't know!" she screamed, and he backed away. "I've never seen him dead, never held him in my arms. All I have is William's word that those sad little bones belong to him. And even he doesn't know. No one knows. No one!"

"But to go with Godfrey of Broseley—"

"Well, I didn't know, did I? You never told me he'd tried to trick you with a false Tom, so how was I to know? How, Adam?" It bubbled out of her, the fear, the anger, and she screamed and yelled, repeating over and over that the only reason she'd been foolish enough to ride with Godfrey was because her lord husband had chosen not to tell her the truth.

Adam reeled. "Are you saying this is my fault?"

"Yes!" she shrieked, and her heart broke at the way his face crumpled. "Yes!"

Oh God, she'd never seen him cry before, not like this, but before her eyes her husband melted to the floor, covering his face with his hands. She made as if to stand, ignoring her protesting limbs.

"Adam," she began, but he was on his feet, half running for the door. She should have called him back. She should have told him that she didn't blame him. But she did, and so she sank back down, jumping when the door crashed shut in his wake.

After that, he didn't come back. She saw him through the window, a bowed shape that walked this way and that, sometimes with William, sometimes with Meg. She should talk to him, she knew that, but she was too tired, too angry, and instead she avoided him as he avoided her.

Truth be told, she avoided everyone but her children, evading any attempts to discuss her ordeal. Mabel tried. William tried and was violently rebuffed. And Adam, he didn't even try, hovering like a protective presence round her. Silent and watchful, he kept guard. Every night, she heard him enter the solar. Every night, she pretended to sleep. Every night, he settled himself on the window bench, and only then did she dare to drift off.

Chapter 29

Two weeks after Kit's ordeal, they were summoned to court. The messenger's tabard was too large, he sneezed constantly, and the missive he handed to Adam was uncomfortably sticky. The instructions were crisp, Sir Henry's neat hand informing Adam that he and his wife were expected to attend on their king—immediately.

"I'll go alone," he said with a sigh, regarding her from under his hair. He had sent off a carefully worded message to Thomas some days back, and he supposed the earl had chosen to share the content with the king—why else would he recall him?

"I am summoned too." She returned Harry to his wet nurse, wiped Ned's face clean, and kissed their eldest son's brow. Not their eldest, Adam reminded himself. Their firstborn was dead, buried in their graveyard.

Adam acquiesced. Maybe a long ride would give them opportunity to heal the rift between them, a chasm of unspoken recriminations, of withheld tears, that had them both in a stranglehold. And besides, Kit needed to be up and about, regain her confidence. Not that the court was the best choice of venue to do so, but the king would not be gainsaid, and this matter with Godfrey needed to be addressed.

The weather was pleasant. That, Adam thought some days later, effectively summed up their recent travels. His wife rode a yard or so ahead of him, her back straight, her veil lifting in the breeze. He didn't know what to say to her, so he reduced his communication to the essentials, twisting inside at how hurt she looked. Rage bloomed in his chest when she flinched at the sight of unknown, swarthy men. She'd ridden constantly on her guard, her hand gripping the handle of her little dagger so hard the knuckles whitened, and he had tried to tell her she was safe, that he would never allow anyone to hurt her.

"He did," she'd replied curtly, and he died inside at her tone, at the unspoken accusation that it was all his fault. And, dear God, it was. If he'd told her about Godfrey and Tom, she would never have believed that accursed hound when he dangled the bait of their son, resurrected, in front of her. And if he'd killed him last time they met, then Godfrey would never have touched his wife. And now…

He swallowed down on bile and glanced at his wife. She'd arranged her veil so it covered the angry scar, but he knew it pained her—not only physically. He rode closer. His hand rose of its own accord, wanting to touch her cheek and tell her it didn't matter: he loved her. But he didn't quite dare to, and Kit rode silent and stiff, eyes on anything but him. With a sigh, Adam let his arm fall. This silence was tearing them apart, but God alone knew how to breach it—he didn't.

The king had taken the opportunity offered by his mother's absence in Scotland to visit his uncle Norfolk in Framlingham. They arrived just after vespers, riding along the glittering mere before clip-clopping over the deep, dry moat and under the recently restored gatehouse. No sooner had they dismounted but a page came running, instructing Adam to present himself to his lord. He apologised to Kit before hastening off towards the lord's chambers—rooms turned over to house the king.

Kit watched him go, thinking that he needed a haircut. He looked scruffier than usual—but then he'd done so for weeks, ever since he'd found her. This terrible, terrible silence, it was drowning them, and she had no notion how to break it, what to say.

She followed yet another page to the chamber allotted to them, helped Gavin order their chests and few belongings, and then she just sat there, staring out at the busy, enclosed bailey below.

"My lady?" Gavin appeared at the door. "We are expected in the hall."

Reluctantly, she got to her feet, following him down the steep stairs that led to the bailey. They passed the chapel, cut across the open space, and entered the hall, Gavin setting off at pace to join his fellow squires at one of the more distant tables.

Kit just stood there. The hall was full of people, and for an instant she considered fleeing to the safety of her room. On the dais, the king was already in his chair, Queen Philippa sitting beside him. She scanned the large room for Adam, found him just below the dais, deep in conversation with Sir Henry. As she watched, Sir Henry clapped him on the shoulder and dragged him off to a waiting table. Probably relieved to escape her presence, she thought bitterly, and she wheeled on her toes, making for the door. A hand on her arm, and there was Earl Thomas, as always splendidly—if soberly—attired. Midnight blue suited him, his clothes complemented by the heavy gold collar round his neck, studded with gems.

"Lady Kit, at last. Welcome to Framlingham." He guided her to a table set to the side, helped her sit, and called for wine before sitting down beside her.

"Are you well?" he asked, studying her intently.

"As well as can be expected." She turned her head to the side, a futile attempt to hide her disfigured cheek. Thomas shook his head.

"None of that, Kit. You know I find you attractive," the earl said with a gentle smile. "Now perhaps more than ever." He touched her scar. "But I am not sitting here as your admirer, I am sitting here as your friend." He took her hand. "Have you told anyone what happened?"

Kit shook her head. The one person she wanted to tell—should tell—she had shoved away with her angry recriminations. Her eyes stuck on Adam, who was sitting some distance away, his back to her. He was nursing a goblet of wine, shoulders rounded as if he was carrying the weight of the world on his shoulders.

"He blames himself," she said instead, nodding in the direction of her husband. As did she—however unfairly.

"Of course he does," the earl said. "Your ordeal is his fault, or so he thinks."

"To some extent, it was."

Thomas' brows rose. "Ah. You blame him too."

Kit squirmed under his perceptive eyes. "Yes."

"He didn't tell you about that false Tom because he was trying to protect you," the earl said, and that had shame burning through her. "He didn't want you to go through the heartbreak of having hope rekindled only to have it brutally quashed."

Kit bit her lip, trying to stop it from wobbling. Thomas took her hand. "You're going to have to forgive him, Kit. And soon—for your sake, as much as for his."

She nodded and wiped at her cheeks. "I know."

"But you can start by telling me," Thomas suggested, kneading her hand. He gave her a slight smile. "I am a good listener."

Kit wasn't sure she wanted to. But his eyes were full of concern, his hands were warm and comforting, and she was drowning in these dark recollections. She brushed at her eyes. "I might cry again."

"Women cry all the time in my presence. I have that effect on the ladies."

That made her laugh, albeit shakily. "You must be a dismal seducer."

"I break their hearts. Only one breaks mine." He squeezed her hand. "Will you tell me?"

Kit took a deep breath. She took two. And then, finally, she began to talk of her experiences at the hands of that damned Godfrey of Broseley.

Adam finished his wine and sighed. The hall was emptying of people, and he should follow suit, collect his wife, and retire to yet another night of silence. He stood, stretched, and looked about for Kit. She was sitting some distance away, holding hands with Thomas. Holding hands! She had not as much as touched him, her husband, for weeks.

Adam gave neither the earl nor Kit the opportunity to say anything. He gripped Kit's arm and lifted her to her feet.

"Adam!" she protested.

"We are leaving. My lord." He inclined his head to Thomas, lacing his voice with ice. To his irritation, the earl grinned. Adam scowled and set off for the door, dragging Kit along.

"You're hurting me," Kit said, pulling at his hold.

He loosened his grip. "I will not have my wife sitting in the lap of another man," he said, steering her through the hall.

"I was not! I was talking to him—a most novel experience these days, to have a man care enough to listen to me."

Adam gave her a little shake. "I care! But you have made it very clear you cannot stand the sight of me."

"You blamed me! Me! And if you truly cared, wouldn't you have tried to talk to me?"

Her words sank like shards of glass into his heart. How could she think he didn't care for her? Every damned night, he'd held vigil at her bed, waiting until he assumed she was asleep before entering their chamber.

"That is unfair," he said in a low voice. "How am I to talk to someone who flees at my approach? Avoids my very presence? You've been shunning me, sweeting, and it's been killing me."

"Killing you?" She wheeled away from him. "It is me who is dying inside. It is me who is marked for life."

Adam stood beside her, not knowing quite what to say. After a couple of heartbeats, she sighed, and without a backward look hastened towards the exit, her long skirts dragging over the rush mats.

"Kit! Wait." He caught up with her just by the door. The torch in the sconce above them gasped in the draught, sooty light illuminating her scarred face. He set a careful finger to her damaged cheek. She trembled under his touch, and he had no idea if it was out of desire or revulsion. Dearest Lord! How could he have let it come to this, that his wife regarded him with apprehension?

"All of what he did to you…" He choked, had to clear his throat, having no real idea of what that miscreant scum of a man had done to her—but he'd had plenty of time to imagine it. "It was my fault." He bowed his head, waiting for her recriminations.

"Yours?" Her voice shook.

"I should have told you about the lad. I should have kept you safe. Instead…" He drew in a long breath. "He took you. He hurt you, he…"

"What?"

"He had his way with you," he whispered, his heart breaking. His Kit, helpless as another man violated her.

"He tried."

"Tried?"

"He…" Her voice faltered. "He did a lot of things." Kit licked her lips. "But not that."

"Why didn't you tell me?"

"Why didn't you ask?"

"That first night, you ordered me out of the room," he reminded her. "I wanted to hold you, to comfort you and be there for you, but you…" He coughed a couple of times. "You looked at me in terror, and I thought…I thought you'd never forgive me. And then, the next day, you screamed at me it was all my fault – and you were right. I had the opportunity to kill him, but I didn't. How can I ever forgive myself for that? How can you?" He averted his face, incapable of meeting her eyes.

"It wasn't your fault." Kit's hand brushed at his. "It was Godfrey's." He looked down, opened his hand and splayed his fingers. She slid her fingers into his, and he tightened his hold, still with his eyes on their interlaced fingers.

"I'm so sorry," he said. "I should have insisted that you tell me, I should have held you as you did, but those first few days you didn't want to talk, and if I tried to approach you, you flinched." He lifted their hands to his mouth and kissed her fingers, one by one. "I didn't know what I was supposed to do. How does one comfort a woman who has been vilely abused? I tried, sweeting, but I did it all wrong, didn't I?"

"As did I." She sighed. "I couldn't stand to see you stagger about like a wounded bear when it was me, not you, who was hurt."

Adam groaned out loud. He enveloped her in an embrace, and she was as stiff as a newel post at first, but slowly she softened, her body fitting into his. Adam rested his chin on the top of her head and closed his eyes.

"It was as if he'd ripped my heart out. Every bruise on your skin, every cut—I felt them ten times over."

"My bruises?" She leaned back to look at him. "When did you see them?"

"Who do you think carried you home, sweeting? Who bathed you and dressed your injuries? Do you truly think I would have let anyone—anyone at all—touch you after what you had just gone through?" He gathered her close, inhaling her scent. "I hated myself," he admitted to the top of her head. "I thought you did too."

There was a soft snort, a half-choked sound he interpreted as a sob. Kit stood on her toes, eyes glittering with tears. "Fools, the both of us."

"Aye." All those nights when he'd sneaked in to watch her sleep, and all he'd wanted was to slide into bed beside her, hold her and reclaim her, but he'd worried she'd scream in terror. "Every night, I've sat by your bed."

"I know. And it made me feel safe to have you there." She rested her face against his chest, and he stroked her softly over her head, her back.

"Will you…" He cleared his throat. "Will you accompany me to our chamber, my dearest lady?"

"Gladly."

They were shy around each other. Adam busied himself lighting candles from the taper. Kit was hesitant as she undressed, so he turned his back on her as he undid his belt and drew the blue tunic over his head. He concentrated on the drawstring of his braies, undid his hose, and after some moments of consideration pulled off his shirt as well. He could hear her breathing, and suddenly her hands slid round his waist. Her breasts pressed against his back; he twisted round to face her.

"Will you tell me what he did to you?" He fiddled with her braid, releasing her hair to spill in waves of dark, dark red around her shoulders.

"Now?"

"Now." He captured her eyes, dark and unreadable in the light of the candles. His hands slid down to her buttocks, pressing her closer, close enough that she should feel safe and loved. With a little sigh, Adam counted the days since he had last held her like this.

"I—"

He put a finger to her lips, swept her up into his arms, and carried her over to the bed. Moments later, she was on her side, him a protective curve around her back, his mouth at her nape.

"Tell me."

So she did, her voice low as she recounted the events of those terrible days in which Adam had been convinced he'd never see her again. He didn't say a word, he just held her, swallowing repeatedly as she described how Godfrey had mistreated her, defiled her.

"He said you'd be glad to be rid of me."

"Sweeting," he murmured. "He lied—you know that, don't you?"

Kit shrugged.

Adam rolled her over to face him. "I love you." He kissed the scar that decorated her cheek. "So very much do I love you."

"Even if I am bastard-born? Ugly and scarred?" she said through her tears.

"Even so. But you know that already." He tugged at a lock of her hair. "And as to ugly, it suffices to see how men gawk at you to know that isn't true."

"They do?"

"I could mention several. Thomas comes first on the list." He scowled, and Kit laughed and wiped at her eyes.

"And what do you think?" she asked, pressing her scarred cheek into the pillow.

"Me?" Adam kissed her nose. "Need you ask?" A soft brushing of lips, no more, but when she gripped at his hair, he deepened the kiss. Her hands slid down to his shoulders. He released her mouth to breathe.

"I think I am a fortunate man," he said, dipping his head to kiss her again. Gently, he reminded himself. Very, very gently. The contour of her thigh, of her hip—he slid his hand over her skin, fingers splayed. Up to her waist, his hand lingering there while he sucked ever so softly on her lower lip, dropped kisses on her eyes, her brows. She sighed his name, the bed swaying as she shifted closer. His fingers travelled over her ribs, up to her breasts. He looked at her, she nodded, and he cupped her breast, brushing his thumb over her nipple. Slowly. Gently. She leaned into his touch, and here at last came her hands, sliding up and down his arm, over his chest.

There was a wordless exclamation when he took her nipple in his mouth, another when his fingers slid through the thick curls that adorned her mound, found her cleft. Gently. Moist and warm, and she raised her hips.

A sigh escaped her when he kissed his way downwards. His tongue darted out to taste her. Again, and she squirmed below him. Adam took hold of her hips to keep her still. Gently? Slowly? Not now, not when she shifted from side to side, her voice hoarse as she called out his name.

His heart pounded, his member was thick with his arousal. Not yet, not yet, not until she shattered under his mouth, until she clawed at his back, begging him to come inside of her. Her hips rose and fell, she gyrated below him, and he drove her over the edge, holding her as all of her shook below him.

When he slid inside of her, she cupped his face and kissed him. His wife. His beautiful Kit. His woman. His. Only his. Kit. His, his, his, his. Kit.

Chapter 30

After mass the next morning, King Edward came over to Kit. At first, he didn't say anything, eyes narrowing as he took in her new scar.

"Men like that deserve to hang," he finally said. "But in Broseley's case, I think I'd rather have him flayed—alive." He placed a light hand on Kit's forearm. "Are you recovered, my lady?"

Kit shared a fleeting smile with Adam. Last night had laid quite a number of ghosts to rest, and for the first time since the June day when she'd been abducted, she'd slept without disturbing dreams.

"As well as can be expected, my lord."

"Good. We must talk." King Edward led the way to his rooms. To be correct, these were Earl Thomas' rooms, decorated with heavy tapestries depicting hunting scenes. Braziers, plump cushions in the window seats, a small collection of books, a well-worn chess set—all in all, the lord's solar was a comfortable space, two large armchairs facing a hearth that now, in full summer, was decorated with flowers and greenery rather than a fire.

The door that led to the lord's bedchamber stood ajar, and Kit had a glimpse of rumpled bedding and a naked leg before the king shut the door a tad too firmly. She smiled: Queen Philippa was not an early riser, and from the look of things, the preceding night had been lively enough to require a further few hours of sleep.

"Is he working alone?" the king asked, sitting down in one of the chairs. Lancelot padded over to sit beside him, resting his huge head in his master's lap.

"Who, Godfrey?" Adam remained standing. "I think not. Someone knows the old king is alive—"

"Too many know!" the king interrupted. "You yourself told my uncle Norfolk, and God knows how many of Mortimer's men have blabbed."

286

"—and that someone—or someones—think it will benefit them to free the former king and return him to his throne," Adam continued, ignoring the king's little outburst.

"Well, we can't have that, can we? I have seen my father buried, and I have no wish to see him resurrected. I am the king now, and two kings in one realm is one king too many." Edward tugged at Lancelot's ear. "Besides, my father may have been a good man, but he was a dismal king."

Edward nibbled at a nail, eyes lost in the carpet adorning the wide floorboards. "I will be a different sort of king—very different."

"What do we do?" Adam asked.

"More precisely, what can we do? We must wait until my lady mother and Mortimer return. After all, only they know where my father is held." The king frowned. "I suspect he is at Corfe. And even if the rebels know, they'll never get him out of there."

"Depends on who they have on their side, my lord," Adam said. "Maybe they have a castellan or two in their thrall."

Edward yawned. "Mortimer chooses his men with care. They'll be able to handle whatever may happen in the coming few weeks. But we need a final solution to this problem, one that ensures no one ever sets my father at the head of a rebellious horde." He gave Kit a crooked smile. "And no, Lady Kit, I am not proposing to have my father murdered, so you need not look shocked."

"Well, that is a relief, my lord," Kit said, feeling her cheeks heat.

"Yes, it is, isn't it?" The king stood. "And now, if you excuse me, I have a wife to wake." He gave Kit a boyish smile, eyes an uncommonly vivid shade of blue. "Did you know she is ticklish?" His smile widened into a grin. "Everywhere, Lady Kit—and I do mean everywhere."

"I shall have to take your word for it," Kit replied. "I have no intention of finding out for myself."

The king exploded into laughter. He was still laughing as he left the room.

"He is much happier when his lady mother is not around," Kit commented as she followed Adam back out into the sunlight.

"Aye." He took her hand, steadying her down the stairs. "Queen Isabella does not tolerate late risers—or, I believe, ticklish daughters-in-law. Not enough decorum."

The following days were pleasant enough. Adam was once again more or less constantly in the king's presence, the rift between them bridged if not entirely healed, and so Kit was left to her own devices, unwilling as yet to resume her duties to Philippa. The other ladies might not say anything to her, but their looks and whispered comments, that avid expression on their faces when they inspected Kit, was more than she could bear.

"They hope for juicy scandal," Queen Philippa said when Kit shared this with her. "Excitement at a once removed."

"I can assure you there was little excitement, my lady. There was terror and pain, humiliation and blood."

Queen Philippa leaned forward, light fingers touching Kit's cheek. "I can see that, Lady Kit. And I wish with all my heart that it had not happened to you."

"Thank you, my lady." For some odd reason, her throat congested, tears springing to her eyes. The queen politely looked away.

"What will you do with the boy?"

"Tom?" Kit finished wiping at her eyes. "He will remain with us at Tresaints." She smiled. "I have never seen a lad consume quite so much food before. Mabel says he has worms, but I myself think it is rather that he has never had the opportunity to eat his fill before. Sad, isn't it?"

"Not for him, not anymore." Queen Philippa wandered over to the large arched window and sat down on the window seat. "I hope to give my husband many such sons. Voracious lads, as eager for their food as for adventure."

"Amen to that, my lady." Kit studied the queen surreptitiously. Was she carrying? She hoped not—a girl of fourteen would find the birthing difficult.

The room filled with the queen's ladies, all of them chattering thirteen to the dozen, and Kit shifted on her feet.

"Go," Queen Philippa said. "Leave me to handle these witless hens." She made a shooing motion with her hands, and after one more reverence, Kit made her escape.

With so much time at her disposal, Kit had ample opportunity to explore the castle. Kit was entranced by Framlingham—not so much by the structure itself, no matter how much Adam lauded the impressive walls and the excellent defences, but rather by the setting, starting with the mere. In the early morning, the flat expanse of water was shrouded with veils of fog. At midday, it mirrored the massive castle. And in the evenings, the setting sun coloured the water a deep gold.

She was sitting by the water one morning when she was joined by Earl Thomas. With a groan, he flung himself down on the grass beside her.

"The longer he stays, the deeper the hole he digs in my larders," he said. "My lady wife will never let me hear the end of it."

"Your lady wife? Is she here?" At last! Kit was curious about the elusive countess.

"No. She remains in Thetford with our children."

"Why do you never bring her to court?" Kit asked, immediately regretting her question. Thomas looked away.

"I have in the past. My brother was kind to her, but Alice is easily intimidated—especially by Queen Isabella."

"But wouldn't she want to come?"

"Not really. Besides, she is far too aware of her lowly birth." He sounded bitter. "As am I, of course."

"So why did you wed her?"

Thomas rolled his eyes. "Love, Lady Kit. Or maybe it was lust."

"Lust?" Kit snorted. "The son of a king would not marry a commoner for lust—he would not have to."

He smiled, no more.

"And do you love her still?"

Yet again, that little smile. His little finger brushed against hers a couple of times before he abruptly stood up and left.

She heard more about the countess from the servants. A snippet here, another there, and Kit was left with an image of a kindhearted lady who had entranced the earl with her soft voice and huge eyes.

"A sweet lady," one of the maids confided to her. "But very shy—and very much in awe of her lord husband."

"Ah." A man like Earl Thomas required a companion who could offer more than soft breasts and adoring looks. She felt a twinge of pity. A rash act—as she heard it, the countess had been a radiant beauty in her youth—and now he was shackled to her for life.

"I fear our little queen has overindulged on chivalric romances," Thomas said, smiling fondly at Queen Philippa, for the evening in a creation adorned with roses and hearts.

"As has our king." Adam laughed. "St George again?"

"Poor little page," Thomas said, "that dragon's head has him bowing under the weight."

The hall was full of light and music. There was dancing and wine, high youthful voices raised in song and laughter.

"Makes me feel ancient," Sir Henry commented, tugging at the worn sleeves of his tunic.

"You are ancient," Adam said, clapping him on the shoulder. "Close to two score ten."

"Well, you're not exactly dewy with youth either," Sir Henry snapped, rising to greet Kit with quite the elegant bow.

In difference to the queen, Kit had opted for simplicity, the wreath of budding roses that adorned her head complementing her green kirtle. A single rose was tucked into her neckline, she smelled of crushed lavender and mint, and when she moved, the sheer material of her long veil billowed around her.

"A celebration of love is always nice," she said when Thomas complained that this was all too much.

"Love?" Thomas laughed. "Ned is more into the quest aspect of things, don't you think?"

"Aye, all he can think of is killing the dragon." Adam grinned when the poor page stumbled. "Not much of a dragon, if you ask me."

"But the queen..." Kit waved a hand in the direction of Queen Philippa.

"Ah yes: the goddess of love." Thomas chuckled. "It seems to me Philippa is more interested in what happens *after* the dragon is slayed, while Ned thinks no further than destroying the evil beast, thereby dazzling us all with his prowess at arms." A sly look at Adam was accompanied by yet another chuckle. "I heard you had him flat on his arse last time he challenged you."

"Aye." A sensitive subject. So far, the king had shown little inclination to trade blows with Adam, preferring to train with his growing circle of companions. Adam smiled crookedly. None of the fledgling earls and barons would ever truly challenge their liege, and so King Edward emerged victorious from every bout.

"Talking of the devil," Sir Henry said in an undertone, a discreet nod in the direction of the king, who was making unsteady progress in their direction.

"Uncle. Lady Kit." He bowed, overbalanced, and almost fell over Kit's lap. Adam heaved him upright.

"Too much wine, my lord?"

"Too much wine, my lord," the king mimicked before burping. "So what if I've had too much wine? Who are you to judge, Sir Adam? Who? Have you my burdens? My sorrows? My..." He hiccupped loudly, lifted his silver goblet. "A toast, my lords. To my hapless sister, as of today wed to a puling child of four." He drank, hiccupped again. "So wrong. A princess wed to the son of a rebellious knave." He snickered. "But the groom won't like it when I take his crown, will he?" Edward shook his head. "Oh no, he won't." He blinked, swaying on his feet.

"Ned." Thomas rose and placed an arm round his nephew. "Let's get you to your bed."

"Bed." King Edward winked. "I like my bed—and my lady wife." He patted Thomas' chest. "Like you," he mumbled. "Like " He gave them a bemused look. "Love." He nodded. "My lady love." He pointed in the direction of his queen. "Bed." He crooked his finger, as if beckoning his

291

wife towards him. "Bed!" he hollered before collapsing into a fit of giggles.

It took Adam and Thomas to get the king across the bailey and up the stairs to his chambers. By the time they'd tucked him in, he was snoring heavily, flushed with too much wine.

"He'll never forgive his beloved Maman for this damned treaty," Thomas commented in an undertone, an eye on Montagu and Stafford, who had insisted on coming along to ensure the king was safely put to bed. "Mark my words: Scotland will fester into something very nasty—Lancaster almost broke out in boils last we had words about it." He jerked his head in the direction of the door, preceding Adam.

"And what is your opinion?" Adam asked once they were standing in the darkened bailey.

"Mine? I don't give a rat's arse about Scotland. I do, however, dislike the way things were handled." Thomas set his jaw. "Matters of such import should be discussed among more than Queen Isabella and her lover. Lancaster will not stand for this much longer—and neither will I." He glanced at Adam. "I just thought you should know."

"Thank you," Adam said with heavy sarcasm. "Such knowledge will truly fill my nights with pleasant dreams." He scowled at his friend. "I have enough to handle as it is, and now you choose to whisper of treason?"

"Treason?" Thomas straightened up. "This is not about treason, it's about usurpation of power!"

"By the queen or Lord Mortimer?"

Thomas closed his eyes for an instant. "Both. But it is him they blame." There was a glimmer of humour in his eyes. "The dowager queen, you see, is a woman—and we all know just how weak and defenceless they are."

"They are," Adam said curtly. "Damned defenceless when faced with a brute. Ask my wife."

Thomas held up his hands. "I didn't mean it like that. What happened to Kit…" He cleared his throat. "But we were talking about the dowager queen, and whatever else she might be, she is neither frail nor vulnerable."

Adam sank back against a nearby wall. "God's blood, but I am tired of all this!"

"Aren't we all?" Thomas joined him, and they stood like that, side by side, faces raised to the darkness of the July sky.

It had been late by the time Adam had come to bed the previous night. Too much wine, too many hours spent discussing with Thomas, and when he'd entered the room, Kit was fast asleep. He'd managed to undress and wash without waking her, had even succeeded in slipping into bed without Kit as much as batting an eyelid—though truth be told, it was too dark to see if she did.

He woke to a morning hazy with foggy sunshine, Kit's half of the bed cold and empty. He dressed and went in search of her—not all that difficult as his wife had a fondness for water. Nor was it difficult to guess why she was up and about at this early hour. While she never spoke of her ordeal, there were moments when she'd still, eyes acquiring a faraway look, hands clasping together, and he would know she was thinking of that damned accursed Godfrey. At other times, her hand rose to touch her new scar, and more than once he'd come upon her wiping at her eyes, even if she insisted it was nothing—a mote of dust, no more.

The inner bailey was sunk in relative silence. The priest was making for the chapel to celebrate prime, a couple of maids were talking in low voices as they made for the buttery. The large main gate was firmly closed—it was locked and barred at sunset, opened after prime—so Adam made for the other gate, the rather impressive western gate that jutted out of the walls, its narrow passage long enough to force any attackers to approach in single file while open to attack from above as well as from the sides.

The guards nodded a good morning before standing aside to allow him to step outside. Before him, the mere glittered in the returning light. Beyond it stretched the earl's hunting grounds, an endless expanse of forest that served to keep the earl's table supplied with everything from venison to boar. The mere contributed as well: already a boat was out on the water, two men pulling at a net.

293

Adam strolled along the shore, wrinkled his nose as he passed the dovecote and its cooing inhabitants, and came upon his wife sitting by the water, her head cradled on her knees. He sat down beside her and gathered her close. She snuggled up to him, and he rested his cheek against her head.

"Why don't you wake me?" he asked after a while.

"Whatever for? So that neither of us sleep?" She sighed. "I hate him for this, for having me see spectres in every shadow, jump when someone approaches in the dark."

"It takes time," he said, wishing he had Godfrey of Broseley in front of him so that he could slice him to pieces, bit by bit.

"It's been close to a month." She pressed her cheek against his chest. "And still, this is the only place where I feel safe, with the sound of your heart under my ear."

Chapter 31

They went to York, where Queen Isabella and Lord Roger were preparing for the parliament demanded by Lancaster back in June. Now it seemed the earl had no intention of attending, and neither did the king's uncles. Adam fixed a brooding look on the back of the king, riding some distance ahead of him. Was Thomas sliding into Lancaster's camp? Dear God, were they about to live through yet another season of bloody war?

"Lancaster is no match to Mortimer in the field," Sir Henry said when Adam shared his concerns. "But yes, I fear you are right: Lancaster is done with being relegated from the place he considers his by an upstart Marcher lord."

"And Kent and Norfolk?" Thomas had bowed out of riding to York on a flimsy excuse related to a supposedly ailing child.

Sir Henry waved away a fly from his palfrey's neck. "It would kill our young liege to have to face his uncles on a battlefield."

And me, Adam thought, closing his eyes at the disturbing image of seeing Thomas come charging against him.

"That is not an answer."

"There is no answer. Do you think me some sort of seer?" Sir Henry gave Adam an irritated look. "But if you want my opinion, I think Norfolk dislikes Lancaster. Kent, however, is easily wooed by promises of grandeur and influence."

Very much in line with Adam's assessment. Kent had been at Ludlow but kept his distance from Mortimer; he'd been at Worcester and spent most of his time in deep conversation with Lancaster. Where before Kent had been one of Queen Isabella's most ardent admirers, lately he'd done little more than bow politely in her direction, although to be fair that could have more to do with a jealous wife than a change of allegiance.

"Our Lord Edmund has never quite known what leg to stand on in this ongoing conflict. First, he was for the former king, then he offered his services to Queen Isabella, and now, disgruntled, no doubt, by having Mortimer outshine him, he turns to Lancaster." Sir Henry used his thumbnail to dislodge something from between his teeth. "He'd never do anything to intentionally harm his nephew—but it is fortunate, I think, that Edward of Caernarvon is safely dead and not imprisoned somewhere."

"How so?" Adam asked, managing to sound only vaguely interested.

"A dashing earl and an imprisoned king?" Sir Henry smiled. "It isn't only our young king who has a fondness for chivalric tales, dear Adam." He nodded and clucked his mount into a trot, calling for Prince John to wait for him.

There was an uncomfortable churning in Adam's bowels. Thomas knew the king was still alive—and dear God, it was Adam who had told him. Would he have told his brother? No, he tried to tell himself, Thomas had given his word. As had Adam, he reminded himself, and look how well he'd held to it. The rest of the long ride to York he spent mulling all of this over, sharing his thoughts with no one—not even with Kit.

Yet again, Queen Isabella had appropriated the Dominican friary for her own use, insisting the castle was too uncomfortable and dreary. She looked careworn, her normally smooth brow adorned by two permanent little furrows, and she'd taken little care of her appearance, clad in a simple dark kirtle with a matching surcoat. With her white veil, devoid of any jewels, she looked verily like a nun—an extraordinarily beautiful nun, to be sure—the impression further reinforced by the fact that she was at her prayers when King Edward, followed by Adam, entered her rooms.

"Son," she said, holding out her arms, and something in her voice and face had the king hastening to embrace her. Adam politely turned his back, pretending great interest in the opposite wall, as whitewashed as all the rest.

"So." The queen released her son. "Why this haste to see me? And this early in the morning?"

The king looked beyond her, to the door that led to her bedchamber. "Is Mortimer not here? He needs to be here too."

"He is in the church, praying for the soul of his departed son," the queen said.

"His son, my lady?" A Mortimer lad dead? Adam mumbled a hasty prayer.

"Roger. Died most unexpectedly, as we hear it." The queen crossed herself. "May he be taken into the grace of our Lord, poor lad." She looked away. "A dead son, a lost daughter. We have little to be merry about at present."

"And worse is to come. Maman, this is urgent. Can we not have him fetched?"

She gave the king a reproving look. "He is praying for his dead child, Edward. What can possibly be more important?"

"A resurrected king?"

"What?" Queen Isabella paled.

"You heard." The king summed up the recent events related to Godfrey of Broseley and Kit. He was halfway through when Lord Roger entered, looking as if he hadn't slept for days. Heavy pouches under red-rimmed eyes, the shadow of grey stubble on his cheeks, a mouth set in a downward curve—Adam's heart went out to him. Even Edward seemed affected, clearing his throat before offering his condolences.

"Thank you, my lord." Lord Roger made for the little table containing a pitcher of wine—sweet and spiced no doubt, as this was how he preferred it early in the morning. "So Broseley is still making mischief, eh?"

Adam stiffened. Lord Roger lifted a hand, no more. "I am sorry for what happened to Lady Kit, and I did not mean to imply her suffering was minor." He turned to the queen. "What do we do, my lady?"

She moved closer, her hand floating up to touch his shoulder, slide down his arm to clasp his hand. Lord Roger gave her a brief smile, drew her close, and for an instant leaned his forehead against hers. Two, three inhalations at most, and then the queen moved away, Mortimer straightened up, and the king closed his mouth.

Lord Roger poured himself some wine. "So, to the matter at hand. Any suggestions?"

"We smuggle him out of the country," Edward said, sitting down in the only chair available. "Exile him, never to return." His voice shook, lashes sweeping down to hide his eyes.

Isabella's brows rose, two well-plucked, dark arcs. "And do you think he will agree to that?"

"It must surely be better than rotting in a dungeon!" King Edward snapped.

"How many times must I tell you? He is not locked up in a dungeon, he lives in comfortable captivity at Corfe." Queen Isabella gave her son an exasperated look. Lord Roger sipped his wine, dark eyes unreadable.

"And to whom would we entrust this delicate task?" Lord Roger asked.

"Well, that's easy." Edward helped himself to a wafer from a little platter. "To Adam, of course."

"Me?" Adam took a step backwards.

"Who better?" Edward tilted his head to the side. "No one would expect me to entrust such a sensitive matter to a lowly knight."

Adam bristled at his tone but held his tongue.

"Even less to one travelling on pilgrimage with his wife," the queen said, and Adam threw her a grateful look. He had no intention of going anywhere without Kit, not so soon after her ordeal.

"His wife? Lady Kit?" Edward tugged at an imaginary beard. "Yes, that would add to the disguise." He looked at his mother. "This must be done with the greatest of stealth."

Mortimer did not like it. That much was apparent, dark eyes flashing from Adam to the king and back again.

"I agree we need to smuggle him away," Lord Roger said, pouring some more wine. "What I do not like is entrusting this to Adam. I have good men of my own to oversee such a delicate operation."

"It is my father, and I prefer to place his life in the hands of men I trust." Edward met Adam's eyes. "Implicitly." But not with everything, Adam amended silently.

"Trust?" Lord Roger's voice dripped ice. "What is it you are insinuating?"

"The king was dead, then he was not. A ruse, Lord Mortimer, a ruse contrived by you and my lady mother." The king got to his feet, and it came as a shock to Adam to see him standing beside Lord Roger. The lad was as tall and broad as Mortimer—a man rather than a boy. "A necessary ruse, perhaps. But also a ruse that leaves me in your power."

"It leaves you in power," Mortimer protested. "A dead king cannot reclaim his throne."

"But he isn't dead—we both know that. And so, should you choose to release him..." Edward set his hands to his neck and made a strangling sound.

Lord Roger looked at him as if he'd lost his wits. "Release him? That would be suicide, my lord."

"Maybe. Maybe not. After all, you could wrest some promises from him first."

"Promises? From him?" Isabella snorted.

"If you think Edward of Caernarvon would ever treat with me, then you're a fool. More importantly, do you think I am fool enough to forget your sire is incapable of holding to an oath? God's blood, if he'd had some constancy in him, none of this would ever have happened!" Mortimer looked to the west. "Had Edward of Caernarvon been half the king his father was, I'd have been at Wigmore rather than at court. Mine would have been a life like my father's and his father's before him— the king's loyal servant, no more." He sighed, his face softening.

"Isn't that what you are now?" Edward asked.

Mortimer gave him a long look. "I try to be. I hope to be."

"Good. And as such, you will of course cooperate on this venture." The king's face set in a smug smile.

"Outplayed, eh?" Lord Roger inclined his head. "Your pleasure is mine, my lord."

Queen Isabella swirled across the room. "You're playing with fire, Edward. To have your father at large—"

"I can't keep him locked up for the rest of his life! Besides, as long as he is here, there is always the risk that someone will free him, have him head up a rebellion."

A swift look passed between Lord Roger and the queen. Adam shivered. Edward of Caernarvon had as much chance of escaping Mortimer's custody alive as did a fly on a frog's sticky tongue.

"And how will you stop him from leading a rebellion once you've set him free?" the queen asked.

Edward gave her a long look. "Money, my lady mother. I find it works with most people, don't you?"

Adam had to smile. An elegant thrust to the jugular, leaving the queen uncharacteristically flushed and flustered.

"What do you propose, my lord?" Mortimer asked.

The king looked pleased and returned to his chair. "We will need an impostor. Whoever believes my father—the former king—is being held at Corfe, must continue thinking so."

"People do know what he looks like," Lord Roger pointed out.

"As long as he is tall, fair, and bearded, he will do." King Edward drummed his fingers on the armrests of his chair. "If you could find a corpse to bury in his stead, surely you can find a lookalike?" Bright blue eyes bored into Mortimer, fingers tightening around the carved lion heads that adorned the armrests.

"I can." Mortimer made for the door. "I shall have a writ ready in an hour, an instruction that our anonymous guest at Corfe be released into Adam's care."

"Your writ? Surely, my writ is enough!"

"Not in this matter, my lord." Lord Roger bowed. "The men charged with the former king's safety are my men—only my men."

"Corfe." Kit looked at him. "You and me?"

"Aye, sweeting. Just you and me—and Egard. No one else."

She pursed her lips. "And what are we to do at Corfe?"

"Free the former king," Adam replied, and his wife gasped. He shook his head. "Not quite free him. We are to smuggle him out of the country." He sat down beside her. "As pilgrims, on our way to Canterbury. And from there we are to go to France."

"And will he come with us?"

"I do not think he will have much of a choice." Adam caressed the hilt of his dagger. "Any attempt to flee, and we are to kill him." There was a hole the size of a millpond in this plan as there was nothing to stop the erstwhile king from revealing who he was once he was outside England. Philippe of Valois would be delighted to have a potential pretender to the English throne at his court, and there were several former Despenser men in France, bitter men who would do anything to be allowed to return home. On the other hand, King Edward was offering more than generous terms—and a chance of freedom.

"Kill him?" Kit moved closer. "Could you do that? A defenceless man?"

"I have my orders."

"Ah." She oozed reproach.

He took hold of her, gave her a little shake. "Of course I can't!" he growled. "So we'd best pray he makes no such attempt. Because if he does, and I do not stop him, we are as good as dead, sweeting." The king had been more than clear on this, every inch the ruler, not the son. A lion in the making, and God save those he chose to savage with his claws. Adam crossed himself.

"Tell them you can't." Kit pressed against his side. "Tell them—"

"What, sweeting? There's no choice here—I am the king's man and must do as he tells me." He gave her a bleak smile. "At least we will be riding together."

"Together." She entwined her fingers with his and rested her head against his shoulder. "You and I, my dearest lord and husband. Always you and I."

Chapter 32

Ten days later, Kit held in her horse before the dilapidated little inn just south of Wareham that had been designated as their meeting point.

"Here?" She threw a longing look back the way they had come. Wareham sported a few fine inns along the Frome, while this place looked about to collapse where it stood.

"Out of the way," Adam replied with a grunt. "Not much custom."

"One wonders why." Kit slid off her mare. "I think I prefer sleeping in the open." Beyond Wareham was forested ground, and she'd be as comfortable under a large tree as in this badly listing building.

"It's because of the ground," Egard said. "Fools, to build on sand."

"It's not the sand's fault that it smells of shit." Adam looked towards the south. "Once we have our fourth companion, I say we ride for the woods. We can buy food along the way."

Kit threw a nervous look at the packhorse. At present, it carried a minor fortune in gold florins and French ecus d'or. Enough, according to Adam, to see a man well clothed and fed for several years—even a man with such discerning tastes as their former king.

Adam sent Egard inside for beer and bread, and then they sat outside, waiting.

"There." Egard stood up, pointing to the south.

A smudge, no more, but soon enough Kit could make out a heavily loaded cart accompanied by three men on horseback. The cart trundled along, jolting over ruts and holes. The sun glinted off helmets and chain-mail, and the closer they got, the more apparent it was that the men were on full alert, gauntleted hands gripping the hilt of their swords.

"Where's the k—"

"Shh!" Adam jerked his head in the direction of the inn. "Egard, go inside and make sure our dear innkeeper is adequately distracted."

"No need," the innkeeper said, appearing from behind the henhouse. "I am a Mortimer man." He grinned. "The real innkeeper is presently visiting with his chickens."

Kit recognised the man riding first as Sir John Maltravers, yet another of Mortimer's loyal men.

"Adam." Maltravers nodded in greeting but remained astride.

"John."

They sized each other up in silence. Adam handed over Lord Roger's writ. Maltravers cracked the seal, read it, and stuffed it into his pouch.

"I do not think this is a good idea," Maltravers said.

"Neither do I, but who asks us?" Adam looked from one to the other of Maltravers' men. "Best make sure they keep their mouths shut."

"Oh, I will." The saddle creaked as Maltravers shifted. He raised a hand, and the driver dropped off the cart and hurried round to lower the tail board. Several barrels rolled off—empty, to judge from how they bounced when they landed in the dirt.

"Careful, man!" Maltravers rode his horse closer.

There was a muffled sound from a large chest placed right in the middle of the cart.

Adam cursed. "You've put him in a chest?"

"Better than a barrel. It's not as if I've had much time to plan this, is it?" Maltravers nodded at the driver, who fiddled with the locks on the chest. The lid swung open, and out sprang a wild-haired creature, snarling like an animal at bay. He held a thin sliver of wood in his hand, eyes so wide the bright blue irises were completely surrounded by bloodshot white. The driver yelped and fell over backwards, Maltravers shouted out an order, and his two other men converged on the cart, swords half-drawn.

"Stop!" Kit yelled, shoving past Adam. The man—their former king—was terrified, his heavily bearded face whipping back and forth between the men-at-arms. Kit undid her cloak.

"My lord," she said, carefully approaching the cart. "Please, my lord, don't be afraid. We mean you no harm."

"No harm?" The man cackled, his hold on the futile piece of wood tightening.

"Kit." Adam put a hand on her arm. She brushed him off, taking yet another step towards the quivering man.

"My lord," she repeated. "You are to come with us—with me." She was close enough to touch him now, stood on her toes to offer him her cloak.

"I am to live?" Sir Edward's voice quavered as he wrapped Kit's cloak around his shivering frame.

"That is entirely in your hands." Maltravers rode his horse closer. "You heard the proposal: you uphold your end, the king will uphold his."

"So it was no ruse?" Sir Edward licked his lips.

"No ruse." Adam stepped forward. "I give you my word."

Sir Edward peered at him, gave a short bark of laughter. "Well, well, if it isn't the honourable Adam de Guirande." He leaned forward and spat Adam in the face. "You took him! You carried him to his death!"

"I did as I was ordered to do." Adam wiped his face clean. "Despenser deserved to die."

"But not like that," the former king moaned.

Adam's face hardened. "Tell that to Lord Badlesmere, to Clifford and Mowbray. Tell it to all the women left widows after your ruthless assizes, all the orphans left destitute in the trail of Despensers' grasping hands. Tell it to—"

"No time for all that now." Maltravers fixed the former king with a hard look. "Do I have your word that you will comply with the proposal?"

"Do I have a choice?" Sir Edward snapped.

"No." Maltravers pointed back the way they'd come. "It is either Corfe or this. And do not even think of going back on your word—wherever you go, there will be a shadow following."

"How comforting," Sir Edward retorted, "at least I know I'll not die alone." He exhaled. "You have my word." He descended from the cart, looked at the deserted inn, the saddled horses. "Are we to stay here long?" He threw Maltravers a baleful look. "I would prefer to leave as soon as possible."

"We leave when I say we do," Adam told him. Maltravers grinned, bowed courteously in the direction of Kit, and rode off the way he'd come, his men falling in behind him.

Adam sent Egard off to get some hours sleep and settled himself just to the side of the little fire, sufficiently hidden by the shadows to remain unseen should anyone come prowling. The bags with gold were at his back, his sword was within reach, and just in case, he had a stout staff as well. He had the distinct sensation they'd been followed, whether by brigands or potential rebels he had no idea, but whatever the case, he was taking no chances. Come the morrow, Sir Edward would cease to be and instead become Brother Edward, complete with a neat tonsure.

Not that the former king was readily recognisable. Adam had been more than taken aback by the screaming apparition that emerged from the chest, seeing nothing of the elegant king he had once known. Golden curls had become a matted mess of greying hair, months of inactivity had resulted in a general softening of limbs and posture. Sir Edward walked with a slight stoop and was uncommonly pale for this time of year, which had Adam concluding he had not been out much lately.

Something moved. Adam gripped the staff, relaxed when he saw it was Sir Edward, sitting up. And then the man was on the move, darting with surprising speed towards the horses. He grunted when Adam brought him down, shrieked in protest when Adam grabbed him by the hair and hauled him back towards the fire.

"Next time, I'll use my sword instead," Adam growled, throwing Sir Edward to his knees. Some yards away, Kit half sat up, blinked, and lay back down again. Egard was wide awake, flitting by them soundlessly on his way to check the restless horses.

"Surely, you'd expect me to try," Sir Edward said.

"Well, I never did put much of a value on your given word." Adam spat to the side. "Once an oath-breaker, always an oath-breaker."

"I could say the same. You promised you'd hold yourself to my son, and here you are running errands for that whoreson Mortimer."

"For Mortimer?" Adam found a wineskin, uncorked it, and took a couple of swallows. "Oh no. I am here at the request of King Edward."

"A traitorous wife and a traitorous son." Sir Edward stretched for the wine. "What is the world coming to?"

"As you make your bed, you lie in it." Adam belched. Damned sour stuff, that. "Do not blame others for your own failings."

Sir Edward laughed. "Ah yes, that is me. Inept and a constant disappointment—from the day I was born." He stretched out on the ground and poked at the embers of the fire. "I do not remember much of my mother. I was only six when she died, still too young to see her more than half a dozen times a year." He shrugged. "My sisters all speak fondly of her, but as it is, the only parent I remember is my father, and he and I were mostly like oil and water."

"Your father was a great king," Adam said.

"By all accounts, a good father as well. But a harsh father when it came to his eldest surviving son, the runt that lived when precious, golden Alphonso died." A sudden flaring of the fire lit up Sir Edward's face, accentuating the high cheekbones and scruffy beard. "I was never good enough," he said. "Where other young men raced to the lists, I preferred to build and row, learn how to shoe a horse and bend the fiery iron to my will. Not, I might add, pursuits my father approved of. And then there was Piers."

"Ah yes, the Gascon upstart you gave the earldom intended for your brother."

Sir Edward gave him a sour look. "You wouldn't understand."

Adam didn't reply, one eye on Sir Edward's hand, snaking ever so discreetly towards the staff Adam had thrown to the ground. Besides, the man was right: he wouldn't understand—not the preference for handsome men, not the willingness to have those favourites rule him.

Something rustled. A twig snapped, followed by the muted sound of feet approaching at a run. Adam leapt to his feet, sword in one hand, dagger in the other.

"Here!" Sir Edward yelled, "I'm—" Egard slammed him to the ground just as half a dozen or so men charged into the clearing. One man died instantly, Adam's sword lopping off his head. From what little he could see, these were men of the woods—except that they wore mail beneath their rough tunics.

Adam grunted when one of the men landed a glancing blow on his chest. Thank the Lord he had heeded Kit's advice and worn his coat of plates! Kit? He used his sword to parry the blow of the man in front of him, stabbed at his face with his dagger. The man collapsed, howling. One downward thrust with his sword and the man was dead. Kit? Where was she? Egard yelled a warning, and Adam threw himself to the ground to avoid the swipe of an axe. Close enough that he could smell the steel edge swishing by his cheek. Moments later, the man fell face forward, Egard's sword buried in his brain. Up. Adam was up, and there was only one man left standing. The ruffian made as if to retreat. Adam attacked. No survivors, not from this. It was an uneven fight, Adam being twice the size of the fool facing him. A swipe to the legs and the man sank to his knees, pleading for his life. The rest was quick and messy, spraying Adam with blood and gore. Kit. He made for the fire.

"Sir!" Egard yelled, and Adam whirled to see their erstwhile king legging it, making for the trees.

"Get him!" Adam stood no chance against a hale man—not on foot. "Kit?" Her cloak and blanket lay in a heap on the ground. "Kit?" His voice rose.

"Here." She stood up from behind a bramble, long shoots covered with thorns that caught on his sleeve when he made to help her. She took his hand, released it abruptly. "You're bleeding!"

"Not so that it hurts." He led her back towards their camp, kicked life in the fire, and had her sit down close. She stared at him. He wiped at his face, his hand coming away even bloodier than before.

Egard came back, dragging a spitting and cursing Sir Edward with him.

"Sit," Adam snarled. "And while you do so, think of any reason why I should let you live after tonight."

Kit inhaled, clasped her arms around her knees, but didn't say anything.

"Why?" Sir Edward shook as if with the ague. "I ran because they were trying to kill me. Me!"

"You? Don't be a fool, they—"

"He's telling the truth," Kit interrupted. "One of them made straight for him with his axe."

"Aye," Egard said. "He didn't reckon with having his nose broken by a staff, though."

"Or his neck severed by a sword." Sir Edward grinned at Egard. "I owe you my life, I think."

"But…" Adam surveyed the little glade. Six dead men, lying as they had fallen. "You called out to them!"

"Happens I thought they were here to rescue me, not murder me." Sir Edward threw some more wood on the fire. Adam set light to a branch and beckoned for Egard to follow him. They went from corpse to corpse. Nothing to identify the men, no distinctive colours, no badges—just six unfamiliar faces, most of them looking as they'd been living rough for quite some time. Adam straightened up, shared a concerned look with Egard.

"Who wants him dead?" he murmured.

"Everyone, my lord." Egard spat to the side. "Mortimer, the young king…" He shrugged. "And there are plenty of men who have not forgotten what Despenser did to them in the name of his king."

"But they didn't know about this venture." Adam clenched his jaw. Lord Roger knew. King Edward knew, as did Queen Isabella. And God knew how many at Corfe knew. A mess.

Egard prodded at the closest corpse. "Or maybe they did. Not everyone's silence can be bought."

They left the clearing some hours later. Six shallow graves, a deeper pit containing weaponry, and Adam was weary to the bones. Kit had washed his face as well as she could, but there was blood in his hair, on his clothes, and the shallow gash on his arm was still seeping.

"Creative," Sir Edward said, breaking the silence.

"How so?"

"To first offer me my freedom and then take the opportunity to murder me when I am well away from Corfe. It smells of Mortimer."

"Or your son," Adam told him harshly.

Sir Edward looked away. "I trust you understand if I say I'd prefer it to be Mortimer."

"Too honourable." Kit sounded as tired as Adam felt. "Lord Mortimer would not lower himself to such."

"And my son might?"

Kit shook her head. "I can't see it. He's too young, too full of tales of chivalry and good deeds."

"And yet it is he who has ordered me to be spirited away, isn't it?" Sir Edward frowned down at a tear in his tunic.

"Aye." Adam held in his horse, looked up and down the deserted road before beckoning for them to ride over it, disappearing into the woods on the opposite side.

"He doesn't want a rival king at hand, not now, not when he's finally beginning to comprehend just how much power a strong king can wield," Sir Edward said. "That hunger for power he has from his mother, not from me. The question is, how far would he go to ensure he sits safe on his throne?"

None of them replied. At long last, Sir Edward cleared his throat. "I still think it is Mortimer. Or Maltravers."

Chapter 33

"There." Kit took a step back, wiping the razor clean. The man before her was transformed, no traces of the former king visible in this gaunt, rather harsh face.

"It feels unfamiliar." Sir Edward ran his hand over his clean-shaven face. "Since I became a man, I've always had a beard." He touched his head. "And a full mane of hair."

Not so any longer, the matted mess having been cut down to a neat little fringe round a new tonsure. He had not liked it at first, protesting angrily when Adam explained just how he was to disguise himself.

But now, after a long bath in which Kit had attended to him—chaperoned by a surly Adam who did not understand why Edward of Caernarvon couldn't wash himself like he had done—he had resigned himself, sitting quietly while Kit shaved him. The shirt Adam had procured was too large, flapping round a frame that consisted of little muscle and much bone.

"It's not as if I've been fed swan and venison," Sir Edward commented, frowning down at his thin legs. Kit handed him a pair of clean braies and looked away while he busied himself putting them on.

"Neither is it bread and water, like you did with Lord Roger," Adam retorted. "And he was never offered clean clothes or a bath while he was your prisoner, was he?" He finished drying his hair and threw the towel to land with the others.

"Always this Mortimer." Sir Edward threw Adam a sly glance. "One could almost think you besotted with him."

Adam's hands clenched and he took a couple of threatening steps towards Sir Edward.

Kit intercepted him. "Ignore him."

"Yes, please do. Everyone else has been doing that for the last few years." Sir Edward scowled. "Me, an anointed king, held a prisoner. Unlawfully, I might add."

"You expected a trial?" Adam sneered. "Maybe like the one Despenser got?"

"A travesty!" Sir Edward was on his feet, eyes on fire. "The verdict was a given."

"It was." Adam rubbed a hand over his face, a tremor running through him. Sir Edward sagged down on the stool.

"It was bad, wasn't it?"

Adam just nodded.

"Poor Hugh." Sir Edward turned the ring he carried on his little finger around. "He was always afraid of dying badly."

"He didn't." Adam shoved the door open. "We leave within the hour," he said over his shoulder, the door banging in his wake.

"I take it Sir Adam did not relish witnessing Hugh's death as much as he thought he would." Sir Edward's eyes narrowed. "Quite the spectacle, they told me."

"I did not see it, thank the Lord." Kit shook out the heavy friar's robe and handed it to him. The black Dominican robe leant him an air of austerity—and piety.

"Brutes." Sir Edward adjusted the heavy belt.

"He died no differently to those you condemned to death for treason."

"The difference being that he was no traitor." Sir Edward slipped on the heavy sandals and wiggled his toes.

"That is a matter of perspective, and whether for treason or not, Despenser deserved to die."

"Well, we will never agree on that, will we?"

"No. But then you were always glaringly blind to his obvious faults."

Sir Edward's mouth twisted. "No, I wasn't. But I needed him and loved him, and so…" He looked away. "There was another side to him, you know. With me, he was ever tender, always there to comfort me when I so required." Sir Edward opened his hands, fingers splayed. "He loved me." Long fingers braided together, and he studied his clasped hands for a long time. "And I loved him." There were tears in his eyes when he looked at Kit. "They say such love is a sin. They say…" He cleared his throat. "I just loved him. How can that be wrong?"

"He wasn't executed for buggering the king," Adam said harshly when Kit shared this conversation with him. They were now safely installed in yet another inn, this time on the northern outskirts of Poole, with Egard and Sir Edward snoring on pallets while Adam and Kit had the bed, a modicum of privacy offered by the thick if worn bed hangings. All the same, they kept their voices down.

"Despenser died for a variety of sins, most of them to do with greed, not lust." He fidgeted in bed, complaining that it was too hot to lie entombed in all this fabric—even more so when Kit had insisted they light the headboard candle.

The little room was stifling to begin with, and with the shutters firmly closed, it was hot enough to make a pig sweat. Nor did it help that they'd supped on onion soup, or that Egard farted as regularly as an old dog. Kit kicked off the bedclothes and rolled over on her belly, propping herself up on her elbows. There'd been no opportunity to talk to Adam properly since the incident last night, and she'd spent most of their day's ride thinking things over.

"Was it Mortimer, you think?"

Adam sighed and covered his face with his arm. "I don't know." The anguish in his voice had her shifting closer. "The man who raised me, who taught me everything I know about how to be good and honourable, he would never do something like that."

"Sometimes, expediency serves the greater good." Kit brushed a hand through his hair, releasing the faint scents of soapwort and chamomile. "But I can't see Mortimer doing this—not for Sir Edward's sake, but for yours."

"Mine?" Adam half sat up.

"You'd never have forgiven yourself if he'd been killed, and Mortimer knows that." Kit smiled at how relieved he looked.

"Who, then?" He turned towards her. "Not the king, Kit. Surely, he wouldn't—" She set a finger to his lips.

"We will never know," she told him. "It could have been Maltravers."

"Not without Lord Roger knowing."

"Or one of his men. Or Queen Isabella, to protect her son."

"Once again, not without Lord Roger knowing."

Kit laughed softly, pressing her lips to his throat. "Men can be such fools at times. Do you really think she'd share her intentions with him, knowing he'd object?"

Adam relaxed against the pillows. "You truly don't think Lord Roger did it?"

"Your precious Lord Roger is ruthless and ambitious. He is not above using guile to vanquish his adversaries—I dare say he does so all the time—but foul murder?" Kit shook her head. She kissed him again, sliding on top of him to snuff out the candle. Her chemise rode up, she tugged at his shirt, and it was bare skin against bare skin, groin against groin.

"Kit! Not now," he admonished, but his arms tightened round her, contradicting his words.

"They're asleep, and we will be very quiet," she whispered, and already he was hard. "I need you." The sight of him covered in blood had unnerved her, haunting her for most of the day. It could have been him dead, all of them slaughtered by a group of men who had no interest in leaving living witnesses behind.

Adam gripped her head and kissed her—lips bruising hers, tongue forceful as it claimed her mouth. He rolled her over. The straw in the mattress rustled, and for a heartbeat or two they held still, listening. Their companions went on snoring, but there were no other sounds. Adam covered her mouth with his when he entered her. A gentle rocking, no more, and the bed creaked, the straw rustled. Kit did not care. She had her man in her arms. His hair tickled her face, his breath warmed her skin. She widened her legs, and he sank that much deeper, his weight holding her still.

"Sweeting," he murmured in her ear. Slowly, he eased out. Just as slowly, he surged back in. A steady, relentless pace, and inside of her the heat built, all of her contracting round the strength and size of him. She inhaled, sank her fingers into his arms, and there was his mouth, swallowing down whatever sounds she made as she found her release.

They were on their way again just after dawn. Adam led the way, Sir Edward and Kit rode side by side, and last of all came

Egard. In difference to the preceding day, it was drizzling, which allowed for all of them to ride with their hoods up—a good thing, according to Adam, who kept a watchful eye on anyone too close to them.

Only once they'd left Poole safely behind did Adam agree to stop and break their fast, a brief meal of bread and ale before they were on their way again. The rain had stopped, and the August day was warm enough to make Kit unclasp her cloak, folding it together before fastening it behind the cantle of her saddle. A gust of wind caught her veil, lifting it to fly behind her. Beside her, Sir Edward stilled.

"What happened to your face?"

Kit clapped a self-conscious hand over her scarred cheek. "Despenser," she said, and Sir Edward's cheeks reddened.

"Hugh? No, I find that hard to believe."

"Believe what you want. This scar is a reminder of the night when your tenderhearted favourite attempted to rape me."

"Rape you?" Sir Edward's voice shook. He rode closer. "You lie. That is a new scar."

"Not all of it." Kit told him. "But yes, you're right: that last cut I got some weeks ago, courtesy of Godfrey of Broseley." She studied him carefully, but from the blank expression on his face, this was not a name he recognised.

"Ah." He rode in silence for a while. "A man who attacks a lady is a dishonourable man."

Kit looked away. "Like you did with Lady Badlesmere?"

"I never touched her! Nor did I let anyone harm her, I just—"

"Locked her up and kept her on a pittance. Like you did with Lady Joan." She adjusted her veil, winding the loose ends round her neck to keep it in place.

"Their men were rebels," Sir Edward said coldly. "Dishonoured by their own actions."

"Dishonoured?" Kit laughed. "Are you saying men like Lord Mortimer have no honour?"

"Honour?" Edward scowled. "It's Mortimer's damned prickly sense of honour that has caused all this, isn't it? Accusing me of breaking my word, of dishonouring my coronation oaths. So yes, he has honour—*had* honour." He glanced at her. "Not anymore, though. Not now that he spends his nights with that faithless whore Isabella."

"You pushed her away," Kit said. "Year after year of having her influence curtailed as you favoured the Despensers—always the Despensers—over her."

Edward's countenance reddened. At long last, he turned to look at her. "She is my wife. She owes me obedience and allegiance."

"As you owe her to treat her fairly." Kit suppressed a little burst of laughter, uncomfortable in being cast as Queen Isabella's defender. "But before all this, was she not also honourable?"

"Aye," Edward replied with a sigh. "She was. Beautiful and learned, and as full of honour as any knight."

Kit nodded, no more. "And yet she and Mortimer dare the censure of the world, the fires of hell everlasting. Do you believe that is an easy thing?"

"Easy? It is lust, plain and simple."

"No, it is passion, a consuming fever. Both of them know there will be a price to pay; neither of them can help it, drawn as moths to a burning flame." Kit urged her palfrey into a trot. "What they have is an affliction, my lord, not a blessing."

"Are you saying they deserve my compassion? For betraying me? Ousting me from my throne and seducing my son into treason?"

"I dare say England is the better for it."

Sir Edward hawked and spat to the side. "I never asked to be king."

They rode in silence after that, Sir Edward lost in his own thoughts.

"I don't know." Adam looked at Egard and then back at the road. "Maybe we should ride round it."

"It would take us several days, m'lord," Egard protested.

"If there is to be a second attempt, it will be there." Adam nodded at the forest and shifted in his saddle.

315

"As yet, no one knows the first attempt failed," Sir Edward put in.

"No." Adam wanted this over and done with, see the former king safely on his way to France and be done with it. But to ride into the New Forest was to play right into the hands of a would-be ambushing party. "I should have hired some men at Christchurch."

"Not an option, m'lord."

"No, heaven forbid that someone recognise their king in this lanky friar," Sir Edward muttered. He cast Adam a look. "Is it me or your wife you fear for?"

"My wife." Adam gnawed his lip, eyes on where Kit had disappeared behind a screen of shrubs to relieve herself.

"So we ride swiftly, with her in our midst," Sir Edward suggested. "I'll need a weapon, of course."

Adam snorted. "And what is to stop you from turning a blade on one of us?" His hold on his sword relaxed when Kit stepped into sight, skirts held high as she made her way back to them through the high grass.

"On you?" Sir Edward blinked. "God's teeth, man, do you take me for a fool? If we are attacked, it is me they want to kill!"

"And if he tries anything, I'll bury my blade in him," Egard added laconically.

"Hmm." Adam dismounted to help Kit up on her horse. "Fine, you can have a sword."

They rode in close formation, Kit in their midst. Not a word, Adam scanning their right, Egard their left. Now and then, Sir Edward cleared his throat, and out of the corner of his eye, Adam saw him gripping the hilt of the sword he'd been given.

They arrived in a hamlet called Brockenhurst in less than an hour. Not that the motley collection of cottages made Adam feel any more secure. Rather the reverse, in fact, what with the gawping villagers. A friar with a sword was in itself enough to have them staring, and when they caught sight of Adam's hauberk, several of them shrank into the protective shadows of the houses.

Kit drew her horse to a stop. "I used to pass by here every summer." She pointed south. "That way Lymington and the sea."

"Lymington? And what would a lady like you do there?" Sir Edward asked.

"Help in the saltworks," Kit replied, kicking her horse into a trot. "We ride for Lyndhurst, I suppose."

"M'lady, wait." Egard caught up with her. "Might make sense to ride beside the road rather than on it," he said, directing himself to Adam. The road ran straight in front of them, bordered by trees. Anyone coming down the road would be visible at a great distance to someone lurking among the trees. Adam's scalp itched.

"You lead," he told Egard. "And keep your eyes wide open."

"Always do, m'lord. Have found it helps to see where you're going."

It was slow going, a careful passing through the dappled shade beneath the trees. On foot, they walked in single file, Egard well ahead while Adam led both Egard's and his horse. When Egard held up his hand, they all halted, and Adam handed the reins of the horses to Sir Edward, moving as soundlessly as he could to join Egard. His man pointed. Some distance ahead was a glade. And in that glade, something moved.

Adam backed up forty or fifty yards. He gestured for Kit and Sir Edward to stay with the horses. Sir Edward nodded and drew his sword. Kit's eyes were huge, but she held her dagger steadily enough. He turned on his toes and padded after Egard.

Three men. From the looks of things, they'd been here for some days, blankets and other gear visible among the undergrowth. At present, they were all focussed on the road, one holding a bow, his companion hefting an axe, while the third was leaning against a tree, a sword balanced across his knees.

"This is a waste of time," one of them growled.

"Well-paid waste of time," the man with the sword said. "Three more days, and then we are free to go. Until then, we remain here, on the lookout for four travellers, one of whom is a woman."

"I wouldn't mind one of those," the older of the bowmen said, making a lewd gesture.

"You know our orders. If they come, we kill them. All of them, even the woman with the scar."

Dearest God! Adam gripped Egard's shoulder. Who? Not Lord Roger—he would never do something like this. Or maybe he would. Adam no longer knew, the world as he knew it turned upside down. Someone had callously ordered their murder. And he could only come up with three names: Lord Roger, Queen Isabella, or King Edward.

Beside him, Egard had nocked an arrow. He raised his brow in an unspoken question. Adam nodded, the arrow flew, and before anyone had time to react, Egard had sent of yet another arrow. Two men, skewered through their uncovered necks. They made a lot of noise as they went down, one of them shrieking like a cut pig before the sound ended in a gurgle.

"Shit!" The man with the sword flew to his feet. "Help!" he yelled, and there were several sets of feet pounding across the road. Moments later, Adam and Egard were fighting for their lives, an uneven five against two.

Back to back, they cut and thrust and swiped. One went down. Egard exclaimed, fell to his knees, and there was blood on the grass, an axe slicing through the air. At the last moment, Egard rolled towards the axe man. More blood, and now there were three. Adam wiped at his eyes. Blood was dripping from his brow, and something had nicked him over the shoulder, an odd straining sensation that made it difficult to raise his sword.

He slipped, his bad foot giving way. A flashing blade, and he parried. Again, and the jarring sensation through his shoulder had his sword dipping towards the ground. The man in front of him sneered and raised his blade. Death stared Adam in the face, small eyes alight with bloodlust. There was a crunching sound, and where there had been a neck, there was now an open wound, blood spraying madly over Adam, over the dying man, and over Sir Edward, both hands gripping the hilt of his sword.

Some time later, it was over. The last two men were as dead as their companions, one of them nailed to the ground by Sir Edward's sword through his midriff. The glade looked and smelled like a slaughterhouse. Adam staggered over to a nearby tree, braced himself against it, and inhaled several gulps of steadying air, dispelling the dizzy sensation that had his vision blurring, his legs dipping.

"Kit?" he asked.

"With the horses." Sir Edward pulled his sword free and wiped the blade on the tunic of one of the dead. "She should not see this."

That made Adam laugh. He could only imagine what he himself looked like, but their disguised friar looked as if he'd rolled himself in a tub of blood, and as to Egard, something had hit him straight over his large and misshapen nose, causing a fountain of blood down his front.

"Your leg?" he asked.

Egard grimaced. "Bad."

"And you?" Adam asked Sir Edward.

"Unscathed—a nick or two, no more." Sir Edward slipped an arm round Egard. "We'd best get going."

"Leave them here?" Adam looked at the dead men. All men deserved to be buried.

"No time, no strength. Frying friars, but you weigh like an ox!" Sir Edward gasped, half dragging, half supporting Egard.

A mute Kit rose to her feet at their approach. Not a sound, not a word as she hurled herself into Adam's arms, her hands already inspecting his face, the cut through his left brow. He winced, his right shoulder protesting under her weight, and she released him as if scalded.

"You're hurt!"

"He'll live," Sir Edward said. "Egard, however, needs immediate help."

A reprimand that had Kit's face reddening. Adam touched her cheek, no more, in a silent assurance that he was not seriously harmed

"See to Egard, sweeting."

They arrived at Lyndhurst just before nightfall. Adam had his arm in a sling, Egard's leg had been tightly bandaged from groin to knee, and they'd scrubbed the worst of the blood off their faces and hands. Not all of it, to judge from the shock on the steward's face.

"Brigands," Adam told him. "Seven men to bury further up the road." He dug about in his pouch, produced his royal writ. The steward made big eyes at the royal seal, bid them welcome to Queen Isabella's manor, and asked them what they needed.

"Hot water," Kit said. "Yarrow, meadowsweet, comfrey, and salt. And some burnt wine or vinegar if you have it."

"Yes, yes, of course, my lady." The steward led the way to their quarters.

She began with Egard. Sir Edward sat beside them, holding the big man's hand as Kit first set his nose, then washed the deep gash in his thigh, using so much salt Egard's eyes squished together. After all this washing, she sewed him up, packing the leg in fragrant poultices before she bandaged him with clean strips of linen.

"Now you." She had Adam sit down and helped him undress. His shoulder blade was throbbing, and her soft hands, the heat of the wet rag she used to wash him, had him holding his breath. "It's none too bad," she said, but her voice was shaking.

He set a hand to her thigh and squeezed. "I've had worse, sweeting." She rested her forehead against his, inhaled, and went on with her ministrations.

Once his shoulder had been seen to, she washed his face. Gently, carefully, she rubbed away the last of the dried blood. Strong fingers inspected his nose, his cheekbones, lingered over his slashed brow, already scabbing nicely.

"Who?" she whispered.

"I don't know. But I have decided on a change of plans." He caught hold of a lock of her hair, wound it round his finger. "We no longer make for Dover."

"Wise move," Sir Edward said from the opposite side of the room. "We're not in shape to fight off yet another set of assassins."

Chapter 34

They stayed in Lyndhurst for four days, with Adam and Sir Edward taking turns to keep guard by their door. Having a royal writ ensured they got what they asked for, so when Adam requested a cart and a drover to see them to Hythe, the steward fell over his feet in his eagerness to comply—or be rid of them.

Egard protested volubly at being transported on the flatbed of the cart, but Kit insisted he should stay off the leg for some days yet, and Adam did not dare to tarry. A whole day of travelling through narrow roads, and at last they saw the Southampton Water, the opposite shore but a ferry ride away.

"To Netley?" the ferryman asked, counting the coins Adam had given him.

"Aye." He led the horses aboard, two at the time.

"And then on to Southampton?" the drover asked as he helped Sir Edward get Egard out of the cart. Adam nodded. No, they were not going to Southampton, but best cover their tracks, just in case.

By the time they'd made it over to the other side, Egard was covered with cold sweat. An entire day being jostled back and forth had not aided his recovery, and it was amidst much cursing he hobbled to the abbey's gatehouse, leaning heavily on his crutches.

"The infirmary?" Adam glowered at the monk. "For how long?"

"Three days at least. Whoever saw to the original wound has done a good job, but the man needs to rest." Two sharp eyes studied Adam. "You look as if you could do with some as well."

"No time," Adam snapped.

"No choice," the monk retorted. He swept off, a flurry of white and black. Like a giant magpie, Adam reflected before joining his two remaining fellow travellers for the evening meal.

"It might have worked to our benefit," Kit said some days later. "Three days here, and they don't know where we are." She helped him tighten the girth on her palfrey.

Adam grunted, no more.

Thank the Lord, Egard was fit enough to sit astride, and soon enough they were on their way to Portsmouth.

"And then what?" Sir Edward asked.

"You take ship to Bordeaux—or elsewhere," Adam said. A bustling port, Portsmouth handled most of the trade from Bordeaux, wine coming to England, wool and mutton going the other way.

"Ah." Sir Edward scratched at his head. The tonsure was no longer quite as neat as it had been. "And I take it this is not in line with your instructions."

"If I follow them, chances are we'll all end up dead."

Sir Edward nodded. "So what's to stop me from revealing who I am once I am in France?" He smiled. "Especially in Bordeaux."

"I am," Egard said. "I'll be coming with you."

"You will?" Sir Edward's smile widened into a grin. "A longing for adventure, dear Egard?"

"I've had my fill of adventure, m'lord. But I wouldn't mind seeing a bit more of the world. One never knows when death catches up with you."

They all crossed themselves. "As God ordains." Sir Edward stood in his stirrups, looking about at the patchwork of harvested fields and meadows. "Will I ever see England again?"

"I fear not, my lord." Adam held in his horse, allowing their former king to take in the landscape around them. Kit and Egard ambled along, the packhorse in their wake.

"And my sons, my daughters? Will I ever see them again?"

Adam made a helpless gesture. "In God's hands."

"God? More like in the hands of that treacherous wife of mine—and her lover, may he wake up poxed."

Adam held his tongue. In some years, it would neither be the queen nor Lord Roger ruling England, it would be this man's son. But even then, Adam suspected the son would not welcome the presence of his sire.

"Exiled." Sir Edward exhaled. "I will walk like a man without a shadow—no past, no future."

"That is up to you, my lord. The past, the present, it is gone as we speak, but the future lies as yet unchartered."

Edward gave him a crooked smile. "A philosopher, Sir Adam?"

Adam shrugged and pulled the billowing cloak tight around him.

"Will he make a good king, my son?" Sir Edward's question came out of the blue, surprising Adam.

"Aye, I think he will." Better than his father, of that Adam was sure, seeing in his young master the skills required to threaten when needed, but mostly to manipulate and cajole, preferring the carrot to the stick. Most of all, this young king of theirs would never allow a single baron to rise above the others—which did not bode well for Lord Roger.

"A good king does not allow himself to be ruled by a whore," Edward said acidly. "Neither does he bend to the will of an upstart baron."

"Or to that of his favourites," Adam retorted, stung into defence of his lord.

Edward clenched his hand, studying nails that were no longer well cared for. "They're dead," he said flatly. "They've paid for their supposed sins." He fixed bright eyes on Adam. "One day, my son will tire of his leading reins."

"Aye." Adam looked away. "Soon enough, the eaglet will resent those who keep him leashed."

"And once he does, he will smite them." Sir Edward grinned. "I cannot wait."

Such sentiments were to be expected from the man who lost his crown because of Lord Roger and the queen, but all the same, the words had Adam's bowels turning to water.

Sir Edward cuffed him lightly on his injured shoulder. "It puts you in an untenable position, doesn't it?" He sounded curious rather than compassionate. "You love Mortimer—and you love my son."

"I do."

"It's either one or the other, Adam. Personally, I hope Mortimer dies as Hugh did."

323

Adam chose not to reply. Instead, he changed the subject. "What will you do next?"

Sir Edward collected the reins and set the horse to a trot. "I'm not sure. For the first time in my life, I have no one to please but myself. No expectations I can never live up to, no constant quibbling with this baron or the other." He pointed at a gull wheeling overhead. "For once, I am free, de Guirande, truly free to be the man I am." He threw Adam a look. "I think I'll start by visiting the pope. I've always wanted to see Avignon." With that, he urged his mount into a canter.

Edward of Caernarvon wore nondescript brown hose, a tunic of an indeterminate shade of green, and a simple hooded mantle that matched his hose. "I could melt into nonexistence in a forest," he jested, adjusting the hat he'd insisted on wearing to cover his head.

"Except you'll be on a ship," Kit reminded him.

"I will." He looked over at Egard, as plainly dressed as he was. Both carried coins sewn into their clothes, tucked into various pouches on their persons, stuffed into the leather bags Egard had found to use as satchels. "I am glad he is coming with me."

"He'll see you safe, my lord." Kit smiled at him. "As long as you hold to your promise, of course."

"Oh, I will." Sir Edward shook himself. "A new life, Lady Kit. Not many men get the opportunity to reinvent themselves."

"May it be a good life, my lord." She dropped into a deep reverence, and he took a step back, looking surprised. "May God keep you safe."

"And you," Sir Edward replied, gesturing for her to rise. He pulled off one of his rings and handed it to her. "For my daughter-in-law, when she has presented my son with an heir." Kit closed her hand around it, feeling its weight.

"I will keep it safe until then."

There'd been no shortage of vessels from which to choose. Sir Edward had refused setting foot on any of the ships flying the Hanseatic pennant, saying he had no desire to end up in the northern wilds of Europe.

"All they eat is herring," he said with a grimace. "I say such fare is bad enough during Lent."

So instead, they'd found berths on one of the cogs destined for Bayonne, a stout enough vessel captained by a Cornish man who'd said little but "aye" and "no".

They made their farewells on the quay. Egard turned the colour of a beet when Kit embraced him, grinned when Adam slapped him on the back, and promised to do his best to make sure no one else broke his nose. Sir Edward bowed to Kit, shook Adam's hand, and, just before he stepped onto the gangway, he crouched, setting the palm of his hand to the ground.

"One last touch," he said with a rueful smile, and his eyes glistened with tears. And then he was gone, leading the way aboard with Egard hobbling after him. Kit and Adam remained on the quay until the cog was safely on its way, a heaving thing that dipped and rose as it left the protected waters of the harbour. And all the while they stood there, they could see the dwindling speck that was their former king, standing in the aft and staring back at the country he would never again return to.

"Home?" Adam asked once the ship had dropped out of sight.

"Home." She nestled into him. "He is not a bad man."

"No. He was just a dismal king."

The ride to Tresaints was uneventful. After one last night in Worcester, they returned home on a cloudy August afternoon, the air heavy with thunder and rain.

"I can't stay for more than a day or so," Adam sighed as they turned up the long lane. "I am expected back to report on my venture."

"Do you want me to ride with you?" she asked, but he could hear it in her voice, see it in how eagerly she studied their approaching home, that Kit would prefer to remain here, at least for some weeks. Truth be told, so would he, but he had no choice. The king's instructions had been explicit. Once he had concluded his mission, he was to present himself at court to update his lord and master.

"I do, but I think it best you stay here." He smiled. "We have children who have need of their mother. And a foundling," he added, nodding in the direction of the little lad approaching them at a run with Meg yelling at him to wait for her.

Kit slid off her horse and ran to meet the children, arms held wide. Meg barged into her. Tom held back, sliding to a stop some feet away. There was a marked difference between this clean and well-fed lad and the urchin Adam had first met back in June. Thick fair hair fell to his shoulders, his previously pinched expression had converted into the round cheeks typical of childhood, and there was even a hesitant smile on his face. His eyes, however, remained wary, darting from Kit to Adam and back again.

Adam dismounted and handed the reins to Tom. "Will you take him to the stables for me?" The lad lit up, took hold of the reins, and strutted off, as proud as a peacock.

"A future stable boy?" Kit asked, lifting Meg to sit on her hip.

"We'll see." He hoisted Meg out of her mother's arms, threw her straight up, and kissed her all over once he'd caught her again. His daughter smelled of milk and grass, of honey and bread.

"Again!" Meg demanded, squirming like an eel in his arms. Adam complied before settling her atop his shoulders. He held out his hand to Kit, and together they walked the last stretch of the lane, on one side bordered by the hornbeams, on the other by a ditch and brambles dotted with ripening hips.

"He must have grown a foot!" Kit crouched before Ned, who hid his face against the folds of Mabel's skirts.

"Not likely, m'lady," Mabel snorted. She disengaged Ned from her skirts and gave him a gentle push in the direction of Kit. Instead, the laddie turned towards Adam. His son and heir, dark red hair peeking from under his coif. Adam lifted Meg to the ground and knelt, holding out a hand to the toddler, who negotiated cobbles and puddles while clutching a rag doll to his chest. He never made it.

"My papa!" Meg shoved Ned, sending him sprawling in the dirt. Ned bawled, struggling to rise. Meg made as if to clamber into Adam's arms, but he shook his head, holding her at a distance.

"Help your brother."

Meg set her mouth in a stubborn line, blue eyes flashing. It made him want to laugh, reminding him as it did of Kit when she was aggravated. But he didn't. Instead, he lowered himself until he could look Meg in the eyes. "You heard," he said, stopping Kit from lifting Ned up with a quick look.

"He fell," Meg tried. Adam just looked at her. "He's a baby!" she wailed. "He fell."

"Girls that lie go to bed without their sweetmeats," Adam told her, "and likely with a smarting arse."

Meg hiccupped, hands settling protectively on her rear.

"Help him up. And you will apologise to him as well."

Meg's lower lip jutted. "He fell."

"Very well." In a flash, he had his daughter over his knee. Three smart smacks and she was back on her feet, howling in anger. "Bed," Adam ordered. "Act a babe and expect to be treated like a babe."

"Papa!" She kicked at him. Adam swung her up and handed her to Mabel.

"Bed," he said. "Now."

"Home." Kit's voice shook with amusement. She handed him his eldest son. "Some years from now, it is likely him shoving her."

"Or one of his younger siblings." He smiled at her. "I am right, am I not?"

She lowered her eyelashes. Thick and dark, they fluttered like butterflies against her cheeks. A nod, no more, her hand slipping down to her belly. He took her hand and pressed a soft kiss to her palm.

"I am glad, my lady. Now, how about we find our other son?"

His children, his horses, his walls, and his stores—he'd inspected them all, and Adam felt content as he settled in the large armchair reserved for the lord of the manor and nodded for Stephen to pour him some wine.

"A good harvest," he said to William, who had ridden in just before sunset, having spent most of the day with the flocks pastured in the farther meadows.

"We'll not starve this winter," William agreed, digging into the stew. He broke off a piece of bread. "We've had some sheep stolen, though."

"Ah. Some of your converts?" Adam teased, his laughter converted into a grunt when William elbowed him—hard.

"Not a jesting matter." William scowled. "Outlaws, likely. Plenty of them around these days, what with all these recent years of upheaval." He lowered his voice, a cautious eye on Kit, who was presently deep in conversation with Mabel and John. "As I hear it, Lancaster and that ingrate Thomas Wake are fanning the flames of discontent in London."

"They are?" Adam looked at his brother. "And how do you know?"

"Friends. Literate friends." William grinned. "Remember that wine merchant we stayed with back in 1323—old Laurence?"

"Aye."

"Well, he remains a Mortimer man—and he does not like how Hamo de Chigwell and Henry Luytens speak out against Lord Roger, blaming him for every ill that has befallen their city."

"The Londoners have always played by their own rules. Think themselves above the rest of us." Adam sipped at his wine. "Let's see how well they do on the field, eh? Rabble, William. Give me four score men and I'll have them bleating their worthless vows of loyalty to the king and Lord Roger."

William's brows rose. "You underestimate them. The London merchants may be useless in the field, but they have the gold to buy themselves an army. More importantly, they are presently buying Lancaster one."

"And does Lord Roger know?"

"He does." William shoved his bowl away. "And I'll send a report with you tomorrow." He clasped Adam's hand. "Must you leave so soon?"

"I must."

"Urgent?"

"It is." Adam needed advice, and if there was one person whom he trusted implicitly, it was William. Kit and William—the only two people he'd trust with anything. Once, that list had been longer, but these days…Like his young king, he thought with a crooked smile, reluctant to place trust in anyone but his wife and brother. "If I tell you something, you must swear never to tell."

"You forget I am a priest."

"I am not talking about confession." Adam frowned, trying to recall when last he'd been shriven. Far too many months ago, he reckoned, but best not tell William, or his brother would insist on having Adam confess to him—something Adam found uncomfortable at best.

"Neither am I," William said. "But why not take this conversation to the chapel? Fewer ears and all that."

Kit looked up as they left, lips pursing slightly. "Will you be long?"

"No." He leaned over her. "About as long as it takes for you to get ready for bed, my lady."

"Single-minded man," she murmured, setting a hand to his cheek. "Are you going to tell him?"

"Aye."

"Good."

The chapel was deserted and dark, the single candle Kit ordered to be kept lit for her children spreading a wavering halo of light on the altar. Adam suggested they sit on one of the two benches and leaned back against the cool wall, and then he began to talk.

By the time he was done, William was so agitated he could not keep still.

"You must be wrong!" He rose, did a little turn round the chapel, came back to sit on the bench. "Wrong, Adam."

"And yet I bear the scars to prove I was attacked."

"By brigands aiming to free that erstwhile king of ours!"

Adam just shook his head. "I heard them, William. They had instructions to kill us all. All—including Kit."

"Mother of God!" William was on his feet again, pacing back and forth. His dark robes swirled around him, hairy shins visible under the billowing fabric. "But who—" he interrupted himself. "No." He gave Adam a beseeching look. "No, Adam."

Adam shrugged. He'd prefer it not to be true either.

"It could be someone who overheard," William said. "Half a sentence there, another here, and maybe someone thought to rid himself of two enervating flies at the same time: the former king and the present king's favourite knight."

"Me?" Adam laughed. "I don't think I am King Edward's favourite." But the weight in his chest lifted at William's words. Maybe he was right—except that whoever had planted those assassins had known exactly what route Adam intended to take.

"Then you are blind, deaf, and dumb." William sat down beside him. "The king loves you, Brother. And so does Lord Roger."

"Which leaves the queen." Adam had to laugh at the horrified expression on William's face—an instant of mirth before he recalled just how serious this matter was.

"The queen? She is a good woman."

"Some call her an adulterous she-wolf," Adam reminded him.

William scowled. "Aye, this matter with Lord Roger…" He shook his head. "To live openly in sin—it will cost them in the hereafter. But from there to murder—that is a giant leap, Adam."

Adam gave him a tired look. "So who, William? The king I'd give my life for? The lord I love with all my heart?"

"Someone else." William pursed his lips. "And whatever the case, you can never voice these suspicions, not to anyone. Should anyone ask, you were attacked by brigands, outlaws out to plunder you and carry off your fair wife." He closed his hands, muttered something in Latin. "Witnesses," he said slowly. "Whoever ordered this done wanted there to be no loose ends."

"And now there are." Adam shifted his sore shoulder. "So how long before someone sticks a knife in me?"

William shook his head. "As long as you play the guileless fool and stick to the story of having been attacked by brigands, that won't happen—I think." He frowned. "Two ambushes, you said?"

"Aye, but only one that anyone knows about. We buried the first six ourselves."

"Good." William fixed his eyes on the heavy crucifix that adorned the altar. "And Kit? How did she take all this?"

"Badly." Adam sighed. "She will not speak much of it, but I can see it gnaws at her."

"I will talk to her."

Adam gave him a cool look. "I am fully capable of doing that myself. She is my wife and should share her fears with me, not with you."

William rolled his eyes. "And if her fears are for you?"

Chapter 35

They'd ridden hard, making for York, but met up with the royal party just south of Doncaster.

"We're heading for London," Montagu told Adam. "Unrest among the merchants, it seems."

"Lancaster," Adam replied. "He's making mischief wherever he goes."

"He is?" Montagu's brows rose. "Alternatively, he has some justification for his grievances. The most powerful baron in the land should be given a say in the government."

"Lancaster is not the most powerful baron," Adam said.

"No." Montagu dragged the vowel out. "And maybe that's the rub, eh? Not that I am much taken with Lancaster—haughty old bastard who seems to think the sun shines out of his own arse."

Adam burst out in laughter, Montagu grinned, set a finger to his hat, and pointed Adam in the direction of the king.

King Edward was sitting with his wife on his lap, her dark hair shielding them both. She squealed when his hand went roving under her skirts, squealed even more when Adam cleared his throat.

"Adam!" Edward looked flustered, lips red and swollen. Philippa giggled and fled.

"My king," Adam bowed, waiting while Edward adjusted his clothes, moving somewhat gingerly.

"Wine?" Edward looked Adam up and down. "You look as if you could do with some."

"It's been a long ride, my lord." Truth be told, he'd have preferred some cider, but he accepted the cup the king handed him.

"So?" King Edward asked after ensuring they were out of earshot from the other people in the room.

"Should we not have your lady mother and Lord Mortimer here as well?"

332

Edward studied his cup. "Mortimer is not himself. That dead son of his has him quite unbalanced." He looked up, those blue eyes he shared with his father meeting Adam's. "I did not think to say this, but his grief is a terrible thing to see, makes me want to offer him comfort, even."

"Losing a child is difficult, my lord. I pray you never have to experience the pain of doing so."

Edward nodded. "He's lost two in a matter of weeks."

"Two?"

"Didn't you hear? His youngest, John, died in a joust down in Shrewsbury. Now," he continued, "what of our other matter?"

Adam had spent the last few minutes attempting to assess his young king. Nothing in his face or demeanour indicated surprise at seeing Adam alive—a fact that had Adam exhaling in relief.

"Well?" Edward demanded. "And why are you gawking at me like that? Do I have something on my face?"

"Red lips?" Adam teased. He cleared his throat. "The matter has been concluded, my lord."

"So he is gone?" The king set down his cup and went over to stand in front of the empty hearth, his back to Adam.

"He is."

"And I will never see him again," the king said softly.

"Likely not, my lord." Adam approached him. "Two kings in one realm make for uncomfortable nights."

"Aye." Edward sighed deeply. "I just wish…"

"I know, my lord." Adam set a careful hand on his lord's shoulder, offering comfort should he want it. Instead, Edward moved away.

"I fear I am too old to be coddled out of my black moods," he said, still with his back to Adam. "Will you tell Lord Mortimer and my lady mother?"

"As you wish, my lord."

"I'm not sure he wants to see you." Richard stood in front of the door leading to Mortimer's rooms, arms crossed.

"Oh, I can assure you he does." Adam took a step forward. Richard did not budge.

"He's not himself at present."

333

"He cannot afford not to be." Adam pushed Richard aside. "There is too much discontent, too much muttering of rebellion, for Lord Roger to submerge himself in grief." He scowled at Richard, who scowled right back, a lock of bright red hair falling over his forehead. "If Lancaster wins, Lord Roger will have even more to grieve over."

"Lancaster?" Richard snorted. "That prickly old bastard? He couldn't best Lord Roger if he tried."

"No? And what of these rumours that the Earl of Kent has joined him, that our dear Archbishop supports him?"

"You forgot Norfolk," Richard said. "Your dear friend seems to be hovering round Lancaster as well."

With that parting shot, Richard stood aside.

Mortimer was sitting at his desk, shoulders bowed. The quill lay unused, the room was sunk in darkness, the shutters firmly closed against the brightness of the day outside.

"Out," he growled.

"My lord," Adam began, and Mortimer whirled.

"I said, out!" The inkpot came flying. Adam ducked. It crashed against the wall, black ink staining the whitewash.

"Adam?" Lord Roger blinked. "Is that you?"

"It is." He crossed over to the desk, knelt before Mortimer. "I just heard about John, my lord. I am so sorry—for you and Lady Joan."

Lord Roger's face sagged. Broad shoulders shook uncontrollably, and Adam did the only thing he could: he embraced the man.

Some while later, Lord Roger was restored to his normal self. A haggard version, to be sure, but he listened intently as Adam informed him of the success of his mission—leaving out any mentions of brigands. His face clouded when Adam turned the matter to the Londoners.

"That Hamo de Chigwell really has it in for me. Ever since he condemned me to death all those years ago, he's viewed me askance."

"I suppose he fears retribution."

"As he should—now more than ever." Mortimer chewed his lip. "Well, none of this is news. Alicia has proved quite useful, keeping us well-informed as to the machinations of the London merchants. They've promised Lancaster enough gold to field six hundred men."

Adam sat back and stretched out his legs. "This is bad, isn't it?"

"It is. Not as bad as back in 1322, nor will I let it become worse. But aye, it is bad. And according to Alicia, the rumour that the old king is alive is flying through London, with various voices raised demanding that he be released and reinstalled." Mortimer smirked. "No chance of that now."

"No." Adam regarded him from under his lashes, fighting the urge to tell Lord Roger about the ambushes. "So what next?"

"The king must be convinced that Lancaster is out to do more but rattle his sword. At present, our liege seems to find this amusing, not quite comprehending just what danger his realm is facing."

"War—again." Adam rubbed at his face.

"But it will not come to that." Lord Roger studied his ink-stained fingers. "My lady the queen and I are taking adequate measures."

Lord Roger promised Adam he'd inform the queen, and Adam was at last free to go. The first thing he did was find a priest. Six deaths weighed heavily on his conscience, no matter how unavoidable. The priest listened, eyes going quite round before he absolved him with a muttered comment that despite all life being sacred, some men deserved life less than others. But he gave Adam an extensive penance: sixty days of daily prayers for the souls of the men he had killed.

Adam exited the chapel, found Gavin, and set off in search of food and sleeping quarters. With his squire at his heels, he had just turned a corner when he crashed into Robert de Langon and Ralph Stafford.

"Damn it, man!" Robert snarled. "Watch where you're going!" He lifted his face. "De Guirande!" He blanched. "What are you doing here?"

"Serving our king." Why was Robert looking as if he'd seen a ghost? "Are you ailing?"

"Me?" Robert laughed—a grating whinnying that sounded contrived. "No, no, of course not. But running into you is a painful experience." He gestured at Adam's breastplate. "Why all the armour?"

"Uncertain times," Adam replied, rubbing at his sore shoulder.

"Ah yes, of course. You've been riding the country on some errand or other, haven't you?" Stafford said and made as if to sidle by.

"Me?" Adam shook his head. "I've been home, taking care of my lands."

"Have you?" Stafford's mouth curled into a little smile. "Well, that should not take you long, should it, de Guirande?"

"Can't take you all that long either." Pompous bastard! Aye, Stafford was a baron, but a rather impoverished one. With a loud sniff, Stafford stalked away, Robert hurrying after him like a tame dog.

"You weren't home, my lord," Gavin said in an undertone.

"Yes, I was." Adam swung to face his squire. "Of course I was, Gavin. Surely, you remember that?"

Gavin's mouth wobbled into a smile. "Aye, my lord. Now that you mention it…"

"Good." Adam beckoned him closer. "Anyone asks, you swear on everything holy that we were both at Tresaints, y'hear?"

"Aye, my lord."

The evening meal was a morose affair. The king and his little queen retired early and Lord Roger conducted an intense discussion with Bishop Burghersh, Queen Isabella sitting slightly to the side. Their dowager queen appeared out of sorts, snappish in her communication with her ladies, just as sharp with the poor lad responsible for keeping her goblet filled with wine. She'd greeted Adam with an inclination of her head, no more, before continuing towards the high table, her ladies near on tripping over their feet as they attempted to keep up.

Adam ate, drank, conversed with Montagu, and longed for home. When Montagu excused himself, Adam decided to leave as well, following the king's friend through the hall. At the door, he turned, looking for Gavin. Instead, he found Robert de Langon staring at him, an unreadable expression on his face. Adam raised his brows. Robert looked away.

"Coming?" Montagu asked.

"Aye." One last look at Robert and he ducked outside.

"Why here?" King Edward tugged at the sleeve of his fine silk tunic and trudged across the grass.

"Why not here, my liege?" Bishop Burghersh gestured at the surrounding abbey grounds. "Where better to meet and parley with an upstart subject than in the presence of our Lord?"

Spoken like a true man of God, Adam reflected, walking a couple of paces behind them. Not that there was anything particularly peaceful about their company, with Adam and his men in full battle gear and armed to the teeth—a precaution Lord Roger had insisted on.

Lord Roger was already waiting for the king, flanked by Queen Isabella and Richard. They'd arrived in good time for the proposed meeting here at Barlings Abbey, a last attempt to heal the breach between Lancaster and Mortimer before it exploded into violence and death. Not that Adam held any hopes that it would work—Lancaster had crossed a line when he openly began promoting rebellion.

"So where is he?" King Edward was peevish, fidgeting like a lad of four. "Who does he think he is, to keep me waiting?"

"Lancaster is Lancaster," Queen Isabella muttered. "In his own opinion, the most important peer of the realm."

There was a commotion in the distance. Adam shielded his eyes. Lord Roger rose on his toes. "My God!" he said. "What is that?"

"An army, my lord. He's brought a goddamned army." Adam gestured for his men to form a tighter circle round the king.

Henry of Lancaster made a splendid entrance. While he left most of his men outside the abbey, he rode in accompanied by men-at-arms and various noblemen, their banners flying in the wind. Nowhere were Norfolk's lions—or Kent's—and Adam unclenched his hand from the hilt of his sword, shook blood into his fingers before resuming his previous position.

Dressed in silk and velvet, heavy robes that dragged over the grass as he approached them, the earl looked every inch the wealthy peer he was, all the way from his shoes in red and gold to the red silk hose that matched his tunic, its hem embroidered with lions rampant. Here was a man of royal blood, all of him proclaimed, a man far better suited to guide their young king than Mortimer, for the day in understated grey.

"So?" Henry of Lancaster said once he was within speaking distance. "What have you to offer this time?" He was wearing chain-mail under his clothes, one hand gripping the decorated pommel of his sword.

"Offer?" Lord Roger raised a brow. "Should you not begin by greeting your king adequately?"

Lancaster turned to the king. "My liege." A barely perceptible bow.

King Edward took a step forward. "My lord Lancaster, have you come to submit, repent your traitorous actions, and beg for peace?"

"What?" Lancaster squeaked, his face acquiring a deep red hue. "I have come to take my rightful place at your side—rid you of your false advisers."

"My mother?" Edward asked mildly.

"The dowager queen is no fit counsel for a king!" Lancaster straightened up. "It is I, as the first peer of the realm, that should control this regency, not a woman who cavorts openly with her lover."

Edward took yet another step towards him with Adam shadowing his every move. "Beware," Edward said. "I will have no one speak ill of my lady mother. No one, Lancaster."

Lancaster laughed. "Everyone already does! And as to her lover…" He spat in the dust.

"I do have a name," Lord Roger said. "And we haven't invited you to parley to have you cast aspersions on Queen Isabella or myself. You are here so that you may reconsider before it is too late."

"Reconsider?" Lancaster turned to smirk at his entourage. Adam recognised several of the men present, most of them minor lords of the north. Notably absent was Henry Percy, as was Neville, and in their stead, Thomas Wyther stood closest to the earl. Not a man Adam had heard anything complimentary about, but he was a renowned fighter, big and burly with a heavy auburn beard.

Right at the back, he caught sight of a familiar, ageing face, and such was Adam's surprise he couldn't quite stop an exclamation. Sir Henry Beaumont riding with Lancaster? The king's former guardian met his eyes, flushed, and averted his face.

Lancaster gestured at his distant troops. "I have not brought all those men for show," he said, his voice dropping into a growl. "Either you submit to me, Mortimer, or I will have them tear you apart."

"How dare you?" King Edward strode forward. "You stand here, before your king, and threaten violence?"

"If that is what it takes." Lancaster sneered. "The kingdom needs me at its helm, not them. I am the one who should rule in your stead, not him, half-Welsh mongrel that he is!"

Lord Roger's mouth curled into a smile. "Not quite half," he drawled. He met Adam's eyes, blinked once, and Adam nodded, quietly ordering his men to form yet another circle, this time round Lancaster and his armed companions.

"He should be banned from court!" Lancaster stabbed a finger in the direction of Lord Roger. "An erstwhile traitor, a—"

"Traitor to whom?" Edward interrupted. "To me?"

"To the former king!"

"Whom you helped depose," Edward reminded him. "You were as eager as anyone else in having him locked away, which makes you as much a traitor as Lord Mortimer. More, even, as your king was also your cousin."

"I was promised a seat on the council!" Lancaster roared.

"You have a seat on the council," Queen Isabella replied. "Is it our fault you've repeatedly refused to attend? Just as you recently refused to be present at York for parliament?"

"A farce!" Lancaster said.

"My parliament, a farce?" Edward asked.

"The council." Lancaster scowled. "It is them—your mother and Mortimer—who rule, not me."

"And so you choose to rise in rebellion instead," Edward stated. "Rebelling against me, your king." He swept Lancaster's companions with a harsh look. "I see before me a collection of traitors, do I not?"

"Traitors?" Lancaster blustered.

"What else to call you?" King Edward demanded. "You come here with an army at your back. I should have you struck in chains this very moment—all of you!"

"Try, and my men will smite you dead!" Lancaster nodded at one of his men, who raised his horn.

"What?" Queen Isabella exclaimed, and Adam's hold on his sword tightened. He'd lop off Lancaster's head himself.

"How dare you?" Edward crowded Lancaster, the earl near on falling as he retreated before the angered king. "You threaten regicide?" He scowled, turned to look at Lancaster's companions. "Is that what you are? Regicides?" There was a collective mumble, a lot of ducked heads and shuffling feet.

"We do as we must," Lancaster said, straightening up. Yet again, he gestured at the man with the horn.

"But not before your blood seeps into the ground," Lord Roger told him. "Your man sets lips to that horn, and I can assure you none of you leave here alive. None of you." He glared at the herald, who lowered his horn, looking from Lancaster to Mortimer. "As to what happens then, when your men see their leaders cut down, I do not know, but I know one thing for sure. You, Lancaster, will die first."

"I have a safe-conduct!" Lancaster said, taking a step back. He and his companions formed a knot of gaily coloured garments.

"A safe-conduct? You threaten your king!" King Edward yelled, and Lancaster jumped. "Order your men gone, and I will allow you to leave."

"Or cut me down."

"You have my word." Edward pulled his sword. "What is it to be, Lancaster?" All around, the king's men followed suit.

Lord Roger drew his own blade, placing himself in front of the queen. Lancaster's men tightened their formation, blades appearing everywhere. Adam took a step forward, gestured for his men to do the same.

Other than the sounds of weapons being drawn, there was silence. Lancaster licked his lips. King Edward not as much as twitched, his sword pointing steadily at the earl.

Lancaster gestured to his herald. "Have them stand down."

Only once one of Adam's men had verified that the earl's men were marching away did King Edward sheath his sword. Adam did not follow suit; neither did his men-at-arms. This was not over yet, not until Lancaster and his companions were safely gone.

"Go," Edward said. "And best reconsider before it is too late."

Lancaster and his men retreated to their horses. Once astride, they set off, all except Lancaster, who halted his horse some distance away. "We are not done!" he yelled before setting spurs to his horse.

"You should have killed him when you had the chance," Queen Isabella said to Lord Roger.

"Kill him?" Lord Roger shook his head. "He came with a safe-conduct, my lady. It would be dishonourable to kill him."

"But pragmatic." The queen gazed after Lancaster. "Sometimes, honour is overrated."

"Not to me," Lord Roger replied, and Edward nodded in agreement before striding over to clasp Mortimer's hand.

"You were right," he said, sounding like a dazed child. "He's planning a rebellion."

"So we must squash it." Lord Roger bowed. "And we will."

"Uncomfortable," Edward said to Adam as they made their way back to their horses.

"Very, my lord." Adam gave him a reassuring smile. "But it will not come to anything."

"We shall see. He wants to control me. Everyone wants to control me, so why should he be any different?" There was a quaver to his voice, a wetness to his eyes, that Adam pretended not to notice. "At least Mortimer has a vested interest in keeping me alive."

Chapter 36

"No." Kit gave William a mulish look. "He belongs here, with us."

"One cannot steal a child. If the boy has relatives in Gloucester, then we must take him to them."

"His mother is dead, he doesn't know his father, and now you tell me it would be better for him to grow up with his uncle?"

"Family, Kit. I'm just proposing that I ride down to Gloucester and see if I can find his kin."

"And then what?" Kit looked at Tom, playing among the apple trees with Meg. "He has a home here."

"He may have a good home there—and if nothing else, they deserve to know he is still alive." William patted her hand. "You should be able to relate to that."

She snatched her hand back. If she squinted or avoided registering Tom's brown eyes, she could almost imagine him the son she'd lost.

Kit leaned back against the bench. Autumn had come suddenly—or so it seemed to her. A fortnight into September, and the sunlight was already that golden hue that presaged shorter days and longer shadows. Heavy dew coated the ground in the morning, and come evening the breeze had a nippy edge to it. The dried peas had already been harvested, the onions were curing in garlands from the beams of the main barn, and come October they'd dig the parsnips out of the ground and stack them in crates filled with straw and sawdust. A good year, all in all, with Mall more than happy to send some of the produce down to the market in Worcester—including some of her precious honey.

Tom came running over, bowed, and presented Kit with an apple. He grinned before darting off to continue helping the apple-pickers, looking nothing like the waif she'd first met back in June.

"I'll go with you," she said. "And unless the uncle is a godly man, Tom stays here with us."

"As you wish." William turned his face up to the sun. "I wonder how Adam is faring."

Kit sighed. "So do I." She gnawed at her lip and crossed her arms over her chest. "Did he offer you his confession?"

"Me?" William smiled. "My brother prefers not to burden me with his sins."

"Oh."

"What is it?"

"It's just...to see him like that, all covered with blood and gore. I'd never realised just how good he was at killing." Kit made a face. "At least six lives on his conscience, and it did not seem to bother him."

"What choice did he have? They attacked you, didn't they?"

"They did. But all the same..."

"How can it surprise you that he is good at killing? Adam lives by his sword—has done so since he first rode into battle with Lord Roger. It is his skill with his weapons that has raised him to what he is, a knight in the service of the king."

"I know. I suppose it's the contrast. The man who killed the outlaws is very different from the man I welcome to my bed. There he is always gentle, always caring, always..." She broke off at William's grin and studied her hands, loosely clasped in her lap. The older she got, the more daring she'd become in bed—both in giving and taking. She craved his presence, needed the satisfaction only Adam could give her. She brushed her hand over the contour of her thigh, wishing it was his touch, not hers.

A hard poke to her ribs recalled her to the here and now. "Lust," William said sternly. "A cardinal sin, Kit."

"Love." She turned to face him. "Carnal love, assuredly, but it is always love between me and Adam. Always."

In response, William cupped her cheek. "He is a fortunate man, my brother."

She covered his hand with her own. "Have you ever..." No. She couldn't possibly ask a priest that!

343

"Have I ever what?" He retook his hand, his mouth twitching. "Struggled with lust?"

Kit worried at a loose thread on her sleeve. "You're a man, so surely—"

"Of course I have," he cut her off. "Especially when I was younger." He sighed. "Oxford was a nest of temptation for one such as me, newly come from the back of beyond. But I was there to become a priest, and I owed it to my benefactor to remain pure." He stood. "We leave for Gloucester tomorrow."

It took them several days to reach Gloucester, and the closer they got, the happier Kit was that she'd ridden with an escort. Men on horseback, men on foot, men with bows and men with swords—they were all making their way to the city.

"Lord Mortimer is assembling an army," one of the men they passed informed them. "Trouble in the east, and he, wise man that he is, calls on us, his people, to help him."

"Trouble? What sort of trouble?" Kit asked.

"How am I to know? I was just told to present myself—and the pay is good, or so they say."

"Lancaster," William said in a hushed voice to Kit. "This all smells of brewing conflict."

"Is Adam here, do you think?"

"I don't know. But we can find out."

It took them ages to get through the toll gate that spanned the northern approach, and then there was yet another gate to pass before they were within the city walls. To her right, Kit could see the towers of St Peter's, and further to the west was St Oswald's Priory, where she and Adam had stayed when they'd been here for King Edward's funeral. She crossed herself, wondering who the nameless wretch might be that had been buried in the king's name.

"I'll find us room and board," William said, wrinkling his nose at Kit's suggestion that they stay in one of the various inns that lined the North Gate. He jerked a thumb in the direction of the abbey. "The good monks will surely have room in their guest hall."

William and two of their men took care of the horses, leaving Kit on foot with Tom and one of Adam's older men, Simon, at her back.

"Take care of your mistress," William told Tom before disappearing into the crowd. Tom pressed himself closer to Kit, wary eyes studying the people that surrounded them.

"Do you recognise anyone?" Kit asked, gravitating towards a nearby stall and the displayed bolts of linen. Tom shook his head, his heavy hair covering his eyes. "But you've been here before, haven't you?" Kit continued. He nodded, tightening his hold on her kirtle. "Tom." She crouched before him. "I will not leave you unless you want me to. But we must at least try and find your uncle—Father William is right in that."

"Don't like him. He kicked out me Mams."

"He did?"

"Aye. Said she was lewd and full of sin." Tom sniffed. "Said he had neither room nor bread to share with a whore and her bastard get."

"Ah." Kit straightened up. "Well, I suppose that means you'll be returning with us to Tresaints." Tom gave her a radiant smile—but refused to let go of her skirts.

William returned just as Kit was concluding her purchases. "The king isn't here, and if so, neither is Adam. Queen Isabella is here, though, as is Lord Roger." He brightened. "Maybe we could present ourselves to them."

"We have no reason to do so." Kit handed the various bolts of cloth to Simon. "We're just here for Tom." She leaned closer and shared what Tom had told her about his uncle. William shrugged.

"The mother was a whore. No God-fearing man wants such a woman under his roof."

"And the child?" Kit beckoned a pie vendor over. Still warm, the pies broke apart to reveal a rich, spicy stew within, and Kit bought half a dozen, distributing them among her companions.

"He did wrong by Tom," William admitted, blowing at his food.

"So we tell him we have Tom and ride right back home."
She gave him a triumphant smile. "Tomorrow."

William had found them lodgings at St Peter's Abbey. What
with all the people presently in Gloucester, they were lucky to
find beds at all, the little monk in charge of the guest lodgings
told them.

"It's all these pilgrims," he said.

"Pilgrims?" William asked.

"Yes, come to pray at the tomb of the king." The monk
rubbed his hands together. "Anyway, no rooms free, but there
are beds in the main hall—women on one side, men on the
other."

They found beds, but it was too early to retire, so at
William's suggestion, he and Kit left Tom with the men and
went for a little walk, skirting the surprisingly large crowds
that were waiting to enter the abbey church, there to visit the
tomb of King Edward, second of that name.

"A farce," Kit muttered, adjusting her veil to cover all her
hair and shadow her face. "All these people, and God alone
knows who is buried in that coffin." She looked to the south,
wondering where Sir Edward and Egard might be by now.
Would they have reached Avignon? When she asked William,
he thought it likely, a yearning tone to his voice.

They entered a tavern, William guiding them to sit at
a small table just by the door. There were plenty of other
women there—albeit none of them with a priest—and Kit
relaxed, throwing curious looks at a nearby party consisting
of four men. She could see they were wearing chain-mail, the
odd glint of metal catching the light when they moved, and
although they were unarmed, they were clearly on their guard,
speaking little with each other while they ate and drank.

"Soldiers for Lord Roger?" she asked William, helping herself
to a fritter. Hot. She inhaled a couple of times through her mouth,
had to gulp down some cider to soothe it. One of the men saw
and winked. She smiled back, miming a burning mouth.

"Soldiers, at any rate," William replied, more interested in
the fritters. Kit shoved the platter in his direction and sat back.

346

In a corner, a man was playing a vieille, singing to himself. A woman strolled past, hair uncovered, and one of the men at the neighbouring table whistled. The wench moved closer, leaning forward to display her generous bosom. The man took hold of her wrist, pulled her into his lap, and the wench shrieked and giggled, the man groped and laughed. The man reminded her of a ferret, small bright eyes in a small pointed face.

William muttered something.

"I've seen whores before," Kit assured him. Out of the corner of her eye, she saw the ferret-man stand, one hand grabbing the woman's posterior.

"No." Low and sharp, the command had ferret-man sinking back down. "We stick together," the speaker continued.

"Yes, my lord," ferret-man said, and Kit was suddenly all that more interested in this group of men. But she kept her eyes on the table, noted that William had grown very still.

"Fool!" the low voice hissed. Stools scraped against the floorboards, Kit raised her mug as if to drink, throwing a casual look in the direction of the four men, now making their way to the door.

"Come on!" William hissed. "We have to follow them."

"We do?" But she stood all the same.

"They're not what they seem." He was already at the door. "Men like that, sporting no badges, no colours—very strange."

"Maybe they're mercenaries." She stepped over the high threshold, shivering in the chill of the evening air.

"If they were, the wench would have been swiving them, one by one." William steadied her over the gutter. "There," he added in an undertone, and then he set off, the skirts of his robe flapping round his legs. Kit hurried along as well as she could in her pattens, attempting to keep to the side and in the shadows.

In front of them, the four men were walking quickly in the direction of the abbey.

"They could be travellers."

"Aye. Or they are spies." William came to a halt. "They could be staying at St Peter's—if so, a stroke of luck."

"Luck?"

He grinned. "Makes it easier to keep an eye on them."

"No." Kit took hold of him. "You will do nothing that puts you at risk. Those men are soldiers, and should they be here as spies, they'll not hesitate to slit your throat."

William snorted. "I've done this before, Kit. I dare say I'll manage."

The men were not in the main hall. William told Kit to go to bed, disappeared for a while, and returned looking disgruntled. He caught Kit's eyes, made a helpless gesture, and lay down on his pallet. Not here, then, Kit thought, yawning into her pillow.

She couldn't sleep. Kit shifted from side to side on the narrow pallet, turned this way and that. At long last, she gave up and sat up. Everywhere sleeping people, some on their back snoring heavily, others curled on their sides. A woman beside her was sprawled quite indecently, a man some beds away was muttering in his sleep. Tom's fair head stuck out from beneath a mountain of blankets, and William's pallet was empty.

Empty? Kit stood and moved closer. Yes, most definitely empty, nor was there any sign of William elsewhere. Fool of a man! Kit found her shoes, tucked the dagger she never travelled without into her belt, and exited the hall. The passage was sunk in shadow, a single torch illuminating the main entrance. The large door stood slightly ajar, and after some consideration Kit squeezed through the narrow gap.

Dark. Cold. She pressed her back against the wall and waited for her eyes to adapt to the night. Buildings took shape, the previously uniform dark shifted into dark shadows and somewhat less dark shadows—sufficient to make out the trees and shrubs. To her far right, there was a faint flicker of light, accompanied by the muted sounds of men talking in hushed tones. Kit slipped closer, and the smell of horses and manure identified the low building as a stable.

Harness jangled. Was someone stealing the horses? Kit rose on her toes to see. A hand came over her mouth, and she kicked and thrashed.

"It's me!" William hissed. He set his mouth to her ear. "It's them. They're leaving. And I've heard enough to know they're Lancaster's men."

When they were finally allowed in to see Mortimer the next morning, he agreed. He gave William a condescending smile. "Not something we don't know, William."

"But here! Spies, my lord."

Kit rolled her eyes. She'd told him repeatedly there was no real reason for them to insist on seeing Mortimer, but William had been adamant, eyes shining with fervour. Clearly, life at Tresaints was not exciting enough.

"As we have spies in Lancaster's camp." Mortimer swept his robe closer round him. They'd had him pulled from his bed, and he was only in his shirt, the robe donned hastily. Through the doorway, Kit caught a glimpse of a bed, red sheets shimmering in the returning light. An outflung pale arm, a cascade of dark hair—Kit averted her eyes.

"You seem much recovered," Mortimer said, directing himself to Kit. "I am glad." Without awaiting her permission, he set his hand to her face, turning it so that her damaged cheek was illuminated. "It heals."

"But it will always be there." A misshapen cross—the sign of a heretic. It filled her with shame, and sometimes with fear, like when the monks at St Peter fixed her with beady eyes.

"Roger?" The soft voice came from the chamber within. William concentrated on his footwear. Mortimer's eyes lit up.

"You must excuse me. My lady requires my presence."

"Of course, my lord." She made as if to leave.

"Wait for us in the hall," Mortimer ordered. "We'll be down shortly."

"Shortly is relative, it would seem," William murmured to Kit when Queen Isabella and Lord Mortimer finally swept into the hall. They'd broken their fast on cheese and wafers, and Kit had even taken the opportunity to close her eyes for a moment.

But now she rose before making a deep reverence before the queen.

"Lady Kit!" Queen Isabella extended her hands in greeting. "I am pleased to see you looking so well after all those recent harrowing events." She pulled Kit with her to one of the window seats, calling for wine.

"Harrowing, my lady?" Kit was not about to give anything away, no matter that the queen's bright green eyes were boring into her. Verily like a cat, at times, was Queen Isabella, and this made Kit think of Flea and how he'd toy with his prey before finally killing it.

"My steward told me all about it." The queen sipped at the heated wine, the rich fragrance of cinnamon and cloves wafting Kit's way. "Covered in blood, as he tells it—even the friar travelling with you." She smiled slightly. "Friar," she repeated, chuckling to herself.

"Not his blood," Kit said. "But yes, you are right: we were attacked by outlaws."

"Ah." The queen ran a finger round the rim of her goblet. "Outlaws? Are you sure?"

Kit put on her most confused face. "What else would they be, my lady?

"These days, one never knows." The queen studied her intently. "And Adam and Egard managed to kill them all?"

"Egard and Adam are quite the formidable fighters, my lady."

"Yes. How fortunate—for you."

"Indeed, my lady."

"And the friar?" The queen waved away the page who came to replenish her goblet.

"Gone elsewhere, my lady." Kit looked away. "To a new life, he said."

"A new life." Queen Isabella set down her goblet. "Let us hope he holds to that."

Chapter 37

After the events at Barlings Abbey, Mortimer and the queen had departed in haste towards the southwest, there to muster an army. Bishop Burghersh was dispatched to London to try and knock some sense into the Londoners, and the king made for Cambridge, a slow tedious trip what with Queen Philippa and her women, their various litters and carts.

When he wasn't leading the fore-riders, Adam amused himself by hovering round Robert de Langon—difficult to do as Robert did his best to give Adam a wide berth. If anything, this made Adam even more determined in his pursuit, wondering why the man went the colour of whey whenever they met. He had his suspicions, and there were nights he spent tossing this way and that as he tried to comprehend just who had ordered their deaths.

If Robert was involved, that pointed mostly to the king—and that had something like a cold fist tightening round Adam's heart—but Robert, just like Stafford, admired Queen Isabella and was as likely to be found in her proximity as in the king's during long evenings of drinking and entertainment. This had Adam leaning towards it all being the queen's idea—but would she be that ruthless?

There was really no point in analysing all this as, no matter what Adam suspected, he could never prove anything. Besides, William was right: even with proof, such accusations could result in a swift death. Adam took to sleeping with his dagger under his pillow, which did little to improve his sleep.

While Robert fled at his approach and Stafford preferred others to Adam, Will Montagu was a friendly presence with whom Adam shared most of his free time—and his quarters.

"Do you truly think all this security is necessary?" Montagu asked one night. "Scouts, guards—one could think you were in charge of a military operation."

"And if Lancaster comes swooping down?"

"Do you think he would?" Montagu cut another slice of cheese.

"After Barlings Abbey? Aye." Adam shifted on his rump. "If I were him, I'd take the first opportunity offered to lay hands on the king. Without the king, Queen Isabella and Lord Mortimer would be fighting uphill."

"Hmm." Montagu yawned. "Not necessarily a bad thing."

"You think Lancaster a better man than Mortimer? Truly?"

"No." Montagu sounded grudging. "Mortimer is competent—however overbearing. Lancaster is simply overbearing." He shook his head. "It's inexplicable how he can have sired a son as likeable as young Grosmont."

"Maybe the lad takes after his mother." Adam had only met Henry Grosmont twice: as a young lad back in 1324, when Lancaster's son accompanied his father to Woodstock, and last year, when young Grosmont briefly joined the Scottish campaign. His impression was of a quiet man who preferred to have his sword speak for him.

Montagu yawned and slouched in his seat, one long leg hooked over the other. He scratched at his dark beard, as neatly coiffed as his long hair, and yawned again. A recent father, he'd been yawning since he returned to court some days back— in between regaling anyone who would listen with detailed descriptions of this miracle come to earth, his son.

"Is Lady Kit recovered?" Montagu asked.

"As much as one can recover from the fears of having been locked up alone and in the dark."

Montagu nodded and steered their conversation to other things. They spent a pleasant few hours discussing horses, the foibles of breeding wives, dogs, and how best to disarm a man with a poleaxe. The brazier spread a pleasant glow, the wine was good, and Adam was just recounting his recent clash of wills with Meg when one of his sentries barged into the room.

"Men!" he gasped. "Some ten miles off, riding hard."

Adam leapt to his feet. "Who?"

The sentry shook his head. "Not sure. But they're many and come armed, my lord."

"The king." Adam snapped his fingers at Montagu. "Get him up and dressed—and the queen." He was already outside, half running to the stables. "Saddle the horses," he ordered one of the stable lads.

"All of them?"

"All. Now. Gavin! Gavin, get your arse down here!"

Gavin tumbled from the hayloft, already pulling on his tunic. "My lord?"

"Arm up. Make sure all the men do."

"What is happening, my lord?"

"I don't know. But I aim to find out." He was out again, making for his quarters while yelling for two of his scouts.

"I need you to ride as close to them as you can," he instructed, pulling his gambeson over his head. "I want numbers, banners—anything you can see."

"But it's dark," one of the scouts said.

"Aye, but they'll not be riding blind, will they?" Adam jerked his head towards the door. "Go!"

"Adam?" King Edward tumbled into the room, half-dressed. "What is the meaning of this?"

"Armed men, my lord—riding at speed towards us." He had his hauberk on, looked about for his coat of plates.

"Spawns of Satan!"

Adam raised his brows, no more. "We must ride, my lord. Best get dressed—and armed." He buckled on his sword belt, picked up his gauntlets, and took a firm hold of the king, propelling him towards the door.

Edward tore free. "What? Now? Shouldn't we fight them instead?"

"Fight them? I have three score men. Not much to throw in the face of a determined enemy." Adam hurried them along the covered passage, making for the king's chambers.

"But Philippa! I can't leave her."

"She will have to ride with us." Adam pushed the king inside, began throwing garments at him.

"And her ladies?" Edward shook out the leather breeches he preferred to wear when riding long distances and pulled them on.

"Her ladies? God's blood, my lord—we can't take them with us!" Adam inhaled. "This is a priory, my lord. If we are gone, chances are they'll set off in pursuit of us, not stay behind to ravage the ladies and plunder the monks."

The little courtyard was a cacophony of noise. Horses, loud men, the shrill sound of frightened women—it made Adam's ears ache. Montagu had somehow managed to chase the queen out of her bed, and he was at present hoisting her astride a little dappled mare. Queen Philippa was all eyes and a pale, pinched face, but she nodded when Montagu spoke to her, hands firm on the reins.

The king was horsed, the flaring light of the torches reflecting off his chain-mail. Montagu, Stafford, Neville, and Ufford formed a tight group round the king and his queen.

Adam mounted Raven, did a swift count of his men. All mounted, all armed, albeit not as impeccably as he would normally demand.

"We ride west!" the king yelled, standing in his stirrups.

"We must ride now," Adam replied, and the king set his horse to a trot, then a canter. Adam gave Raven his head, urging the stallion on. Once he was abreast with the king, he leaned over. "No need to waste their strength, my lord."

"No, no, you're right." Edward slowed his stallion to a trot. "Who?"

"I don't know—yet."

Montagu rode up to join them. "You truly think they mean us harm?"

"I don't know, but better safe than sorry." Adam looked down the column. On his orders, they were riding without light—a risk, but better than advertising their presence. "I'll form a rear guard, something to distract their fore-riders."

"You do that." Edward glanced over his shoulder. "I'll lead with Montagu."

Adam held in Raven, allowing most of their party to overtake him and pass on into the dark. Right at the end, he found Gavin and his six Tresaints men-at-arms, together with ten or so more.

"We ride rear," he said, and they halted their horses. They set off again in two groups, one on either side of the road, at present no more than a pale ribbon against the darkness of the meadows and fields that bordered it.

A horse came galloping at speed behind them. Two horses. The scouts? Adam allowed them to pass before charging after them.

"My lord!" one of them gasped, throwing back his cloak to reveal the royal arms.

"What did you find?"

"Close to ten score," the scout replied, his companion nodding beside him. "Well-mounted, but they've been riding for some time, so their horses are flagging."

"Who?" Adam asked.

The other scout licked his lips. "Lancaster," he said hoarsely. "He himself rides with them."

"Damn!"

They rode all night. Come dawn, several of the riders wanted to stop for a rest, but King Edward would not have it, urging them to ride on. Adam couldn't agree more: the further they rode this first stretch, the higher the probability they'd evade their pursuers.

"We make for Salisbury," King Edward informed him. "My lady mother said they were going there first."

"That's a long ride," Adam said.

"Don't tell me things I already know! Have you got another suggestion?"

"No, my lord." Adam stroked Raven over his neck. They were walking the horses, a long line of silent men atop tired mounts. Only two women rode with them, Queen Philippa and her Flemish nurse, who looked remarkably unperturbed despite the recent upheaval. Philippa no longer looked like a fearful doe, but she shivered in the chilly air despite being wrapped in a hooded cloak Adam recognised as Montagu's.

"I shall have his balls for this, and if anything happens to Philippa..." Edward threw an unguarded look at his wife. For an instant, his mouth wobbled.

"Nothing will happen to her—or to you, my lord." Adam met the king's eyes. "Not while I'm alive."

"I know, Adam." The king smiled. "My most loyal knight will never let me down."

Adam's cheeks heated.

Beside him, de Langon snickered. "Such big words, Sir Adam," he said in an undertone. "Let's see what you do once the enemy is upon us."

"Are you questioning my honour?" Adam rode Raven straight at him.

"I'm saying that only God knows what a man will do when death stares him in the face."

"How would you know? Have you ever lived through that experience?"

"No," de Langon admitted sullenly.

"No, I thought as much. A prancing little lord, knighted in some unimportant skirmish because his rich father greased a couple of palms." Adam rode that much closer. "I, on the other hand, was made a knight on a field that looked like a charnel house—dead and wounded everywhere. And quite a few had died at my hand—after trying to kill me." He spat to the side. "I have stared death in the face, de Langon. I know what I will do. So speak for yourself, not for me."

Montagu laughed. "That put you in your place, didn't it, dear Robert?"

"I have to see to our rear," Adam said, turning Raven. "Maybe you'd care to ride with us, de Langon. After all, that's where we will see battle first if they catch up with us." De Langon made no move to accompany him. "No, I thought as much. You strike me as one of those who prefer paying others to bleed and die for you."

"How dare you!" de Langon began, his hand closing on the hilt of his sword.

Adam ignored him. "My lord." He inclined his head to the king and rode off, laughing silently when he heard the king tear into de Langon, along the lines that he would not have someone questioned de Guirande's loyalty and bravery.

Chapter 38

Queen Isabella insisted Kit remain with her in Gloucester, saying she had need of female companionship. There was no way Kit could refuse. After arranging for Tom and her men to return home to Tresaints, she and William moved into the castle. Not that she saw much of William, who was absorbed into Mortimer's administrative office, beaming happily whenever she did see him. The man was wasted as a priest in the depths of the Worcestershire countryside: William needed a grander purpose.

Kit, on the other hand, was kept busy in the queen's apartments. Too old-fashioned, too dark, too cold—Queen Isabella was less than pleased with her rooms, complaining about everything from the old painted furniture to the lack of tapestries and carpets. The walls were found dull and dreary, and soon enough the queen had the castellan bowing and scraping as he promised to ensure the rooms were refurbished as soon as possible.

"White walls, dotted with blue fleurs-de-lis and a border of English lions, gold on red," Queen Isabella ordered. "And find me something to hang on the walls and lay on my floors immediately—surely, a town the size of Gloucester has some merchants of high-quality items?"

The castellan scurried off to do as the queen commanded. Queen Isabella sank down in the single good chair and extended her feet towards the warmth of the hearth. New shoes in leather inlaid with silver and green peeked from beneath the queen's skirts, for the day a matching green.

"The English have no sense of style," Queen Isabella commented. "It is fortunate my son has me to ensure his royal apartments are furnished as they should be."

"Yes, my lady." In Kit's private opinion, Edward did not much care about his surroundings—he was too young for such.

357

Truth be told, she suspected the queen was as uninterested as her son; all these efforts expended on her rooms were merely an attempt to distract herself from the real possibility of looming war. Every day, Mortimer's men came riding in from all over the country, and from the way Mortimer's face had acquired an almost permanent frown, Kit surmised the news was not good. Lancaster, it seemed, was determined to push things to the limit, as manifested by his recent behaviour at Barlings Abbey.

Three days later, a cloaked shape came galloping into the bailey, accompanied by two men-at-arms. It sufficed for Kit to hear the voice to have her wincing. Her half-sister Alicia had a distinctive, shrill voice, and she was presently haranguing the poor lad who'd run forward to hold her horse. Alicia dismounted and took off over the uneven and wet cobbles, making for the hall. She undid her cloak as she went, and beneath she was in various shades of blue silk, an elegant girdle adorning her middle, several rings on her hands.

Still as thin as always, still with that long face dominated by sharp cheekbones and a blade for a nose, she swept up the stairs and demanded she be taken to the queen. If she noticed Kit, she ignored her, passing her without as much as a glance. Kit fell in behind her, curious as to Alicia's haste.

A page opened the door to the queen's solar, and Alicia pushed by him. Other than the queen and Lord Mortimer, the room was empty of all but Richard, who rose when he saw his sister—both his sisters—entering.

"Lancaster is riding to snatch the king," Alicia said without any preamble, and both the queen and Mortimer stilled. Alicia inhaled. "I came as quickly as I could."

"When?" Queen Isabella asked.

"They set off ten days ago," Alicia said. "Or so I understood from what Hamo and Henry were discussing."

"Ten days!" The queen whirled, extending a hand to Mortimer. "If he succeeds…"

"He will not," he said, but from his sudden pallor, he was saying this as much to reassure himself as her. "Adam will know better than to do without sentries."

Alicia's lip curled. "De Guirande? Begging your pardon, my lord, but however skilled he is, there is little he can do against two hundred mounted men-at-arms."

"Two hundred?" The queen stumbled, Lord Mortimer's arm shot out, closing round her elbow.

"We must set our trust to Adam—and Ned. That son of yours has more than his share of courage and wits."

Queen Isabella gave him a tremulous smile. "If Lancaster has Edward…"

Dearest God, Adam would die before allowing Lancaster to carry his lord away. Kit pressed her hands to her belly, made it over to a stool, and sat down. The room was whirling around her. She heard Mortimer tell the queen not to despair, saw Queen Isabella straighten up and square her shoulders, and then the queen and Mortimer were gone, Mortimer barking orders to Richard over his shoulder.

Kit braced her hands against her thighs and concentrated on her breathing. She knew nothing for sure, she reminded herself, and Adam was a wily captain. A couple of steadying breaths, and she was collected enough to raise her face—only to meet Alicia's cold eyes.

"Sister," she said. "I hear you are to be congratulated on the birth of a daughter."

"Congratulate me?" Alicia sounded as if she'd swallowed a bucket of gravel. "A puny girl-child is nothing to celebrate."

"A child is a child."

Alicia snorted. "I have other matters to deal with." Her mouth curled into something resembling a smile. "Some of us are destined to play an important role in the ongoing events."

"We are," Kit agreed, thinking of her recent adventures with Sir Edward.

"You?" Alicia sniffed. "You're not the one who risks her life spying on Queen Isabella's behalf." She sucked in her lip, causing her to look eerily like her dead mother. "I fear I may have backed the wrong horse. Lancaster is amassing quite the army."

"Lord Mortimer will pound Lancaster to dust."

"Unless he has the king," Alicia reminded her with a nasty smile. "One of them, at any rate."

"One of them? Is there more than one?"

"Lancaster is saying the old king is still alive, imprisoned somewhere."

Kit managed a laugh. "Am I to take it he believes in fairies as well?"

"No." Alicia threw her a sour look. "He believes in the Earl of Kent." She adjusted her veil. "A handsome man, the earl." She smiled. "As is dear Adam."

"Dear Adam?" Kit echoed.

"He has a fondness for me, your husband."

"For you?" Kit shook her head. "I find that unbelievable."

"And yet he held me in his arms—in front of the queen and her ladies." Alicia gave Kit a spiteful look. "Maybe he doesn't care for you as much as you think."

"Or maybe you've just imagined it all," Kit bit back.

"Me?" Alicia laughed. "Why don't you ask Adam?" She smirked. "Well, I can't be sitting here with you any longer. I must find the queen and ask her what more she needs from me—she values my services."

"I am sure she does. Spies are hard to find—or trust." With that rather elegant put down, Kit sailed away, fuming at Alicia's comments about Adam—and praying her husband would return to her unharmed.

Everything hurt: his thighs, his arse, his damned foot, his back. Adam shifted gingerly in his saddle and sneezed. The king drew his stallion to a halt.

"Salisbury, at last!" he said, nodding towards the distant spire rising loftily towards the sky.

"Aye, my lord." Four days since their panicked escape, and here they were, Lancaster outpaced. Long hours in the saddle had left them tired and grimy, snatched hours of sleep led to frayed tempers, and days of pottage swallowed in haste had Adam's stomach rumbling. God's blood, but he needed a bed!

The king had recovered quickly from his initial shock, not so the little queen, who'd grown paler with each day. But she was a brave thing, their queen, pasting a wide smile on her face whenever the king looked her way. The moment he turned his back, her mouth drooped, and Adam had the impression she was in discomfort, but his every attempt at finding out more had been rebuffed by the queen's formidable Flemish woman.

They rode into Salisbury in tight formation, causing severe disruption among the gawking residents. The king smiled and waved, the people cheered, and Adam fell back, smiling at how well their king handled the crowds. His shoulders relaxed, and he was already daydreaming of feather mattresses and plump pillows when the king rode up to him.

"They're not here! Mortimer and my mother are in Gloucester—with the men they've mustered." He halted his horse, studying the teeming courtyard. "We must ride on."

"Now?" Adam threw a longing look at the guest lodgings that stood opposite the cathedral.

"Tomorrow. At dawn." The king's brows pulled together. "Philippa needs a full night's sleep."

"Aye, my lord." Another night of being constantly on his guard, of having scouts and sentries posted. The close was walled, but it wasn't built to withstand a determined onslaught, more to erect a boundary between the cathedral and the adjoining cloisters and the somewhat less religious life that went on beyond.

"Is he still on our heels?" the king asked.

"No. But a full night resting…" Adam left the rest unsaid.

"It is a risk we have to take." Edward dismounted. "I must see to Philippa."

"Yes, my lord."

By compline, the king and his wife were safely abed, and Adam had divided up his tired men in three groups, sending out the first to man the gates and set up sentries gazing ever northwards. The others he sent to bed, and then he went to find his scouts.

Gavin looked up when he entered, then returned his attention to the food. Hot soup, stale bread—the monks had not been prepared for such an influx of visitors. Gavin's cheeks were covered by reddish bristles, his tunic and hose were spattered with mud, and the cloak he'd thrown to the side was just as dirty—and damp. But despite all this, Adam's squire was in high spirits, proud of his new role among the other scouts.

Good men, all of them, and now he had to tell them to forget about warm beds and sweet dreams; instead, they'd have another night outside. None of them complained. They just nodded and finished their food, shrugged on their cloaks, and went to find fresh horses—from the bishop's stables.

Thank the Lord it was an uneventful night. The scouts returned at dawn, having seen neither hair nor hide of Lancaster, but the king insisted they press on. And so they did, covering the remaining distance to Gloucester in a few blurred days. With the king in front, they entered the city through the north gate and trotted towards the castle. It was rainy and windy, the king's banner flapped overhead, and the guards at the main gate to the castle stood to the side. They were expected—Adam's fore-riders had done their job.

Into the bailey, and there were men everywhere. Lads appeared as if by miracle to take care of the horses, and here came Mortimer, cutting through the assembled men like a knife through a knob of butter.

"My lord?" He came to a halt in front of the king. "Are you unharmed?"

King Edward nodded and turned round to receive his wife. "I am. No thanks to Lancaster." He turned to face Mortimer. "Do whatever you have to do to break him, you hear?"

"Hopefully, we will talk him to his senses," Lord Roger said, greeting Adam with a flicker of a smile. "If not Lancaster, at least his allies."

"I don't care what you do. Just stop him." Edward took his wife's hand. "My lady needs a bath and a bed."

"Your rooms have been prepared, my lord." Mortimer gestured towards the keep. "And for the rest of you, there is food and ale in the hall. Plenty of ale." A half-hearted cheer went up—they were all simply too tired.

Lord Roger took hold of Adam's arm. "Truly? Eight days from Cambridge?"

"Aye. With Lancaster snapping at our heels, what else could we do? We—" Whatever else he was going to say was wiped clean out of his mind. Kit—here! She was standing at the entrance to the keep, strands of red hair whipping round her face. He took a step towards her, took two, and remembered Lord Roger was still there.

"Go on." Mortimer shoved him gently. "We can talk later."

It had been gone vespers when the king and his companions came clattering across the drawbridge and into the lower ward. The king was first off his horse, but Kit's attention was on the distinctive black stallion and its rider. He was wet, he was dirty, his shoulders slumped, and when he dismounted, his bad leg dipped beneath him, testament to just how tired he was. But he was here, and he was alive, and she should go to him, but instead she remained where she was, standing just by the entrance to the keep.

Mortimer clapped Adam on the shoulder, Adam nodded and said something, looked up, saw her, and the look on his face was priceless. She took a step forward. He came striding towards her, took the stairs two treads at the time, and then she was in his arms, and he smelled of sweat and mud, his cheeks covered by a bristling beard that scratched her skin when he kissed her. She didn't care. He tasted too much of onion and garlic. She didn't care. He was cold and wet. She didn't care.

Half an hour later, he was clean and dry, holding her hand as they made for the hall. The king was already there, looking as well-scrubbed as one of Mall's big pots.

"Philippa?" Kit asked.

"She's been poorly these last few days," Adam replied. "What she needs is her bed and plenty of possets."

Adam ate. And ate. He drank. He ate some more, and then Montagu came over and dragged him off, saying Mortimer and the king required his presence. A long discussion ensued, and Kit was just considering whether to retire to the little room she was to share with Adam when he at last stood and started making his way back to her. Midway there, he came to a halt. Alicia said something to him, her long-fingered hand gripping his sleeve. He should have brushed it off. Instead, he bent down to hear whatever it was Alicia was saying, and Kit left.

He had no idea what had his wife taking off like that, but he knew better than to not go after her, taking the stairs two treads at a time to compensate for her speed.

"What's the matter?" he asked when he caught up with Kit just as she entered their little chamber.

"The matter?" She turned on him. "Alicia is the matter."

"Alicia?"

"She says you've embraced her."

"Taken out of context, but aye, I comforted her. The poor woman was falling apart."

"Poor woman?" Kit kicked at him. "Since when does Alicia deserve to be described thus?"

"Since she's been wed to an abusive husband who covers her with bruises." Adam crossed his arms over his chest. "You cannot truly believe I have a fondness for her."

"No." She gave him a sullen look. "Not her."

"Not her? What is that supposed to mean?"

Kit looked away.

"Kit?" He leaned forward, wound a lock of hair round his finger, and tugged.

"It's just that you are such a virile man. When we are together, not a day passes without you bedding me. And I see the girls and women look at you—they do, Adam—so now and then I wonder how you handle months away from me."

In response, Adam held up his hand and wiggled his fingers.

"Adam!"

"You asked, sweeting." He gave her a curious look. "Surely, you do so as well." Kit ducked her head, looking at anything but him. He laughed. "I see you do," he teased, drawing her close enough to kiss her nose. "So tell me, does it feel the same as when I touch you?"

She shook her head.

"Good." He pulled her close enough to kiss.

She played coy at first, mouth soft but closed. He wouldn't have that—not from his Kit. He increased his efforts, his lips and tongue demanding entrance. With a little sigh, she gave way, and Adam tasted honeyed wine and almonds. A warm, tender mouth, and her breath came in audible gasps when he released her.

Kit licked her lips, eyes wide and unfocussed. Adam sat down on a stool, lifted her onto his lap, and went back to kissing her. Hands tightened in his hair, breasts pressed against his chest, and heat flew through his veins. He adjusted her to straddle him and she obliged, pressing down on him in a way that had him groaning in her mouth.

"There's too much cloth between us," he grumbled, shoving at her heavy skirts. Impossible to get her close enough, feel the warmth radiating off her skin. There: his fingers slid over her garter, moved upward over her thighs. Kit rocked against him, the stool shifted, and he widened his legs to keep her still. Such soft skin—like the finest of silks, but hot rather than cool. Kit moaned, and now it was her tugging at the folds of fabric that separated them, at his tunic and his shirt.

"Now!" Her breath tickled his neck, her lips left damp impressions, and he lifted her to stand. Kit swayed on her feet. He caught her, tumbling her on top of the bed. These clothes…No, no time for such, not now. Wait—Adam took a deep breath. There was always time.

"Adam?" She half sat up.

He reached for her veil. It drifted to the side. Her braid, as thick as his forearm, he unravelled slowly. So much hair; thick and gleaming, it fell to her waist.

"You are beautiful." Even in the weak light, he could see her blush, and it made him smile. "Such beauty must be properly appreciated," he continued, sliding fingers down the column of her neck to her cotehardie, a thing in green velvet adorned with a series of small carved buttons. One button at a time, and the swell of her breasts rose and fell.

The fire in the grate crackled, the bed creaked as she shifted beneath his fingers, but otherwise there was silence, her eyes never leaving his. As it should be: his wife loved him—

was loved by him—with her eyes wide open so that he could read in them just what she was feeling, what she needed and wanted.

He rubbed the green velvet between his fingers as he took off the cotehardie. He undid the lacings on her kirtle. The back of his hand grazed her chest. She inhaled. The kirtle was off, the heavy wool sighing as it landed on the floor. Through the sheer fabric of her shift, the contours of her body were clearly visible, as were the dark curls that adorned her mound.

Linen. Rougher on the fingers, on her nipples. His mouth left damp patches over her breasts. The way she moaned when he kissed her cleft through the fabric, how she tasted and smelled…Adam's cock throbbed heavily, his balls contracting with need. But not yet.

At last. She, naked, her hair spread out across the pillow. He slid a finger inside, and she was hot and slick. She reached for him, he batted away her hands. Not yet.

He did not disrobe completely. Uncooperative fingers fumbled with his belt. His tunic tangled round his head before he tore it loose. He left his hose on, undid his braies, and hefted the heavy weight of his balls in his hand a couple of times before covering her welcoming body with his.

Ah, God! Her insides clenching round him, her hands clutching at his hair so hard it hurt. His head spun. His cock sank into her. Deep. Hard. Her hissed inhalations, the sound of his name, a breathless repeated "Adam" in his ear. Deeper. Harder. She cried out his name, and he covered her mouth with his, stealing her breath and her voice from her as she shook beneath him.

There was a spot just behind her ear where she was ticklish. She snorted with laughter when Adam nuzzled her there, him reluctant to roll off, his member still buried in her. Her arms came round his back, holding him to her as if she would never let him go. Adam relaxed in her embrace.

"I love you," she whispered.

Adam lifted his head sufficiently to look at her. "Most appropriate, my lady. A good wife should hold her lord and husband in high esteem." She slapped his buttocks, he growled and pinned her to the bed, one large hand easily holding both of hers. He kissed the corner of her mouth, her nose, her eyes. "I love you too," he murmured. "My sun, my moon, my everything."

He really should say things like that more often, Adam reflected, wiping a tear away from her cheek. He rolled over on his back, and she rested her head on his shoulder, listening as he told her about the recent escape from Lancaster.

"Damned man," he said. "Even without the king under his control, Lancaster aims to do battle—or so it would seem. Alicia tells of an impressive army."

"I'm not sure one should trust Alicia—or everything she says."

Adam looked down his nose at her. "Trust her? Who on God's Earth would do that? But the information she gives verifies what Lord Roger has heard from others." He sighed. "Hopefully, Lord Roger's attempts at soothing all those ruffled feathers will pay off. If Lancaster comes to parliament in Salisbury, chances are we'll sort this without resorting to arms."

Chapter 39

Lancaster did not come to Salisbury, declaring that unless his demands were met—principally that Mortimer be banished from court and he himself be given the authority he should have as formal head of the king's council—he would not deign to honour the assembly with his presence. Even worse, neither the Earl of Kent nor the Earl of Norfolk made an appearance at the Salisbury Parliament, leaving the king devastated and Adam with a constant gripe in his belly. This year of our Lord 1328 would end badly. Things were coming to a head, and when news reached them of how Lancaster's man Thomas Wyther had murdered a minor northern lord for remaining loyal to his king, King Edward's eyes narrowed into streaks of blue.

"Damn the man! I shall see him hang for that!"

"Who? Wyther or Lancaster?" Mortimer asked.

"Both! But at least Wyther."

"Hanging Lancaster will do you little good, my lord," Lord Roger said. "Him you need to crush and humiliate."

Edward gave him an appraising look. "He'd have your head off in an instant should he have the opportunity."

Lord Roger shrugged. "Maybe. But I have no intention of giving him one. Besides, the man is your most powerful earl, and one does best to tread carefully around such."

"My most powerful earl?" King Edward gave Lord Roger a smile that was all teeth, no warmth. "I thought you were, my dear Earl of March."

"You flatter me, my lord," Lord Roger replied. "I am but your humble servant."

"Humble," King Edward muttered to Lord Roger's back as he moved away, surrounded by the Bishops of Lincoln and Hereford. "I dare say Roger Mortimer does not even know how to spell that word."

Adam did not say anything, standing to the side while the king and his companions snickered. It had caused quite the tempest when Queen Isabella had told her son it was time he rewarded Lord Mortimer for his loyal service by making him an earl.

For days, the king and his mother had engaged in a battle of wills, a whispered, angered discussion that had the king looking as if he'd mistakenly drunk vinegar instead of wine, while the queen went about with an uncharacteristically high colour and eyes as brittle as shards of mullion glass. At last, the king had given in—but insisted that if Mortimer was to be made an earl, so was Prince John.

"One earl each, Maman. Don't you find it fair?"

"They're your earls—both of them."

"Lord Mortimer serves but one master," King Edward said coldly. "Himself—and his mistress."

For an instant, Queen Isabella's hand hung in the air, quivering. Edward had raised his brows and stood his ground, flashing eyes daring his mother to slap him.

And so now the realm had three new earls, one the underage Earl of Cornwall, another the imposing Earl of March, and the third the new Earl of Ormond, young James Butler being a loyal companion to the king—and the heir to half of Ireland.

These days, however, the talk was not so much about the new earls or the recently concluded parliament. It was about Lancaster and his determination to vanquish Mortimer on the battlefield. Where Mortimer had mustered in Gloucester, Lancaster had done so in London, and the latest reports had him moving towards Winchester, near on apoplectic after hearing of Lord Mortimer's new title.

Lancaster on his own did not much worry Adam, no matter how many men he might have, but the thought of Thomas riding with him…No, it made Adam's bowels turn to water. If he were to face his friend across the field of battle, would he be able to raise his sword against him? Even slay him?

He did not share these thoughts with anyone but his brother—not even with Kit, being afflicted by a burst of puce-green jealousy when he'd watched her near on collapse upon hearing Norfolk was now thought to be among the rebels.

"You're being foolish," William admonished him. "She is as concerned as you are at the notion that you and Earl Thomas should meet in battle. She knows how much you love the man."

"And so does she, apparently."

"She does. As a friend, Adam."

They were walking side by side through the busy Salisbury market. Kit was supposed to have come with them, but Queen Philippa had requested her presence, and so they'd left without her, Adam promising to buy her some trinket or other as a consolation. Garters, he'd decided upon seeing the beautifully embroidered lengths of silk ribbons, and now he had two pairs in his pouch—one in green, the other in blue.

There were men-at-arms everywhere. Lord Roger—Earl Roger—was taking no chances, ensuring the royal arms were prominently displayed on the tabards of his men.

"Spies," he'd told Adam laconically earlier. "I fear we are infested with them, and I intend to catch some."

A young lad walked by offering roasted chestnuts. William gave him a farthing and helped himself to a dozen, offering some to Adam, who had his mouth full of hot chestnuts when he saw the group of men come riding from the north gate.

"Damn!" he said, spitting chestnuts over the cobbles.

"What?" William asked.

"That's Thomas Wake," Adam told him. "And that," he added, pointing at one of the men riding behind Wake, "is Broseley." He was already halfway across the market square, hands clenched into fists.

William pulled him to a stop. "You can't do anything to him, Adam. They're riding under a flag of truce."

Adam tore free of his brother's hands. "No? Watch me— I'm going to rip him apart, limb by limb."

"You can't." William fixed him with a stern look. "Not now."

Adam closed his eyes, inundated by a rage so hot he feared it was causing steam to leak out of his ears and nose. Broseley—here but untouchable. He watched Wake's men as they picked their way through the market, evidently making for the cathedral close.

"What he did to Kit…" Adam lurched into a trot, following Wake.

"I know." William kept pace beside him. "And of course he must be adequately punished—in accordance with the law."

"Not good enough." Adam wanted to beat Broseley to a pulp that twitched and clung to life before finally finishing him off by plunging a dagger into his stomach—a slow, painful death.

Thomas Wake was come to parley. By the time Adam and William made it back to the bishop's palace, Wake and his men were kicking their heels in the bishop's hall, waiting for the king and Lord Roger to make an appearance. As Adam entered, he walked straight across the hall to stand in front of Godfrey, whose eyes opened wide.

"I will have your hide for what you did to my wife," Adam said in a low voice. "I will see you dead before I'm done—and it will not be an easy death, that I promise."

He was shoved aside by Thomas Wake.

"How dare you threaten one of my men?" Wake blustered.

"I did not take you for a man who rode with murderer, my lord, but then I didn't take you for a traitor either," Adam replied. Wake paled, opened his mouth to say something, but desisted when the door flew open.

In marched the king and Lord Roger, surrounded by at least a score of armed men—enough that Wake's eyes flitted to his own little group of men.

"You have a nerve, to show yourself here, Cousin," Mortimer said. Beside him, the king nodded, eyes studying each and every one of Wake's men with such intensity they shuffled on their feet. At the sight of Godfrey of Broseley, the king's eyes darted to Adam.

Wake stood up straight. "I'm not here to talk to you—I'm here to parley with the king."

"Ah." Mortimer waited until the king was seated before sitting down in the only other chair. He crossed his legs and adjusted the fall of his robes. "Go on, we are all ears."

"The king, not you!" Wake repeated. King Edward raised his brows and steepled his hands in front of him before turning to Mortimer.

"Tell him that any business he wishes to conduct he'll have to handle with you. I do not lower myself to dealing with traitorous dogs."

If before Wake had been pale, now he went a bright red. "Traitorous? My liege, I—"

The king held up his hand. "And you can also tell him that I have issues with being in the presence of a would-be murderer, an abductor and abuser of innocent women. Does my lord Wake condone men who repeatedly break the law?"

Godfrey of Broseley trembled.

Wake turned to study Broseley. "Truly?"

"Most definitely. But we can deal with that whoreson later." Mortimer sounded bored. "So what do you want?"

"There must be a way to avoid this confrontation," Wake began. Yet again, the king cut him off.

"Of course there is. You must submit and beg for mercy."

Wake coloured. "Not a response Lancaster will like, my lord."

"Well, it is all the response he will get. We have already promised that there will be no loss of life for those who return to the king's peace—barring those we have named, like that accursed Thomas Wyther and the king's former guardian Sir Henry Beaumont, now turned traitor." Mortimer stood, an imposing figure in his dark robes, even more so when one saw the hauberk he was wearing beneath and the sword at his side. In comparison, Wake looked puny. "But the king's patience is not limitless. At some point, those who persist in this rebellion may well find themselves facing an accusation of treason—and we all know how traitors die, don't we, Cousin?"

Wake licked his lips. "Lancaster is a stubborn man."

The king gave him a wolfish grin. "So am I." With no further words, he rose and left the room, the heavy cloak edged with fur swirling round him. Every inch the king, Adam thought with pride, all the way from his fair hair adorned by the circlet of gold to the soft boots in bright red.

"Well, I suppose this concludes things, doesn't it?" Mortimer looked Wake up and down. "I do hope you come to your senses before it's too late, Cousin. I'd hate to have to witness the hanging, drawing, and quartering of a close relative."

Wake coughed. Mortimer laughed.

"You have an hour to leave the town," Mortimer said. "Best make haste. Oh, and as to Broseley, I'd like you to leave him behind."

Adam took a step closer to Broseley, who shrank away, hands gripping the hilt of his sword.

"Leave him behind?" Wake shook his head. "I can't do that. He's pledged himself to me and my protection."

"Ah. So you run with outlaws these days, do you?" Lord Roger strolled over to where Adam was standing and placed a cautionary hand on his arm.

"No. But my honour requires I take him with me. I shall deal with him myself."

"Good. He deserves to hang—as a minimum." Mortimer gestured at the door. "Go on. And do convey my warmest regards to my fellow earl." He chuckled. "Lancaster is a fool—and he will lose."

"How can you be so sure?" Wake demanded.

"How?" Mortimer's eyes glittered. "Simple, dear cousin. I fight for my life—and that of all those I hold dear." He set a light hand on the pommel of his sword. "We ride to London in a week. It is best for all if Lancaster does not attempt to block us."

Whatever Wake told Lancaster, it did not seem to have led to any change in the earl's position. From what Kit had heard, he remained in Winchester, determined to stop the king and Mortimer from reaching London. Men kept riding back and forth, one day Thomas Wake, the other that weasel of a man the Archbishop of Canterbury, both attempting to broker a treaty.

In general, most of the bishops had been swayed by Lord Roger's promises of dealing leniently with the erstwhile rebels, going so far as to swear on the archbishop's crozier that he would spare Lancaster's life. But it did not go down well that the further the crisis developed, the more it became evident who was in charge. It was not the young king, nor was it his mother—no, this time round the undisputed ruler was the newly belted Earl of March, and he no longer made any attempts to hide the fact.

"He's playing with fire," Kit said with a little sigh, sitting down beside William. At the high table, Queen Philippa greeted her husband before sitting down, all dimples and smiles.

"Our Lord Mortimer is destined for great things," William replied, grabbing a roasted rib from a passing platter.

"As is our king," Kit pointed out, her gaze on Mortimer, who sat side by side with Queen Isabella, the tawny velvet of his robes contrasting with his dark eyes and hair. He laughed and talked, ate and drank, but all the while he was scanning the hall, as if constantly on his guard. These days, he went nowhere without a small personal guard—four men who followed him as closely as his shadow.

On the other side of Queen Isabella, King Edward was deep in conversation with his wife. Kit had to smile at the way he speared a morsel of meat and offered it to Philippa, oblivious to all but her. Or rather pretending to be oblivious. Their king and his close circle of companions might be rowdy and seemingly more given to carousing than politics, but from what Adam told her, the late-night conversations tended to veer towards the state of the realm, the king showing a remarkable grasp of politics in these discussions.

"And bitterness," Adam had added last night. "With his mother for being so grasping, with Lord Roger for taking unto himself all powers that belong with the regent, with his uncles for betraying him, and with Lancaster for being obdurate."

"Is Mortimer doing that?" she'd asked.

"He is. At present, I don't see that there is an alternative. King Edward's very crown is in danger, and for Lord Roger to defend it, he must control all resources." Adam had settled himself in her arms, his head a warm weight on her shoulder.

"The question is, will Lord Roger relinquish all those powers once Lancaster is vanquished?"

"And what do you think?"

There'd been a loud exhalation. "I think no, sweeting. A man like Lord Roger to taste the nectar of absolute power—I fear it is quite addictive."

It may be addictive, but power did seem to come with substantial drawbacks, or so Kit thought, watching Mortimer's tense stance, the way his fingers drummed at the table.

She was distracted from her inspection of the baron by Adam, who sat down beside her and slipped an arm round her waist. Lately, he was something of a grim protective presence—even more so when they'd received word that no sooner had Wake left Salisbury but Godfrey had set heels to his mount and fled.

"We ride tomorrow," Adam told her. "To Winchester and then to London."

"And Lancaster?" Kit asked.

"Well, if he's still in Winchester, we'll squash him there." Adam sounded unconcerned, his hand tightening on the hilt of his eating knife. He avoided any further questions by popping a dried fig in his mouth. Kit picked at a small cluster of raisins while studying him under her lashes.

There was a commotion by the door. In came Alicia Luytens, accompanied by a woman clutching an infant and three men-at-arms. She ordered her companions to wait and marched towards the high table. Shadow and light played over the sharp planes of her face, causing her to look like an avenging angel—a harsh angel, failing dismally in such qualities as mercy and compassion.

"My lady," she said, sweeping Queen Isabella a deep reverence. "My lord," she added, addressing Mortimer. The king's brows shot up, and beside Kit, Adam made an exasperated sound. Alicia, however, seemed not to notice, her attention focussed on Queen Isabella. "I have news."

"Not here," Mortimer said, standing up. "My liege," he added, addressing the king with a bow that had Alicia's face turning the colour of a scalded ham, "will you honour us with your presence?"

King Edward stood and made for the adjoining chamber with his mother, Mortimer, and Alicia at his heels. A hush descended on the hall, all eyes riveted on the closed door. It opened.

"Monmouth, de Guirande, Montagu—get over here," Mortimer ordered, and Adam flew to his feet, as did Montagu. Some tables away, Robert de Langon scowled, as did Stafford and Ufford. Kit turned to William.

"Now what?"

They found out soon enough. Adam and Richard erupted from the room some minutes later, yelling for their men to get ready to leave within the hour. Out came Montagu, hastening over to the king's other companions. Whatever he said had them on their feet, making for the door.

Adam stopped for an instant beside Kit. "London is about to rise in favour of Lancaster. They've elected that swine Hamo as their mayor." He stooped and kissed her brow. "We ride in haste, sweeting. You will travel with the queens." He turned to William. "Take care of her, Brother."

"Always." William clasped his brother's hand. "Ride with God, Adam."

She saw him once more in the large courtyard. Already astride, he was commanding his men into neat lines, four men abreast. So many men, so many restive horses, and all she could see was her Adam. As if sensing her, he turned. A hand over his heart, a slight bow, and he was off. But she could swear she had heard him whisper "I love you" despite the jangling of harnesses and armour.

Once the men were gone, a foreboding silence settled over the remaining women. Queen Philippa set her ladies to packing, Queen Isabella supervised the preparation of litters and carts, and Kit was sent this way and that.

Come evening, they assembled for prayers with Queen Isabella's chaplain. Philippa excused herself soon after, and it was Kit and Alicia and Queen Isabella, plus some of the queen's serving women.

"So where do you go from here?" Queen Isabella asked Alicia. She bit into a pear, fruit juice dribbling down her chin.

"Go?" Alicia looked confused. "Why, I stay here, my lady. With you."

"With me?" The queen finished wiping her chin. "Why would I want you here? Am I to forget you once came close to poisoning me?"

"But..." Alicia sank in on herself, thin shoulders bowing. "Where am I to go?"

"Not my concern," the queen said. "Maybe you could dress in sackcloth and ashes and return to your husband."

"Her husband?" Kit ignored Alicia's forbidding look and pulled back her sleeve, displaying bruises and scratches. "And what will he do if he finds out she's betrayed him and his friends?"

"Kill me," Alicia groaned, reclaiming her arm.

Queen Isabella tapped her foot. "Then go somewhere else. Once we've dealt with Lancaster, we can surely handle Master Luytens."

"Go where?" Alicia sank down to the floor.

Kit inhaled. No, she didn't want to, but she had to. "You could stay at Tresaints."

"With you?" Alicia sneered. "I think not. The house my father bequeathed to his common-born whore is not a place I want to ever see or visit."

"Suit yourself." She had offered and been refused. Kit could do no more.

Chapter 40

Mortimer sent the Sheriff of Hampshire to warn Lancaster he was coming.

"One last attempt at avoiding armed conflict," he explained to the king. "At least for now." He gestured at their men. "Good men, but at present we are too evenly matched, Lancaster and I—us. We need more time, my lord, and it is the general who chooses wisely when to engage who carries the day."

King Edward nodded, no more. "And if Lancaster remains in Winchester?"

"Then we will fight." Lord Roger glanced at Adam. "It will be bloody, but your men will fight to the death for you."

"The death?" the king repeated in a breathless voice. "Do you think it will come to that?"

"Not for you, my lord. But for me, yes." Lord Roger rose in his stirrups. "Damn it, where is that sheriff?" He clapped a hand to his hat and urged his horse into a canter, leaving the king with Adam.

"Whatever else one can say about Mortimer, one cannot call him a coward," the king said.

"No, my lord." Adam watched as Lord Roger galloped past the front riders, four men falling in behind him. "He has always faced the challenges life has thrown him bravely."

"As a true knight should." Edward shaded his eyes. "And there, it seems, comes the sheriff."

"Wake is doing his best," the sheriff said once the king and Adam joined him and Mortimer. "He's begging Lancaster to leave before it is too late." He wiped at his wet face. "Wake fears for his life—all their lives—should your men descend on them."

"And rightly so. We are done dancing around with these rebels." King Edward looked at Mortimer. "I say we prevaricate no more."

"As you wish, my lord." Mortimer called for one of his squires to find the sheriff a fresh horse. "One last chance, John. Tell Wake we are coming—at speed."

The sheriff gave a weary nod, no more, before transferring to his new mount.

They plodded on, advancing in good order. Adam rode back and forth along the columns, talking to his men, here a jest, there an encouraging pat on the shoulder. They made camp within sight of the walls of Winchester. Tomorrow, they'd enter the town, and depending on what Lancaster chose to do, it could be a full-out battle.

Come dawn, Adam was awaiting his orders when one of their scouts came riding back.

"They're pulling out," he said. "Lancaster has already left."

"Good." Lord Roger pulled on his gauntlets. "We march. Now."

By the time Adam and his men reached the town, most of Lancaster's men were gone. But not all, and in some places violence flared, Lancaster's stragglers fighting like cornered rats. Come evening, Winchester was safely back under royal control, and messengers were dispatched with haste to the two queens.

"We wait for them before we proceed further," Lord Roger decided, and the king gave him a sour look but acquiesced.

One day in Winchester and they were on the road again, approaching London from the south. A sequence of grey and wet November days followed, and Adam huddled under his heavy sheepskin cloak, glad that for once Kit had listened to him and agreed to travel in one of the litters.

From the reports they received, the Londoners were in a right frenzy. Hamo de Chigwell was no longer the mayor, having been replaced by a John de Grantham, and the closer they got to London, the more numerous the various messengers from the London burghers, declaring their joy at welcoming the king and Lord Mortimer to the city.

"Pah!" Lord Roger crumpled the last obsequious message and fed it into the brazier. "Like sheep, the lot of them. They're lining up, eager to be fleeced if that ensures they're not slaughtered."

The king laughed. "So what do we do?"

"Oh, we start by fleecing them," Lord Roger replied. "And then, when the time is right, we slaughter some of them—as a warning of what happens when merchants attempt to meddle in the governance of your realm."

Montague gave an approving nod. "Serve them right. Can't have upstart commoners thinking they should have a voice, can we?"

It did not take long to pacify London—not when the new mayor was falling over his feet to prove just how loyal he and all his fellow merchants were to Mortimer. The court moved into the Tower, and in less than a week Mortimer had his men in all crucial positions responsible for law and order in the sprawling city. The Londoners themselves were forbidden to bear arms—on pain of death. And in all this, one Henry Luytens ended up very dead, his corpse bobbing like an overlarge piece of flotsam in the Thames.

"Me?" Adam asked when Richard requested he accompany Richard to the sheriff.

"We're family. That's why they contacted me."

"Not my family," Adam muttered but agreed to go with him all the same.

"Murdered," the sheriff concluded laconically, covering Luyten's face. "God knows what he was doing out and about in the middle of the night. But whatever it was, it ended with a dagger in his gullet."

"Ah," Adam said, studying his brother-in-law. "And how do we know it was at night?"

"His steward vouches for his master's presence in his house at curfew." The sheriff plucked at his protruding bottom lip. "One of Lancaster's pet dogs, as I hear it. Maybe that's what got him killed. Well, we will never know, will we?"

"No," Richard agreed, wiping his hands on his fine new gown. "As I hear it, he was not a nice man."

"Not much, no. As per the neighbours, that poor wife of his walked about decorated with bruises." The sheriff narrowed his eyes. "Maybe she did it."

"Alicia?" Richard emitted a bark of laughter. "I think not. She is far away from here, and too gentle, too frail to even consider hurting someone."

"If you say so." The sheriff shrugged.

"You did it," Adam stated as they walked back to the Tower.

"I had to." Richard studied his hands. "Alicia was right: I was so eager to get her off my hands I did not care what sort of ogre she ended up with. And so…" He turned aside, steadying himself against a wall. "God's blood," he said weakly. "I did not think it would be so different to kill a man in cold blood versus killing an enemy in the heat of a battle."

"I hope Alicia will be adequately grateful. With her husband dead, she becomes quite the rich widow."

"Aye." Richard was back to looking at his hands, turning them this way and that, as if fearing to find blood on them. "But I don't intend to tell her what I did."

"No, that would be foolish. One never knows when she would use such information against you."

Richard didn't protest. He just scowled.

Kit was not pleased at being back in the Tower. The old fortress woke too many memories of those years when Despenser had lorded over all England, the then king too lazy and besotted to deny his favourite anything. Besides, she longed for her children, and recently she'd taken to slipping into the chapel whenever she could, praying that her children and her home be safe despite the unrest that yet again stalked the country.

"I thought I'd find you here."

Kit started, turning to face the king. "My lord."

He joined her in front of the altar. "I remember having words with my father in here," he said, crossing himself. "I was angry at him for how he was treating Maman."

"You were always a gallant son."

"To her. Not necessarily to him." King Edward dropped his gaze to the floor. "How was he?"

Kit threw a cautious look over her shoulder. The chapel was empty, the few candles illuminating nothing more than the bright red-and-white pillars that strove upwards to meet the painted ceiling.

"Relieved, I think," she replied after a while. "Mind you, he was angry as well—mainly with Lord Mortimer and your mother."

"The Babylon whore," he said bitterly.

"That's harsh, my lord."

"Probably." He glanced at her. "She can't help it, trapped in a love as poisonous as it is magnificent."

"Very eloquent."

"It will not end well," he said. "How can it?"

"I know." She gnawed her lip. "But they don't—not yet. They still believe that somehow the love they share will keep them safe."

"It's not only love," he reminded her. "It is greed and ambition. My lady mother has found the perfect mate in Lord Mortimer, and together they wish to dominate the world."

Kit smiled. "Not the entire world, my lord."

"No. Only my part of it." He grimaced. "So, my fath—" He broke off. "Sir Edward," he added in a hushed voice.

"Hale enough," Kit said. "And by the time we bid him farewell, I think he was looking forward to his new adventure. He saw it as an opportunity at a new life, my lord. Not many men get second chances with their lives."

He smiled, dashing at his eyes. "I miss him. So many years since I last saw him, and sometimes I fear that I'll forget what he looks like."

"You won't, my lord." She set a careful hand on his arm. "And if you forget, all you need to do is look at your own reflection."

"Am I that like him?"

She pretended to study him. "Well, now that there is something growing on your face that resembles a beard rather than tufts of misplaced hair, yes, you do."

He laughed, stroking his cheeks. "It suits me, doesn't it?" He grew serious. "If nothing else, it makes me look older than I am."

"Being too young is a fault that corrects itself, my lord."

"Hopefully, before it's too late," he muttered. "So," he continued in his normal voice, "do you wish for a boy or a girl this time round?"

"I wish for a healthy child, my lord." She patted herself on her stomach, now visibly rounded.

"Amen to that." He crossed himself again, waited while she did the same, and escorted her out of the chapel and into the weak sunlight outside. "Philippa lost a child on that long ride," he blurted.

"Truly?"

"She…" He scuffed at the ground, and she was suffused with a wave of tenderness for this half man, half boy. "She was late," he mumbled. "Well over a week. And then all that horseback riding…"

"No." Kit shook her head. "Rarely is a planted child dislodged by a ride. And at her age, her courses need not be as regular as they become as she grows to maturity." She gave him a stern look. "She's too young, my lord."

A vivid wave of red tinged his cheeks and his ears. "She wants my child," he said, pride leaking out of every word.

"Of course she does. But not yet. For her sake, be careful, my lord."

"Be careful?" There was a twinkle in his eyes. "Would you care to elucidate on that, Lady Kit?"

"No." She wagged a finger at him. "Talk to a man, my lord."

He grinned. "Poor Adam. He becomes terribly embarrassed when I ask him about things like this."

Kit just laughed. "Somehow, I think you know much more about these matters than you let on."

"What can I say? Cousin Louis was a good teacher."

Once Mortimer had sorted things in London, they set off due west. This time, Kit insisted on riding, which gave her opportunity to talk to both her brother and her husband. Richard was subdued—understandably in view of Henry Luytens—and it took her quite some time to coax a little smile from him.

"Adam?" He laughed. "No, I will not name my newborn son after your husband."

"A good name," Kit protested.

"Maybe so. Maud has her heart set on Gilbert, for her father." Richard tweaked his cloak into place. "I am of a mind to allow her to choose. Two sons in something more than one year—she deserves something back."

"Your heart perhaps?" Kit suggested.

"My heart?" Richard shook his head. "Taken, I fear."

"By Lord Roger," Adam supplied as Richard galloped off.

"Surely, a heart has room for more than one love?" Kit protested.

"Aye. And he is fond of Maud—just as he is fond of you. But whatever passion he has he expends on his lord." He gave her a little smile. "I used to feel the same: Lord Roger was the sun in my existence. Until you."

"Until me." She leaned over to set her gloved hand atop his. "My lord, keeper of my heart."

"As it should be."

"Yes." Kit stared after her brother, who had now reached Lord Roger. "Poor Maud."

"Poor Richard." Adam nodded in the direction of Queen Isabella. "Behold Lord Mortimer's sun."

Chapter 41

December began badly. When Adam hurried into his lord's chambers, still muddy after his recent exercises in the tiltyard, he was met by a trembling king, eyes like glowing sapphires in a face devoid of any colour.

"Read." The king handed Adam a document.

"Sweetest Virgin," Adam muttered under his breath as he scanned the letter. Not this. He'd taken some comfort at hearing neither Kent nor Norfolk had been present in Winchester, but with this document the two earls were definitely siding with the rebels, calling all to come to London and discuss the serious matters of the king being in breach not only of his coronation oath but also of the laws as laid down by the Magna Carta.

"And there, between the lines, everyone can read that my uncles hold me responsible for my father's unlawful imprisonment—and that he is still alive!" The king kicked at a cushion, sending it flying to hit the recently painted wall.

In accordance with Queen Isabella's instructions, the royal chambers at Gloucester had been refurbished, but somehow Adam suspected that neither the smell of fresh paint nor the rich colours of the new fabrics were of any comfort whatsoever to his young king, standing very straight and somehow so alone in the middle of a room containing at least half a dozen people.

"The old king is dead," Lord Roger said from his perch in a window. "We buried him a year ago—here."

"Stop it!" The king whirled. "We both know—"

"We know nothing," Queen Isabella interrupted, her voice dripping ice. "Your royal father is dead and buried. Let those that claim otherwise produce proof in the shape of a living, breathing king." She went to join Lord Roger in the window seat. "This is war, is it not?"

"It is." Lord Roger sighed. "But not yet. Give me one or two more weeks."

"And then what?" the king demanded. "Aim you to make war on my uncles?"

"I will make war on whoever threatens your throne, my lord. Hopefully, your uncles will come to their senses before it is too late."

"Or maybe I should do as they say." Edward straightened up. "Maybe I should have you and my mother exiled and attend this London conference, requesting that my uncles help me lead this kingdom—not you."

Lord Roger studied his nails. "Maybe you should." He stood, shaking out the skirts of his robes. "Is that your wish, my lord? Because all you have to do is say the word, and I will leave—today. But my men go with me, and I will not go peaceably into exile. Why should I, when all I've ever attempted is to heal this realm of yours from the grievous wounds imposed by your incompetent father?" He nailed the king with a look so black it made Adam's innards quiver in recognition. While rarely roused, an enraged Mortimer was a sight that had men, dogs, and horses fleeing his presence.

"Roger." Queen Isabella was at his side. "He didn't mean it like that."

"He didn't? To me it sounded most genuine. Your ungrateful whelp is finding his teeth and his claws. So be it— let him fight his own battles." Lord Roger shook off the queen. "Let's see just how long he survives without us, eh?" He took a step towards the king. "So, my lord, how will you deploy your five score men to defend yourself and your little wife? And do you truly think Lancaster—or Norfolk and Kent—have any intention of letting you rule?"

"They're my uncles! They love me, and—"

"Love?" Lord Roger yanked the document out of Adam's hands. "Is this love? Is it? To me, it smells of treason—and let's not forget Norfolk has a claim of his own on the throne. How many would not prefer having an adult man as a king to a half-grown lad like you?"

"Thomas?" Edward shook his head. "No, Thomas would not do that to me."

"He just has!" Lord Roger roared, and the king jerked as if slapped.

"Roger." Queen Isabella took hold of him again. "That's enough, my lion."

Lion? More like a vicious Welsh dragon, but with a loud curse Mortimer retreated to his window seat, sitting down with his back to the room, eyes on what little he could see through the thick glass.

A heavy silence fell. Mortimer continued to stare out of the window. Queen Isabella sat down and studied her son.

"What do we do?" Edward asked the room at large. Adam held his tongue, as did Richard and Maltravers, lounging against a wall. Bishop Burghersh cleared his throat, opened his mouth, but at a look from Queen Isabella thought better of it.

"Maman," Edward finally said. "I need help."

"You do? Just now, it seemed to me you wished me gone from your life, banished forever."

Adam had to hand it to her. The queen knew just how to sink a dagger into a man's heart and twist.

The king took a step towards her. "I did not mean it, not like that."

"And yet Roger is right: that is what you said." She gave him a cool look, long fingers tapping at the wrought armrests of the chair. The king fidgeted. Adam looked away, uncomfortable with how young and forlorn he looked.

"I apologise," the king said after some moments of silence. He bowed to his mother. "I did not mean to suggest I could do without your help or presence."

Queen Isabella nodded, no more, gesturing at Lord Roger. Something flared in the king's eyes, his chin came up in wordless defiance. The queen waited. The king agonised. Adam wished he could leave, not wanting to witness this humiliation of his lord.

At long last, the king cleared his throat. "My apologies to you too, Earl Roger."

To Mortimer's credit, he did not demand more than that. He rose, approached the king, and bowed deeply. "Your servant always, my lord."

387

But he wasn't. All those present knew it was one man in charge of the kingdom, and that man was not their sixteen-year-old king.

"That maggot of an archbishop deserves to be dipped in honey and left for the ants," Lord Roger growled some days after Christmas, tossing the long letter to Adam. "Threaten us with excommunication indeed! I'll show him—I'll show them all!"

It had been a dismal Christmas, the only source of cheer being Kit's presence and the long hours of darkness in which Adam could retire to be only with her. They'd sent William back to Tresaints, and soon enough Kit would return there as well—sooner if war broke out—there to await the birth of their next child. But for now, she was here at Warwick with the court, spending her days with Queen Philippa while Adam had his men exercising in the large outer bailey or spent time in the tiltyard with the king.

As always, King Edward escaped into strenuous mock-fighting to work the edge of an ever-present simmering anger. As always, his preferred sparring partner was Adam, even if now and then he'd challenge one of his other companions.

"They never dare to defeat me," he explained in a curt voice. "You never let me win."

"But you win all the same at times," Adam replied, rubbing at his right arm, still sore from the king's blow.

"Not as often as I'd like."

"More often than I like," Adam retorted, and for an instant his lord had grinned, looking like the young lad he was.

"Adam?" Lord Roger snapped his fingers in front of Adam's nose, recalling him to the cold chamber. Warwick was not as well-appointed as Gloucester, and as a consequence Lord Roger had been given a set of small and dark rooms, quite some distance from Queen Isabella's more spacious accommodation.

"Simon was Lancaster's choice for the archbishop," Bishop Burghersh said calmly. "Of course he's going to side with the man to whom he owes his preferment."

"And even when Lancaster is defeated, that damned Mepeham will remain the archbishop." Lord Roger made a face.

"Yes. Unless you murder him—but that would be most imprudent. Look what happened to Henry II and St Thomas." Bishop Burghersh smothered a yawn.

"I am not in the habit of murdering anyone," Lord Roger replied, standing up. "Time to end all this before it spirals totally out of control." He called for a clerk. "Adam, arrange for a messenger to ride for London, another to ride to Lancaster—wherever he may be."

After dinner, Lord Mortimer requested that the king, the two queens, and the king's captains and closest companions remain in the hall. Only once the other men and women had left did Lord Roger stand.

"I've declared war on the rebels." He paused, bowed slightly in the direction of the king. "In your name, of course." He smiled at Queen Isabella. "As we speak, messengers are on their way to London and Lancaster. I've given them one more chance to submit to your mercy. Any man who returns to your peace by Twelfth Night will be pardoned. Let's see how many will be wise enough to accept that offer."

"And my uncles?" the king asked.

"Last I heard, Norfolk and Kent are with Lancaster. If they choose to fight or not is up to them." Lord Roger made for the door. "We ride for Kenilworth at dawn. And then on to Leicester."

If looks could kill, Mortimer would have been dead before he reached the door, several pairs of eyes throwing darts at his broad back. Not the king, who seemed submerged in the contemplation of the empty trencher in front of him. But Montagu, Stafford, and all the rest, they shifted and muttered, saying it was not right that Mortimer should take it upon himself to declare war in the king's name.

"What choice did he have?" Adam asked.

"Well, look who always leaps to Mortimer's defence," de Langon sneered, elbowing Montagu, who scowled at him.

"It was not an attempt at defence. It was a question," Adam replied calmly. "Unless you want Lancaster to crush us all and impose his rule on the king, what else can be done but declare war?"

"Maybe Lancaster would be a better choice," Ufford said.

"Maybe cows fly," Adam retorted. "The man is as proud as Lucifer, and as greedy."

Montague nodded. "Not a better alternative, I agree. But Mortimer is acting as if he were the king." He kept his voice low, a cautious eye on the king, who was talking to his mother.

"He is acting on behalf of the king," Adam tried, even if deep down he agreed.

"See?" de Langon said. "Once a Mortimer man, always a Mortimer man."

"Take that back." Adam's voice rose. "I'll not have a useless, spiteful little lordling cast aspersions on my honour."

"Your honour?" De Langon laughed—but took the precaution of retreating so that there was a table between him and Adam. "And what honour is there in wedding the discarded scraps from Lord Mortimer's bed? That scar-faced wife of yours is said to have been like a bitch in heat when she was younger—always slobbering over Mortimer."

The blow to de Langon's back sent him face first into the table.

"Lady Kit to you," the king said. "And I'll have you know she is a good and virtuous lady—a lady I count as a friend and cherish as if she were a sister."

"My lord," de Langon stammered, hands to his bleeding face. "I didn't mean to insult—"

"Yes, you did." The king looked him up and down. "I frankly have no recollection of how you came to join my household, but as of now you are no longer welcome. I expect you gone by nightfall."

"But my lord," de Langon bleated to no avail. The king was gone, striding over to where his wife was waiting for him.

"Best get packing," Montagu said, standing up. "Can't say I'll be sorry to see you go, de Langon."

"Your fault!" de Langon yelled, pointing at Adam. "If only those incompetent—" He broke off, glaring at Adam.

"If only what?" Adam asked.

"Nothing." De Langon spat at him. "I hate you! One day…"

"Go." Adam took a step closer. "And if you're not gone by nightfall, I will personally make you pay for those slurs on my wife."

"Make me pay?" de Langon kept his distance, cradling his face. "You have that wrong, de Guirande, it will be me making you pay."

Adam lunged. De Langon fled, squealing.

Montagu snickered. "Best watch your back, dear Adam."

"A mouse threatening a wolf," Stafford commented before getting to his feet. "Best get started with the preparations. You heard Mortimer. We leave at dawn."

Late that same night, a page came to fetch Adam, saying the Earl of March required his presence.

"Now?" Adam grumbled, getting out of his bed. He promised Kit he'd be back as quickly as he could, at which she grunted something unintelligible.

Lord Roger was alone.

"Ah, Adam." He patted at the stool beside him. "Everything ready for tomorrow?"

"It is." Adam gave him a wary look. Rarely did Lord Roger overimbibe, but his glassy eyes and wet mouth indicated tonight was an exception.

"Good, good." Lord Roger sighed profoundly. "War, Adam. How could it come to this?" He gestured at the nearby table, piled with writs and documents. "I work hard, long hours expended on the safety of this realm, and what do I get? Ingratitude." He smacked his lips. "Rebels. A bad year," he continued, pouring himself yet another goblet of wine. Adam eyed him cautiously.

"My sons, my boys, dead." Lord Roger drank. "Roger gone, John as well, —and now that fool of an earl! Who does Lancaster think he is?"

"A peer of the realm, my lord," Adam replied. "And they do not love you—not anymore."

"They have never loved me," Lord Roger muttered. "But it suffices if they fear me." He stretched. "And they will. By God, they will. I shall ruin Lancaster, and after him, I'll do the same to whoever challenges my authority."

"A dangerous path to tread, my lord." Adam moved the wine out of reach. "Conciliation is surely a better approach."

"And you think I haven't tried?" Lord Roger gave him a bleary look. "Have I not shown myself to be reasonable and fair? Did I not promise them their lives despite their treasonous acts?" He belched. "Faithless, the lot of them—including our dear boy-king." He shook his head. "Faithless. Damn them all," he mumbled, his head dipping towards the table. "Life used to be so simple. Now it is all so complicated, and sometimes I get lost in all the dark." He gave Adam a wry smile. "And I miss my Joanie." He placed a finger to his lips. "Shhh. Best not tell my lady love that." He wobbled to his feet. *My lady love,* he carolled, and he had a good voice, deep and musical. "Two ladies, one man. One crown, two men. A mess. Such a mess."

"My lord." Adam made a grab for Lord Roger. "Best we get you to bed. We rise with the cocks tomorrow."

"Rise with the cocks," Lord Roger repeated, weaving his way to the bed. "Rise and fight."

Once he'd assured himself Lord Roger was fast asleep, Adam returned to his wife. This time, she was wide awake.

"Is he ailing?"

"No." He pulled her close. "He is maudlin—and drunk. At times, all that responsibility is too much, I reckon."

"Especially as he receives little gratitude." She stroked Adam's cheek. "He deserves some, I think."

"Aye." He nestled closer, sliding one hand under her shift to cup her breast. "I wish you weren't leaving me tomorrow."

"Your decision, not mine," she reminded him with an edge to her voice. He propped himself up on an elbow.

"I can't have you riding with an army, sweeting." He'd arranged for an escort to see her home safely.

"I know." She wound her arms around his neck. "But I don't like it…"

"When we are apart," he filled in with a smile. "I'll be back with you soon enough."

"You think Mortimer will prevail?"

"Aye." Of this he was certain. "He will win this battle. The question is whether he will win the war." He fell back against the pillows. "They've pushed him into a corner, sweeting. Lord Roger can never relinquish his power, not anymore. Because the moment he does, the disgruntled peers will come after him, and that is a risk he cannot take." He tightened his hold on her. "But I don't want to spend these remaining hours with you talking about Lord Roger."

"No?" She kissed his neck. "So what does my husband want?"

"You."

Chapter 42

Come dawn, Kit bid Adam a teary farewell in their little room. Adam kissed her thoroughly, but his mind was already elsewhere, with his men, his horses. Once astride, he turned, hoping for a last sight of her, and there she was, standing at the entrance of the keep. She blew him a kiss. He bowed, setting his hand to his chest. As always, his gesture made her smile.

Most of the women were remaining behind, but not so Queen Isabella, who rode side by side with Lord Roger. An impressive lady, Adam thought, catching a glimpse of the sword she was carrying. Likely, she could use it as well.

The ride to Kenilworth was uneventful, but the garrison refused the king entry. King Edward was furious, Mortimer was unsurprised, and Queen Isabella suggested they continue with their plan and ride for Leicester. Two more days on the road, and it was cold and wet, the king's mood growing fouler by the moment. Once in Leicester, Mortimer's instructions were short and to the point.

"Destroy it all—but leave the people their lives."

Before the king's astounded eyes, Mortimer's men set to work, and over the coming days every building was destroyed, the skies darkened by the acrid smoke from the burnt homes and stables. Women wept and begged, children wailed, but nothing stopped the methodical destruction.

Cows, sheep, pigs, and chickens—all killed. The fishponds were drained, leaving the fish to die flapping in the mud, and even the deer in the forest were hunted and slain, carcasses stacked atop of each other. Meagre winter stores were raided, what little remained of last year's harvest thrown outside to rot, and it turned Adam's stomach, but he did as ordered, knowing full well just how effective a measure this was. Despairing, starving people made bad soldiers and sullen tenants, and hopefully Lancaster would have his hands full repairing the damage done.

The inhabitants wept and begged, but Mortimer told the people to take it up with their rebellious lord. This was retribution for Lancaster's treachery, and as such the now destitute people should go to him for compensation.

"Wilful destruction!" the king paced back and forth. Adam heaved a silent sigh: at times, he was remarkably innocent, this king of theirs. What did he think war was but destruction and pillage?

"What better way to force him to do battle?" Mortimer replied. "Our spies tell us Lancaster is already on the move."

"But all those people," the king groaned. "They'll starve before the new harvest is in. Look at them, Mortimer—how can you turn babes out to live off air and water?"

"Hopefully, they'll find refuge in a nearby convent—the friars will do what they can." Mortimer sounded irritated. "It is always thus in war. The innocents bleed and die."

"And all those men—dead!"

"Yes." Mortimer crossed himself. "That was most unfortunate, but you'd best take that up with Percy. It was his men who massacred those peasants, not mine."

"They were marching to join Lancaster," Percy protested. "And they weren't exactly defenceless." Percy sported several bruises and gashes, and from what Adam had heard, he'd been as involved as his men in killing the peasants.

"Still." The king gave him a black look. "Slaughtered. Like pigs."

"Blame it on Lancaster," Mortimer said. "His people, suffering because of his ambition and greed."

"Hmm." The king gave Mortimer a long look. "And now to where?"

"We go south. To Northampton."

Adam was patrolling the outer perimeter of their camp in Northampton when the shout went up, Gavin yelling that there were men approaching at full gallop, banners flapping overhead.

"Who?" Adam demanded, already calling his men into formation.

"Don't know," Gavin said. "Too far away to see."

Adam squinted. A cloud of dust, no more, above which he could vaguely make out two squares of...red? Dearest God! Lancaster was storming towards them!

"Sound the alarm," he ordered, and at the sound of the horn, men came tumbling out of tents. Adam watched with approval as his men donned armour and rushed to form lines. All that training had paid off, and now all he had to do was hope they were strong enough to withstand the approaching army.

"My lord!" Gavin tugged at his sleeve. "Not an army, my lord, and those are not Lancaster's banners."

Adam clambered atop a barrel, peering in the direction of the approaching riders. Three lions, gold on scarlet, but one banner with a border of white, the other with an argent bar across the top. "Norfolk!" he yelled. "That's Norfolk and Kent, and they carry a flag of truce as well." He leapt off his perch. "I must tell the king."

The king already knew. He stood as still as a statue as his pages struggled with his armour, and only once he was adequately armed, his sword at his side, did he follow Adam outside.

"Shit," the king muttered. "It's cold enough to freeze my balls off." He pulled his cloak closer. "Do you think they come to submit?"

"Why else?" Adam gave the king an encouraging smile before placing his men in a protective half circle round the king, Lord Roger, and Queen Isabella. All three stood still and silent as the two earls dismounted. They must have ridden like the hounds of hell, to judge from the state of their horses and the purple shadows under their eyes. Or maybe it was fear that had them looking pale and haggard, one sporting dark, unshaven cheeks, the other gilded bristles.

They stood for a moment by their horses, as if girding themselves before an unpleasant ordeal. Thomas said something to his brother. Kent nodded and clasped his brother's hand.

Together, the brothers began their slow approach towards the king, bareheaded and with their swords carried unsheathed by their side.

"My liege." Thomas of Norfolk bent knee and offered the king his sword. Kent mirrored his movement. "We ask that you take us into your peace and accept our homage."

King Edward stepped forward. "Why should I do that? You've already broken your oaths to me."

Thomas winced. "Look, Ned—"

"My liege, to you," King Edward interrupted. "We have gone too far for loving nicknames, don't you think?"

"Damn it," Thomas said, "don't make this more difficult than it has to be."

"Difficult?" King Edward set his foot to his uncle and sent him sprawling in the wet grass. "You were going to make war on me, and you talk about things being difficult?"

"My dearest liege." Thomas righted himself, standing on his knees. "I beg you forgive us. Please," he added, bowing his head. Once again, Kent followed suit.

The king left them there for some time. Long enough that Adam could see the tremor that flew through Edmund of Kent, blue eyes darting sideways in an attempt to catch his brother's eyes.

"You're forgiven." Edward gripped Thomas by the elbow and pulled him upright, did the same to Kent. "But if there is a next time, you will die—as traitors should."

One by one, he embraced his uncles and exchanged the kiss of peace, but when Thomas attempted to tighten the embrace, the king stepped back, shaking his head.

"I'm afraid it will take some time for me to trust you again," he said in a tone that had Adam's heart cracking. "I loved you," the king went on, so low only those closest could hear. "I trusted you and looked up to you. And this is how you rewarded me."

"Ned," Thomas groaned. "We never meant you any harm! We just "

"Rose in rebellion," the king cut him off. "Wrote a document in which you describe me as an oath-breaker." He nodded. "Minor things, all in all." He turned his back on his uncles. "And now what, my Earl of March?"

"Now we go for Lancaster. I'm sure your uncles will be more than happy to tell us where he is."

"Bedford." Edmund of Kent studied the large camp, the drawn-up men-at-arms. "You'll annihilate him."

"Maybe. Maybe not." Mortimer gave him a cold smile. "It is up to the king. My lord," he continued, "I recommend we ride for Bedford. Now."

"Very well." Edward sighed. "Let's end this once and for all."

"Now?" Edmund of Kent looked at the sky. "It will be dark in some hours."

"As far as I know, men can walk as well in the dark as in daylight." Mortimer clapped his hands and moved away, surrounded by his captains.

Thomas and his brother were left standing as the camp erupted with activity. The brothers shared a long look, and then Edmund hitched his shoulders.

"We best prepare as well."

"Aye." Thomas retrieved his sword. Adam walked over to him.

"It is good to see you again. I've missed you sorely these last few months."

Thomas nodded. "And I you, Adam." But his eyes were on Mortimer and the queen, and there was little love there. Adam felt rebuffed. He cleared his throat and went to find his men.

"Adam?" Thomas called him back.

"Aye?"

"Shall we ride together? Like friends should?"

Adam responded with a broad smile. "Like friends."

When they set off an hour or so later, Queen Isabella rode with them, having donned armour like any man.

"You can't!" The king stared when his lady mother appeared in hauberk and assorted pieces of plate. "It's not seemly, Maman!"

"That man threatens my son. I am entitled to ride against him."

To be quite correct, Lancaster was more of a threat to the queen and Lord Roger, but Adam felt it unwise to point that out.

"Lord Mortimer," the king said. "Please make her see sense."

"My lady queen does as she pleases, my lord." Mortimer smiled at the queen. "And in my opinion, she looks quite magnificent."

"Looks?" the king snorted. "And what if there is fighting? What then?"

"Then I will die in her defence if necessary," Lord Roger said.

Other than the queen, the next surprise was that Mortimer intended to cover the whole distance in one go.

"Impossible," Edmund of Kent said.

"Nothing is impossible. It is but a matter of pace and endurance," Mortimer retorted. "The element of surprise should never be underestimated."

The king rose in his stirrups and studied the marching men-at-arms. "Can they do it?"

"They can," Adam answered in Mortimer's stead—after all, many of them were his men.

"Good." The king nodded at Mortimer. "We do as the earl suggests." He'd been referring to Mortimer as the earl at every opportunity, and every time he did, Norfolk and Kent looked as if they'd eaten nettles. From the way the king studied his uncles, their reaction had not gone unnoticed—not by him nor by Mortimer.

"Not the way I'd imagined celebrating Twelfth Night," Thomas commented, shrinking into his cloak. He threw a bleak look at the surrounding countryside. Denuded trees raised their branches against a pale blue sky, last year's leaves crunching underfoot as they rode in tight formation towards the southeast.

"I don't think anyone would exchange festivities for this," Adam replied. "But with rebellious earls at large, what is the king to do?"

Thomas gave him a sour look. "You may or may not believe me, but I would never have taken the field against Ned. Never. Riding against one anointed king was quite enough."

"But necessary at the time," Adam reminded him.

"Happens men will say the same about Lancaster's effort in some years." Thomas rode his horse closer. "And my brother? Have you any news of him?"

"He's riding over there." Adam pointed at Edmund.

"My other brother."

"He is dead, remember?" Adam warned. "Best for all things stay that way."

"I was hoping for some reassurance, no more," Thomas muttered. "I do not expect you to divulge secrets—not to me, the would-be traitor."

Adam cast a quick look around. "Last I heard, he was well." He held up his hand at the eager look on Thomas' face. "No. Please don't ask me anything more. Please."

Thomas nodded. "Fair enough. And thank you."

Mortimer had the men and horses settling into a steady pace. When daylight waned, torches were lit, the men continuing to march, with now and then a short break to eat and drink. The king rode at the head, flanked by Mortimer and his mother. Some paces behind came Adam and Thomas, together with Edmund of Kent, Montague, and Stafford. There was little conversation, and as the night grew colder and darker, they all retreated into their own thoughts. There was no moon to light their way, only a sky that glittered with stars as cold as the night around them. Adam's breath plumed, and he could no longer feel the toes of his feet.

"Has Kit recovered from her ordeal?" Thomas suddenly asked, breaking the silence.

"She has." Adam smiled at the thought of his wife. Had she been anywhere close, he'd have warmed his freezing feet in her bed, and she'd have squealed in protest. "And your wife?"

Thomas gave him one of those characteristic crooked smiles. "Alice? She is hale." They fell back into silence.

"Adam?" Mortimer beckoned him forward. Adam urged Raven into a trot, easing him back into a steady walk once he was abreast with Mortimer.

"My lord?"

The king rode up on his other side. "Uncle Edmund just asked me where we were keeping my father," he said in a low voice.

"Ah." Adam shot a look at Earl Edmund, presently riding side by side with Queen Isabella.

"Has Norfolk asked you?" Lord Roger asked.

"No." Not an outright lie, seeing as Thomas had only asked for news of his brother.

"Good." King Edward threw a look at his uncles. "It seems we've been quite successful in spiriting my father out of the country. A well-kept secret—and that is how it must stay, to convince everyone he is truly dead."

Not so well-kept. After all, unless the person who had planned the ambushes had also taken part in them—and Adam held that to be highly unlikely—someone other than the king, Mortimer, the queen, and Maltravers knew something important had been afoot last summer. Adam chewed his lip. To tell them might risk his life. To not tell them… Damn! He had to tell them. "I fear someone knows—or has reason to suspect."

"What?" the king hissed.

"Explain." Lord Roger urged his horse in a trot. Adam and the king followed suit, creating a gap to the closest riders.

Hesitantly, Adam told them about the ambushes, the thirteen dead men, his conviction that the purpose of those ambushes had been to kill them.

"All?" the king croaked. "Even Lady Kit?"

"All, my lord," Adam replied, relieved by the king's horrified reaction.

"But why haven't you told us this before?" the king asked.

"Because he didn't know who might have ordered it," Lord Roger said. "In fact, he still doesn't know. It could be me, the queen, or you, my liege." If anything, he sounded amused.

"Me? You suspect me?" The king's voice shook.

Adam shrugged. What was he to say? They rode in stony silence for a while

"Damnation!" Lord Roger met Adam's eyes. "I swear on my soul that it wasn't me."

401

"Or me!" The king rose in his stirrups, looking back at his mother. "Or Maman." He turned to glare at Adam, as if daring him to disagree.

"A conundrum, to be sure," Lord Roger said, casting a fleeting look in the direction of the queen. "We'll speak of it later. For now, we concentrate on Lancaster."

Just before dawn, three men rode in to say Lancaster's camp had been sighted. Mortimer held up his hand in command, the signal was mirrored down the line, and the entire army ground to a standstill. A hushed conference took place, Mortimer and King Edward shoulder to shoulder as they discussed how to deploy the troops. Orders were given, and men melted away into the chilly half-light, some to deal with the sentries, others to take up distant positions.

By the time the sun rose, Mortimer had Lancaster's camp surrounded. At his signal, the heralds blew their horns, startling the sleeping enemy. Havoc erupted. Men spilled from the tents, some brandishing swords, the majority unarmed. Screams, men running madly, some towards the baggage train, others towards the horses.

Wake emerged from his tent, bare-legged and struggling with his coat of plate. He yelled and pointed, but no one was listening, not when Mortimer gave the signal to advance. From all sides, Mortimer's men converged on the camp, marching in formation. At Mortimer's command, they came to a halt. An impressive show of force, this disciplined and silent army, moving as a single entity.

"Lancaster!" Mortimer yelled. "We are here to do you battle in the name of the king."

The tent flap to the central pavilion was thrown back. Out stepped Lancaster, in a gown and little else. Mortimer looked at the king and nodded. King Edward spurred his horse forward, Mortimer on one side, Queen Isabella on the other. Lancaster's mouth fell open.

"Yield or die," the king said, the sun glinting on his naked blade.

With the expression of a man witnessing his own execution, the earl knelt in the mud in front of his king's horse. Mortimer flashed the queen a smile before raising his arm to the skies in a victorious gesture.

"Who to threaten him now?" Thomas murmured in Adam's ear. "Look at him, your Marcher lord. The single most powerful man in the kingdom, our king his puppet." He nodded at Lancaster. "Will he have him killed, do you think?"

"I don't know. I don't think so—he's promised the archbishop he'll let Lancaster live."

"Fool. He should kill him." Thomas smiled, a brittle thing consisting mostly of teeth. "In fact, he should kill all of us."

"What?" Adam turned to face his friend.

"If Mortimer aims to rule, he will have to do so." Thomas regarded Adam steadily. "The Earl of March is no friend of mine, Adam. Not anymore." He nodded in the direction of their king, sitting silent and pale on his horse. "It is him I serve. Soon enough, serving him will require opposing Mortimer— and the dowager queen." He leaned closer, his voice a whisper. "What will you do then, Adam de Guirande?"

"I serve the king," Adam replied hollowly.

Something akin to compassion flashed through Thomas' eyes. "But you love them both."

"I do. God help me, but I do."

Chapter 43

It was over. For now, Adam qualified, watching as one by one the rebellious lords approached the king and bent their knee before him. Not one of them to die—bar those four Mortimer had specifically named in the message he sent off before marching on Kenilworth—but quite a few would be severely impoverished, some of them quailing when they heard the fine imposed on them.

Lancaster was standing beside the king, forced to watch as the men he had lured into rebelling were issued financial punishment sufficient to cripple them for years to come. Not that he'd come out of things unaffected, having been bound over for the astronomical sum of eleven thousand pounds. For a man who made at best two hundred fifty pounds a year, as Adam did, the amount was incomprehensible.

On the other side of the king stood Mortimer, resplendent in his new earl's robes. A heavy gold collar adorned his chest, there were rings on every other finger, jewels sparkling when he moved. In comparison to Lord Roger, even the king looked dim—despite the red of his attire.

"He outshines them all, doesn't he?" Thomas commented. He too was in his earl's robes, and while not as gaudy as Mortimer, he drew more than his share of appreciative looks, mainly from the ladies. Adam, in a new burgundy gown, felt quite drab beside him.

"His victory," Adam said. "And you must admit he has advocated surprising leniency."

"Of course he has. To do otherwise would be to enrage the barons. Nothing is quite as dangerous as a cornered dog—well, with the exception of a pack of cornered dogs." Thomas nodded in the direction of Lancaster. "He's finished. It'll take him years to recover financially, and he has been ailing for months. His eyes."

"Ah." Adam had wondered at Grosmont's constant presence beside his father.

"He's fortunate in his son." Thomas looked at Lord Roger. "I don't see his sons anywhere."

"No. Geoffrey is back in France, and Edmund is at Wigmore with his wife and baby son." It pained Lord Roger that none of his numerous family had braved the journey to attend his triumph here at Westminster. Not that he'd said anything, but after finding Lord Roger pacing the wall walk and staring to the southwest, Adam had drawn his own conclusions. At heart, Lord Roger was a lonely man, hiding behind a shield of aloofness—and the queen.

"Off back home?" Thomas asked once they'd escaped the great hall.

"Tomorrow." Adam cast a look at the sky. "If I ride hard, I'll make it home before Candlemas."

"For long?"

"At home?" Adam shook his head. "I am expected at Woodstock in a fortnight." He rubbed at his neck. "The king won't countenance releasing me from his service." It had been a difficult discussion, King Edward refusing to listen to any of Adam's arguments. And in punishment for having dared to raise the issue, he'd shortened Adam's leave, saying he needed him back as soon as possible. It had left Adam angry and hurt, and these last few days he'd avoided the king like the plague.

"Of course not. Men like you don't grow on trees, and Ned is too fond of you to want to see you go." Thomas clapped him on the back—as hard as always. "Besides, I told him not to. Attending court without you would be dreadfully dreary."

"You did?" Adam was torn between being pleased and being irritated. Thomas pulled him aside and nodded at the king, presently exiting the hall surrounded by what looked like a gaggle of peacocks.

"That's the future, Adam. Those are the men who will shape the world of tomorrow, together with our king. You and I…" He paused, set a hand to his heart, and sighed. "Well, we are past it."

"Talk for yourself. Neither Montague nor Stafford are spring chickens—they're your age, only a couple of years younger than me."

"They don't act our age. They act his age." Thomas smiled at his nephew. "Anyway, that's why I want you to stay with him, at least for some more years. I'd be very lonely without you to share my thoughts with." He spoke casually, at odds with the intent look in his eyes.

"As long as we stay off the subject of women," Adam muttered, and Thomas burst out laughing.

It wasn't only Thomas who expressed his pleasure at Adam's continued service with the king. Just as he was tightening the girth one last time—Raven had the nasty habit of blowing himself up—a hand gripped Adam by the shoulder. He didn't need to turn to know who it was.

"My lord," he said, cinching the girth. He and Lord Roger had had heated words some days back regarding the fact that Godfrey of Broseley remained at large as well as the as yet unsolved matter of the ambushes. To Adam's frustration, it had been Lord Roger's conclusion that it was likely Godfrey had fled the country and that it would be impossible to identify who had ordered the attempted murders. Nor did Lord Roger think it much mattered—whoever had done so had nothing to gain by trying again, not now that Sir Edward was safely gone. Adam did not agree, nor had he liked how evasive Mortimer had been. The more he mulled it over, the more Adam concluded the queen was somehow involved, which would explain Mortimer's reluctance to investigate further. The queen...Adam suppressed a little shiver. Would she have ordered all of their deaths?

"I just wanted to wish you safe travels." Lord Roger stroked Raven over his nose. "I hear you requested to be released from your service."

"I did. Too old for all this." Adam led Raven out of the stable.

Lord Roger smiled. "Too old? Then what am I? Decrepit?"

"We're different, my lord. You thrive on this—the glamour, the power, the intrigues—while I only need one thing: my Kit and my home."

"That's two things," Lord Roger corrected with a smile.

"Not really. Kit is my home." Adam swung himself up in the saddle and sat looking down at Lord Roger, who patted him on the thigh.

"God's speed, Adam. Both in the coming and the going—and I for one am right glad to know you will be back." He squinted up at Adam. "You're very dear to me, Adam de Guirande—have been since the night I found you beaten half to death."

"As are you to me, my lord." Adam swallowed a couple of times. "But you already know that, don't you?"

"I think I do." Lord Roger smiled. "Go on. Best ride off before we both burst into tears like silly women."

Adam laughed. "A fate worse than death—what would it do to our reputations?" He inclined his head and urged Raven into a trot.

Six days later, he was back at Tresaints. It seemed an eternity since he'd last seen his home—even longer since he'd seen his children, who all seemed to have sprouted into new little beings. Meg had grown tall and shy, Ned was a sturdy toddler, and little Harry was no longer all that little, wide grey eyes studying him with open curiosity.

As always, his wife had met him halfway up the lane. As always, he'd dismounted and walked back hand in hand with her. But once in the bailey, she'd released him, allowing him the time to greet his sons and daughter before coming to claim yet another kiss. She looked radiant, round like a pear and as rosy as a dewy dog rose.

"Twins," Mabel told him in passing, lifting Harry off the ground with one hand while steadying Ned with the other. For a woman old enough to be Adam's grandmother, she was surprisingly agile—and fast, grabbing Ned before he managed to escape her.

"Twins?" He placed a large hand on Kit's belly. "Truly?"

"Mabel says so." Kit covered his hand with her own. "We'll know in some months."

"Know?" Mabel snorted. "We already know. I know."

Kit sniffed. "You're not infallible, Mabel."

"When it comes to babies, aye, I am." Mabel sniffed. "And they're boys," she added triumphantly.

"God help us," Kit said to her back. "Two lads? Ned is already tearing the place apart, and once Harry masters the art of walking, I dare say he'll join in." She patted her stomach. "Truth be told, I am a bit fearful. Harry's was not an easy birth, and to have Mabel going on and on about there being two…"

He nodded, no more, wishing he could assure her he'd be here, but such a promise was not in his gift. She leaned back against his chest; he slipped his hands round her waist to rest on her expanding girth.

"He just submitted?" she asked, eyes on their children, who were now in the orchard, playing under the bare trees.

"He did."

"And will he try again?"

"Lancaster? No. He is well and truly crushed."

She turned in his arms. "And Thomas?"

"He made his peace with the king, him and his brother both." He was not entirely pleased by the obvious relief in her face. "You care for him, don't you?"

"Thomas?" She nodded. "Does that bother you?"

"It shouldn't. But it does, seeing as he looks at you as a starving wolf would eye a lamb."

Kit laughed. "Let him try anything, and he may be surprised to find even lambs can have horns."

"They do?"

"No." She shoved at him. "As you well know." She grew serious. "And the king? How is he?"

Adam sighed. "Wary. Of his uncles, of Lancaster—and of Lord Roger." He looked to the southwest, the horizon a collection of flowing hills outlined against the grey January sky. "I asked him to release me from his service. He refused."

Her mouth softened into a smile. "Are you surprised?" She stood on her toes to brush at his hair, and he leaned into her touch.

"I just…" he began. He was done with all that—he wanted to be with her, set down permanent roots here, in this place that meant so much to her.

"I know. But Edward has need of you. He's still a lad, coping in a world of adults, and for various reasons he does not trust easily." Warm lips pressed against his. "I can share you with him some more years. Some."

Adam rested his forehead against hers. "Some." Until the king had reached his majority, he thought, and something dark and toothy unfurled in his belly. A king intent on claiming his powers, an earl grown fond of ruling in the king's stead: not the best of combinations.

"Adam?" Kit held his face between her hands. "What is it?"

"Nothing." He took a determined breath. God alone knew what the future might hold, so there was no point in speculating. He smiled down at her. "Truly, sweeting, it was nothing." He tightened his hold. "Shall we go inside?"

Her mouth curved. "I thought you'd never ask."

Hand in hand, they made for the manor and the privacy of the solar. For now, everything else would keep. For now.

Historical Note

In February of 1327, a very young Edward III was crowned, thereby beginning what would become one of the longer and more successful reigns in English history. But the early years were difficult, especially as the former king, Edward II, was still alive, if imprisoned. Being only fourteen, Edward was not considered old enough to rule in his own name, and so his mother Queen Isabella, and her favourite, Roger Mortimer, became regents – in itself a situation that caused disquiet and unrest among the rest of the English barons.

One of the first matters to sort were the Scots. Mortimer and Isabella had treated with the Scots prior to invading in 1326, and once they were safely installed, the Scots demanded that the promises made be fulfilled, notably that a peace treaty be struck recognising Scotland as a sovereign state. To reinforce the message, James Douglas led men over the border to burn and pillage, a not-so-subtle reminder that Scotland was a power to be reckoned with. As described in this book, the young king and various of his nobles were eager to teach the Scots a lesson, and so began the debacle that ended with an almost successful attempt by the Scots to abduct Edward III. Ultimately, this paved the way for the treaty that was further cemented by marrying little Princess Joan to the equally young Prince David. Edward III never wanted the treaty and would go on to make war on the Scots some years later.

When it comes to the matter of Edward II's fate, I have gone out on a limb: while various historians these days believe that Edward II did not die in September of 1327, many still insist he did. For the purpose of my story – and also because I find the arguments put forwards by historians such as Kathryn Warner and Ian Mortimer feasible and intriguing – I have chosen to allow Edward II an extended lease on life. The man, it seems to me, deserves it.

As to Queen Isabella and Roger Mortimer, I have painted a picture of a couple very much in love – not only with power but also with each other. Two strong and ambitious people, alike enough that they would ultimately reinforce their respective flaws and cause their downfall– but when this book closes, they are still far from downfall, confident in their own power. But Edward III has no intention of remaining forever under their control, and so…Well, what happens next will be revealed in the next book in the series, The Cold Light of Dawn, due out early 2018.

I have allowed Thomas of Brotherton a lot of space in this book. For a man born to power and wealth in times of great upheaval, this Earl of Norfolk is a surprisingly invisible character, relegated as being an unimportant and weak man. I have chosen to make something more out of him, finding it difficult to believe that any child born to Edward I and his rather impressive second wife, Princess Marguerite of France, would be so…so…beige. Besides, my Adam needed a friend with some clout.

As always, I must remind my readers that Adam de Guirande is an invented character (unfortunately) as are his wife, his family, the people who serve him. However, his brother-in-law, Richard de Monmouth, did exist, even if he'd have been more than surprised at meeting the family I've given him.

For those among you who know the history of the Hansa inside out, I'd like to say that yes, I am using the term Hanseatic League a bit prematurely, as this name was not established until the 1350's. However, the various Hansa organisations were most certainly a power to be reckoned with – had been since the 12th century – and instead of mentioning the Lübeck Hansa or the Hamburg Hansa, I have chosen to go with the Hanseatic League.

For those interested in reading more about this period, I warmly recommend Kathryn Warner's excellent books about Edward II and his queen as well as Ian Mortimer's book The Greatest Traitor.

The King's Greatest Enemy continues in

The Cold Light of Dawn.

"I know exactly how you feel." Kit stroked the panting ewe over her head. "Two babies, kicking at you from the inside in their haste to meet the world."

"You should not be out here," old John said. "A lady like you, so close to her time, and here you are, kneeling among the sheep."

"Every lamb that is born healthy adds to our wealth." Kit sat back on her heels. "Besides, it is near on six weeks before I am due. What would you have me do? Remain in the solar and indulge in baked goods and dried fruit?"

"Better than being here, in the mud." But John smiled. "What does Mabel say?"

"You know her." Kit set her hands to the ground and heaved herself upright without overbalancing. "She nags."

"Ah. Well, she has always been good at that." John grinned. "God knows she kept the rest of us in good order, despite being only a year or two older than me."

Kit nodded, no more, attempting to catch her breath.

"My lady?" John hovered. Kit waved him away, watching as he dropped back down to help the second of the little lambs into the world.

"Kit!" William came striding over the pasture, all long legs and flapping gown. "What are you doing out here? Adam would have my guts for not keeping a better eye on you." He gestured at the sky, as yet mostly dark, albeit that a faint line of pink tainted the eastern horizon. "You should be sleeping!"

"Tell that to the ewes." Kit rubbed at her back. "They mostly lamb at night."

William took hold of her arm. "To bed, Kit. Mabel says—"

412

"Mabel says this, Mabel says that." Kit snorted. "Truth be told, Mabel has no idea what she's talking about. It's not as if she's ever carried a child or birthed it, is it?"

"Not necessarily out of choice, my lady," John said.

"No." Kit spread her hands in an apologetic gesture. "You're right: that was uncalled for."

"Inside," William said. "Bed. Now."

With no further protest, Kit accompanied him. Besides, her toes were freezing, and she needed to relieve herself.

They stopped at the little chapel. Kit glanced at William, they shared a little smile and entered. The building was the oldest on the manor—or so Kit's mother Alaïs had always maintained—a small whitewashed space in which the painted decorations were kept to a minimum. Not that any of this was visible in wavering glow of the single candle burning on the altar, Kit did not need light to know exactly where the statues of the three saints were—they sat just inside the door, St Winifride, St Wulfstan and St Odo. A Welsh saint, a French saint and an English one—apt in a manor built by a Norman knight upon returning from the Crusades.

William sank into his own thoughts before the altar. Kit clasped her hands over her swollen belly and wondered what Adam might be doing. She fidgeted, bumping into William. As tall as her husband, William also had the same fair hair and similar build as his brother, but where decades of earning his living with his sword had left Adam a collection of compact muscles, William had ink-splotched fingers and a tendency to squint—this after years of peering at documents and Holy Scripture.

Presently, he was Tresaints' resident priest—and Adam's steward, overseeing an ever-growing combination of pastures, woodlands and fields. Being in the king's service came with its rewards, and God knew they needed it: with all these children, more land was always welcome.

Beside her, William was praying, and she fell in, adding her voice to the whispered Latin.

"Amen," he finished, and she echoed him before crossing herself. There was enough light in the chapel now for her to make out the Holy Virgin as she stood beside her Son on the triptych that adorned the altar. Kit whispered yet one more prayer, this one directed to the Virgin; "See me and my babes safe through the coming ordeal." It seemed to her the painted Virgin smiled.

Some hours later, Kit was in the kitchens, discussing food with Mall. There was plenty of salted herring left, and at present two dozen were soaking in cold water prior to being cooked. "Pottage with leeks," Mall said, "and split peas." She smacked her lips. "Will go well with the herring."

In Kit's considered opinion little went well with herring, but she nodded all the same.

"Mistress?" Tom the Foundling almost fell into the kitchen. "There are people coming down the lane. John said to fetch you."

Kit rose, steadying herself against the table. "People?"

"One of them's a lady, and she has the prettiest palfrey I've ever seen, and—"

"A lady, Mama," Meg interrupted, jumping up and down. "A real lady, and she has—"

Kit waved the children silent. "A lady?" She made for the door, Meg skipping beside her.

"A pretty, pretty lady," Meg warbled, her dark braids jumping up and down. "Will they stay?"

"We shall see." In her head, Kit was already considering how to lodge these unknown guests.

"Ah, there you are." William looked anything but happy. "We have visitors."

"So I heard. Who?" She accompanied him over the little bailey towards the gate.

"You'll never guess," he said, just as the first rider came through the gate. Kit's belly cramped and she took an instinctive step closer to William.

"What's she doing here?"

Beside her, Meg gasped in admiration, eyes riveted to the lady clad in green and blue, the hood of her mantel thrown back to reveal a veil in the sheerest of linen.

"I am sure we will find out." William set a hand to her back for an instant, sufficient support for Kit to stiffen her spine.

"Sister," Kit offered reluctantly when the neat little mare came to a halt in front of her. Alicia Luytens and she shared a father, but where Alicia had been born in wedlock, Kit was the child of an illicit union, the damage further compounded—at least in Alicia's eyes—by the fact that Kit's mother was a salter's daughter.

Alicia did not reply, narrow face set in an unreadable expression as she gazed at her surroundings. "My father was born here," she said to her male companion as she dismounted. "Imagine that! Such humble beginnings." She landed lightly on her feet, made as if to enter the manor house, but Kit blocked her way.

"I do not recall inviting you," Kit said icily.

"You didn't. I came anyway—to see." Thinly plucked brows rose in arcs as she took in Kit's rounded state. "Another one? Really, some breed like rabbits, don't they?" She laughed, tugging at her dark green mantle, a beautiful thing edged with squirrel fur. Gloves of a matching green covered her hands, and the silk in her blue skirts rustled when she moved. In comparison, Kit's everyday russet was drab and unflattering, straining over her large belly.

"Why are you here?" William planted himself in front of Kit, arms crossed over his chest.

"Why not? Widow Luytens had a penchant to see her father's birthplace." Her companion threw the reins of his horse to one of his servants and strolled forward. "Small, but with potential," he said, studying the recently refurbished manor house. He was dressed for travel, sensible clothes in good grey worsted and a heavy cloak lined with fleece. His dark hair fell in soft waves to his shoulders, a neat beard covered his cheeks, and eyes as cold and hard as pebbles alighted for an instant on Kit before he reverted to scrutinising the various buildings. The nerve of him! Kit wanted to spit him in the face.

"And you are?" William asked.

"That," Kit said, "is Robert de Langon—recently dismissed from the king's service for slandering me." To Kit's satisfaction, this had de Langon paling. "And in view of what you said, you are not welcome here at Tresaints—either of you."

415

Alicia snickered and made a new attempt to reach the manor house. John surged forward, accompanied by his grandsons.

"Best leave," John said. "My mistress does not want you here."

"Maybe that is not for her to say," Robert de Langon said. "After all, Tresaints was part of Katherine de Monmouth's dowry, not the impostor's."

"And I was short-changed by my brother." Alicia swept the neat bailey yet another lingering look. "I should be compensated. I am looking at marrying again." She simpered at Robert.

"Fortunately, my father amended the contracts," Kit said. "Everything is in legal order—as confirmed by the late Earl of Pembroke."

"I have rights!" Alicia hissed. "This is fine land and a good manor. Why should you have it and not me? I shall make claims on my brother, and then we'll see."

"You do that." Something knotted itself in Kit's belly, but she succeeded in sounding unperturbed. "But your quarrel is with him, not with me."

"Knowing Richard, he'll not part with anything of his to compensate me," Alicia said.

"Knowing you, you don't deserve any compensation." Kit looked Alicia up and down. "You look in the best of spirits despite being so recently bereaved. But then, I suppose you were more than thrilled at hearing your husband was dead."

"He abused me!" Alicia hissed.

"Ah, is that why you had him killed?" Kit said, noting out of the corner of her eye how Robert took a step back from Alicia.

"I did not!" Pale blue eyes glared at Kit.

"So you say." Kit studied her sister. "And have you told Robert about your foiled attempt to poison Queen Isabella and Earl Roger?"

"I…" Alicia spluttered, throwing a look at Robert.

"Is this true?" Robert said.

"She misconstrues." Alicia's face, always an unfortunate collection of angles and sharp planes, tightened into a grimace.

She sniffed and wiped at her long nose. "I was blackmailed. My mother's life hung in the balance."

"Not a great loss to the world," Kit muttered. Lady Cecily inhabited quite a few of Kit's rare nightmares, an apparition dominated by a nose as sharp and long as Alicia's, and a mouth set in a permanent snarl.

"She was my mother!" Alicia scowled.

"I can but commiserate," Kit retorted. "And now I must bid you leave."

"What, no hospitality offered to weary travellers?" Robert de Langon asked.

"You are no friend of my husband—or of me. Neither is Alicia, so the answer is no." Kit raised her chin and stared him down.

At long last he sighed. "We'd best get going," he said to Alicia. "It's quite the ride to Worcester." Once he was astride, he looked down at Kit. "I trust you were not lying about the contracts. Such things are easy to check—and I must of course look out for the interests of my wife-to-be."

"It will not avail you if you do." Kit even managed a cold smile. "Good day to you. I shall be sure to tell my husband of your visit. I dare say he will be less than pleased." She took a step forward. "It would be foolish to anger Adam de Guirande. He has the ear of the king—you do not."

De Langon sneered. "For now."

The moment they were gone, Kit turned on John. "As of now, the gate is kept closed. Always."

"Yes, my lady." John was already halfway to the gate, yelling orders. Meg and Tom scampered after him.

"What was that?" William asked.

"Intimidation." Kit clenched her hand to stop it from shaking. "I must send word to Adam—and Richard."

"Richard?"

"The contracts name Katherine de Monmouth, not me. They will have to be rewritten."

"Or amended." William took hold of her shoulders. "Calm down, Kit."

"My home!" She placed her hands over her heaving stomach. "This is my home, William!"

"And so it will remain." He drew her close enough to kiss her forehead. "It will." Kit rested against him, eyes closed. Long, slow breaths, and the loud thumping of her heart calmed.

"It's all very odd," she said once she'd regained her composure. "Alicia and de Langon, does Richard know?" She scraped at a spot of wax on the sleeve of William's gown.

"She's a wealthy widow. As a widow, she can arrange her affairs as it pleases her—and it seems Robert de Langon does."

"They suit." Kit straightened up. "May they find what they deserve in each other."

"God help them," William muttered. "De Langon is from Gascony, isn't he?"

"He is. A minor lordling who hoped his father's generous gifts to the new king would ensure an exalted position among the king's friends." Kit crouched to wipe her youngest son's face. Harry beamed up at her, pudgy—and dirty—fingers gripping at her skirts. "But as Adam tells it, Edward rarely noticed his presence—or absence."

"Ah. That must be difficult."

"He's not a nice man." Kit took hold of William's offered hand and hauled herself upright. "He doesn't deserve any compassion."

"All men deserve compassion," William admonished. He winked. "Some less than others, to be sure."

About the Author

When Anna is not stuck in the 14th century, chances are she'll be visiting in the 17th century, more specifically with Alex and Matthew Graham, the protagonists of the best-selling, multiple award winning, series The Graham Saga. This series is the story of two people who should never have met – not when she was born three centuries after him. A fast-paced blend of love, drama and adventure, The Graham Saga will carry you from Scotland to the New World and back again.

For more information about Anna and her books, please visit www.annabelfrage.com or pop by her blog https://annabelfrage.wordpress.com

Lightning Source UK Ltd.
Milton Keynes UK
UKOW04f1517120118
316035UK00001B/185/P